Edward Earl of Derby, Edward Earl of Derby

The Iliad of Homer rendered into English blank verse

Edward Earl of Derby, Edward Earl of Derby

The Iliad of Homer rendered into English blank verse

ISBN/EAN: 9783743463448

Manufactured in Europe, USA, Canada, Australia, Japa

Cover: Foto ©Andreas Hilbeck / pixelio.de

Manufactured and distributed by brebook publishing software (www.brebook.com)

Edward Earl of Derby, Edward Earl of Derby

The Iliad of Homer rendered into English blank verse

THE
ILIAD OF HOMER

RENDERED INTO ENGLISH BLANK VERSE.

TO WHICH ARE APPENDED

TRANSLATIONS OF POEMS ANCIENT AND MODERN.

By EDWARD EARL OF DERBY.

EIGHTH EDITION.

IN TWO VOLUMES.—Vol. II.

LONDON:
JOHN MURRAY, ALBEMARLE STREET.
1871.

LIST OF BOOKS.

VOLUME II.

CONTENTS OF TRANSLATIONS.

From the Latin.

From the French.

From the Italian.

CONTENTS. vii

HOMER'S ILIAD.

BOOK XV.

NOW when the Trojans had recrossed the trench
  And palisades, and in their headlong flight
Many had fallen by Grecian swords, the rest,
Routed, and pale with fear, made head awhile
Beside their cars; then Jove on Ida's height   5
At golden-thronèd Juno's side awoke;
Rising, he saw the Trojans and the Greeks,
Those in confusion, while behind them pressed
The Greeks, triumphant, Neptune in their midst:
He saw too Hector stretched upon the plain,   10
His comrades standing round; senseless he lay,
Drawing short breath, blood gushing from his mouth;
For by no feeble hand the blow was dealt.
  Pitying, the Sire of Gods and men beheld,
And thus, with sternest glance, to Juno spoke: 15
"Juno, thou subtle mischief, thy base fraud
Hath Hector quelled, and Trojans driven to flight:
Nor know I but thyself mayst reap the fruit,
By shameful scourging, of thy vile deceit.
Hast thou forgotten how in former times   20
I hung thee from on high, and to thy feet
Attached two ponderous anvils, and thy hands
With golden fetters bound, which none might break?

There didst thou hang amid the clouds of Heaven;
Through all Olympus' breadth the Gods were wroth; 25
Yet dared not one approach to set thee free.
If any so had ventured, him had I
Hurled from Heaven's threshold, till to earth he fell,
With little left of life. Yet was not quenched
My wrath on godlike Hercules' account,   30
Whom thou, with Boreas, o'er the watery waste
With fell intent didst send; and tempest-tossed,
Cast him ashore on Coös' fruitful isle.
I rescued him from thence, and brought him back,
After long toil, to Argos' grassy plains.   35
This to thy mind I bring, that thou mayst learn
To cease thy treacherous wiles, nor hope to gain
By all thy lavished blandishments of love,
Wherewith thou hast deceived me, and betrayed."
He said; and terror seized the stag-eyed Queen; 40
Who thus with wingèd words addressed her Lord:
"By Earth I swear, and yon broad Heaven above,
And Stygian stream beneath, the weightiest oath
Of solemn power to bind the blessed Gods;
By thine own sacred head, our nuptial bed,   45
Whose holy tie I never could forswear;
That not by my suggestion and advice
Earth-shaking Neptune on the Trojan host,
And Hector, pours his wrath, and aids the Greeks;
In this he but obeys his own desire,   50
Who looks with pity on the Grecian host
Beside their ships o'erborne; and could my words
Prevail, my counsel were to shape his course,
O cloud-girt King, obedient to thy will."

She said; the Sire of Gods and men, well pleased, 55
Her answer heard, and thus with gracious smile:
"If, stag-eyed Queen, in synod of the Gods
Thy counsels shall indeed with mine agree,
Neptune, how strong soe'er his wish, must change
His course, obedient to thy will and mine; 60
And if in all sincerity thou speak,
Go to the assembled Gods, and hither send
Iris, and Phœbus of the silver bow;
That she may to the Grecian camp repair,
And bid that Neptune from the battle-field 65
Withdraw, and to his own domain retire;
While Phœbus Hector to the fight restores,
Inspiring new-born vigour, and allaying
The mortal pains which bow his spirit down;
Then, heartless fear infusing in the Greeks, 70
Put them to flight, that flying they may fall
Beside Achilles' ships; his comrade then,
Patroclus, he shall send to battle forth
To be by Hector slain, in front of Troy;
Yet not to fall till many valiant youths 75
Have felt his prowess; and, amid the rest,
My son, Sarpedon; by his comrade's death
Achilles roused to rage shall Hector slay;
Thenceforth my counsel is, that from the ships
The Trojan force shall still be backward driven, 80
Until at length, by Pallas' deep designs,
The Greeks possess the lofty walls of Troy.
Yet will not I my anger intermit,
Nor suffer other of the immortal Gods
To aid the Greeks, till Peleus' son behold 85

His wish accomplished, and the boon obtained
I promised once, and with a nod confirmed,
That day when sea-born Thetis clasped my knees,
And prayed me to avenge her warrior son."

 Thus he; the white-armed Queen of Heaven submiss 90
His mandate heard; and from the Idæan mount
With rapid flight to high Olympus sped.
Swift as the mind of man, who many a land
Hath travelled o'er, and with reflective thought
Recalls, "here was I such a day, or here,"   95
And in a moment many a scene surveys;
So Juno sped o'er intervening space;
Olympus' heights she reached, and in the house
Of Jove appeared amid the assembled Gods.
They at her coming rose, with golden cups   100
Greeting their Queen's approach; the rest she passed,
And from the hand of fair-faced Themis took
The proffered cup, who first had run to meet,
And thus with wingèd words addressed the Queen:

 "Juno, why com'st thou hither? and with looks 105
Of one distraught with fear? hath Saturn's son,
Thy mighty Lord, thus sore affrighted thee?"
To whom the white-armed Goddess, Juno, thus:

 "Forbear thy questions, Themis; well thou know'st
How haughty and imperious is his mind;   110
Thou for the Gods in haste prepare the feast;
Then shalt thou learn, amid the Immortals all,
What evil he designs; nor all, I ween,
His counsels will approve, or men, or Gods,
Though now in blissful ignorance they feast." 115

 She said, and sat; the Gods, oppressed with care,

Her farther speech awaited; on her lips
There dwelt indeed a smile, but not a ray
Passed o'er her darkening brow, as thus her wrath
Amid the assembled Gods found vent in words: 120
    "Fools are we all, who madly strive with Jove,
Or hope, by access to his throne, to sway,
By word or deed, his course; from all apart,
He all our counsels heeds not, but derides;
And boasts o'er all the immortal Gods to reign   125
In unapproached pre-eminence of power.
Prepare then each his several woe to bear;
On Mars e'en now, methinks, the blow hath fallen;
Since in the fight, the man he loves the best,
And boasts his son, Ascalaphus, is slain."   130
    She said; and Mars, enraged, his brawny thigh
Smote with his hands, and thus, lamenting, spoke:
    "Blame not, ye Gods, who on Olympus dwell,
That to the Grecian ships I haste, to avenge
My slaughtered son, though blasted by Heaven's fire 135
'Twere mine 'mid corpses, blood, and dust to lie."
    He said, and gave command to Fear and Flight
To yoke his car; and donned his glittering arms.
Then from the throne of Jove had heavier wrath
And deeper vengeance on the Immortals fallen,   140
But Pallas, in alarm for all the Gods,
Quitting in haste the throne whereon she sat,
Sprang past the vestibule, and from his head
The helmet lifted, from his arm the shield;
Took from his sturdy hand, and reared upright,   145
The brazen spear; then with reproachful words
She thus assailed the impetuous God of War:

"Frantic, and passion-maddened, thou art lost!
Hast thou no ears to hear? or are thy mind
And sense of reverence utterly destroyed?   150
Or heard'st thou not what white-armed Juno spoke,
Fresh from the presence of Olympian Jove?
Wouldst thou, thine evil destiny fulfilled,
By hard constraint, despite thy grief, be driven
Back to Olympus; and to all the rest   155
Confusion and disaster with thee bring?
At once from valiant Trojans and from Greeks
His thoughts would be diverted, and his wrath
Embroil Olympus, and on all alike,
Guilty or not, his anger would be poured.   160
Waive then thy vengeance for thy gallant son;
Others as brave of heart, as strong of arm,
Have fallen, and yet must fall; and vain the attempt
To watch at once o'er all the race of men."

Thus saying, to his seat again she forced   165
The impetuous Mars: meanwhile, without the house,
Juno, by Jove's command, Apollo called,
And Iris, messenger from God to God;
And thus to both her wingèd words addressed:

"Jove bids you with all speed to Ida haste;   170
And when, arrived, before his face ye stand,
Whate'er he orders, that observe and do."

Thus Juno spoke, and to her throne returned;
While they to spring-abounding Ida's heights,
Wild nurse of forest beasts, pursued their way;   175
The all-seeing son of Saturn there they found
Upon the topmost crag of Gargarus,
An incense-breathing cloud around him spread.

Before the face of cloud-compelling Jove
They stood; well-pleased he witnessed their approach 180
In swift obedience to his consort's words,
And thus to Iris first his speech addressed:
  "Haste thee, swift Iris, and to Ocean's King
My message bear, nor misreporting aught,
Nor aught omitting; from the battle-field   185
Bid him retire, and join the assembled Gods,
Or to his own domain of sea withdraw.
If my commands he heed not, nor obey,
Let him consider in his inmost soul
If, mighty though he be, he dare await   190
My hostile coming; mightier far than he,
His elder born; nor may his spirit aspire
To rival me, whom all regard with awe."
  He said; swift-footed Iris, at the word,
From Ida's heights to sacred Ilion sped.   195
Swift as the snow-flakes from the clouds descend,
Or wintry hail before the driving blast
Of Boreas, ether-born; so swift to Earth
Descended Iris; by his side she stood,
And with these words the Earth-shaking God addressed;
  "A message, dark-haired Circler of the Earth,   [200
To thee I bring from Ægis-bearing Jove.
He bids thee straightway from the battle-field
Retire, and either join the assembled Gods,
Or to thine own domain of sea withdraw.   205
If his commands thou heed not, nor obey,
Hither he menaces himself to come,
And fight against thee; but he warns thee first,
Beware his arm, as mightier far than thou,

Thine elder born; nor may thy spirit aspire   210
To rival him, whom all regard with awe."
    To whom in towering wrath the Earth-shaking God:
" By Heaven, though great he be, he yet presumes
Somewhat too far, if me, his equal born,
He seeks by force to baffle of my will.   215
We were three brethren, all of Rhæa born
To Saturn; Jove and I, and Pluto third,
Who o'er the nether regions holds his sway.
Threefold was our partition; each obtained
His meed of honour due; the hoary Sea   220
By lot my habitation was assigned;
The realms of Darkness fell to Pluto's share;
Broad Heaven, amid the sky and clouds to Jove;
But Earth, and high Olympus, are to all
A common heritage; nor will I walk   225
To please the will of Jove; though great he be,
With his own third contented let him rest;
Nor let him think that I, as wholly vile,
Shall quail before his arm; his lofty words
Were better to his daughters and his sons   230
Addressed, his own begotten; who perforce
Must listen to his mandates, and obey."
    To whom swift-footed Iris thus replied:
" Is this, then, dark-haired Circler of the Earth,
The message, stern and haughty, which to Jove   235
Thou bidd'st me bear? perchance thine angry mood
May bend to better counsels; noblest minds
Are easiest bent; and o'er superior age
Thou know'st the avenging Furies ever watch."
    To whom Earth-shaking Neptune thus replied;   240

"Immortal Iris, weighty are thy words,
And in good season spoken; and 'tis well
When envoys are by sound discretion led.
Yet are my heart and mind with grief oppressed,
When me, his equal both by birth and fate,　　245
He seeks with haughty words to overbear.
I yield, though with indignant sense of wrong.
But this I say, nor shall my threat be vain:
Let him remember, if in my despite,
'Gainst Pallas', Juno's, Hermes', Vulcan's will,　　250
He spare to overthrow proud Ilion's towers,
And crown with victory the Grecian arms,
The feud between us never can be healed."

The Earth-shaker said, and from the field withdrew
Beneath the ocean wave, the warrior Greeks　　255
His loss deploring; to Apollo then
The Cloud-compeller thus his speech addressed:

"Go straight to Hector of the brazen helm,
Good Phœbus; for beneath the ocean wave
The Earth-shaker hath withdrawn, escaping thus　　260
My high displeasure: had he dared resist,
The tumult of our strife had reached the Gods
Who in the nether realms with Saturn dwell.
Yet thus 'tis better, both for me and him,
That, though indignant, to my will he yields;　　265
For to compel him were no easy task.
Take thou, and wave on high thy tasselled shield,
The Grecian warriors daunting: thou thyself,
Far-darting King, thy special care bestow
On noble Hector; so restore his strength　　270
And vigour, that in panic to their ships,

And the broad Hellespont, the Greeks be driven.
Then will I so by word and deed contrive
That they may gain fresh respite from their toil."
    He said, nor did Apollo not obey   275
His Sire's commands; from Ida's heights he flew,
Like to a falcon, swooping on a dove,
Swiftest of birds; then Priam's son he found,
The godlike Hector, stretched at length no more,
But sitting, now to consciousness restored,   280
With recognition looking on his friends;
The cold sweat dried, nor gasping now for breath,
Since by the will of Ægis-bearing Jove
To life new wakened; close beside him stood
The Far-destroyer, and addressed him thus: 285
"Hector, thou son of Priam, why apart
From all thy comrades art thou sitting here,
Feeble and faint? What trouble weighs thee down?"
    To whom thus Hector of the glancing helm
With faltering voice: "Who art thou, Prince of Gods, 290
Who thus enquirest of me? know'st thou not
How a huge stone, by mighty Ajax hurled,
As on his comrades by the Grecian ships
I dealt destruction, struck me on the breast,
Dashed to the earth, and all my vigour quelled?   295
I deemed in sooth this day my soul, expired,
Should see the dead, and Pluto's shadowy realm."
    To whom again the far-destroying King:
"Be of good cheer; from Saturn's son I come
From Ida's height to be thy guide and guard;   300
Phœbus Apollo of the golden sword,
I, who of old have thy protector been,

Thee and thy city guarding. Rise then straight;
Summon thy numerous horsemen; bid them drive
Their flying cars to assail the Grecian ships: 305
I go before; and will thy horses' way
Make plain and smooth, and daunt the warrior Greeks."
  His words fresh vigour in the chief infused.
As some proud steed, at well-filled manger fed,
His halter broken, neighing, scours the plain,   310
And revels in the widely-flowing stream
To bathe his sides; then tossing high his head,
While o'er his shoulders streams his ample mane,
Light-borne on active limbs, in conscious pride,
To the wide pastures of the mares he flies;   315
So vigorous, Hector plied his active limbs,
His horsemen summoning at Heaven's command.
  As when a rustic crowd of men and dogs
Have chased an antlered stag, or mountain goat,
That 'mid the crags and thick o'ershadowing wood 320
Hath refuge found, and baffled their pursuit:
If, by the tumult roused, a lion stand,
With bristling mane, before them, back they turn,
Checked in their mid career; even so the Greeks,
Who late in eager throngs were pressing on,   325
Thrusting with swords and double-pointed spears,
When Hector moving through the ranks they saw,
Recoiled, and to their feet their courage fell.
To whom thus Thoas spoke, Andræmon's son,
Ætolia's bravest warrior, skilled to throw   330
The javelin, dauntless in the stubborn fight;
By few surpassed in speech, when in debate
In full assembly Grecian youths contend:

He thus with prudent speech began, and said:
"Great is the marvel which our eyes behold, 335
That Hector see again to life restored,
Escaped the death we hoped him to have met
Beneath the hands of Ajax Telamon.
Some God hath been his guard, and Hector saved,
Whose arm hath slacked the knees of many a Greek: 340
So will he now; for not without the aid
Of Jove, the Lord of thunder, doth he stand
So boldly forth, so eager for the fight.
Hear then, and all by my advice be ruled:
Back to the ships dismiss the general crowd; 345
While of our army we, the foremost men,
Stand fast, and meeting him with levelled spears,
Hold him in check; and he, though brave, may fear
To throw himself amid our serried ranks."
He said; they heard, and all obeyed his words; 350
The mighty Ajax, and Idomeneus
The King, and Teucer, and Meriones,
And Meges, bold as Mars, with all their best,
Their stedfast battle ranged, to wait the assault
Of Hector and his Trojans; while behind, 355
The unwarlike many to the ships retired.
The Trojan mass came on, by Hector led
With haughty stride; before him Phœbus went,
His shoulders veiled in cloud; his arm sustained
The awful Ægis, fearful to behold, 360
Bright-flashing, hung with shaggy tassels round;
Which Vulcan, skilful workman, gave to Jove,
To scatter terror 'mid the souls of men.
This on his arm, the Trojan troops he led.

Firm stood the mass of Greeks; from either side   365
Shrill clamours rose; and fast from many a string
The arrows flew, and many a javelin, hurled
By vigorous arms; some buried in the flesh
Of stalwart youths, and many, ere they reached
Their living mark, fell midway on the plain,   370
Fixed in the ground, in vain athirst for blood.
While Phœbus motionless his Ægis held,
Thick flew the shafts, and fast the people fell
On either side; but when he turned its flash
Full in the faces of the astonished Greeks,   375
And shouted loud, their spirits within them quailed,
Their fiery courage borne in mind no more.
As when two beasts of prey, at dead of night,
With sudden onset scatter wide a herd
Of oxen, or a numerous flock of sheep,   380
Their keepers absent; so unnerved by fear
The Greeks dispersed; such panic 'mid their ranks,
That victory so might crown the Trojan arms,
Apollo sent; and as the masses broke,
Each Trojan slew his man; by Hector's hand   385
Fell Stichius and Arcesilas; the one,
The leader of Bœotia's brass-clad host,
The other, brave Menostheus' trusted friend.
Æneas Medon slew, and Iasus;
Medon, the great Oïleus' bastard son,   390
Brother of Ajax; he in Phylace,
Far from his native home, was driven to dwell;
Since one to Eriopis near akin,
His sire Oïleus' wife, his hand had slain:
And Iasus, the Athenian chief, was deemed   395

The son of Sphelus, son of Bucolus.
Polydamas amid the foremost ranks
Mecistes slew, Polites Echius,
Agenor Clonius; while from Paris' hand
An arrow, 'mid the crowd of fugitives   400
Shot from behind, beneath the shoulder struck
Dëiocus, and through his chest was driven.
These while the Trojans of their arms despoiled,
Through ditch and palisades promiscuous dashed
The flying Greeks, and gained, hard-pressed, the wall;   405
While loudly Hector to the Trojans called
To assail the ships, and leave the bloody spoils:
"Whom I elsewhere, and from the ships aloof
Shall find, my hand shall doom him on the spot;
For him no funeral pyre his kin shall light,   410
Or male or female; but before the wall
Our city's dogs his mangled flesh shall tear."
He said; and on his horses' shoulder-point
Let fall the lash, and loudly through the ranks
Called on the Trojans; they with answering shout   415
And noise unspeakable, urged on with him
Their harnessed steeds; Apollo, in the van,
Trod down with ease the embankment of the ditch,
And filled it in; and o'er it bridged a way
Level and wide, far as a javelin's flight   420
Hurled by an arm that proves its utmost strength.
O'er this their columns passed; Apollo bore
His Ægis o'er them, and cast down the wall;
Easy, as when a child upon the beach,
In wanton play, with hands and feet o'erthrows   425
The mound of sand, which late in play he raised;

So, Phœbus, thou, the Grecian toil and pains
Confounding, sentest panic through their souls.
Thus hemmed beside the ships they made their stand,
While each exhorted each, and all, with hands　　430
Outstretched, to every God addressed their prayer:
And chief, Gerenian Nestor, prop of Greece,
With hands uplifted toward the starry Heaven:
　"O Father Jove! if any e'er to Thee
On corn-clad plains of Argos burnt the fat　　435
Of bulls and sheep, and offered up his prayer
For safe return; and thine assenting nod
Confirmed thy promise; O remember now
His prayer; stave off the pitiless day of doom,
Nor let the Greeks to Trojan arms succumb."　　440
　Thus Nestor prayed; loud thundered from on high
The Lord of counsel, as he heard the prayer
Of Neleus' aged son; with double zeal,
The Trojans, as the mind of Jove they knew,
Pressed on the Greeks, with warlike ardour fired.　　445
As o'er the bulwarks of a ship pour down
The mighty billows of the wide-pathed sea,
Driven by the blast, that tosses high the waves,
So down the wall, with shouts, the Trojans poured;
The cars admitted, by the ships they fought　　450
With double-pointed spears, and hand to hand;
These on their chariots, on the lofty decks
Of their dark vessels those, with ponderous spars,
Which on the ships were stored for naval war,
Compact and strong, their heads encased in brass.　　455
　While yet beyond the ships, about the wall
The Greeks and Trojans fought, Patroclus still

Within the tent of brave Eurypylus
Remaining, with his converse soothed the chief,
And healing unguents to his wound applied,   460
Of power to charm away the bitter pains;
But when the Trojans pouring o'er the wall,
And routed Greeks in panic flight he saw,
Deeply he groaned, and smiting on his thigh
With either palm, in anguish thus he spoke: 465
  "Eurypylus, how great soe'er thy need,
I can no longer stay; so fierce the storm
Of battle rages; but the attendants' care
Will all thy wants supply; while I in haste
Achilles seek, and urge him to the war;   470
Who knows but Heaven may grant me to succeed?
For great is oft a friend's persuasive power."
He said, and quickly on his errand sped.
  Meanwhile the Greeks, in firm array, endured
The onset of the Trojans; nor could these   475
The assailants, though in numbers less, repel;
Nor those again the Grecian masses break,
And force their passage through the ships and tents.
As by a rule, in cunning workman's hand,
Who all his art by Pallas' aid has learnt,   480
A vessel's plank is smooth and even laid;
So level lay the balance of the fight.
Others round other ships maintained the war,
But Hector that of Ajax sought alone.
For that one ship they two unwearied toiled;   485
Nor Hector Ajax from his post could move,
And burn the ship with fire; nor he repel
The foe who came protected by a God.

Then noble Ajax with his javelin smote
Caletor, son of Clytius, through the breast,   490
As toward the ship a blazing torch he bore;
Thundering he fell, and dropped his hand the torch.
But Hector, when his eyes his kinsman saw
By the dark vessel, prostrate in the dust,
On Trojans and on Lycians called aloud: 495
  " Trojans and Lycians, and ye Dardans, famed
In close encounter, in this press of war
Slack not your efforts; haste to save the son
Of Clytius, nor let Greeks his arms possess,
Who 'mid their throng of ships has nobly fallen."   500
At Ajax, as he spoke, his gleaming spear
He threw, but missed his aim; yet Lycophron,
His comrade, of Cythera, Mastor's son
(Who flying from Cythera's lovely isle
With guilt of bloodshed, near to Ajax dwelt),   505
Standing beside the chief, above the ear
He struck, and pierced the brain: from the tall prow
Backward he fell, his limbs relaxed in death.
Then Ajax, shuddering, on his brother called:
  "Good Teucer, we have lost a faithful friend,   510
The son of Mastor, our Cytheran guest,
Whom as a father all revered; who now
Lies slain by noble Hector. Where are then
Thine arrows, swift-winged messengers of fate,
And where thy trusty bow, Apollo's gift?"   515
  Thus Ajax; Teucer heard, and ran in haste,
And stood beside him, with his bended bow,
And well-stored quiver: on the Trojans fast
He poured his shafts; and struck Pisenor's son,

Clitus, the comrade of Polydamas,   520
The noble son of Panthöus; he the reins
Held in his hand, and all his care bestowed
To guide his horses; for, where'er the throng
Was thickest, there in Hector's cause, and Troy's,
He still was found; but o'er him hung the doom   525
Which none might turn aside; for from behind
The fateful arrow struck him through the neck;
Down from the car he fell; swerving aside,
The startled horses whirled the empty car.
Them first the King Polydamas beheld,   530
And stayed their course; to Protiaon's son,
Astynöus, then he gave them, with command
To keep good watch, and still be near at hand;
Then 'mid the foremost joined again the fray.
Again at Hector of the brazen helm   535
An arrow Teucer aimed; and had the shaft
The life of Hector quenched in mid career,
Not long the fight had raged around the ships:
But Jove's all-seeing eye beheld, who watched
O'er Hector's life, and Teucer's hopes deceived.   540
The bow's well-twisted string he snapped in twain,
As Teucer drew; the brass-tipped arrow flew
Wide of the mark, and dropped his hand the bow.
Then to his brother, all aghast, he cried:
"O Heaven, some God our best-laid schemes of war 545
Confounds, who from my hands hath wrenched the bow,
And snapped the newly-twisted string, which I
But late attached, my swift-winged shafts to bear."
    Whom answered thus great Ajax Telamon:
"O friend, leave there thine arrows and thy bow,   550

Marred by some God who grudges our renown;
But take in hand thy ponderous spear, and cast
Thy shield about thy shoulders, and thyself
Stand forth, and urge the rest, to face the foe.
Let us not tamely yield, if yield we must,   555
Our well-built ships, but nobly dare the fight."
    Thus Ajax spoke; and Teucer in the tent
Bestowed his bow, and o'er his shoulders threw
His fourfold shield; and on his firm-set head
A helm he placed, well-wrought, with horsehair plume, 560
That nodded, fearful, o'er his brow; his hand
Grasped the firm spear, with sharpened point of brass:
Then ran, and swiftly stood by Ajax' side.
Hector meanwhile, who saw the weapon marred,
To Trojans and to Lycians called aloud: 565
    "Trojans and Lycians, and ye Dardans famed
In close encounter, quit ye now like men;
Against the ships your wonted valour show.
E'en now, before our eyes, hath Jove destroyed
A chieftain's weapon. Easy 'tis to trace   570
O'er human wars the o'erruling hand of Jove,
To whom he gives the prize of victory,
And whom, withholding aid, he minishes,
As now the Greeks, while we his favour gain.
Pour then your force united on the ships;   575
And if there be among you, who this day
Shall meet his doom, by sword or arrow slain,
E'en let him die! a glorious death is his
Who for his country falls; and dying, leaves
Preserved from danger, children, wife, and home,   580
His heritage uninjured, when the Greeks

Embarking hence shall take their homeward way."
His words fresh courage roused in every breast.
Ajax, on the other side addressed the Greeks:
"Shame on ye, Greeks! this very hour decides   585
If we must perish, or be saved, and ward
Destruction from our ships; and can ye hope
That each, if Hector of the glancing helm
Shall burn our ships, on foot can reach his home?
Or hear ye not, how, burning to destroy   590
Our vessels, Hector cheers his forces on?
Not to the dance, but to the fight he calls;
Nor better counsel can for us be found,
Than in close fight with heart and hand to join.
Better at once to risk or die, or live,   595
Than thus remain pent up beside our ships,
In dire distress, by meaner men beset."
His words fresh courage roused in every breast.
Then Hector vanquished Perimedes' son,
Schedius, the Phocian chief; on the other side   600
Laödamas, Antenor's noble son,
The foot commanding, was by Ajax slain;
While of his arms Polydamas despoiled
Cyllenian Otus, friend of Phyleus' son,
The proud Epeians' leader; Meges saw,   605
And rushed upon him; but Polydamas,
Stooping, the blow evaded; him he missed;
For Phœbus willed not Panthöus' son should fall
In the front rank contending; but the spear
Smote Crœsmus through the breast; thundering he fell, 610
And from his corpse the victor stripped his arms.
Him Dolops, son of Lampus, spearman skilled,

Well trained in every point of war, assailed
(The son of Lampus he, the prince of men,
Son of Laomedon); from close at hand   615
Forward he sprang, and thrust at Meges' shield;
But him the solid corslet which he wore,
With breast and back-piece fitted, saved from harm:
The corslet Phyleus brought from Ephyra,
By Selles' stream; Euphetes, King of men,   620
Bestowed it as a friendly gift, to wear
In battle for a guard from hostile spears;
Which from destruction now preserved his son.
Next Meges struck, with keen-edged spear, the crown
Of Dolops' brass-bound, horsehair-crested helm,   625
Severing the horsehair plume, which, brilliant late
With crimson dye, now lay defiled in dust.
Yet fought he on, and still for victory hoped;
But warlike Mencläus to the aid
Of Meges came; of Dolops unobserved   630
He stood, and from behind his shoulder pierced;
The point, its course pursuing, through his breast
Was driven, and headlong on his face he fell.
Forthwith advanced the two to seize the spoils;
But loudly Hector on his kinsmen called;   635
On all, but chief on Icetäon's son,
The valiant Melanippus; he erewhile,
In far Percote, ere the foes appeared,
Pastured his herds; but when the ships of Greece
Approached the shore, to Ilion back he came;   640
There, 'mid the Trojans eminent, he dwelt
In Priam's house, beloved as Priam's son.
Him Hector called by name, and thus addressed:

" Why, Melanippus, stand we idly thus?
Doth not thy slaughtered kinsman touch thy heart? 645
See how they rush on Dolops' arms to seize;
Then on! no distant war must now be waged,
But hand to hand, till or the Greeks be slain,
Or lofty Troy, with all her children, fall."
　He said, and led the way; him followed straight 650
The godlike chief; great Ajax Telamon
Meanwhile the Greeks encouraged to the fight,
And cried, " Brave comrades, quit ye now like men;
Bear a stout heart; and in the stubborn fight
Let each to other mutual succeour give;　　　　　655
By mutual succour more are saved than fall;
In timid flight nor fame nor safety lies."
　He said; his words sank deep in hearts resolved
On firm defence; as with a wall of brass
The ships they guarded; though against them Jove 660
Led on the Trojans; Meneläus then
With stirring words Antilochus addressed:
" Antilochus, than thou, of all the Greeks
Is none more active, or more light of foot;
None stronger hurls the spear; then from the crowd 665
Spring forth, and aim to reach some Trojan's life."
　Thus saying, he withdrew; fired by his words,
Forth sprang the youth, and poised his glittering spear,
Glancing around him; back the Trojans drew
Before his aim; nor flew the spear in vain;　　　　670
But through the breast it pierced, as on he came,
Brave Melanippus, Icetäon's son.
Thundering he fell, and loud his armour rang.
Forth sprang Antilochus, as springs a hound

Upon a fawn, which from its lair disturbed   675
A hunter's shaft has struck, and quelled its powers;
So, Melanippus, sprang to seize thy spoils
The stout Antilochus; but not unmarked
Of Hector's eye, who, hastening through the press,
Advanced to meet him; waited not the attack,   680
Bold warrior as he was, Antilochus,
But trembling fled: as when a beast of prey,
Conscious of evil deed, amid the herd
The guardian dog or herdsman's self has slain,
And flies, ere yet the avenging crowd collect;   685
So fled the son of Nestor; onward pressed,
By Hector led, the Trojans; loud their shouts,
As on the Greeks their murderous shafts they poured:
Yet turned he, when his comrades' ranks he reached.
Then on the ships, as ravening lions, fell   690
The Trojans: they but worked the will of Jove,
Who still their courage raised, and quelled the Greeks;
Of victory these debarred, and those inspired;
For so he willed, that Hector, Priam's son,
Should wrap in fire the beakèd ships of Greece,   695
And Thetis to the uttermost obtain
Her over-bold petition; yet did Jove,
The Lord of Counsel, wait but to behold
The flames ascending from the blazing ships:
For from that hour the Trojans, backward driven,   700
Should to the Greeks the final triumph leave.
With such design, to seize the ships, he fired
The already burning zeal of Priam's son;
Fiercely he raged, as terrible as Mars
With brandished spear; or as a raging fire   705

'Mid the dense thickets on the mountain side.
The foam was on his lips; bright flashed his eyes
Beneath his awful brows, and terribly
Above his temples waved amid the fray
The helm of Hector; Jove himself from Heaven   710
His guardian hand extending, him alone
With glory crowning 'mid the host of men;
But short his term of glory; for the day
Was fast approaching, when, with Pallas' aid,
The might of Peleus' son should work his doom.   715
Oft he essayed to break the ranks, where'er
The densest throng and noblest arms he saw;
But strenuous though his efforts, all were vain:
They, massed in close array, his charge withstood;
Firm as a craggy rock, upstanding high,   720
Close by the hoary sea, which meets unmoved
The boisterous currents of the whistling winds,
And the big waves that bellow round its base;
So stood unmoved the Greeks, and undismayed.
At length, all blazing in his arms, he sprang   725
Upon the mass; so plunging down, as when
On some tall vessel, from beneath the clouds
A giant billow, tempest-nursed, descends:
The deck is drenched in foam; the stormy wind
Howls in the shrouds; the affrighted seamen quail 730
In fear, but little way from death removed;
So quailed the spirit in every Grecian breast.
    As when a ravening lion on a herd
Of heifers falls, which on some marshy mead
Feed numberless, beneath the care of one,   735
Unskilled from beasts of prey to guard his charge;

And while beside the front or rear he walks,
The lion on the unguarded centre springs,
Seizes on one, and scatters all the rest;
So Hector, led by Jove, in wild alarm   740
Scattered the Grecians all; but one alone,
Brave Periphetes, of Mycenæ, slew;
The son of Copreus, whom Eurystheus sent
His envoy to the might of Hercules;
Far nobler than the father was the son;   745
In speed of foot, in warlike might, in mind,
In all, among Mycenians foremost he:
Who now on Hector fresh renown conferred;
For, backward as he stepped, against the rim
Of the broad shield which for defence he bore,   750
Down reaching to his feet, he tripped, and thus
Entangled, backward fell; and as he fell,
Around his temples clattered loud his helm.
Hector beheld, and o'er him stood in haste,
And with his spear transfixed his breast, and slew 755
Before his comrades' eyes; yet dared not one,
Though grieving for their comrade's loss, advance
To rescue; such of Hector was their awe.
They fronted now the ships; the leading prows
Which first were drawn on shore, still barred their way; 760
Yet on they streamed; and from the foremost ships,
Now hardly pressed, the Greeks perforce retired;
But closely massed before the tents they stood,
Not scattered o'er the camp; by shame restrained,
And fear; and loudly each exhorted each.   765
Gerenian Nestor chief, the prop of Greece,
Thus by their fathers singly each adjured:

"Quit ye like men, dear friends; and think it shame
To forfeit now the praise of other men;
Let each man now his children and his wife,   770
His fortunes and his parents, bear in mind;
And not the living only, but the dead;
For them, the absent, I, your suppliant, pray,
That firm ye stand, and scorn disgraceful flight."
His words fresh courage roused in every breast;   775
And from their eyeballs Pallas purged away
The film of darkness; and on every side,
Both toward the ships and toward the level fight,
Clear light diffused; there Hector they discerned,
And all his comrades, those who stood aloof,   780
And those who near the ships maintained the war.
Then was not Ajax' mighty soul content
To stand where stood the other sons of Greece;
Along the vessels' lofty decks he moved
With haughty stride; a ponderous boarding-pike,   785
Well polished, and with rivets well secured,
Of two and twenty cubits' length, he bore.
As one well-skilled in feats of horsemanship,
Who from a troop of horses on the plain
Has parted four, and down the crowded road,   790
While men and women all in wonder gaze,
Drives toward the city; and with force untired
From one to other springs, as on they fly;
O'er many a vessel's deck so Ajax passed
With lofty stride, and voice that reached to Heaven, 795
As loudly shouting on the Greeks he called
To save their ships and tents: nor Hector stayed

Amid the closely-bucklered Trojan ranks;
But, as upon a flock of birds, that feed
Beside a river's bank, or geese, or cranes,   800
Or long-necked swans, a fiery eagle swoops;
So on the dark-prowed ship with furious rush
Swept Hector down; him Jove with mighty hand
Sustained, and with him forward urged the crowd.
Fierce round the ships again the battle raged;   805
Well might ye deem no previous toil had worn
Their strength, who in that dread encounter met;
With edge so keen, and stubborn will they fought.
But varying far their hopes and fears: the Greeks
Of safety and escape from death despaired;   810
While high the hopes in every Trojan's breast,
To burn the ships, and slay the warlike Greeks:
So minded each, opposed in arms they stood.
   On a swift-sailing vessel's stern, that bore
Protesiläus to the coast of Troy,   815
But to his native country bore not thence,
Hector had laid his hand; around that ship
Trojans and Greeks in close encounter met.
The arrow's or the javelin's distant flight
They waited not, but, fired with equal rage,   820
Fought hand to hand, with axe and hatchet keen,
And mighty swords, and double-pointed spears.
Many a fair-hilted blade, with iron bound,
Dropped from the hands, or from the severed arms,
Of warrior chiefs; the dark earth ran with blood: 825
Yet loosed not Hector of the stern his hold,
But grasped the poop, and on the Trojans called:

"Bring fire, and all together loud and clear
Your war-cry raise; this day will Jove repay
Our labours all, with capture of those ships, ,   830
Which hither came, against the will of Heaven,
And which on us unnumbered ills have brought,
By our own Elders' fault, who me, desiring
Even at their vessels' sterns to urge the war,
Withheld, and to the town the troops confined.   835
But Jove all-seeing, if he then o'erruled
Our better mind, himself is now our aid."
    Thus he: they onward pressed with added zeal;
Nor Ajax yet endured, by hostile spears
Now sorely galled; yet but a little space,   840
Back to the helmsman's seven-foot board he moved,
Expecting death; and left the lofty deck,
Where long he stood on guard; but still his spear
The Trojans kept aloof, whoe'er essayed
Amid the ships to launch the unwearied flames;   845
And, loudly shouting, to the Greeks he called:
    "Friends, Grecian heroes, ministers of Mars,
Quit ye like men! dear friends, remember now
Your wonted valour! think ye in your rear
To find supporting forces, or some fort   850
Whose walls may give you refuge from your foe?
No city is nigh, whose well-appointed towers,
Manned by a friendly race, may give us aid;
But here, upon the well-armed Trojans' soil,
And only resting on the sea, we lie   855
Far from our country; not in faint retreat,
But in our own good arms, our safety lies."

He said; and with his sharp-edged spear his words
He followed up; if any Trojan dared,
By Hector's call inspired, with fiery brand 860
To assail the ships, him with his ponderous spear
Would Ajax meet; and thus before the ships
Twelve warriors, hand to hand, his prowess felt. 863

BOOK XVI.

THUS round the well-manned ship they waged the war:
　Meanwhile by Peleus' son Patroelus stood,
Weeping hot tears; as some dark-watered fount
Pours o'er a eraggy rock its gloomy stream;
Aehilles, swift of foot, with pity saw,　　　　　　　5
And to his friend these wingèd words addressed:
　"Why weeps Patroclus, like an infant girl,
That prays her mother, by whose side she runs,
To take her up; and, elinging to her gown,
Impedes her way, and still with tearful eyes　　　10
Looks in her faee, until she take her up?
Even as that girl, Patroelus, such art thou,
Shedding soft tears: hast thou some tidings brought
Touehing the general weal, or me alone?
Or have some evil news from Phthia eome,　　　　15
Known but to thee? Menœtius, Actor's son,
Yet surely lives; and 'mid his Myrmidons
Lives aged Peleus, son of Æaeus:
Their deaths indeed might well demand our tears:
Or weep'st thou for the Greeks, who round their ships　20
By death their former insolenco repay?
Speak out, that I may know thy eause of grief."
　To whom, with bitter groans, Patroelus thus:
" O son of Peleus, noblest of the Greeks,
Achilles, be not wroth! such weight of woe　　　　25

The Grecian camp oppresses; in their ships
They who were late their bravest and their best,
Sore wounded all by spear or arrow lie;
The valiant son of Tydeus, Diomed,
Pierced by a shaft, Ulysses by a spear,   30
And Agamemnon's self; Eurypylus
By a sharp arrow through the thigh transfixed;
For these, the large resources of their art
The leeches ply, and on their wounds attend;
While thou, Achilles, still remain'st unmoved.   35
Oh, be it never mine to nurse such hate
As thou retain'st, inflexibly severe!
Who e'er may hope in future days by thee
To profit, if thou now forbear to save
The Greeks from shame and loss? Unfeeling man! 40
Sure Peleus, horseman brave, was ne'er thy sire,
Nor Thetis bore thee; from the cold grey sea
And craggy rocks thou hadst thy birth; so hard
And stubborn is thy soul. But if the fear
Of evil prophesied thyself restrain,   45
Or message by thy Goddess-mother brought
From Jove, yet send me forth with all thy force
Of Myrmidons, to be the saving light
Of Greece; and let me to the battle bear
Thy glittering arms, if so the men of Troy,   50
Scared by thy likeness, may forsake the field,
And breathing-time afford the sons of Greece,
Toil-worn; for little pause has yet been theirs.
Fresh and unwearied, we may drive with ease
To their own city, from our ships and tents,   55
The Trojans, worn and battle-wearied men."

Thus prayed he, all unwisely; for the prayer
He uttered, to himself was fraught with death;
To whom, much grieved, Achilles, swift of foot:
"Heaven-born Patroclus, oh, what words are these!   60
Prophetic warnings move me not, though known;
Nor message hath my mother brought from Jove;
But it afflicts my soul, when one I see
That basely robs his equal of his prize,
His lawful prize, by highest valour won;   65
Such grief is mine, such wrong have I sustained.
Her, whom the sons of Greece on me bestowed,
Prize of my spear, the well-walled city stormed,
The mighty Agamemnon, Atreus' son,
Hath borne by force away, as from the hands   70
Of some dishonoured, houseless vagabond.
But let the past be past; I never meant
My wrath should have no end; yet had not thought
My anger to abate, till my own ships
Should hear the war-cry, and the battle bear.   75
But go, and in my well-known armour clad,
Lead forth the valiant Myrmidons to war,
Since the dark cloud of Trojans circles round
The ships in force; and on the shingly beach,
Pent up in narrow limits, lie the Greeks;   80
And all the city hath poured its numbers forth
In hope undoubting; for they see no more
My helm among them flashing; else in flight
Their dead would choke the streams, if but to me
Great Agamemnon bore a kindly mind: 85
But round the camp the battle now is waged.
No more the hands of valiant Diomed,

The Greeks protecting, hurl his fiery spear;
Nor hear I now, from his detested lips,
The shout of Agamemnon; all around   90
Is heard the warrior-slayer Hector's voice,
Cheering his Trojans; with triumphant cries
They, from the vanquished Greeks, hold all the plain.
Nathless do thou, Patroclus, in defence
Fall boldly on, lest they with blazing fire   95
Our ships destroy, and hinder our retreat.
But hear, and ponder well the end of all
I have to say, and so for me obtain
Honour and glory in the eyes of Greece;
And that the beauteous maiden to my arms   100
They may restore, with costly gifts to boot.
The ships relieved, return forthwith; and though
The Thunderer, Juno's Lord, should crown thine arms
With triumph, be not rash, apart from me,
To combat with the warlike sons of Troy;   105
(So should my name in less repute be held;)
Nor, in the keen excitement of the fight
And slaughter of the Trojans, lead thy troops
On toward the city, lest thou find thyself
By some one of the immortal Gods opposed;   110
For the far-darting Phœbus loves them well;
But when in safety thou hast placed the ships,
Delay not to return, and leave the rest
To battle on the plain: for would to Jove,
To Pallas and Apollo, that not one,   115
Or Greek or Trojan, might escape from death,
Save only thou and I; that so we two
Alone might raze the sacred towers of Troy."

Such converse held they; while by hostile spears
Hard pressed, no longer Ajax might endure;   120
At once by Jove's high will and Trojan foes
O'ermastered; loud beneath repeated blows
Clattered around his brow the glittering helm,
As on the well-wrought crest the weapons fell;
And his left arm grew faint, that long had borne   125
The burthen of his shield; yet nought availed
The press of spears to drive him from his post;
Labouring he drew his breath, his every limb
With sweat was reeking; breathing space was none;
Blow followed blow, and ills were heaped on ill.   130
   Say now, ye Nine, who on Olympus dwell,
How first the fire assailed the Grecian ships.
   Hector approached, and on the ashen spear
Of Ajax, close behind the head, let fall
His mighty sword; right through he clove the wood; 135
And in his hand the son of Telamon
The headless shaft held bootless; far away,
Loud ringing, fell to earth the brazen point.
Ajax, dismayed, perceived the hand of Heaven,
And knew that Jove the Thunderer had decreed   140
To thwart his hopes, and victory give to Troy.
Slow he retired; and to the vessel they
The blazing torch applied; high rose the flame
Unquenchable, and wrapped the poop in fire.
The son of Peleus saw, and with his palm   145
Smote on his thigh, and to Patroclus called:
"Up, nobly born Patroclus, car-borne chief!
Up, for I see above the ships ascend
The hostile fires; and lest they seize the ships,

And hinder our retreat, do thou in haste   150
Thine armour don, while I arouse the troops."
   He said: his dazzling arms Patroclus donned:
First on his legs the well-wrought greaves he fixed,
Fastened with silver clasps; his ample chest
The breastplate of Achilles, swift of foot,   155
Star-spangled, richly wrought, defended well;
Around his shoulders slung, his sword he bore,
Brass-bladed, silver-studded; next his shield
Weighty and strong; and on his firm-set head
A helm he wore, well-wrought, with horsehair plume 160
That nodded, fearful, o'er his brow; his hand
Grasped two stout spears, familiar to his hold.
One spear Achilles had, long, ponderous, tough;
But this he touched not; none of all the Greeks,
None, save Achilles' self, that spear could poise;   165
The far-famed Pelian ash, which to his sire,
On Pelion's summit felled, to be the bane
Of mightiest chiefs, the Centaur Chiron gave.
Then to Automedon he gave command
To yoke the horses; him he honoured most,   170
Next to Achilles' self; the trustiest he
In battle to await his chief's behest.
The flying steeds he harnessed to the car,
Xanthus and Balius, fleeter than the winds;
Whom, grazing in the marsh by ocean's stream,   175
Podarge, swift of foot, to Zephyr bore:
And by their side the matchless Pedasus,
Whom from the capture of Eëtion's town
Achilles bore away; a mortal horse,
But with immortal coursers meet to vie.   180

Meantime Achilles, through their several tents,
Summoned to arms the warlike Myrmidons.
They all, like ravening wolves, of courage high,
That on the mountain side have hunted down
An antlered stag, and battened on his flesh :   185
Their chaps all dyed with blood, in troops they go,
With their lean tongues from some black-watered fount
To lap the surface of the dark cool wave,
Their jaws with blood yet reeking, unsubdued
Their courage, and their bellies gorged with flesh ;   190
So round Pelides' valiant follower thronged
The chiefs and rulers of the Myrmidons.
Achilles in the midst to charioteers
And bucklered warriors issued his commands.
Fifty swift ships Achilles, dear to Jove,   195
Led to the coast of Troy ; and ranged in each
Fifty brave comrades manned the rowers' seats.
O'er these five chiefs, on whom he most relied,
He placed, himself the Sovereign Lord of all.
One band Menestheus led, with glancing mail,   200
Son of Sperchius, Heaven-descended stream ;
Him Peleus' daughter, Polydora fair,
A mortal in a God's embrace compressed,
To stout Sperchius bore ; but, by repute,
To Borus, Periercs' son, who her   205
In public, and with ample dower, espoused.
The brave Eudorus led the second band,
Whom Phylas' daughter, Polymele fair,
To Hermes bore ; the maid he saw, and loved,
Amid the virgins, mingling in the dance   210
Of golden-shafted Dian, Huntress-Queen ;

He to her chamber access found, and gained
By stealth her bed; a valiant son she bore,
Eudorus, swift of foot, in battle strong.
But when her infant, by Lucina's aid,   215
Was brought to light, and saw the face of day,
Her to his home, with ample dower enriched,
Echecles, son of Actor, bore away;
While him the aged Phylas kept, and nursed
With tender care, and cherished as his own.   220
The brave Peisander, son of Mæmalus,
The third commanded; of the Myrmidons,
Next to Pelides' friend, the noblest spear.
The fourth, the aged warrior Phœnix led;
The fifth, Alcimedon, Laerces' son: 225
These with their chiefs arranged in order due,
Achilles thus with stirring words addressed:
  "Ye Myrmidons, forget not now the vaunts
Which, while my wrath endured, ye largely poured
Upon the Trojans; me ye freely blamed;   230
'Ill-omened son of Peleus, sure in wrath
Thou wast conceived, implacable, who keep'st
Thy comrades here in idleness enforced!
'Twere better far our homeward way to take,
If such pernicious rancour fill thy soul!'   235
Thus ye reproached me oft! Lo! now ye have
The great occasion which your souls desired!
Then on, and with brave hearts the Trojans meet!"
  His words fresh courage roused in every breast;
And more compact, beneath their monarch's eye,   240
Their ranks were formed; as when a builder lays
The closely-fitting stones, to form the wall

Of some great house, and brave the winds of Heaven;
So close were fitted helm and bossy shield;
Buckler on buckler pressed, and helm on helm,　　245
And man on man; the horsehair plumes above,
That nodded, fearful, from the warriors' brows,
Each other touched; so closely massed they stood.
Before them all stood prominent in arms
Two chiefs, Patroclus and Automedon,　　250
Both with one thought possessed, to lead the fight
In the fore-front of all the Myrmidons.
　　Achilles then within his tent withdrew,
And of a gorgeous coffer raised the lid,
Well-wrought, by silver-footed Thetis placed　　255
On board his ship, and filled with rich attire,
With store of wind-proof cloaks, and carpets soft.
There lay a goblet, richly chased, whence none,
But he alone, might drink the ruddy wine,
Nor might libations thence to other Gods　　260
Be made, save only Jove; this brought he forth,
And first with sulphur purified, and next
Washed with pure water; then his hands he washed,
And drew the ruddy wine; then standing forth
Made in the centre of the court his prayer,　　265
And as he poured the wine, looked up to Heaven,
Not unbeheld of Jove, the lightning's Lord:
　"Great King, Dodona's Lord, Pelasgian Jove,
Who dwell'st on high, and rul'st with sovereign sway
Dodona's wintry heights; where dwell around　　270
Thy Sellian priests, men of unwashen feet,
That on the bare ground sleep; thou once before
Hast heard my prayer, and me with honour crowned,

And on the Greeks inflicted all thy plagues;
Hear yet again, and this my boon accord.   275
I 'mid the throng of ships myself remain;
But with a numerous force of Myrmidons
I send my comrade in my stead to fight:
On him, all-seeing Jove, thy favour pour;
Strengthen his heart, that Hector's self may learn   280
If, e'en alone, my follower knows to fight,
Or only then resistless power displays,
When I myself the toil of battle share.
And from our vessels when the foe is driven,
Grant that with all his arms and comrades true   285
He may in safety to the ships return."
    Thus prayed he; Jove, the Lord of counsel, heard,
And half his prayer he granted, half denied:
For from the ships the battle to repel
He granted; but denied his safe return.   290
His prayers and offerings ended, to the tent
Achilles turned again, and in the chest
Replaced the cup; then issuing forth, he stood
Before the tent; for much he longed to see
The Greeks and Trojans join in battle strife.   295
They who in arms round brave Patroclus stood
Their line of battle formed, with courage high
To dash upon the Trojans; and as wasps
That have their nest beside the public road,
Which boys delight to vex and irritate   300
In wanton play, but to the general harm;
Them if some passing traveller unawares
Disturb, with angry courage forth they rush
In one continuous swarm, to guard their nest:

E'en with such courage poured the Myrmidons   305
Forth from the ships; then uproar wild arose,
And loud Patroclus on his comrades called:
"Ye valiant Myrmidons, who boast yourselves
Achilles' comrades, quit ye now like men;
Your ancient valour prove; to Peleus' son,   310
Of all the Greeks the noblest, so shall we,
His faithful followers, highest honour give;
And Agamemnon's haughty self shall mourn
The slight on Grecia's bravest warrior cast."
His words fresh courage roused in every breast.   315
Thick on the Trojan host their masses fell;
While loud the fleet re-echoed to the sound
Of Grecian cheers; but when the Trojans saw,
Blazing in arms, Mencetius' godlike son,
Himself, and follower; quailed the spirits of all;   320
Their firm-set ranks were shaken; for they deemed
Achilles had beside the ships exchanged
His wrath for friendship; and each several man
Looked round, to find his own escape from death.
Then first Patroclus aimed his glittering spear   325
Amid the crowd, where thickest round the ship
Of brave Protesiläus, raged the war;
And struck Pyræchmes, who from Amydon,
From the wide-flowing stream of Axius, led
The horsehair crested Pæons; him he struck   330
Through the right shoulder; backwards in the dust,
Groaning, he fell; around him quailed with fear
His Pæons all, such terror in their ranks
Patroclus threw, their bravest leader slain,
The foremost in the fight; the crowd he drove   335

Far from the ships, and quenched the blazing fire.
There lay the half-burnt ship; with shouts confused
The Trojans fled; and from amid the ships
Forth poured the Greeks; and loud the clamour rose.

    As when around a lofty mountain's top   340
The lightning's Lord dispels a mass of cloud,
And every crag, and every jutting peak
Is plainly seen, and every forest glade;
And the deep vault of Heaven is opened wide;
So when the Greeks had cleared the ships of fire,   345
They breathed awhile; yet ceased not so the strife;
For not in headlong panic from the ships
The Trojans by the valiant Greeks were driven,
But, though perforce retiring, still made head.

    Then of the chiefs, as wider spread the fight,   350
Each singled each; Menœtius' noble son
First threw his pointed spear, and on the thigh
Struck Arëilochus, in act to turn;
Right through the point was driven; the weighty spear
Shattered the bone, and prone to earth he fell.   355
The warlike Meneläus aimed his spear
Where Thoas' breast, unguarded by his shield,
Was left exposed; and slacked his limbs in death.
Phyleus' brave son, as rushed Amphiclus on,
Stood firm, with eye observant; then the attack   360
Preventing, through his thigh, high up, where lie
The strongest muscles, smote; the weapon's point
Severed the tendons; darkness closed his eyes.
Of Nestor's sons, Antilochus, the first,
Atymnius wounded, driving through his flank   365
The brazen spear; prone on his face he fell.

Then, burning to avenge his brother's death,
Stood Maris o'er the corpse, and hand to hand
Engaged Antilochus; but ere a blow
Was struck, the godlike Thrasymedes drove   370
Through his right shoulder, with unerring aim,
His glittering spear; the point his upper arm
Tore from the muscles, shattering all the bone:
Thundering he fell, and darkness closed his eyes.
So to the shades, by those two brethren's hands   375
Subdued, Sarpedon's comrades brave were sent,
The sons of Amisodarus, who reared
 The dread Chimæra, bane of mortal men.
On Cleobulus, wounded in the press,
Ajax Oïleus sprang, and captive took,   380
Alive; but sudden on his neck let fall
His hilted sword, and quenched the fire of life.
The hot blood dyed the sword; the darkling shades
Of death, and rigorous fate, his eyes o'erspread.
Then Peneleus and Lycon, hand to hand,   385
Engaged in combat; both had missed their aim,
And bootless hurled their weapons; then with swords
They met; first Lycon on the crested helm
Dealt a fierce blow; but in his hand the blade
Up to the hilt was shivered; then the sword   390
Of Peneleus his neck, below the ear,
Dissevered; deeply in his throat the blade
Was plunged, and by the skin alone was stayed;
Down drooped his head, his limbs relaxed in death.
Meriones by speed of foot o'ertook,   395
And, as his car he mounted, Acamas
Through the right shoulder pierced; down from the car

He fell; the shades of death his eyes o'erspread.
Full on the mouth of Erymas was thrust
The weapon of Idomeneus; right through,   400
The white bones crashing, passed the brazen spear
Below the brain; his teeth were shattered all;
With blood, which with convulsive sobs he blew
From mouth and nostril, both his eyes were filled;
And death's dark cloud encompassed him around.   405
Thus slew the Grecian leaders each his man.

As ravening wolves, that lambs or kids assail,
Strayed from their dams, by careless shepherds left
Upon the mountain scattered; these they see,
And tear at once their unresisting prey;   410
So on the Trojans fell the Greeks; in rout
Disastrous they, unmanned by terror, fled.
Great Ajax still, unwearied, longed to hurl
His spear at Hector of the brazen helm;
But he, well skilled in war, his shoulders broad   415
Protected by his shield of tough bull's hide,
Watched for the whizzing shafts, and javelins' whirr.
Full well he knew the tide of battle turned,
Yet held his ground, his trusty friends to save.
As from Olympus, o'er the clear blue sky   420
Pour the dark clouds, when Jove the vault of Heaven
O'erspreads with storm and tempest, from the ships
So poured with panic cries the flying host,
And in disordered rout recrossed the trench.
Then Hector's flying coursers bore him safe   425
Far from the struggling masses, whom the ditch
Detained perforce; there many a royal car
With broken pole the unharnessed horses left.

On, shouting to the Greeks, Patroclus pressed
The flying Trojans; they, with panic cries,   430
Dispersed, the roads encumbered; high uprose
The storms of dust, as from the tents and ships
Back to the city stretched the flying steeds;
And ever, where the densest throng appeared,
With furious threats Patroclus urged his course;   435
His glowing axle traced by prostrate men
Hurled from their cars, and chariots overthrown.
Flew o'er the deep-sunk trench the immortal steeds,
The noble prize the Gods to Peleus gave,
Still onward straining; for he longed to reach,   440
And hurl his spear at Hector; him meanwhile
His flying steeds in safety bore away.
    As in the autumnal season, when the earth
With weight of rain is saturate; when Jove
Pours down his fiercest storms in wrath to men,   445
Who in their courts unrighteous judgments pass,
And justice yield to lawless violence,
The wrath of Heaven despising; every stream
Is brimming o'er; the hills in gulleys deep
Are by the torrents seamed, which, rushing down   450
From the high mountains to the dark-blue sea,
With groans and tumult urge their headlong course,
Wasting the works of man; so urged their flight,
So, as they fled, the Trojan horses groaned.
The foremost ranks cut off, back toward the ships   455
Patroclus drove them, baffling their attempts
To gain the city; and in middle space
Between the ships, the stream, and lofty wall,
Dealt slaughter round him, and of many a chief

The bitter penalty of death required. 460
Then Pronöus with his glittering spear he struck,
Where by the shield his breast was left exposed,
And slacked his limbs in death; thundering he fell.
Next Thestor, son of Œnops, he assailed;
He on his polished car, down-crouching, sat, 465
His mind by fear disordered; from his hands
The reins had dropped; him, thrusting with the spear
Through the right cheek and through the teeth he smote,
Then dragged him, by the weapon, o'er the rail.
As when an Angler on a prominent rock 470
Drags from the sea to shore with hook and line
A weighty fish; so him Patroclus dragged,
Gaping, from off the car; and dashed him down
Upon his face; and life forsook his limbs.
Next Eryalus, eager for the fray, 475
On the mid forehead with a mighty stone
He struck; beneath the ponderous helmet's weight
The skull was split in twain; prostrate he fell,
By life-consuming death encompassed round.
Forthwith Amphoterus, and Erymas, 480
Epaltes, Echius, and Tlepolemus,
Son of Damastor, Pyris, Ipheus brave,
Euippus, Polymelus, Argeas' son,
In quick succession to the ground he brought.
Sarpedon his ungirdled forces saw 485
Promiscuous fall before Menœtius' son,
And to the Lycians called in loud reproof:
"Shame, Lycians! whither fly ye? why this haste?
I will myself this chief confront, and learn
Who this may be of bearing proud and high, 490

Who on the Trojans grievous harm hath wrought,
And many a warrior's limbs relaxed in death."
   He said, and from his car, accoutred, sprang;
Patroclus saw, and he too leaped to earth.
As on a lofty rock, with angry screams,   495
Hook-beaked, with talons curved, two vultures fight;
So with loud shouts these two to battle rushed.
The son of Saturn pitying saw, and thus
To Juno spoke, his sister and his wife:
   "Woe, woe! that fate decrees my best-beloved,   500
Sarpedon, by Patroclus' hand to fall;
E'en now conflicting thoughts my soul divide,
To bear him from the fatal strife unhurt,
And set him down on Lycia's fertile plains,
Or leave him by Patroclus' hand to fall."   505
   Whom answered thus the stag-eyed Queen of Heaven:
"What words, dread son of Saturn, dost thou speak?
Wouldst thou a mortal man from death withdraw
Long since by fate decreed? Do what thou wilt;
Yet cannot we, the rest, applaud thine act.   510
This too I say, and turn it in thy mind:
If to his home Sarpedon thou restore
Alive, bethink thee, will not other Gods
Their sons too from the stubborn fight withdraw?
For in the field around the walls of Troy   515
Are many sons of Gods, in all of whom
This act of thine will angry feelings rouse.
But if thou love him, and thy soul deplore
His coming doom, yet in the stubborn fight
Leave him beneath Patroclus' hand to fall: 520
Then, when his spirit hath fled, the charge assign

To Death and gentle Sleep, that in their arms
They bear him safe to Lycia's wide-spread plains:
There shall his brethren and his friends perform
His funeral rites, and mound and column raise,   525
The fitting tribute to the mighty dead."
    Thus she; the Sire of Gods and men complied
But to the ground some drops of blood let fall,
In honour of his son, whom fate decreed,
Far from his country, on the fertile plains   530
Of Troy to perish by Patroclus' hand.
As near the champions drew, Patroclus first
His weapon hurled, and Thrasymedes brave,
The faithful follower of Sarpedon, struck
Below the waist, and slacked his limbs in death.   535
Thrown in his turn, Sarpedon's glittering spear
Flew wide; and Pedasus, the gallant horse,
Through the right shoulder wounded; with a scream
He fell, and in the dust breathed forth his life,
As, shrieking loud, his noble spirit fled.   540
This way and that his two companions swerved;
Creaked the strong yoke, and tangled were the reins,
As in the dust the prostrate courser lay.
Automedon the means of safety saw;
And drawing from beside his brawny thigh   545
His keen-edged sword, with no uncertain blow
Cut loose the fallen horse; again set straight,
The two, extended, stretched the tightened rein.
Again in mortal strife the warriors closed:
Once more Sarpedon hurled his glittering spear   550
In vain; above Patroclus' shoulder flew
The point, innocuous; from his hand in turn

The spear not vainly thrown, Sarpedon struck
Where lies the diaphragm, below the heart.
He fell; as falls an oak, or poplar tall,   555
Or lofty pine, which on the mountain top
For some proud ship the woodman's axe hath hewn;
So he, with death-cry sharp, before his car
Extended lay, and clutched the blood-stained soil.
As when a lion on the herd has sprung,   560
And, 'mid the heifers seized, the lordly bull
Lies bellowing, crushed between the lion's jaws;
So by Patroclus slain, the Lycian chief,
Undaunted still, his faithful comrade called;
"Good Glaucus, warrior tried, behoves thee now   565
Thy spearmanship to prove, and warlike might.
Welcome the fray; put forth thine utmost speed;
Call on the Lycian chiefs, on every side,
To press around, and for Sarpedon fight;
Thou too thine arms for my protection wield;   570
For I to thee, through all thy future days,
Shall be a ceaseless scandal and reproach,
If me, thus slain before the Grecian ships,
The Greeks be suffered of my arms to spoil:
But stand thou fast, and others' courage raise."   575
    Thus as he spoke, the shades of death o'erspread
His eyes and nostrils; then with foot firm-set
Upon his chest, Patroclus from the corpse
Drew, by main force, the fast-adhering spear;
The life forth issuing with the weapon's point.   580
Loosed from the royal car, the snorting steeds,
Eager for flight, the Myrmidons detained.
Deep-grieving, Glaucus heard his voice: and chafed

His spirit within him, that he lacked the power
To aid his comrade; with his hand he grasped   585
His wounded arm, in torture from the shaft
By Teucer shot, to save the Greeks from death,
As on he pressed to scale the lofty wall:
Then to Apollo thus addressed his prayer:

"Hear me, great King, who, as on Lycia's plains, 590
Art here in Troy; and hear'st in every place
Their voice who suffer, as I suffer now.
A grievous wound I bear, and sharpest pangs
My arm assail, nor may the blood be stanched:
The pain weighs down my shoulder; and my hand 595
Hath lost its power to fight, or grasp my spear.
Sarpedon, bravest of the brave, is slain,
The son of Jove; yet Jove preserved him not.
But thou, O king, this grievous wound relieve;
Assuage the pain, and give me strength to urge   600
My Lycian comrades to maintain the war,
And fight myself to guard the noble dead."

Thus as he prayed, his prayer Apollo heard,
Assuaged his pains, and from the grievous wound
Stanched the dark blood, and filled his soul with strength.
Glaucus within himself perceived, and knew,   [605
Rejoicing, that the God had heard his prayer.
First, hurrying here and there, he called on all
The Lycian leaders for their King to fight:
Then 'mid the Trojans went with lofty step,   610
And first to Panthöus' son, Polydamas,
To brave Agenor and Æneas next;
Then Hector of the brazen helm himself;
Approaching, thus with wingèd words addressed:

"Hector, forgett'st thou quite thy brave allies, 615
Who freely in thy cause pour forth their lives,
Far from their home and friends? but they from thee
No aid receive; Sarpedon lies in death,
The leader of the bucklered Lycian bands,
Whose justice and whose power were Lycia's shield; 620
Him by Patroclus' hand hath Mars subdued.
But, friends, stand by me now! with just revenge
Inspired, determine that the Myrmidons
Shall not, how grieved soe'er for all the Greeks
Who by our spears beside the ships have fallen, 625
Our dead dishonour, and his arms obtain."
    He said; and through the Trojans thrilled the sense
Of grief intolerable, unrestrained;
For he, though stranger-born, was of the State
A mighty pillar; and his followers 630
A numerous host; and he himself in fight
Among the foremost; so, against the Greeks,
With fiery zeal they rushed, by Hector led,
Grieved for Sarpedon's loss; on the other side
Patroclus' manly heart the Greeks aroused, 635
And to the Ajaces first, themselves inflamed
With warlike zeal, he thus addressed his speech:
    "Ye two Ajaces, now is come the time
Your former fame to rival, or surpass:
The man hath fallen, who first o'erleaped our wall, 640
Sarpedon; now remains, that, having slain,
We should his corpse dishonour, and his arms
Strip off; and should some comrade dare attempt
His rescue, him too with our spears subdue."
    He said; and they, with martial ardour fired, 645

Rushed to the conflict. When on either side
The reinforced battalions were arrayed,
Trojans and Lycians, Myrmidons and Greeks
Around the dead in sternest combat met,
With fearful shouts; and loud their armour rang.　650
Then, to enhance the horror of the strife
Around his son, with darkness Jove o'erspread
The stubborn fight: the Trojans first drove back
The keen-eyed Greeks; for first a warrior fell,
Not of the meanest 'mid the Myrmidons,　　　655
Epegeus, son of valiant Agacles;
Who in Budæum's thriving state bore rule
Erewhile; but flying for a kinsman slain,
To Peleus and the silver-footed Queen
He came a suppliant; with Achilles thence　　660
To Ilion sent, to join the war of Troy.
Him, as he stretched his hand to seize the dead,
Full on the forehead, with a massive stone
Great Hector smote; within the ponderous helm
The skull was split in twain; prone on the corpse　665
He fell, by life-destroying death subdued.
Grieved was Patroclus for his comrade slain;
Forward he darted, as a swift-winged hawk,
That swoops amid the starlings and the daws;
So swift didst thou, Patroclus, car-borne chief,　　670
Upon the Trojans and the Lycians spring,
Thy soul with anger for thy comrade filled.
A ponderous stone he hurled at Sthenelas,
Son of Ithæmenes; the mighty mass
Fell on his neck, and all the muscles crushed.　　675
Back drew great Hector and the chiefs of Troy;

Far as a javelin's flight, in sportive strife,
Or in the deadly battle, hurled by one
His utmost strength exerting; back so far
The Trojans drew, so far the Greeks pursued.   680
Glaucus, the leader of the Lycian spears,
First turning, slew the mighty Bathycles,
The son of Chalcon; he in Hellas dwelt,
In wealth surpassing all the Myrmidons.
Him, as he gained upon him in pursuit,   685
Quick turning, Glaucus through the breast transfixed;
Thundering he fell; deep grief possessed the Greeks
At loss of one so valiant; fiercely joyed
The Trojans, and around him crowded thick;
Nor of their wonted valour were the Greeks   690
Oblivious, but still onward held their course.
Then slew Meriones a crested chief,
The bold Laogonus, Onetor's son;
Onetor, of Idæan Jove the Priest,
And by the people as a God revered.   695
Below the ear he struck him; from his limbs
The spirit fled, and darkness veiled his eyes.
   Then at Meriones Æneas threw
His brazen spear, in hopes beneath his shield
To find a spot unguarded; he beheld,   700
And downward stooping, shunned the brazen death;
Behind him far, deep in the soil infixed,
The weapon stood; there Mars its impulse stayed;
So, bootless hurled, though by no feeble hand,
Æneas' spear stood quivering in the ground;   705
Then thus in wrath he cried: "Meriones,
 Had it but struck thee, nimble as thou art,

My spear had brought thy dancing ·to a close."
  To whom the spearman skilled, Meriones:
"Brave as thou art, Æneas, 'tis too much   710
For thee to hope the might of all to quell,
Who dare confront thee; thou art mortal too!
And if my aim be true, and should my spear
But strike thee fair, all valiant as thou art,
And confident, yet me thy fall shall crown   715
With triumph, and thy soul to Hades send."
  He said; and him Menœtius' noble son
Addressed with grave rebuke: "Meriones,
Brave warrior, why thus waste the time in words?
Trust me, good friend, 'tis not by vaunting speech, 720
Unseconded by deeds, that we may hope
To scare away the Trojans from the slain:
Hands are for battle, words for council meet;
Boots it not now to wrangle, but to fight."
  He said, and led the way; him followed straight 725
The godlike chief; forthwith, as loudly rings,
Amid the mountain forest's deep recess,
The woodman's axe, and far is heard the sound;
So from the wide-spread earth their clamour rose,
As brazen arms, and shields, and tough bull's hide 730
Encountered swords and double-pointed spears.
Nor might the sharpest sight Sarpedon know,
From head to foot with wounds and blood and dust
Disfigured; thickly round the dead they swarmed.
As when at spring-tide in the cattle-sheds   735
Around the milk-can swarm the buzzing flies,
While the warm milk is frothing in the pail;
So swarmed they round the dead; nor Jove the while

Turned from the stubborn fight his piercing glance;
But still looked down with gaze intent, and mused 740
Upon Patroclus' coming fate, in doubt,
If he too there beside Sarpedon slain,
Should perish by illustrious Hector's hand,
Spoiled of his arms; or yet be spared awhile
To swell the labours of the battle-field.   745
He judged it best at length, that once again
The gallant follower of Peleus' son
Should toward the town with fearful slaughter drive
The Trojans, and their brazen-helmèd chief.
First Hector's soul with panic fear he filled   750
Mounting his car, he fled, and urged to flight
The Trojans; for he saw the scales of Jove.
Then nor the valiant Lycians held their ground;
All fled in terror, as they saw their king
Pierced through the heart, amid a pile of dead;   755
For o'er his body many a warrior fell,
When Saturn's son the conflict fierce inflamed.
Then from Sarpedon's breast they stripped his arms,
Of brass refulgent; these Menœtius' son
Sent by his comrades to the ships of Greece.   760
    To Phœbus then the Cloud-compeller thus:
" Hie thee, good Phœbus, from amid the spears
Withdraw Sarpedon, and from all his wounds
Cleanse the dark gore; then bear him far away,
And lave his body in the flowing stream;   765
Then with divine ambrosia all his limbs
Anointing, clothe him in immortal robes.
To two swift bearers give him then in charge,
To Sleep and Death, twin brothers, in their arms

To bear him safe to Lycia's wide-spread plains: 770
There shall his brethren and his friends perform
His funeral rites, and mound and column raise,
The fitting tribute to the mighty dead."
 He said; obedient to his father's words,
Down to the battle-field Apollo sped 775
From Ida's height; and from amid the spears
Withdrawn, he bore Sarpedon far away,
And laved his body in the flowing stream;
Then with divine ambrosia all his limbs
Anointing, clothed him in immortal robes; 780
To two swift bearers gave him then in charge,
To Sleep and Death, twin brothers; in their arms
They bore him safe to Lycia's wide-spread plains.
 Then to Automedon Patroclus gave
His orders, and the flying foe pursued. 785
Oh much deceived, insensate! had he now
But borne in mind the words of Peleus' son,
He might have 'scaped the bitter doom of death.
But still Jove's will the will of man o'errules:
Who strikes with panic, and of victory robs 790
The bravest; and anon excites to war;
Who now Patroclus' breast with fury filled.
Whom then, Patroclus, first, whom slew'st thou last,
When summoned by the Gods to meet thy doom?
Adrastus, and Autonöus, Perimus 795
The son of Meges, and Echeclus next;
Epistor, Melanippus, Elasus,
And Mulius, and Pylartes; these he slew;
The others all in flight their safety found.
 Then had the Greeks the lofty-gated town 800

Of Priam captured by Patroclus' hand,
So forward and so fierce he bore his spear;
But on the well-built tower Apollo stood,
On his destruction bent, and Troy's defence.
The jutting angle of the lofty wall   805
Patroclus thrice assailed; his onset thrice
Apollo, with his own immortal hands
Repelling, backward thrust his glittering shield.
But when again, with more than mortal force
He made his fourth attempt, with awful mien   810
And threatening voice the Far-destroyer spoke:
    "Back, Heaven-born chief, Patroclus! not to thee
Hath fate decreed the triumph to destroy
The warlike Trojans' city; no, nor yet
To great Achilles, mightier far than thou."   815
    Thus as he spoke, Patroclus backward stepped,
Shrinking before the Far-destroyer's wrath.
Still Hector kept before the Scæan gates
His coursers; doubtful, if again to dare
The battle-throng, or summon all the host   820
To seek the friendly shelter of the wall.
Thus as he mused, beside him Phœbus stood,
In likeness of a warrior stout and brave,
Brother of Hecuba, the uncle thence
Of noble Hector, Asius, Dymas' son;   825
Who dwelt in Phrygia, by Sangarius' stream;
His form assuming, thus Apollo spoke;
    "Hector, why shrink'st thou from the battle thus?
It ill beseems thee! Would to Heaven that I
So far thy greater were, as thou art mine;   830
Then sorely shouldst thou rue this abstinence.

But, forward thou! against Patroclus urge
Thy fiery steeds, and, slaying him, obtain,
If so Apollo will, immortal fame."
    This said, the God rejoined the strife of men;   835
And noble Hector bade Cebriones
Drive 'mid the fight his car; before him moved
Apollo, scattering terror 'mid the Greeks,
And lustre adding to the arms of Troy.
All others Hector passed unnoticed by,   840
Nor stayed to slay; Patroclus was the mark
At which his coursers' clattering hoofs he drove.
On the other side, Patroclus from his car
Leaped to the ground: his left hand held his spear;
And in the right a ponderous mass he bore   845
Of rugged stone, that filled his ample grasp:
The stone he hurled; not far it missed its mark,
Nor bootless flew; but Hector's charioteer
It struck, Cebriones, a bastard son
Of royal Priam, as the reins he held.   850
Full on his temples fell the jagged mass,
Drove both his eyebrows in, and crushed the bone;
Before him in the dust his eyeballs fell;
And. like a diver, from the well-wrought car
Headlong he plunged; and life forsook his limbs.   855
O'er whom Patroclus thus with bitter jest:
" Heaven! what agility! how deftly thrown
That somersault! if only in the sea
Such feats he wrought, with him might few compete,
Diving for oysters, if with such a plunge   860
He left his boat, how rough soe'er the waves,
As from his car he plunges to the ground:

Troy can, it seems, accomplished tumblers boast."
    Thus saying, on Cebriones he sprang,
As springs a lion, through the breast transfixed,   865
In act the sheepfold to despoil, and dies
The victim of his courage; so didst thou
Upon Cebriones, Patroclus, spring.
Down from his car too Hector leaped to earth.
So, o'er Cebriones, opposed they stood;   870
As on the mountain, o'er a slaughtered stag,
Both hunger-pinched, two lions fiercely fight,
So o'er Cebriones two mighty chiefs,
Menœtius' son and noble Hector, strove,
Each in the other bent to plunge his spear.   875
The head, with grasp unyielding, Hector held;
Patroclus seized the foot; and, crowding round,
Trojans and Greeks in stubborn conflict closed.
    As when, encountering in some mountain-glen,
Eurus and Notus shake the forest deep,   880
Of oak, or ash, or slender cornel-tree,
Whose tapering branches are together thrown,
With fearful din, and crash of broken boughs;
So mixed confusedly, Greeks and Trojans fought,
No thought of flight by either entertained.   885
Thick o'er Cebriones the javelins flew,
And feathered arrows, bounding from the string;
And ponderous stones that on the bucklers rang,
As round the dead they fought; amid the dust
That eddying rose, his art forgotten all,   890
A mighty warrior, mightily he lay.
While in mid Heaven the sun pursued his course,
Thick flew the shafts, and fast the people fell

On either side; but when declining day
Brought on the hour that sees the loosened steers,   895
The Greeks were stronger far; and from the darts
And Trojan battle-cry Cebriones
They drew, and from his breast his armour stripped.
Fiercely Patroclus on the Trojans fell:
Thrice he assailed them, terrible as Mars,   900
With fearful shouts; and thrice nine foes he slew:
But when again, with more than mortal force
His fourth assault he made, thy term of life,
Patroclus, then approached its final close:
For Phœbus' awful self encountered thee,   905
Amid the battle throng, of thee unseen,
For thickest darkness shrouded all his form:
He stood behind, and with extended palm
Dealt on Patroclus' neck and shoulders broad
A mighty buffet; dizzy swam his eyes,   910
And from his head Apollo snatched the helm;
Clanked, as it rolled beneath the horses' feet,
The visored helm; the horsehair plume with blood
And dust polluted; never till that day
Was that proud helmet so with dust defiled,   915
That wont to deck a godlike chief, and guard
Achilles' noble head, and graceful brow:
Now by the will of Jove to Hector given.

   Now death was near at hand; and in his grasp
His spear was shivered, ponderous, long, and tough,   920
Brass-pointed; with its belt, the ample shield
Fell from his shoulders; and Apollo's hand,
The royal son of Jove, his corslet loosed.
Then was his mind bewildered; and his limbs

Gave way beneath him; all aghast he stood: 925
Him, from behind, a Dardan, Panthöus' son,
Euphorbus, peerless 'mid the Trojan youth,
To hurl the spear, to run, to drive the car,
Approaching close, between the shoulders stabbed;
He, trained to warfare, from his car, ere this   930
A score of Greeks had from their chariots hurled:
Such was the man who thee, Patroclus, first
Wounded, but not subdued; the ashen spear
He, in all haste withdrew; nor dared confront
Patroclus, though disarmed, in deadly strife.   935
    Back to his comrades' sheltering ranks retired,
From certain death, Patroclus: by the stroke
Of Phœbus vanquished, and Euphorbus' spear:
But Hector, when Patroclus from the fight
He saw retreating, wounded, through the ranks   940
Advancing, smote him through the flank; right through
The brazen spear was driven; thundering he fell;
And deeply mourned his fall the Grecian host.
    As when a lion hath in fight o'erborne
A tuskèd boar, when on the mountain top   945
They two have met, in all their pride of strength,
Both parched with thirst, around a scanty spring;
And vanquished by the lion's force, the boar
Hath yielded, gasping; so Menœtius' son,
Great deeds achieved, at length beneath the spear   950
Of noble Hector yielded up his life;
Who o'er the vanquished, thus, exulting, spoke:
"Patroclus, but of late thou mad'st thy boast
To raze our city walls, and in your ships
To bear away to your far-distant land,   955

Their days of freedom lost, our Trojan dames:
Fool that thou wast! nor know'st, in their defence,
That Hector's flying coursers scoured the plain;
From them, the bravest of the Trojans, I
Avert the day of doom; while on our shores   960
Thy flesh shall glut the carrion birds of Troy.
Poor wretch! though brave he be, yet Peleus' son
Availed thee nought, when, hanging back himself,
With sage advice he sent thee forth to fight:
'Come not to me, Patroclus, car-borne chief,   965
Nor to the ships return, until thou bear
The warrior-slayer Hector's bloody spoils,
Torn from his body;' such were, I suppose,
His counsels; thou, poor fool, becam'st his dupe."
To whom Patroclus thus in accents faint: 970
    "Hector, thou boastest loudly now, that Jove,
With Phœbus joined, hath thee with victory crowned:
They wrought my death, who stripped me of my arms.
Had I to deal with twenty such as thee,
They all should perish, vanquished by my spear: 975
Me fate hath slain, and Phœbus; and, of men,
Euphorbus; thou wast but the third to strike.
This too I say, and bear it in thy mind;
Not long shalt thou survive me; death e'en now
And final doom hangs o'er thee, by the hand   980
Of great Achilles, Peleus' matchless son."
    Thus as he spoke, the gloom of death his eyes
O'erspread, and to the shades his spirit fled,
Mourning his fate, his youth and strength cut off.
    To whom, though dead, the noble Hector thus: 985
"Patroclus, why predict my coming fate?

Or who can say but fair-haired Thetis' son,
Achilles, by my spear may first be slain?"
   He said, and planting firm his foot withdrew
The brazen spear, and backward drove the dead   990
From off the weapon's point; then, spear in hand,
Intent to slay, Automedon pursued,
The godlike follower of Æacides:
But him in safety bore the immortal steeds,
The noble prize the Gods to Peleus gave.   995

BOOK XVII.

NOR was Patroclus' fall, by Trojans slain,
 Of warlike Meneläus unobserved;
Forward he sprang, in dazzling arms arrayed,
And round him moved, as round her new-dropped calf,
Her first, a heifer moves with plaintive moan: 5
So round Patroclus Meneläus moved,
His shield's broad orb and spear before him held,
To all who might oppose him threatening death.
Nor, on his side, was Panthöus' noble son
Unmindful of the slain; but, standing near, 10
The warlike Meneläus thus addressed:

 "Illustrious son of Atreus, Heaven-born chief,
Quit thou the dead; yield up the bloody spoils;
For, of the Trojans and their famed Allies,
Mine was the hand that in the stubborn fight 15
First struck Patroclus; leave me then to wear
Among the men of Troy my honours due,
Lest by my spear thou lose thy cherished life."
 To whom in anger Meneläus thus:
"O Father Jove, how ill this vaunting tone 20
Beseems this braggart! In their own esteem,
With Panthöus' sons for courage none may vie;
Nor pard, nor lion, nor the forest boar,
Fiercest of beasts, and proudest of his strength.
Yet nought avai'ed to Hyperenor's might 25

His youthful vigour, when he held me cheap,
And my encounter dared; of all the Greeks
He deemed my prowess least; yet he, I ween,
On his own feet returned not, to rejoice
His tender wife's and honoured parents' sight.   30
So shall thy pride be quelled, if me thou dare
Encounter; but I warn thee, while 'tis time,
Ere ill betide thee, 'mid the general throng
That thou withdraw, nor stand to me opposed.
After the event may even a fool be wise."   35
He spoke in vain; Euphorbus thus replied:
  "Now, Heaven-born Meneläus, shalt thou pay
The forfeit for my brother's life, o'er whom,
Slain by thy hand, thou mak'st thy boasting speech.
Thou in the chambers of her new-found home   40
Hast made his bride a weeping widow; thou
Hast filled with bitterest grief his parents' hearts:
Some solace might those hapless mourners find,
Could I thy head and armour in the hands
Of Panthöus and of honoured Phrontis place;   45
Nor uncontested shall the proof remain,
Nor long deferred, of victory or defeat."
  He said, and struck the centre of the shield,
But broke not through; against the stubborn brass
The point was bent; then with a prayer to Jove   50
The son of Atreus in his turn advanced;
And, backward as he stepped, below his throat
Took aim, and pressing hard with stalwart hand
Drove through the yielding neck the ponderous spear:
Thundering he fell, and loud his armour rang.   55
Those locks, that with the Graces' hair might vie,

Those tresses bright, with gold and silver bound,
Were dabbled all with blood. As when a man
Hath reared a fair and vigorous olive plant,
In some lone spot, by copious-gushing springs,   60
And seen expanding, nursed by every breeze,
Its whitening blossoms; till with sudden gust
A sweeping hurricane of wind and rain
Uproots it from its bed, and prostrate lays;
So lay the youthful son of Panthöus, slain   65
By Atreus' son, and of his arms despoiled.
As when a lion, in the mountains bred,
In pride of strength, amid the pasturing herd
Seizes a heifer in his powerful jaws,
The choicest; and, her neck first broken, rends,   70
And, on her entrails gorging, laps the blood;
Though with loud clamour dogs and herdsmen round
Assail him from afar, yet ventures none
To meet his rage, for fear is on them all;
So none was there so bold, with dauntless breast   75
The noble Meneläus' wrath to meet.
Now had Atrides borne away with ease
The spoils of Panthöus' son; but Phœbus grudged
His prize of victory, and against him launched
The might of Hector, terrible as Mars: 80
To whom his wingèd words, in Mentes' form,
Chief of the Cicones, he thus addressed:

  "Hector, thy labour all is vain, pursuing
Pelides' flying steeds; and hard are they
For mortal man to harness, or control,   85
Save for Achilles' self, the Goddess-born.
The valiant Meneläus, Atreus' son,

Defends meanwhile Patroclus; and e'en now
Hath slain a noble Trojan, Panthöus' son,
Euphorbus, and his youthful vigour quelled."   90
    He said, and joined again the strife of men:
Hector's dark soul with bitter grief was filled;
He looked amid the ranks, and saw the two,
One slain, the other stripping off his arms,
The blood outpouring from the gaping wound.   95
Forward he sprang, in dazzling arms arrayed,
Loud shouting, blazing like the quenchless flames
Of Vulcan: Meneläus heard the shout,
And, troubled, communed with his valiant heart:
    "Oh, woe is me! for should I now the spoils   100
Abandon, and Patroclus, who for me
And in my cause lies slain, of any Greek
Who saw me, I might well incur the blame:
And yet if here alone I dare to fight
With Hector and his Trojans, much I fear,   105
Singly, to be by numbers overwhelmed;
For Hector all the Trojans hither brings.
But wherefore entertain such thoughts, my soul?
Who strives against the will divine, with one
Beloved of Heaven, a bitter doom must meet.   110
Then none may blame me, though I should retreat
From Hector, who with Heaven's assistance wars.
Yet could I hear brave Ajax' battle cry,
We two, returning, would the encounter dare,
E'en against Heaven, if so for Peleus' son   115
We might regain, and bear away the dead:
Some solace of our loss might then be ours."
    While in his mind and spirit thus he mused,

By Hector led, the Trojan ranks advanced:
Backward he moved, abandoning the dead;   120
But turning oft, as when by men and dogs
A bearded lion from the fold is driven
With shouts and spears; yet grieves his mighty heart,
And with reluctant step he quits the yard:
So from Patroclus Meneläus moved;   125
Yet when he reached his comrades' ranks, he turned,
And looked around, if haply he might find
The mighty Ajax, son of Telamon.
Him on the battle's farthest left he spied,
Cheering his friends and urging to the fight,   130
For sorely Phœbus had their courage tried;
And hastening to his side, addressed him thus:
  "Ajax, haste hither; to the rescue come
Of slain Patroclus; if perchance we two
May to Achilles, Peleus' son, restore   135
His body: his naked body, for his arms
Are prize to Hector of the glancing helm."
  He said, and Ajax' spirit within him stirred;
Forward he sprang, and with him Atreus' son.
Hector was dragging now Patroclus' corpse,   140
Stripped of its glittering armour, and intent
The head to sever with his sword, and give
The mangled carcase to the dogs of Troy:
But Ajax, with his tower-like shield, approached;
Then Hector to his comrades' ranks withdrew,   145
Rushed to his car, and bade the Trojans bear
The glittering arms, his glorious prize, to Troy:
While Ajax with his mighty shield o'erspread
Menœtius' son; and stood, as for his cubs

A lion stands, whom hunters, unaware,   150
Have with his offspring met amid the woods,
Proud in his strength he stands; and down are drawn,
Covering his eyes, the wrinkles of his brow:
So o'er Patroclus mighty Ajax stood,
And by his side, his heart with grief oppressed,   155
The warlike Meneläus, Atreus' son.
   Then Glaucus, leader of the Lycian host,
To Hector thus, with scornful glance, addressed
His keen reproaches: "Hector, fair of form,
How art thou wanting in the fight! thy fame,   160
Coward and runaway, thou hast belied.
Bethink thee now, if thou alone canst save
The city, aided but by Trojans born;
Henceforth no Lycian will go forth for Troy
To fight with Greeks; since favour none we gain   165
By unremitting toil against the foe.
How can a meaner man expect thine aid,
Who basely to the Greeks a prize and spoil
Sarpedon leav'st, thy comrade and thy guest?
Greatly he served the city and thyself,   170
While yet he lived; and now thou dar'st not save
His body from the dogs! By my advice
If Lycians will be ruled, we take at once
Our homeward way, and Troy may meet her doom.
But if in Trojan bosoms there abode   175
The daring, dauntless courage, meet for men
Who in their country's cause against the foe
Endure both toil and war, we soon should see
Patroclus brought within the walls of Troy;
Him from the battle could we bear away,   180

And, lifeless, bring to royal Priam's town,
Soon would the Greeks Sarpedon's arms release,
And we to Ilion's heights himself might bear:
For with his valiant comrades there lies slain
The follower of the bravest chief of Greece.   185
But thou before the mighty Ajax stood'st
With downcast eyes, nor durst in manly fight
Contend with one thy better far confessed."

    To whom thus Hector of the glancing helm,
With stern regard, replied: " Why, Glaucus, speak, 190
Brave as thou art, in this o'erbearing strain?
Good friend, I heretofore have held thee wise
O'er all who dwell in Lycia's fertile soil;
But now I change, and hold thy judgment cheap,
Who chargest me with flying from the might   195
Of giant Ajax; never have I shrunk
From the stern fight, and clatter of the cars;
But all o'erruling is the mind of Jove,
Who strikes with panic, and of victory robs
The bravest; and anon excites to war.   200
Stand by me now, and see if through the day
I prove myself the coward that thou say'st,
Or suffer that a Greek, how brave soe'er,
Shall rescue from my hands Patroclus' corpse."

    He said, and loudly on the Trojans called: 205
" Trojans and Lycians, and ye Dardans, famed
In close encounter, quit ye now like men;
Maintain awhile the stubborn fight, while I
The splendid armour of Achilles don,
My glorious prize from slain Patroclus torn."   210
    So saying, Hector of the glancing helm,

Withdrawing from the field, with rapid steps
His comrades followed, and ere long o'ertook,
Who toward the town Achilles' armour bore;
Then standing from the bloody fight aloof   215
The armour he exchanged; his own he bade
The warlike Trojans to the city bear;
While he, of Peleus' son, Achilles, donned
The heavenly armour, which the immortal Gods
Gave to his sire; he to his son conveyed;   220
Yet in that armour grew not old that son.
Him when apart the Cloud-compeller saw
Girt with the arms of Peleus' godlike son,
He shook his head, as inly thus he mused:
" Ah hapless! little deem'st thou of thy fate,   225
Though now so nigh! Thou of the prime of men,
The dread of all, hast donned the immortal arms,
Whose comrade, brave and good, thy hand hath slain;
And shamed him, stripping from his head and breast
Helmet and cuirass; yet thy latest hours   230
Will I with glory crown; since ne'er from thee,
Returned from battle, shall Andromache
Receive the spoils of Peleus' godlike son."
    He said, and nodded with his shadowy brows;
Then with the armour, fitted to his form   235
By Jove himself, was Hector girt by Mars
The fierce and terrible; with vigorous strength
His limbs were strung, as 'mid his brave allies
He sprang, loud-shouting; glittering in his arms,
To all he seemed Achilles' godlike self.   240
To each and all in cheering tones he spoke,
Mesthles and Glaucus and Thersilochus,

Asteropæus and Hippothöus,
Medon, Deisenor, Phorcys, Chromius,
And Ennomus the seer: to all of these   245
His wingèd words he cheeringly addressed:
" Hear me, ye countless tribes, that dwelling round
Assist our cause! You from your several homes
Not for display of numbers have I called,
But that with willing hearts ye should defend   250
Our wives and infants from the warlike Greeks:
For this I drain my people's stores, for food
And gifts for you, exalting your estate;
Then, who will boldly onward, he may fall,
Or safe escape, such is the chance of war;   255
But who within our valiant Trojans' ranks
Shall but the body of Patroclus bring,
Despite the might of Ajax; half the spoils
To him I give, the other half myself
Retaining; and his praise shall equal mine."   260
    He said; and onward, with uplifted spears,
They marched upon the Greeks; high rose their hopes
From Ajax Telamon to snatch the dead;
Vain hopes, which cost them many a life! Then thus
To valiant Menelaus Ajax spoke: 265
" O Heaven-born Meneläus, noble friend,
For safe return I dare no longer hope:
Not for Patroclus' corpse so much I fear,
Which soon will glut the dogs and birds of Troy,
As for my life and thine I tremble now: 270
For, like a war-cloud, Hector's might I see
O'ershadowing all around; now is our doom
Apparent; but do thou for succour call

On all the chiefs, if haply they may hear."
Thus Ajax spoke: obedient to his word,　　　275
On all the chiefs Atrides called aloud:
　"O friends, the chiefs and councillors of Greece,
All ye that banquet at the general cost
With Atreus' sons, and o'er your several states
Dominion hold; whose honour is of Jove;　　　280
'Twere hard to call by name each single man,
So fierce the combat rages; but let each
And all their aid afford, and deem it shame
Patroclus' corpse should glut the dogs of Troy."
　He said: first heard Oïleus' active son,　　　285
And hastening through the fray, beside him stood.
Next him Idomeneus, with whom there came,
Valiant as Mars, his friend Meriones.
But who can know or tell the names of all,
Who, following, swelled the battle of the Greeks?　290
Onward the Trojans pressed, by Hector led:
With such a sound, as when the ocean wave
Meets on the beach the outpouring of a stream,
Swollen by the rains of Heaven; the lofty cliffs
Resound, and bellows the big sea without;　　　295
With such a sound advanced the Trojan host:
While round Patroclus, with one heart and mind,
The Greeks a fence of brass-clad bucklers raised.
O'er their bright helms the son of Saturn shed
A veil of darkness; for Menœtius' son,　　　300
Achilles' faithful friend, while yet he lived
Jove hated not, nor would that now his corpse
Should to the dogs of Troy remain a prey,
But to the rescue all his comrades stirred.

At first the Trojans drove the keen-eyed Greeks; 305
Leaving the corpse, they fled; nor with their spears
The valiant Trojans reached a single Greek;
But on the dead they seized; yet not for long
Endured their flight; them Ajax rallied soon,
In form pre-eminent, and deeds of arms, 310
O'er all the Greeks, save Peleus' matchless son.
Onward he sprang, as springs a mountain boar,
Which, turning in the forest glade to bay,
Scatters with ease both dogs and stalwart youths;
So Ajax scattered soon the Trojan ranks, 315
That round Patroclus closing, hoped to bear,
With glory to themselves, his corpse to Troy.
Hippothöus, Pelasgian Lethus' son,
Was dragging by the feet the noble dead,
A leathern belt around his ancles bound, 320
Seeking the favour of the men of Troy;
But on himself he brought destruction down,
Which none might turn aside; for from the crowd
Outsprang the son of Telamon, and struck,
In close encounter, on the brass-cheeked helm; 325
The plumèd helm was shivered by the blow,
Dealt by a weighty spear and stalwart hand;
Gushed from the wound the mingled blood and brain,
His vital spirit quenched; and on the ground
Fell from his powerless grasp Patroclus' foot; 330
While he himself lay stretched beside the dead,
Far from his own Larissa's teeming soil:
Not destined he his parents to repay
Their early care; for short his term of life,
By godlike Ajax' mighty spear subdued. 335

At Ajax Hector threw his glittering spear:
He saw, and narrowly the brazen death
Escaped; but Schedius, son of Iphitus,
(The bravest of the Phocian chiefs, who dwelt
In far-famed Panopeus, the mighty Lord   340
Of numerous hosts,) below the collar-bone
It struck, and passing through, the brazen point
Came forth again beneath his shoulder-blade:
Thundering he fell, and loud his armour rang.
    As Phorcys, son of Phænops, kept his watch   345
O'er slain Hippothöus, him Ajax smote
Below the waist; the weighty spear broke through
The hollow breastplate, and the intestines tore;
Prone in the dust he fell, and clutched the ground.
At this the Trojan chiefs and Hector's self   350
'Gan to give way; the Greeks, with joyful shouts,
Seized both the dead, and stripped their armour off.
To Ilion now, before the warlike Greeks,
O'ercome by panic, had the Trojans fled;
And now had Greeks, despite the will of Jove,   355
By their own strength and courage, won the day,
Had not Apollo's self Æneas roused,
In likeness of a herald, Periphas,
The son of Epytus, now aged grown
In service of Æneas' aged sire,   360
A man of kindliest soul: his form assumed
Apollo, and Æneas thus addressed:
    " Æneas, how, against the will of Heaven,
Could ye defend your city, as others now
In their own strength and courage confident,   365
Their numbers, and their troops' undaunted hearts,

I see their cause maintaining; if when Jove
Rather to us than them the victory wills,
With fear unspeakable ye shun the fight?"
    He said: the presence of the Archer-God   370
Æneas knew, and loud to Hector called:
"Hector, and all ye other chiefs of Troy,
And brave Allies, foul shame it were that we,
O'ercome by panic, should to Ilion now
In flight be driven before the warlike Greeks;   375
And by my side, but now, some God there stood,
And told how Jove, the sovereign arbiter
Of battle, on our side bestowed his aid;
On then! nor undisturbed allow the Greeks
To bear Patroclus' body to their ships."   380
    He said, and far before the ranks advanced;
They rallying turned, and faced again the Greeks.
    Then first Æneas' spear the comrade brave
Of Lycomedes struck, Leocritus,
Son of Arisbas; Lycomedes saw   385
With pitying eyes his gallant comrade's fall;
And standing near, his glittering spear he threw,
And through the midriff Apisaon struck,
His people's guardian chief, the valiant son
Of Hippasus, and slacked his limbs in death.   390
He from Pæonia's fertile fields had come,
O'er all his comrades eminent in fight,
All save Asteropæus, who with eyes
Of pity saw his gallant comrade's fall,
And forward sprang to battle with the Greeks;   395
Yet could not force his way; for all around
Patroclus rose a fence of serried shields,

And spears projecting; such the orders given
By Ajax, and with earnest care enforced;
That from around the dead should none retire,　　400
Nor any to the front advance alone
Before his fellows; but their steady guard
Maintain, and hand to hand the battle wage.
So ordered Ajax; then with crimson blood
The earth was wet; and hand to hand they fell,　　405
Trojans alike, and brave Allies, and Greeks;
For neither these a bloodless fight sustained,
Though fewer far their losses; for they stood
Of mutual succour mindful, and support.
Thus, furious as the rage of fire, they fought;　　410
Nor might ye deem the glorious sun himself
Nor moon was safe; for darkest clouds of night
O'erspread the warriors, who the battle waged
Around the body of Menœtius' son:
Elsewhere the Trojans and the well-greaved Greeks 415
Fought, undisturbed, in the clear light of day;
The sun's bright beams were shed abroad; no cloud
Lay on the face of earth or mountain tops;
They but by fits, at distant intervals,
And far apart, each seeking to avoid　　　　420
The hostile missiles, fought; but in the midst
The bravest all, in darkness and in strife
Sore pressed, toiled on beneath their armour's weight.
　　As yet no tidings of Patroclus' fall
Had reached two valiant chiefs, Antilochus　　425
And Thrasymedes; but they deemed him still
Alive, and fighting in the foremost ranks.
They, witnessing their comrades' flight and death,

Fought on apart, by Nestor so enjoined,
When from the ships he bade them join the fray. 430
Great was meanwhile their labour, who sustained,
Throughout the livelong day, that weary fight;
Reeked with continuous toil and sweat, the knees,
And legs and feet, the arms, and eyes, of all
Who round Achilles' faithful comrade fought. 435
As when a chief his people bids to stretch
A huge bull's hide, all drenched and soaked with grease;
They in a circle ranged, this way and that,
Pull the tough hide, till entering in, the grease
Is all absorbed; and dragged by numerous hands 440
The supple skin to the utmost length is stretched;
So these in narrow space this way and that
The body dragged; and high the hopes of each
To bear it off in triumph; to their ships
The Greeks, to Troy the Trojans; fiercely raged 445
The struggle; spirit-stirring Mars himself,
Or Pallas to her utmost fury roused,
Had not that struggle with contempt beheld:
Such grievous labour o'er Patroclus' corpse
Had Jove to horses and to men decreed. 450
  But of Patroclus' fall no tidings yet
Had reached Achilles; for the war was waged
Far from the ships, beneath the walls of Troy;
Nor looked he of his death to hear, but deemed
That when the Trojans to their gates were driven, 455
He would return in safety; for no hope
Had he of taking by assault the town,
With, or without, his aid; for oft apart
His Goddess-mother had his doom foretold,

Revealing to her son the mind of Jove;   460
Yet ne'er had warned him of such grief as this,
Which now befell, his dearest comrade's loss.
   Still round the dead they held their pointed spears,
Fought hand to hand, and mutual slaughter dealt;
And thus perchance some brass-clad Greek would say : 465
   "O friends, 'twere shameful should we to the ships
Ingloriously return; ere that should be,
Let earth engulph us all; so better far
Than let these Trojans to their city bear
Our dead, and boast them of their triumph gained." 470
On the other hand some valiant Trojan thus
Would shout: "O friends, though fate decreed that here
We all should die, yet let not one give way."
   Thus, cheering each his comrades, would they speak,
And thus they fought; the iron clangour pierced   475
The empty air, and brazen vault of Heaven.
But from the fight withdrawn, Achilles' steeds
Wept, as they heard how in the dust was laid
Their charioteer, by Hector's murderous hand.
Automedon, Diores' valiant son,   480
Essayed in vain to rouse them with the lash,
In vain with honeyed words, in vain with threats;
Nor to the ships would they return again
By the broad Hellespont, nor join the fray;
But as a column stands, which marks the tomb   485
Of man or woman, so immovable
Beneath the splendid car they stood, their heads
Down-drooping to the ground, while scalding tears
Dropped earthward from their eyelids, as they mourned
Their charioteer; and o'er the yoke-band shed   490

Down streamed their ample manes, with dust defiled.
The son of Saturn pitying saw their grief,
And sorrowing shook his head, as thus he mused:
  "Ah, hapless horses! wherefore gave we you
To royal Peleus, to a mortal man,   495
You that from age and death are both exempt!
Was it that you the miseries might share
Of wretched mortals? for of all that breathe,
And walk upon the earth, or creep, is nought
More wretched than the unhappy race of man.   500
Yet shall not ye, nor shall your well-wrought car,
By Hector, son of Priam, be controlled;
I will not suffer it; enough for him
To hold, with vaunting boast, Achilles' arms;
But to your limbs and spirits will I impart   505
Such strength, that from the battle to the ships
Ye shall in safety bear Automedon;
For yet I will the Trojans shall prevail,
And slay, until they reach the well-manned ships,
Till sets the sun, and darkness shrouds the earth." 510
  He said, and in their breasts fresh spirit infused;
They, shaking from their manes the dust, the car
Amid the Greeks and Trojans lightly bore.
Then as a vulture 'mid a flock of geese,
Though for his comrade grieved, Automedon,   515
His horses urging, 'mid the battle rushed.
Swiftly he fled from out the Trojan host;
Swiftly again assailed them in pursuit;
Yet speedy to pursue, he could not slay;
Nor, in the car alone, had power at once   520
To guide the flying steeds, and hurl the spear.

At length a comrade brave, Alcimedon,
Laerces' son, beheld; behind the car
He stood, and thus Automedon addressed:
 "Automedon, what God has filled thy mind   525
With counsels vain, and thee of sense bereft?
That with the Trojans, in the foremost ranks,
Thou fain wouldst fight alone, thy comrade slain,
While Hector proudly on his breast displays
The glorious arms of great Æacides."   530
 To whom Automedon, Diores' son:
"Alcimedon, since none of all the Greeks
May vie with thee, the mettle to control
Of these immortal horses, save indeed,
While yet he lived, Patroclus, godlike chief;   535
But him stern death and fate have overta'en;
Take thou the whip and shining reins, while I,
Descending from the car, engage in fight."
 He said; and mounting on the war-car straight,
Alcimedon the whip and reins assumed;   540
Down leaped Automedon; great Hector saw,
And thus addressed Æneas at his side:
 "Æneas, prince and counsellor of Troy,
I see, committed to unskilful hands,
Achilles' horses on the battle field: 545
These we may hope to take, if such thy will;
For they, methinks, will scarcely stand opposed,
Or dare the encounter of our joint assault."
 He said; Anchises' valiant son complied;
Forward they went, their shoulders covered o'er   550
With stout bull's-hide, thick overlaid with brass.
With them both Chromius and Aretus went;

And high their hopes were raised, the warriors both
To slay, and make the strong-necked steeds their prize:
Blind fools! nor destined scatheless to escape   555
Automedon's encounter; he his prayer
To Jove addressed, and straight with added strength
His soul was filled; and to Alcimedon,
His trusty friend and comrade, thus he spoke:

"Alcimedon, do thou the horses keep   560
Not far away, but breathing on my neck;
For Hector's might will not, I deem, be stayed,
Ere us he slay, and mount Achilles' car,
And carry terror 'mid the Grecian host,
Or in the foremost ranks himself be slain."   565

Thus spoke Automedon, and loudly called
On Meneläus and the Ajaces both:
"Ye two Ajaces, leaders of the host,
And, Meneläus, with our bravest all,
Ye on the dead alone your care bestow,   570
To guard him, and stave off the hostile ranks;
But haste, and us, the living, save from death;
For Hector and Æneas hitherward,
With weight o'erpowering through the bloody press,
The bravest of the Trojans, force their way: 575
Yet is the issue in the hands of Heaven;
I hurl the spear, but Jove directs the blow."

He said, and, poising, hurled his ponderous spear;
Full on Aretus' broad-orbed shield it struck;
Nor stayed the shield its course; the brazen point 580
Drove through the belt, and in his body lodged.
As with sharp axe in hand a stalwart man,
Striking behind the horns a sturdy bull,

Severs the neck; he forward plunging, falls;
So forward first he sprang, then backwards fell;   585
And quivering, in his vitals deep infixed,
The sharp spear soon relaxed his limbs in death.
Then at Automedon great Hector threw
His glittering spear; he saw, and forward stooped,
And shunned the brazen death; behind him far   590
Deep in the soil infixed, with quivering shaft
The weapon stood; there Mars its impulse stayed.
And now with swords, and hand to hand, the fight
Had been renewed; but at their comrade's call
The two Ajaces, pressing through the throng,   595
Between the warriors interposed in haste.
Before them Hector and Æneas both,
And godlike Chromius, in alarm recoiled;
Pierced through the heart, Aretus there they left;
And, terrible as Mars, Automedon   600
Stripped off his arms, and thus exulting cried:
"Of some small portion of its load of grief,
For slain Patroclus, is my heart relieved,
In slaying thee, all worthless as thou art."
    Then, throwing on the car the bloody spoils,   605
He mounted, hands and feet imbrued with blood,
As 'twere a lion, fresh from his repast
Upon the carcase of a slaughtered bull.
    Again around Patroclus' body raged
The stubborn conflict, direful, sorrow-fraught: 610
From Heaven descending, Pallas stirred the strife,
Sent by all-seeing Jove to stimulate
The warlike Greeks; so changed was now his will.
As o'er the face of Heaven when Jove extends

His bright-hued bow, a sign to mortal men　　615
Of war, or wintry storms, which bid surcease
The rural works of man, and pinch the flocks;
So Pallas, in a bright-hued cloud arrayed,
Passed through the ranks, and roused each several man.
To noble Meneläus, Atreus' son,　　620
Who close beside her stood, the Goddess first,
The form of Phœnix and his powerful voice
Assuming, thus her stirring words addressed:
　"On thee, O Meneläus, foul reproach
Will fasten, if beneath the walls of Troy　　625
The dogs devour Achilles' faithful friend;
Then hold thou firm, and all the host inspire."
　To whom thus Meneläus, good in fight:
"O Phœnix, aged warrior, honoured sire,
If Pallas would the needful power impart,　　630
And o'er me spread her ægis, then would I
Undaunted for Patroclus' rescue fight,
For deeply by his death my heart is touched;
But valiant Hector, with the strength of fire
Still rages, and destruction deals around:　　635
For Jove is with him, and his triumph wills."
　He said: the blue-eyed Goddess heard with joy
That, chief of all the Gods, her aid he sought.
She gave fresh vigour to his arms and knees,
And to his breast the boldness of the fly,　　640
Which, oft repelled by man, renews the assault
Incessant, lured by taste of human blood;
Such boldness in Atrides' manly breast
Pallas inspired; beside Patroclus' corpse
Again he stood, and poised his glittering spear.　　645

G 2

There was one Podes in the Trojan ranks,
Son of Eëtion, rich, of blameless life,
Of all the people most to Hector dear,
And at his table oft a welcome guest:
Him, as he turned to fly, beneath the waist   650
Atrides struck; right through the spear was driven;
Thundering he fell; and Atreus' son the corpse
Dragged from the Trojans 'mid the ranks of Greece.

Then close at Hector's side Apollo stood,
Clad in the form of Phænops, Asius' son,   655
Who in Abydos dwelt; of all the Allies
Honoured of Hector most, and best beloved;
Clad in his form, the Far-destroyer spoke:

"Hector, what other Greek will scare thee next?
Who shrink'st from Meneläus, heretofore   660
A warrior deemed of no repute; but now,
Alone, he robs our Trojans of their dead;
And in the foremost ranks e'en now hath slain
Podes, thine own good friend, Eëtion's son."

He said; dark grief o'erclouded Hector's brow,   665
As to the front in dazzling arms he sprang.
Then Saturn's son his tasselled ægis waved,
All glittering bright; and Ida's lofty head
In clouds and darkness shrouded; then he bade
His lightning flash, his volleying thunder roar,   670
That shook the mountain; and with victory crowned
The Trojan arms, and panic-struck the Greeks.

The first who turned to fly was Peneleus,
Bœotian chief; him, facing still the foe,
A spear had slightly on the shoulder struck,   675
The bone just grazing: by Polydamas,

Who close before him stood, the spear was thrown.
Then Hector Lëitus, Alectryon's son,
Thrust through the wrist, and quelled his warlike might:
Trembling, he looked around, nor hoped again　　680
The Trojans, spear in hand, to meet in fight;
But, onward as he rushed on Lëitus,
Idomeneus at Hector threw his spear:
Full on his breast it struck; but near the head
The sturdy shaft was on the breastplate snapped:　685
Loud was the Trojans' shout; and he in turn
Aimed at Idomeneus, Deucalion's son,
Upstanding on his car; his mark he missed,
But Cœranus he struck, the charioteer
And faithful follower of Meriones,　　690
Who with him came from Lyctus' thriving town:
The chief had left on foot the well-trimmed ships;
And, had not Cœranus his car in haste
Driven to the rescue, by his fall had given
A Trojan triumph; to his Lord he brought　695
Safety, and rescue from unsparing death;
But fell, himself, by Hector's murderous hand.
Him Hector struck between the cheek and ear,
Crashing the teeth, and cutting through the tongue.
Headlong he fell to earth, and dropped the reins:　700
These, stooping from the car, Meriones
Caught up, and thus Idomeneus addressed:
　"Ply now the lash, until thou reach the ships:
Thyself must see how crushed the strength of Greece."
　He said; and toward the ships Idomeneus　705
Urged his fleet steeds; for fear was on his soul.
Nor did not Ajax and Atrides see

How in the Trojans' favour Saturn's son
The wavering scale of victory turned; and thus
Great Ajax Telamon his grief expressed: 710
"O Heaven! the veriest child might plainly see
That Jove the Trojans' triumph has decreed:
Their weapons all, by whomsoever thrown,
Or weak, or strong, attain their mark; for Jove
Directs their course; while ours upon the plain   715
Innocuous fall. But take we counsel now
How from the fray to bear away our dead,
And by our own return rejoice those friends
Who look with sorrow on our plight, and deem
That we, all powerless to resist the might   720
Of Hector's arm, beside the ships must fall.
Would that some comrade were at hand, to bear
A message to Achilles; him, I ween,
As yet the mournful tidings have not reached,
That on the field his dearest friend lies dead.   725
But such I see not; for a veil of cloud
O'er men and horses all around is spread.
O Father Jove, from o'er the sons of Greece
Remove this cloudy darkness; clear the sky,
That we may see our fate, and die at least,   730
If such thy will, in the open light of day."
    He said, and, pitying, Jove beheld his tears;
The clouds he scattered, and the mist dispersed;
The sun shone forth, and all the field was clear;
Then Ajax thus to Meneläus spoke: 735
    "Now, Heaven-born Meneläus, look around
If haply 'mid the living thou mayst see
Antilochus, the noble Nestor's son;

And bid him to Achilles bear in haste
The tidings, that his dearest friend lies dead."   740
    He said, nor did Atrides not comply;
But slow as moves a lion from the fold,
Which dogs and youths with ceaseless toil hath worn,
Who all night long have kept their watch, to guard
From his assault the choicest of the herd;   745
He, hunger-pinched, hath oft the attempt renewed,
But nought prevailed; by spears on every side,
And javelins met, wielded by stalwart hands,
And blazing torches, which his courage daunt;
Till with the morn he sullenly withdraws;   750
So from Patroclus, with reluctant step
Atrides moved; for much he feared the Greeks
Might to the Trojans, panic-struck, the dead
Abandon; and departing, he besought
The two Ajaces and Meriones: 755
"Ye two Ajaces, leaders of the Greeks,
And thou, Meriones, remember now
Our lost Patroclus' gentle courtesy,
How kind and genial was his soul to all,
While yet he lived—now sunk, alas! in death."   760
    Thus saying, Meneläus took his way,
Casting his glance around on every side,
Like to an eagle, famed of sharpest sight
Of all that fly beneath the vault of Heaven;
Whom, soaring in the clouds, the crouching hare   765
Eludes not, though in leafiest covert hid;
But swooping down, he rends her life away:
So, Meneläus, through the ranks of war
Thy piercing glances every way were turned,

If Nestor's son, alive, thou mightst descry;   770
Him on the field's extremest left he found,
Cheering his friends, and urging to the fight;
He stood beside him, and addressed him thus:
  " Antilochus, come hither, godlike friend,
And woful tidings hear, which would to Heaven   775
I had not to impart; thyself thou seest
How Jove hath heaped disaster on the Greeks,
And victory given to Troy; but one has fallen,
Our bravest, best! Patroclus lies in death;
And deeply must the Greeks his loss deplore.   780
But haste thee to the ships, to Peleus' son
The tidings bear, if haply he may save
The body of Patroclus from the foe;
His naked body, for his arms are now
The prize of Hector of the glancing helm."   785
  He said; and at his words Antilochus
Astounded stood; long time his tongue in vain
For utterance strove; his eyes were filled with tears,
His cheerful voice was mute; yet not the less
To Meneläus' bidding gave his care: 790
Swiftly he sped; but to Läodocus,
His comrade brave, who waited with his car
In close attendance, first consigned his arms;
Then from the field with active limbs he flew,
Weeping, with mournful news, to Peleus' son.   795
Nor, noble Meneläus, did thy heart
Incline thee to remain, and aid thy friends,
Where from their war-worn ranks the Pylian troops
Deplored the absence of Antilochus;

But these in godlike Thrasymedes' charge   800
He left; and to Patroclus hastening back,
Beside the Ajaces stood, as thus he spoke:
" Him to Achilles, to the ships, in haste
I have despatched; yet fiercely as his wrath
May burn toward Hector, I can scarce expect   805
His presence here; for how could he, unarmed,
With Trojans fight? But take we counsel now
How from the field to bear away our dead,
And 'scape ourselves from death by Trojan hands."
      Whom answered thus great Ajax Telamon: 810
" Illustrious Meneläus, all thy words
Are just and true; then from amid the press,
Thou and Meriones, take up in haste,
And bear away the body; while behind
We two, in heart united, as in name,   815
Who side by side have still been wont to fight,
Will Hector and his Trojans hold at bay."
      He said; they, lifting in their arms the corpse,
Upraised it high in air; then from behind
Loud yelled the Trojans, as they saw the Greeks   820
Retiring with their dead; and on they rushed,
As dogs that in advance of hunter youths
Pursue a wounded boar; awhile they run,
Eager for blood; but when, in pride of strength,
He turns upon them, backward they recoil,   825
This way and that in fear of death dispersed.
So onward pressed awhile the Trojan crowd,
With thrust of swords, and double-pointed spears
But ever as the Ajaces turned to bay,

Their colour changed to pale, not one so bold　　830
As, dashing on, to battle for the corpse.
Thus they, with anxious care, from off the field
Bore toward the ships their dead; but on their track
Came sweeping on the storm of battle, fierce,
As, on a sudden breaking forth, the fire　　835
Seizes some populous city, and devours
House after house amid the glare and blaze,
While roar the flames before the gusty wind;
So fiercely pressed upon the Greeks' retreat
The clattering tramp of steeds and armèd men.　　840
But as the mules, with stubborn strength endued,
That down the mountain through the trackless waste
Drag some huge log, or timber for the ships,
And spent with toil and sweat, still labour on
Unflinching; so the Greeks with patient toil　　845
Bore on their dead; the Ajaces in their rear
Stemming the war, as stems the torrent's force
Some wooded cliff, far stretching o'er the plain;
Checking the mighty river's rushing stream,
And flinging it aside upon the plain,　　850
Itself unbroken by the strength of flood:
So firmly, in the rear, the Ajaces stemmed
The Trojan force; yet these still onward pressed,
And 'mid their comrades proudly eminent,
Two chiefs, Æneas, old Anchises' son,　　855
And glorious Hector, in the van were seen.
Then, as a cloud of starlings or of daws
Fly screaming, as they see the hawk approach,
To lesser birds the messenger of death;

So before Hector and Æneas fled,   860
Screaming, forgetful of their warlike fame,
The sons of Greece; and scattered here and there
Around the ditch lay store of goodly arms,
By Greeks abandoned in their hasty flight.
Yet still, unintermitted, raged the war.   865

BOOK XVIII.

THUS, furious as the rage of fire, they fought.
　　Meantime Antilochus to Peleus' son,
Swift-footed messenger, his tidings bore.
Him by the high-beaked ships he found, his mind
The event presaging, filled with anxious thoughts,　　5
As thus he communed with his mighty heart:
　"Alas! what means it, that the long-haired Greeks,
Chased from the plain, are thronging round the ships?
Let me not now, ye Gods, endure the grief
My mother once foretold, that I should live　　10
To see the bravest of the Myrmidons
Cut off by Trojans from the light of day.
Mœnœtius' noble son has surely fallen;
Foolhardy! yet I warned him, and besought,
Soon as the ships from hostile fires were safe,　　15
Back to return, nor Hector's onset meet."
　　While in his mind and spirit thus he mused,
Beside him stood the noble Nestor's son,
And weeping, thus his mournful message gave:
　"Alas! great son of Peleus, woful news,　　20
Which would to Heaven I had not to impart,
To thee I bring: Patroclus lies in death;
And o'er his body now the war is waged;
His naked body, for his arms are now
The prize of Hector of the glancing helm."　　25

He said; and darkest clouds of grief o'erspread
Achilles' brow; with both his hands he seized
And poured upon his head the grimy dust,
Marring his graceful visage; and defiled
With blackening ashes all his costly robes.   30
Stretched in the dust his lofty stature lay,
As with his hands his flowing locks he tore;
Loud was the wailing of the female band,
Achilles' and Patroclus' prize of war,   .
As round Achilles, rushing out of doors,   35
Beating their breasts, with tottering limbs they pressed.
In tears beside him stood Antilochus,
And in his own Achilles' hand he held,
Groaning in spirit, fearful lest for grief
In his own bosom he should sheathe his sword·   40
Loud were his moans; his Goddess-mother heard,
Beside her aged father where she sat
In the deep ocean caves, and wept aloud;
The Nereids all, in ocean's depths who dwell,
Encircled her around; Cymodoce,*   45
Nesæe, Spio, and Cymothöe,
The stag-eyed Halia, and Amphithöe,
Actæa, Limnorea, Melite,
Doris, and Galatea, Panope;
There too were Oreithyia, Clymene,   50

---

* L. 45 et seqq. I hope I may be pardoned for having somewhat curtailed
the list of these ladies, which in the original extends over ten lines of names
only. In doing so, I have followed the example of Virgil, who represents the
same ladies, evidently the *élite* of submarine society (G. 4. 336), in attendance on
Cyrene; and has not only reduced the list, but added some slight touches illus-
trating their occupations and private history: a liberty permissible to an
imitator, but not to a translator.

And Amathea with the golden hair,
And all the denizens of ocean's depths.
Filled was the glassy cave; in unison
They beat their breasts, as Thetis led the wail:
  "Give ear, my sister Nereids all, and learn   55
How deep the grief that in my breast I bear.
Me miserable! me, of noblest son
Unhappiest mother! me, a son who bore,
My brave, my beautiful, of heroes chief!
Like a young tree he throve: I tended him,   60
In a rich vineyard as the choicest plant;
Till in the beakèd ships I sent him forth
To war with Troy; him ne'er shall I behold,
Returning home, in aged Peleus' house.
E'en while he lives, and sees the light of day,   65
He lives in sorrow; nor, to soothe his grief,
My presence can avail; yet will I go,
That I may see my dearest child, and learn
What grief hath reached him, from the war withdrawn."
  She said, and left the cave; with her they went, 70
Weeping; before them parted the ocean wave.
But when they reached the fertile shore of Troy,
In order due they landed on the beach,
Where frequent, round Achilles swift of foot,
Were moored the vessels of the Myrmidons.   75
There, as he groaned aloud, beside him stood
His Goddess-mother; she, with bitter cry,
Clasped in her hands his head, and sorrowing spoke:
  "Why weeps my son? and what his cause of grief?
Speak out, and nought conceal; for all thy prayer 80
Which with uplifted hands thou mad'st to Jove,

He hath fulfilled, that, flying to their ships,
The routed sons of Greece should feel how much
They need thine aid, and deep disgrace endure."
To whom Achilles, deeply groaning, thus: 85
"Mother, all this indeed hath Jove fulfilled;
Yet what avails it, since my dearest friend
Is slain, Patroclus? whom I honoured most
Of all my comrades, loved him as my soul,
Him have I lost: and Hector from his corpse   90
Hath stripped those arms, those weighty, beauteous arms,
A marvel to behold, which from the Gods
Peleus received, a glorious gift, that day
When they consigned thee to a mortal's bed.
How better were it, if thy lot had been   95
Still 'mid the Ocean deities to dwell,
And Peleus had espoused a mortal bride!
For now is bitter grief for thee in store,
Mourning thy son; whom to his home returned
Thou never more shalt see; nor would I wish   100
To live, and move amid my fellow-men,
Unless that Hector, vanquished by my spear,
May lose his forfeit life, and pay the price
Of foul dishonour to Patroclus done."
To whom, her tears o'erflowing, Thetis thus: 105
"E'en as thou sayst, my son, thy term is short;
Nor long shall Hector's fate precede thine own."
Achilles, answering, spoke in passionate grief:
"Would I might die this hour, who failed to save
My comrade slain! far from his native land   110
He died, sore needing my protecting arm;
And I, who ne'er again must see my home,

Nor to Patroclus, nor the many Greeks
Whom Hector's hand hath slain, have rendered aid;
But idly here I sit, cumbering the ground: 115
I, who amid the Greeks no equal own
In fight; to others, in debate, I yield.
Accursed of Gods and men be hateful strife
And anger, which to violence provokes
E'en temperate souls; though sweeter be its taste   120
Than dropping honey, in the heart of man
Swelling, like smoke; such anger in my soul
Hath Agamemnon kindled, King of men.
But pass we that; though still my heart be sore,
Yet will I school my angry spirit down.   125
In search of Hector now, of him who slew
My friend, I go; prepared to meet my death,
When Jove shall will it, and the Immortals all.
From death not e'en the might of Hercules,
Though best beloved of Saturn's son, could fly,   130
By fate and Juno's bitter wrath subdued.
I too, since such my doom, must lie in death;
Yet, ere I die, immortal fame will win;
And from their delicate cheeks, deep-bosomed dames,
Dardan and Trojan, bitter tears shall wipe,   135
And groan in anguish; then shall all men know
How long I have been absent from the field;
Then, though thou love me, seek not from the war
To stay my steps: for bootless were thy speech."

    Whom answered thus the silver-footed Queen: 140
"True are thy words, my son; and good it is,
And commendable, from the stroke of death
To save a worsted comrade; but thine arms,

Thy brazen, flashing arms, the Trojans hold:
Them Hector of the glancing helm himself　　145
Bears on his breast, exulting, yet not long
Shall be his triumph, for his doom is nigh.
But thou, engage not in the toils of war,
Until thine eyes again behold me here;
For with to-morrow's sun will I return　　150
With arms of Heavenly mould, by Vulcan wrought."
　　Thus saying, from her son she turned away,
And turning, to her sister Nereids spoke:
"Back to the spacious bosom of the deep
Retire ye now; and to my father's house,　　155
The aged Ocean God, your tidings bear;
While I to high Olympus speed, to crave
At Vulcan's hand, the skilled artificer,
A boon of dazzling armour for my son."
　　She said; and they beneath the ocean wave　　160
Descended, while to high Olympus sped
The silver-footed Goddess, thence in hope
To bear the dazzling armour to her son.
She to Olympus sped; the Greeks meanwhile
Before the warrior-slayer Hector fled　　165
With wild, tumultuous uproar, till they reached
Their vessels and the shore of Hellespont.
Nor had the well-greaved Greeks Achilles' friend,
Patroclus, from amid the fray withdrawn;
For close upon him followed horse and man,　　170
And Hector, son of Priam, fierce as flame;
Thrice noble Hector, seizing from behind,
Sought by the feet to drag away the dead,
Cheering his friends; thrice, clad in warlike might,

The two Ajaces drove him from his prey.   175
Yet, fearless in his strength, now rushing on
He dashed amid the fray; now, shouting loud,
Stood firm; but backward not a step retired.
As from a carcase herdsmen strive in vain
To scare a tawny lion, hunger-pinched;   180
E'en so the Ajaces, mail-clad warriors, failed
To scare the son of Priam from the corpse.
And now the body had he borne away,
With endless fame; but from Olympus' height
Came storm-swift Iris down to Peleus' son,   185
And bade him don his arms; by Juno sent,
Unknown to Jove, and to the Immortals all.
She stood beside him, and addressed him thus:
  "Up, son of Peleus! up, thou prince of men!
Haste to Patroclus' rescue; whom around,   190
Before the ships, is waged a fearful war,
With mutual slaughter; these the dead defending,
And those to Ilion's breezy heights intent
To bear the body; noble Hector chief,
Who longs to sever from the tender neck,   195
And fix upon the spikes, thy comrade's head.
Up then! delay no longer; deem it shame
Patroclus' corpse should glut the dogs of Troy,
Dishonouring thee, if aught dishonour him."
  Whom answered thus Achilles, swift of foot: 200
"Say, heavenly Iris, of the immortal Gods
Who bade thee seek me, and this message bring?"
  To whom swift Iris thus: "To thee I come
By Juno sent, the imperial wife of Jove;
Unknown to Saturn's son, and all the Gods   205

Who on Olympus' snowy summit dwell."
    To whom again Achilles, swift of foot:
"How in the battle toil can I engage?
My arms are with the Trojans; and to boot
My mother warned me not to arm for fight,   210
Till I again should see her; for she hoped
To bring me heavenly arms by Vulcan wrought:
Nor know I well whose armour I could wear,
Save the broad shield of Ajax Telamon;
And he, methinks, amid the foremost ranks   215
E'en now is fighting o'er Patroclus' corpse."
    Whom answered storm-swift Iris: "Well we know
Thy glorious arms are by the Trojans held:
But go thou forth, and from above the ditch
Appear before them; daunted at the sight,   220
Haply the Trojans may forsake the field,
And breathing-time afford the sons of Greece,
Toil-worn; for little pause has yet been theirs."
    Swift Iris said, and vanished; then uprose
Achilles, dear to Jove; and Pallas threw   225
Her tasselled ægis o'er his shoulders broad;
His head encircling with a coronet
Of golden cloud, whence fiery flashes gleamed.
As from an island city up to Heaven
The smoke ascends, which hostile forces round   230
Beleaguer, and all day with cruel war
From its own state cut off; but when the sun
Hath set, blaze frequent forth the beacon fires;
High rise the flames, and to the dwellers round
Their signal flash, if haply o'er the sea   235
May come the needful aid; so brightly flashed

That fiery light around Achilles' head.
He left the wall, and stood above the ditch,
But from the Greeks apart, remembering well
His mother's prudent counsel; there he stood,   240
And shouted loudly; Pallas joined her voice,
And filled with terror all the Trojan host.
Clear as the trumpet's sound, which calls to arms
Some town, encompassed round with hostile bands,
Rang out the voice of great Æacides.   245
But when Achilles' voice of brass they heard,
They quailed in spirit; the sleek-skinned steeds themselves,
Conscious of coming ill, bore back the cars:
Their charioteers, dismayed, beheld the flame
Which, kindled by the blue-eyed Goddess, blazed   250
Unquenched around the head of Peleus' son.
Thrice shouted from the ditch the godlike chief;
Thrice terror struck both Trojans and Allies;
And there and then beside their chariots fell
Twelve of their bravest; while the Greeks, well pleased, 255
Patroclus' body from the fray withdrew,
And on a litter laid; around him stood
His comrades, mourning; with them, Peleus' son,
Shedding hot tears, as on his friend he gazed,
Laid on the bier, and pierced with deadly wounds: 260
Him to the war with horses and with cars
He sent; but ne'er to welcome his return.
   By stag-eyed Juno sent, reluctant sank
The unwearied sun beneath the ocean wave;
The sun had set, and breathed awhile the Greeks   265
From the fierce labours of the balanced field;
Nor less the Trojans, from the stubborn fight

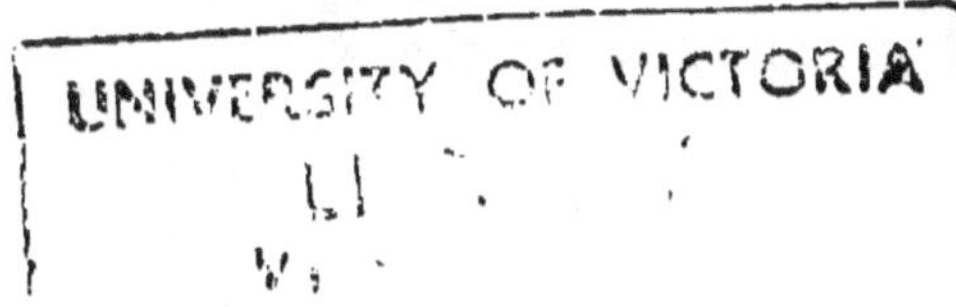

Retiring, from the chariots loosed their steeds:
But ere they shared the evening meal, they met
In council; all stood up; none dared to sit;   270
For fear had fallen on all, when reappeared
Achilles, from the battle long withdrawn.
First Panthöus' son, the sage Polydamas,
Addressed the assembly; his sagacious mind
Alone beheld the future and the past;   275
The friend of Hector, born the selfsame night;
One best in arms, the other in debate;
Who thus with prudent speech began, and said:
    "Be well advised, my friends! my counsel is
That we regain the city, nor the morn   280
Here in the plain, beside the ships, await,
So far removed from our protecting walls.
While fiercely burned 'gainst Atreus' godlike son
That mighty warrior's wrath, 'twas easier far
With the other Greeks to deal; and I rejoiced   285
When by the ships we passed the night, in hopes
We soon might call them ours; but now, I own,
Achilles, swift of foot, excites my fear.
His proud, impetuous spirit will spurn the plain,
Where Greeks and Trojans oft in warlike strife   290
Their balanced strength exert; if he come forth,
Our fight will be to guard our homes and wives.
Gain we the city; trust me, so 'twere best.
Now, for a while, ambrosial night detains
The son of Peleus; but at early morn   295
If issuing forth in arms he find us here,
His prowess we shall know; and happy he
Who, flying, shall in safety reach the walls

Of sacred Troy; for many a Trojan slain
Shall feed the vultures: Heaven avert such fate!   300
But if, though loth, ye will by me be ruled,
This night in council husband we our strength;
While towers, and lofty gates, and folding doors
Close joined, well-fitting, shall our city guard:
Then issuing forth in arms at early morn   305
Man we the towers; so harder were his task
If, from the ships advancing, round the wall
He offer battle; bootless to return,
His strong-necked horses worn with labour vain
In coursing, purposeless, around the town.   310
To force an entrance, or the town destroy,
Is not his aim; and ere that end be gained,
The dogs of Troy upon his flesh shall feed."
    To whom thus Hector of the glancing helm
With stern regard: "Polydamas, thy words   315
Are such as grate unkindly on mine ear,
Who fain would have us to the walls retire.
What? have ye not already long enough
Been cooped within the towers? the wealth of Troy,
Its brass, its gold, were once the common theme   320
Of every tongue; our hoarded treasures now
Are gone, to Phrygian and Mæonian shores
For sale exported, costly merchandise,
Since on our city fell the wrath of Jove.
And now, when deep-designing Saturn's son   325
Such glory gives me as to gain the ships,
And, crowded by the sea, hem in the Greeks,
Fool! put not thou these timid counsels forth,
Which none will follow, nor will I allow.

But hear ye all, and do as I advise: 330
Share now the meal, by ranks, throughout the host;
Then set your watch, and each keep careful guard;
And whom his spoils o'erload, if such there be,
Let him divide them with the general crowd;
Better that they should hold them than the Greeks: 335
And with the morn, in arms, beside the ships,
Will we again awake the furious war.
But if indeed Achilles by the ships
Hath reappeared, himself, if so he choose,
Shall be the sufferer; from the perilous strife   340
I will not shrink, but his encounter meet:
So he, or I, shall gain immortal fame;
Impartial Mars hath oft the slayer slain."
    Thus Hector spoke; the Trojans cheered aloud:
Fools, and by Pallas of their sense bereft,   345
Who all applauded Hector's ill advice,
None the sage counsel of Polydamas!
Then through the camp they shared the evening meal.
    Meantime the Greeks all night with tears and groans
Bewailed Patroclus; on his comrade's breast   350
Achilles laid his murder-dealing hands,
And led with bitter groans the loud lament.
As when the hunters, in the forest's depth,
Have robbed a bearded lion of his cubs;
Too late arriving he with anger chafes;   355
Then follows, if perchance he may o'ertake,
Through many a mountain glen, the hunters' steps,
With grief and fury filled; so Peleus' son,
With bitter groans, the Myrmidons addressed:
    "Vain was, alas! the promise which I gave,   360

Seeking the brave Menœtius to console,
To bring to Opus back his gallant son,
Rich with his share of spoil from Troy o'erthrown;
But Jove fulfils not all that man designs:
For us hath fate decreed, that here in Troy   365
We two one soil should redden with our blood;
Nor me, returning to my native land,
Shall aged Peleus in his halls receive,
Nor Thetis; here must earth retain my bones.
But since, Patroclus, I am doomed on earth   370
Behind thee to remain, thy funeral rites
I will not celebrate, till Hector's arms,
And head, thy haughty slayer's, here I bring;
And on thy pyre twelve noble sons of Troy
Will sacrifice, in vengeance of thy death.   375
Thou by our beakèd ships till then must lie;
And weeping o'er thee shall deep-bosomed dames,
Trojan and Dardan, mourn both night and day;
The prizes of our toil, when wealthy towns
Before our valour and our spears have fallen."   380
     He said, and bade his comrades on the fire
An ample tripod place, without delay
To cleanse Patroclus from the bloody gore:
They on the burning fire the tripod placed,
With water filled, and kindled wood beneath.   385
Around the bellying tripod rose the flames,
Heating the bath; within the glittering brass
Soon as the water boiled, they washed the corpse,
With lissom oils anointing, and the wounds
With fragrant ointments filled, of nine years old;   390
Then in fine linen they the body wrapped

From head to feet, and laid it on a couch,
And covered over with a fair white sheet.
All night around Achilles swift of foot
The Myrmidons with tears Patroclus mourned.   395
    To Juno then, his sister and his wife,
Thus Saturn's son: "At length thou hast thy will,
Imperial Juno, who hast stirred to war
Achilles swift of foot; well might one deem
These long-haired Greeks from thee derived their birth." 400
    To whom in answer thus the stag-eyed Queen:
"What words, dread son of Saturn, dost thou speak?
E'en man, though mortal, and inferior far
To us in wisdom, might so much effect
Against his fellow-man; then how should I,   405
By double title chief of Goddesses,
First by my birth, and next because thy wife
I boast me, thine, o'er all the Gods supreme,
Not work my vengeance on the Trojan race?"
    Such converse while they held, to Vulcan's house,   410
Immortal, starlike bright, among the Gods
Unrivalled, all of brass, by Vulcan's self
Constructed, sped the silver-footed Queen.
Him sweltering at his forge she found, intent
On forming twenty tripods, which should stand   415
The wall surrounding of his well-built house;
With golden wheels beneath he furnished each,
And to the assembly of the Gods endued
With power to move spontaneous, and return,
A marvel to behold! thus far his work   420
He had completed; but not yet had fixed
The rich-wrought handles; these his labour now

Engaged, to fit them, and to rivet fast.
While thus he exercised his practised skill,
The silver-footed Queen approached the house.   425
Charis, the skilful artist's wedded wife,
Beheld her coming, and advanced to meet;
And, as her hand she clasped, addressed her thus:
  "Say, Thetis of the flowing robe, beloved
And honoured, whence this visit to our house,   430
An unaccustomed guest? but come thou in,
That I may welcome thee with honour due."
  Thus, as she spoke, the Goddess led her in,
And on a seat with silver studs adorned,
Fair, richly wrought, a footstool at her feet,   435
She bade her sit; then thus to Vulcan called:
"Haste hither, Vulcan; Thetis asks thine aid."
  Whom answered thus the skilled artificer:
" An honoured and a venerated guest
Our house contains; who saved me once from woe, 440
When by my mother's act from Heaven I fell,
Who, for that I was crippled in my feet,
Deemed it not shame to hide me; hard had then
My fortune been, had not Eurynome
And Thetis in their bosoms sheltered me;   445
Eurynome, from old Oceanus
Who drew her birth, the ever-circling flood.
Nine years with them I dwelt, and many a work
I fashioned there of metal, clasps, and chains
Of spiral coil, rich cups, and collars fair,   450
Hid in a cave profound; where the ocean stream
With ceaseless murmur foamed and moaned around;
Unknown to God or man, but to those two

Who saved me, Thetis and Eurynome.
Now to my house hath fair-haired Thetis come;   455
To her, my life preserved its tribute owes:
Then thou the hospitable rites perform,
While I my bellows and my tools lay by."
    He said, and from the anvil reared upright
His massive strength; and as he limped along,   460
His tottering knees were bowed beneath his weight.
The bellows from the fire he next withdrew,
And in a silver casket placed his tools;
Then with a sponge his brows and lusty arms
He wiped, and sturdy neck and hairy ·chest.   465
He donned his robe, and took his weighty staff;
Then through the door with halting step he passed;
There waited on their King the attendant maids;
In form as living maids, but wrought in gold;
Instinct with consciousness, with voice endued,   470
And strength, and skill from heavenly teachers drawn.
These waited, duteous, at the Monarch's side,
His step supporting; he, with halting gait,
Passed to a gorgeous chair by Thetis' side,
And, as her hand he clasped, addressed her thus: 475
    " Say, Thetis of the flowing robe, beloved
And honoured, whence this visit to our house,
An unaccustomed guest? say what thy will,
And, if within my power, esteem it done."
    To whom in answer Thetis, weeping, thus: 480
" Vulcan, of all the Goddesses who dwell
On high Olympus, lives there one whose soul
Hath borne such weight of woe, so many griefs,
As Saturn's son hath heaped on me alone?

Me, whom he chose from all the sea-born nymphs, 485
And gave to Peleus, son of Æacus,
His subject; I endured a mortal's bed,
Though sore against my will; he now, bent down
By feeble age, lies helpless in his house.
Now adds he farther grief; he granted me   490
To bear, and rear, a son, of heroes chief;
Like a young tree he throve; I tended him,
In a rich vineyard as the choicest plant:
Till in the beakèd ships I sent him forth
To war with Troy; him ne'er shall I behold,   495
Returning home, in aged Peleus' house.
E'en while he lives, and sees the light of day,
He lives in sorrow; nor, to soothe his grief,
My presence can avail; a girl, his prize,
Selected for him by the sons of Greece,   500
Great Agamemnon wrested from his arms:
In grief and rage he pined his soul away;
The Trojans then, all egress from the camp
Debarred, hemmed in the Greeks beside their ships:
They, to implore his aid, their envoys sent   505
With proffers charged of many and costly gifts.
With his own hand to save them he refused;
But, in his armour clad, to battle sent
His friend Patroclus, with a numerous band.
All day they fought before the Scæan gates;   510
And in that day had Ilion been destroyed,
But in the van, Menœtius' noble son,
After great deeds achieved, Apollo slew,
And crowned with glory Hector, Priam's son.
Therefore a suppliant to thy knees I come,   515

If to my son, to early death condemned,
Thou wilt accord the boon of shield and helm,
And well-wrought greaves with silver clasps secured,
And breastplate: for his own, his faithful friend,
By Trojan hand subdued, hath lost; and he,　　520
O'erwhelmed with grief, lies prostrate on the earth."
　Whom answered thus the skilled artificer:
"Take comfort, nor let this disturb thy mind;
Would that as surely, when his hour shall come,
I could defend him from the stroke of death,　　525
As I can undertake that his shall be
Such arms as they shall marvel who behold."
　He left her thus, and to his forge returned;
The bellows then directing to the fire,
He bade them work; through twenty pipes at once 530
Forthwith they poured their diverse-tempered blasts;
Now briskly seconding his eager haste,
Now at his will, and as the work required.
The stubborn brass, and tin, and precious gold,
And silver, first he melted in the fire;　　535
Then on its stand his weighty anvil placed;
And with one hand the hammer's ponderous weight
He wielded, while the other grasped the tongs.
　And first a shield he fashioned, vast and strong,
With rich adornment; circled with a rim,　　540
Threefold, bright-gleaming, whence a silver belt
Depended; of five folds the shield was formed;
And on its surface many a rare design
Of curious art his practised skill had wrought.
　Thereon were figured earth, and sky, and sea,　　545
The ever-circling sun, and full-orbed moon,

And all the signs that crown the vault of Heaven;
Pleiads and Hyads, and Orion's might,
And Arctos, called the Wain, who wheels on high
His circling course, and on Orion waits;   550
Sole star that never bathes in the ocean wave.

And two fair populous towns were sculptured there:
In one were marriage pomp and revelry,
And brides, in gay procession, through the streets
With blazing torches from their chambers borne,   555
While frequent rose the hymeneal song.
Youths whirled around in joyous dance, with sound
Of flute and harp; and, standing at their doors,
Admiring women on the pageant gazed.

Meanwhile a busy throng the forum filled: 560
There between two a fierce contention rose,
About a death-fine; to the public one
Appealed, asserting to have paid the whole;
While one denied that he had aught received.
Both were desirous that before the Judge   565
The issue should be tried; with noisy shouts
Their several partisans encouraged each.
The heralds stilled the tumult of the crowd:
On polished chairs, in solemn circle, sat
The reverend Elders; in their hands they held   570
The loud-voiced heralds' sceptres; waving these,
They heard the alternate pleadings; in the midst
Two talents lay of gold, which he should take
Who should before them prove his righteous cause.

Before the second town two armies lay,   575
In arms refulgent; to destroy the town
The assailants threatened, or among themselves

Of all the wealth within the city stored
An equal half, as ransom, to divide.
The terms rejecting, the defenders manned   580
A secret ambush; on the walls they placed
Women and children mustered for defence,
And men by age enfeebled; forth they went,
By Mars and Pallas led; these, wrought in gold,
In golden arms arrayed, above the crowd   585
For beauty and stature, as befitting Gods,
Conspicuous shone; of lesser height the rest.
But when the destined ambuscade was reached,
Beside the river, where the shepherds drove
Their flocks and herds to water, down they lay,   590
In glittering arms accoutred; and apart
They placed two spies, to notify betimes
The approach of flocks of sheep and lowing herds.
These, in two shepherds' charge, ere long appeared,
Who, unsuspecting as they moved along,   595
Enjoyed the music of their pastoral pipes.
They on the booty, from afar discerned,
Sprang from their ambuscade; and cutting off
The herds, and fleecy flocks, their guardians slew.
Their comrades heard the tumult where they sat   600
Before their sacred altars, and forthwith
Sprang on their cars, and with fast-stepping steeds
Pursued the plunderers, and o'ertook them soon.
There on the river's bank they met in arms,
And each at other hurled their brazen spears.   605
And there were figured Strife, and Tumult wild,
And deadly Fate, who in her iron grasp
One newly wounded, one unwounded bore,

While by the feet from out the press she dragged
Another slain: about her shoulders hung   610
A garment crimsoned with the blood of men.
Like living men they seemed to move, to fight,
To drag away the bodies of the slain.
    And there was graven a wide-extended plain
Of fallow land, rich, fertile, mellow soil,   615
Thrice ploughed; where many ploughmen up and down
Their teams were driving; and as each attained
The limit of the field, would one advance,
And tender him a cup of generous wine:
Then would he turn, and to the end again   620
Along the furrow cheerly drive his plough.
And still behind them darker showed the soil,
The true presentment of a new-ploughed field,
Though wrought in gold; a miracle of art.
    There too was graven a corn-field, rich in grain, 625
Where with sharp sickles reapers plied their task,
And thick, in even swathe, the trusses fell;
The binders, following close, the bundles tied:
Three were the binders; and behind them boys
In close attendance waiting, in their arms   630
Gathered the bundles, and in order piled.
Amid them, staff in hand, in silence stood
The King, rejoicing in the plenteous swathe.
A little way removed, the heralds slew
A sturdy ox, and now beneath an oak   635
Prepared the feast; while women mixed, hard by,
White barley porridge for the labourers' meal.
    And, with rich clusters laden, there was graven
A vineyard fair, all gold; of glossy black

The bunches were, on silver poles sustained; 640
Around, a darksome trench; beyond, a fence
Was wrought, of shining tin; and through it led
One only path, by which the bearers passed,
Who gathered in the vineyard's bounteous store.
There maids and youths, in joyous spirits bright, 645
In woven baskets bore the luscious fruit.
A boy, amid them, from a clear-toned harp
Drew lovely music; well his liquid voice
The strings accompanied; they all with dance
And song harmonious joined, and joyous shouts, 650
As the gay bevy lightly tripped along.
  Of straight-horned cattle too a herd was graven;
Of gold and tin the heifers all were wrought:
They to the pasture, from the cattle-yard,
With gentle lowings, by a babbling stream, 655
Where quivering reed-beds rustled, slowly moved.
Four golden shepherds walked beside the herd,
By nine swift dogs attended; then amid
The foremost heifers sprang two lions fierce
Upon the lordly bull: he, bellowing loud, 660
Was dragged along, by dogs and youths pursued.
The tough bull's-hide they tore, and gorging lapped
The intestines and dark blood; with vain attempt
The herdsmen following closely, to the attack
Cheered their swift dogs; these shunned the lions' jaws,
And close around them baying, held aloof. [665
  And there the skilful artist's hand had traced
A pasture broad, with fleecy flocks o'erspread,
In a fair glade, with fold, and tents, and pens.
  There, too, the skilful artist's hand had wrought, 670

With curious workmanship, a mazy dance,
Like that which Dædalus in Cnossus erst
At fair-haired Ariadne's bidding framed.
There, laying each on other's wrists their hand,
Bright youths and many-suitored maidens danced : 675
In fair white linen these; in tunics those,
Well woven, shining soft with fragrant oils ;
These with fair coronets were crowned, while those
With golden swords from silver belts were girt.
Now whirled they round with nimble practised feet, 680
Easy, as when a potter, seated, turns
A wheel, new fashioned by his skilful hand,
And spins it round, to prove if true it run :
Now featly moved in well-beseeming ranks.
A numerous crowd, around, the lovely dance   685
Surveyed, delighted; while an honoured Bard
Sang, as he struck the lyre, and to the strain
Two tumblers, in the midst, were whirling round.
   About the margin of the massive shield
Was wrought the mighty strength of the ocean stream
   The shield completed, vast and strong, he forged [690
A breastplate, dazzling bright as flame of fire ;
And next, a weighty helmet for his head,
Fair, richly wrought, with crest of gold above;
Then last, well-fitting greaves of pliant tin.   695
   The skilled artificer his works complete
Before Achilles' Goddess-mother laid :
She, like a falcon, from the snow-clad heights
Of huge Olympus, darted swiftly down,
Charged with the glittering arms by Vulcan wrought. 700

BOOK XIX.

NOW morn in saffron robe, from the ocean stream
  Ascending, light diffused o'er Gods and men;
As Thetis, to the ships returning, bore
The gift of Vulcan; there her son she found,
Who o'er Patroclus hung in bitter grief; 5
Around him mourned his comrades; in the midst
She stood, and clasped his hand, as thus she spoke:

  "Leave we, my son, though deep our grief, the dead;
Here let him lie, since Heaven hath doomed his fall;
But thou these arms receive, by Vulcan sent, 10
Fairer than e'er on mortal breast were borne."
The arms before Achilles, as she spoke,
The Goddess laid; loud rang the wondrous work.
With awe the Myrmidons beheld; nor dared
Affront the sight: but as Achilles gazed, 15
More fiery burned his wrath; beneath his brows
His eyes like lightning flashed; with fierce delight
He seized the glorious gift; and when his soul
Had feasted on the miracle of art,
To Thetis thus his wingèd words addressed: 20

  "Mother, the God hath given me arms indeed,
Worthy a God, and such as mortal man
Could never forge; I go to arm me straight;
Yet fear I for Menœtius' noble son,
Lest in his spear-inflicted wounds the flies 25

May gender worms, and desecrate the dead,
And, life extinct, corruption reach his flesh."
    Whom answered thus the silver-footed Queen:
"Let not such fears, my son, disturb thy mind;
I will myself the swarms of flies disperse,   30
That on the flesh of slaughtered warriors prey;
And should he here remain a year complete,
Still should his flesh be firm and fresh as now:
But thou to council call the chiefs of Greece;
Against the monarch Agamemmon there,   35
The leader of the host, abjure thy wrath;
Then arm thee quickly, and put on thy might."
    Her words with dauntless courage filled his breast.
She in Patroclus' nostrils, to preserve
His flesh, red nectar and ambrosia poured.   40
    Along the ocean beach Achilles passed,
And loudly shouting, called on all the chiefs;
Then all who heretofore remained on board,
The steersmen, who the vessels' rudders hold,
The very stewards that served the daily bread,   45
All to the assembly thronged, when reappeared
Achilles, from the fight so long withdrawn.
Two noble chiefs, two ministers of Mars,
Ulysses sage, and valiant Diomed,
Appeared, yet crippled by their grievous wounds.   50
Their halting steps supporting with their spears,
And on the foremost seats their places took.
Next followed Agamemnon, King of men,
He also wounded; for Antenor's son,
Coön, had stabbed him in the stubborn fight.   55
When all the Greeks were closely thronged around,

Up rose Achilles swift of foot, and said:
"Great son of Atreus, what hath been the gain
To thee or me, since heart-consuming strife
Hath fiercely raged between us, for a girl,   60
Who would to Heaven had died by Dian's shafts
That day when from Lyrnessus' captured town
I bore her off? so had not many a Greek
Bitten the bloody dust, by hostile hands
Subdued, while I in anger stood aloof.   65
Great was the gain to Troy; but Greeks, methinks,
Will long retain the memory of our feud.
Yet pass we that; and though our hearts be sore,
Still let us school our angry spirits down.
My wrath I here abjure; it is not meet   70
It burn for ever unappeased; do thou
Muster to battle straight the long-haired Greeks;
That, to the Trojans once again opposed,
I may make trial if beside the ships
They dare this night remain; but he, I ween,   75
Will gladly rest his limbs, who safe shall fly,
My spear escaping, from the battle field."
He said: the well-greaved Greeks rejoiced to hear
His wrath abjured by Peleus' godlike son;
And from his seat, not standing in the midst,   80
Thus to the assembly Agamemnon spoke:
"Friends, Grecian Heroes, Ministers of Mars,
When one stands up to speak, 'tis meet for all
To lend a patient ear, nor interrupt;
For e'en to practised speakers hard the task: 85
But in this vast assembly, who can speak
That all may hear? the clearest voice must fail.

To Peleus' son, Achilles, I my mind
Will frankly open; ye among yourselves
Impart the words I speak, that all may know.   90
Oft hath this matter been by Greeks discussed,
And I their frequent censure have incurred:
Yet was not I the cause; but Jove, and Fate,
And gloomy Erinnys, who combined to throw
A strong delusion o'er my mind, that day   95
I robbed Achilles of his lawful prize.
What could I do? a Goddess all o'er-ruled,
Daughter of Jove, dread Atè, baleful power,
Misleading all; with lightest step she moves,
Not on the earth, but o'er the heads of men,   100
With blighting touch; and many hath caused to err.
E'en Jove, the wisest deemed of Gods and men,
In error she involved, when Juno's art
By female stratagem the God deceived:
When in well-girdled Thebes Alcmena lay   105
In travail of the might of Hercules,
In boastful tone amid the Gods he spoke:
'Hear all ye Gods, and all ye Goddesses,
The words I speak, the promptings of my soul.
This day Lucina shall to light bring forth   110
A child, the future Lord of all around,
Of mortal men, who trace to me their blood.'
Whom answered Juno thus, with deep deceit:
'Thou dost but feign, nor wilt fulfil thy word:
Come now, Olympian, swear a solemn oath   115
That he shall be the Lord of all around,
Who on this day shall be of woman born,
Of mortal men, who trace to thee their blood.'

She said, and Jove, the snare unseeing, swore
A solemn oath; but found his error soon.　120
Down from Olympus' height she sped in haste
To Argos of Achaia; for the wife
Of Sthenelus, the son of Perseus, there,
She knew, was seven months pregnant of a son;
Whom, though untimely born, she brought to light,　125
Staying meanwhile Alcmena's labour-pangs.
To Saturn's son herself the tidings brought,
And thus addressed him: ' Jove, the lightning's Lord,
I bring thee news; this day a mighty man,
By thee ordained to be the Argives' King,　130
Is born, Eurystheus, son of Sthenelus,
The son of Perseus, issue of thy blood;
Well worthy he to be the Argives' King.'
She said: keen sorrow deeply pierced his soul;
Then Até by the glossy locks he seized　135
In mighty wrath; and swore a solemn oath,
That to Olympus and the starry Heaven
She never should return, who all misleads.
His arm then whirling, from the starry Heaven
He flung her down, to vex the affairs of men.　140
Yet oft her fraud remembered he with groans,
When by Eurystheus' hard commands he saw
Condemned to servile tasks his noble son.
So, oft as Hector of the glancing helm
Beside the ships to slaughter gave the Greeks,　145
Back to my mind my former error came.
I erred, for Jove my judgment took away;
But friendly reconcilement now I seek,
And tender costly presents; then thyself

Uprouse thee, and excite the rest to arms,   150
While I prepare the gifts, whate'er of late*
The sage Ulysses promised in thy tent:
Or, if thou wilt, though eager for the fray,
Remain thou here awhile, till from my ship
My followers bring the gifts; that thou mayst see   155
I make my offerings with no niggard hand."
  Whom answered thus Achilles swift of foot:
"Most mighty Agamemnon, King of men,
The gifts thou deem'st befitting, 'tis for thee
To give, or to withhold; but now at once   160
Prepare we for the battle; 'tis not meet
On trivial pretexts here to waste our time,
Or idly loiter; much remains to do:
Again be seen Achilles in the van,
Scattering with brazen spear the Trojan ranks;   165
And ye, forget not man with man to fight."
  To whom in answer sage Ulysses thus:
"Brave as thou art, Achilles, godlike chief,
Yet fasting lead not forth the sons of Greece
To fight the Trojans; for no little time   170
Will last the struggle, when the serried ranks
Are once engaged in conflict, and the Gods
With equal courage either side inspire:
But bid them, by the ships, of food and wine
(Wherein are strength and courage) first partake;   175

---

* L. 151. Χθιζὸς, yesterday. But either the word must have a more extended
signification than is usually given to it, or Homer must here have fallen into an
error; for two complete nights, and one day, that on which Patroclus met his
death, had intervened since the visit of Ajax and Ulysses to the tent of Achilles.
See also l. 215.

For none throughout the day till set of sun,
Fasting from food, may bear the toils of war;
His spirit may still be eager for the fray;
Yet are his limbs by slow degrees weighed down,
Himself by thirst and hunger worn, his knees　　　180
Unable, as he moves, to bear his weight.
But he who, first with food and wine refreshed,
All day maintains the combat with the foe,
His spirit retains unbroken, and his limbs
Unwearied, till both armies quit the field.　　　185
Disperse then now the crowd, and bid prepare
The morning meal; meantime to public view
Let Agamemnon, King of men, display
His costly gifts; that all the Greeks may see,
And that thy heart within thee melt with joy:　　　190
And there in full assembly let him swear
A solemn oath, that he hath ne'er approached
The fair Briseis' bed, nor held with her
Such intercourse as man with woman holds.
Be thou propitious, and accept his oath.　　　195
Then at a sumptuous banquet in his tent
Let him receive thee; that thine honour due
May nothing lack; and so, Atrides, thou
Shalt stand in sight of all men clear of blame;
For none can wonder that insulting speech　　　200
Should rouse the anger of a sceptred King."
　To whom thus Agamemnon, King of men:
"Son of Laertes, I accept thy speech
With cordial welcome: all that thou hast said
Is well and wisely spoken; for the oath,　　　205
I am prepared, with willing mind, to swear;

Nor in the sight of Heaven will be forsworn.
Let then Achilles here awhile remain,
Though eager for the fray; ye too remain,
Until the presents from my tent be brought,   210
And we our solemn compact ratify.
Then this command upon thyself I lay:
That thou the noblest youths of all the Greeks
Select, and bid them from my vessel bear
The gifts, which to Achilles yesternight   215
We promised, and withal the women bring;
And let Talthybius through the host seek out
A boar, for sacrifice to Jove and Sol."
  Whom answered thus Achilles swift of foot:
"Most mighty Agamemnon, King of men,   220
These matters to some future time were best
Deferred, some hour of respite from the fight,
Of rage less fiercely burning in my breast;
But slaughtered now they lie, whom Priam's son,
Hector, hath slain, by Jove to victory led.   225
Ye bid us take our food; if I might rule,
I would to battle lead the sons of Greece,
Unfed, and fasting; and at set of sun,
Our shame avenged, an ample feast prepare;
Till then, nor food nor drink shall pass my lips,   230
My comrade slain; who pierced with mortal wounds,
Turned toward the doorway, lies within my tent,
Amid his mourning friends; while there he lies,
No thought have I for these or aught beside,
Save carnage, blood, and groans of dying men."   235
  To whom Ulysses, sage in council thus:
"O Son of Peleus, noblest of the Greeks,

How far, Achilles, thou surpassest me
In deeds of arms, I know; but thou must yield
To me in counsel, for my years are more,   240
And my experience greater far than thine:
Then to my words incline a patient ear.
Men soonest weary of battle, where the sword
The bloodiest harvest reaps; the lightest crop
Of slaughter is where Jove inclines the scale,   245
Dispenser, at his will, of human wars.
The Greeks by fasting cannot mourn their dead;
For day by day successive numbers fall;
Where were the respite then from ceaseless fast?
Behoves us bury out of sight our dead,   250
Steeling our hearts, and weeping but a day;
And we, the rest, whom cruel war hath spared,
Should first with food and wine recruit our strength;
Then, girding on our arms, the livelong day
Maintain the war, unwearied; then let none   255
Require a farther summons to the field;
(And woe to him who loitering by the ships
That summons hears;) but with united force
Against the Trojans wake the furious war."
He said, and called on noble Nestor's sons,   260
On Meges, Phyleus' son, Meriones,
Thoas, and Lycomedes, Creon's son,
And Melanippus; they together sought
The mighty monarch Agamemnon's tent.
Soon as the word was given, the work was done;   265
Seven tripods brought they out, the promised gifts;
Twelve horses, twenty caldrons glittering bright;
Seven women too, well skilled in household cares,

With whom, the eighth, the fair Briseis came.
Ulysses led the way, and with him brought		270
Ten talents full of gold; the attendant youths
The other presents bore, and in the midst
Displayed before the assembly: then uprose
The monarch Agamemnon; by his side,
With voice of godlike power, Talthybius stood,		275
Holding the victim: then Atrides drew
The dagger, ever hanging at his side,
Close by the scabbard of his mighty sword,
And from the victim's head the bristles shore.
With hands uplifted then to Jove he prayed;		280
While all around the Greeks in silence stood,
Listening, decorous, to the monarch's words,
As looking up to Heaven he made his prayer:
  "Be witness, Jove, thou highest, first of Gods,
And Sun, and Earth, and ye who vengeance wreak 285
Beneath the earth on souls of men forsworn,
Furies! that never, or to love unchaste
Soliciting, or otherwise, my hand
Hath fair Briseis touched; but in my tent
Still pure and undefiled hath she remained:		290
And if in this I be forsworn, may Heaven
With all the plagues afflict me, due to those
Who sin by perjured oaths against the Gods."
  Thus as he spoke, across the victim's throat
He drew the pitiless blade; Talthybius then		295
To hoary Ocean's depths the carcase threw,
Food for the fishes; then Achilles rose,
And thus before the assembled Greeks he spoke:
  "O Father Jove, how dost thou lead astray

Our human judgments! ne'er had Atreus' son 300
My bosom filled with wrath, nor from my arms,
To his own loss, against my will had torn
The girl I loved, but that the will of Jove
To death predestined many a valiant Greek.
Now to the meal; anon renew the war." 305
  This said, the assembly he dismissed in haste,
The crowd dispersing to their several ships;
Upon the gifts the warlike Myrmidons
Bestowed their care, and bore them to the ships
Of Peleus' godlike son; within the tent 310
They laid them down, and there the women placed,
While to the drove the followers led the steeds.
Briseis, fair as golden Venus, saw
Patroclus lying, pierced with mortal wounds,
Within the tent; and with a bitter cry, 315
She flung her down upon the corpse, and tore
Her breast, her delicate neck, and beauteous cheeks;
And, weeping, thus the lovely woman wailed:
  "Patroclus, dearly loved of this sad heart!
When last I left this tent, I left thee full 320
Of healthy life; returning now, I find
Only thy lifeless corpse, thou Prince of men!
So sorrow still, on sorrow heaped, I bear.
The husband of my youth, to whom my sire
And honoured mother gave me, I beheld 325
Slain with the sword before the city walls:
Three brothers, whom with me one mother bore,
My dearly-loved ones, all were doomed to death:
Nor wouldst thou, when Achilles swift of foot
My husband slew, and royal Mynes' town 330

In ruin laid, allow my tears to flow;
But thou wouldst make me (such was still thy speech)
The wedded wife of Peleus' godlike son:
Thou wouldst to Phthia bear me in thy ship,
And there, thyself, amid the Myrmidons,   335
Wouldst give my marriage feast; then, unconsoled,
I weep thy death, my ever-gentle friend!"
    Weeping, she spoke; the women joined her wail:
Patroclus' death the pretext for their tears,
But each in secret wept her private griefs.   340
    Around Achilles thronged the elder men,
Urging to eat; but he, with groans, refused:
"I pray you, would you show your love, dear friends,
Ask me not now with food or drink to appease
Hunger or thirst; a load of bitter grief   345
Weighs heavy on my soul; till set of sun
Fasting will I remain, and still endure."
    The other monarchs at his word withdrew:
The two Atridæ, and Ulyssès sage,
And Nestor and Idomeneus remained,   350
And aged Phœnix, to divert his grief;
But comfort none, save in the bloody jaws
Of battle would he take; by memory stirred,
He heaved a deep-drawn sigh, as thus he spoke:
    "How oft hast thou, ill-fated dearest friend,   355
Here in this tent with eager zeal prepared
The tempting meal, whene'er the sons of Greece
In haste would arm them for the bloody fray!
Now liest thou there, while I, for love of thee,
From food and drink, before me placed, refrain: 360
For ne'er shall I again such sorrow know,

Not though I heard of aged Peleus' death,
Who now in Phthia mourns, with tender tears,
His absent son; he on a foreign shore
Is warring in that hateful Helen's cause: 365
No, nor of his, who now in Scyros' isle
Is growing up, if yet indeed he live,
Young Neoptolemus, my godlike son.
My hope had been indeed, that here in Troy,
Far from the plains of Argos, I alone   370
Was doomed to die; and that to Phthia thou,
Returned in safety, mightst my son convey
From Scyros home, and show him all my wealth,
My spoils, my slaves, my lofty, spacious house.
For Peleus or to death, methinks, e'en now   375
Hath yielded, or, not far from death removed,
Lives on in sorrow, bowed by gloomy age,
Expecting day by day the messenger
Who bears the mournful tidings of my death."
    Weeping, Achilles spoke; and with him wept   380
The Elders; each to fond remembrance moved
Of all that in his home himself had left.
The son of Saturn, pitying, saw their grief,
And Pallas thus with wingèd words addressed:
"My child, dost thou a hero's cause forsake,   385
Or does Achilles claim no more thy care,
Who sits in sorrow by the high-prowed ships,
Mourning his comrade slain? the others all
Partake the meal, while he from food abstains:
Then haste thee, and, with hunger lest he faint,   390
Drop nectar and ambrosia on his breast."
His words fresh impulse gave to Pallas' zeal:

Down, like the long-winged falcon, shrill of voice,
Through the clear sky she swooped : and while the Greeks
Armed for the fight, Achilles she approached,   395
And nectar and ambrosia on his breast
Distilled, lest hunger should his strength subdue ;
Back to her mighty father's ample house
Returning, as from out the ships they poured.
Thick as the snow-flakes that from Heaven descend,   400
Before the sky-born Boreas' chilling blast ;
So thick, outpouring from the ships, the stream
Of helmets polished bright, and bossy shields,
And breastplates firmly braced, and ashen spears :
Their brightness flashed to Heaven ; and laughed the Earth
Beneath the brazen glare ; loud rang the tramp   [405
Of armèd men : Achilles in the midst,
The godlike chief, in dazzling arms arrayed.
His teeth were gnashing audibly ; his eye
Blazed with the light of fire ; but in his heart   410
Was grief unbearable ; with furious wrath
He burned against the Trojans, as he donned
The heavenly gifts, the work of Vulcan's hand.
First on his legs the well-wrought greaves he fixed,
Fastened with silver clasps ; his breastplate next   415
Around his chest ; and o'er his shoulders flung
His silver-studded sword, with blade of brass ;
Then took his vast and weighty shield, whence gleamed
A light refulgent as the full-orbed moon ;
Or as to seamen o'er the wave is borne   420
The watchfire's light, which, high among the hills,
Some shepherd kindles in his lonely fold :
As they, reluctant, by the stormy winds,

Far from their friends are o'er the waters driven;
So from Achilles' shield, bright, richly wrought,   425
The light was thrown. The weighty helm he raised.
And placed it on his head; the plumèd helm
Shone like a star; and waved the hairs of gold,
Thick-set by Vulcan in the gleaming crest.
Then all the arms Achilles proved, to know   430
If well they fitted to his graceful limbs:
Like wings, they seemed to lift him from the ground.
Last, from its case he drew his father's spear,
Long, ponderous, tough; not one of all the Greeks,
None, save Achilles' self, could poise that spear ·   435
The far-famed Pelian ash, which to his sire,
On Pelion's summit felled, to be the bane
Of mighty chiefs, the Centaur Chiron gave.
With care Automedon and Alcimus
The horses yoked, with collars fair attached: 440
Placed in their mouths the bits, and passed the reins
Back to the well-built car: Automedon
Sprang on the car, with shining lash in hand:
Behind, Achilles came, arrayed for war,
In arms all glittering as the gorgeous sun,   445
And loudly to his father's steeds he called:
" Xanthus and Balius, noble progeny
Of swift Podarge, now in other sort
Back to the Grecian ranks in safety bear,
When ye shall quit the field, your charioteer;   450
Nor leave him, as ye left Patroclus, slain."
    To whom in answer from beneath the yoke
Xanthus, the noble horse, with glancing feet:
Bowing his head the while till all his mane

Down from the yoke-band streaming, reached the ground;
By Juno, white-armed Queen, with speech endued: [455
  "Yes, great Achilles, we this day again
Will bear thee safely; but thy day of doom
Is nigh at hand; nor we shall cause thy death,
But Heaven's high will, and Fate's imperious power.   460
By no default of ours, nor lack of speed,
The Trojans stripped Patroclus of his arms:
The mighty God, fair-haired Latona's son,
Achieved his death, and Hector's victory gained
Our speed of foot may vie with Zephyr's breeze,   465
Deemed swiftest of the winds; but thou art doomed
To die, by force combined of God and man."
  He said; his farther speech the Furies stayed.
To whom in wrath Achilles swift of foot:
"Xanthus, why thus predict my coming fate?   470
It ill beseems thee! well I know myself
That I am fated here in Troy to die,
Far from my home and parents; yet withal
I cease not, till these Trojans from the field
Before me fly." He said, and to the front,
His war-cry shouting, urged his fiery steeds.   476

BOOK XX.

ROUND thee, Achilles, by their beakèd ships
　　Stood thus accoutred, eager for the fray,
The sons of Greece; the Trojan host, opposed,
Stood on the sloping margin of the plain.
Then Jove to Themis gave command to call　　5
The Gods to council from the lofty height
Of many-ridged Olympus; to the house
Of Jove she summoned them from every side.
Thence of the Rivers, save Oceanus,
Not one was absent; nor of Nymphs, who haunt　　10
Clear fount, or shady grove, or grassy mead.
They, at the Cloud-compeller's house arrived,
Within the polished corridor reclined,
Which Vulcan's cunning hand for Jove had built.
There were they gathered in the abode of Jöve:　　15
Nor did the Earth-shaking Neptune slight the call,
But came from ocean's depths, and in the midst
He sat, and thus the will of Jove enquired:

　"Why, Lord of lightning, hast thou summoned here
The Gods to council? dost thou aught devise　　20
Touching the Greeks and Trojans? who e'en now
Kindle anew, it seems, the blaze of war."

　To whom the Cloud-compeller, answering, thus:
"The purpose, Neptune, well thou know'st thyself
For which I called ye; true, they needs must die,　　25

But still they claim my care; yet here will I
Upon Olympus' lofty ridge remain,
And view, serene, the combat; you, the rest,
Go, as you list, to Trojans or to Greeks,
And at your pleasure either party aid.   30
For if we leave Achilles thus alone
To fight against the Trojans, not an hour
Will they before the son of Peleus stand.
They dreaded him before; but now, I fear,
Since roused to fury by his comrade's death,   35
He e'en in fate's despite may storm the wall."
    Thus Saturn's son, and quenchless battle roused:
The Gods, divided, hastened to the war:
Juno and Pallas to the ships of Greece,
With them the Earth-shaker, and the helpful God,   40
Hermes, for cunning subtleties unmatched;
And Vulcan too, exulting in his strength,
Yet halting, and on feeble limbs sustained.
Mars of the glancing helm took part with Troy,
And golden Phœbus with his locks unshorn,   45
Latona too, and Dian, Archer-Queen,
Xanthus, and Venus, laughter-loving dame.
    While from the fight of men the Gods abstained,
High rose the Grecian vaunts, as, long withdrawn,
Achilles on the field again appeared;   50
And every Trojan's limbs with terror quaked,
Trembling, as Peleus' godlike son they saw,
In arms all-glittering, fierce as blood-stained Mars.
But when the Immortals mingled in the throng,
Then furious waxed the spirit-stirring strife;   55
Then Pallas raised her war-cry, standing now

Beside the deep-dug trench, without the wall,
Now shouting loud along the sounding beach.
On the other side, as with the tempest's roar,
Mars to the Trojans shouted loud; one while   60
From Ilion's topmost height; anon again
From the fair hill, o'erhanging Simöis' stream.
Thus, either side exciting to the fray,
The immortal Gods unchained the angry war.
Thundered on high the Sire of Gods and men   65
With awful din; while Neptune shook beneath
The boundless earth, and lofty mountain tops.
The spring-abounding Ida quaked and rocked
From her firm basis to her loftiest peak,
And Troy's proud city, and the ships of Greece.   70
Pluto, the infernal monarch, heard alarmed,
And, springing from his throne, cried out in fear,
Lest Neptune, breaking through the solid earth,
To mortals and Immortals should lay bare
His dark and drear abode of Gods abhorred.   75
Such was the shock when Gods in battle met;
For there to royal Neptune stood opposed
Phœbus Apollo with his arrows keen;
The blue-eyed Pallas to the God of War;
To Juno, Dian, heavenly Archeress,   80
Sister of Phœbus, golden-shafted Queen.
Stout Hermes, helpful God, Latona faced;
While Vulcan met the mighty rolling stream,
Xanthus by Gods, by men Scamander called.
Thus Gods encountered Gods: Achilles' soul   85
Meantime was burning 'mid the throng to meet
Hector, the son of Priam, with whose blood

He longed to glut the insatiate Lord of War.
Apollo then, the spirit-stirring God,
Æneas moved Achilles to confront,   90
And filled with courage high; and thus, the voice
Assuming of Lycaon, Priam's son,
Apollo, son of Jove, the chief addressed:
  "Æneas, prince and councillor of Troy,
Where are the vaunts, which o'er the wine-cup late 95
Thou mad'st amid the assembled chiefs of Troy,
That hand to hand thou wouldst Achilles meet?"
  To whom Æneas thus in answer spoke:
"Why, son of Priam, urge me to contend,
Against my will, with Peleus' mighty son?   100
Not for the first time should I now engage
Achilles swift of foot: I met him once,
And fled before his spear, on Ida's hill,
When on our herds he fell; Lyrnessus then
He razed, and Pedasus; me Jove preserved,   105
With strength endowing, and with speed of foot.
Else had I fallen beneath Achilles' hand,
By Pallas aided; who before him moves,
Light of his life, and guides his brazen spear
Trojans and Leleges alike to slay.   110
'Tis not in mortal man with him to fight,
Whom still some God attends, and guards from harm;
And, e'en unaided, to the mark his spear
Unerring flies, unchecked until it pierce
A warrior's breast; yet if the Gods the scale   115
Impartial hold, all brass-clad as he is,
O'er me no easy triumph should he gain."
  To whom the King Apollo, son of Jove:

" Brave chief, do thou too to the immortal Gods
Address thy prayer; men say that thou art sprung 120
From Venus, child of Jove; his mother owns
A humbler origin; one born to Jove,
The other to the aged Ocean God.
On then with dauntless spear, nor be dismayed
By his high tone and vaunting menaces."   125
    His words with courage filled the hero's breast,
And on he sprang, in dazzling arms arrayed;
But not unmarked of white-armed Juno passed,
To meet Achilles through the press of men,
Who thus addressed the Gods, to council called: 130
    "Neptune and Pallas both, bethink ye well
What now should be our course; Æneas comes,
In dazzling arms arrayed, to meet in fight
The son of Peleus; Phœbus sends him forth.
Say, then, shall we, encountering, to retreat   135
Perforce constrain him? or shall one of us
Beside Achilles stand, and give him strength
That he may nothing lack; and know himself
By all the mightiest of the immortal Gods
Beloved, and those how powerless, by whose aid   140
The Trojans yet maintain defensive war?
Therefore, to join the battle, came we all
From high Olympus, that in this day's fight
No ill befall him; though the time shall come
For him to meet the doom, by fate decreed,   145
When at his birth his thread of life was spun.
But if Achilles from a voice divine
Receive not this assurance, he may well
Be struck with fear, if haply to some God

He find himself opposed : 'tis hard for man   150
To meet, in presence visible, a God."
    To whom Earth-shaking Neptune thus replied :
" Juno, thine anger carry not too far ;
It ill beseems thee. Not with my consent
Shall we, the stronger far, provoke to arms   155
The other Gods ; but rather from the field
Retiring, let us from on high survey,
To mortals left, the turmoil of the war.
Should Mars or Phœbus then begin the fight,
Or stay Achilles, and his arm restrain,   160
Then in the contest we too may engage ;
And soon, methinks, will they be fain to join,
Driven from the field, the Synod of the Gods,
Subdued perforce by our victorious hands."
    The dark-haired monarch spoke ; and led the way 165
To the high wall, by Trojans built of old,
With Pallas' aid, for godlike Hercules ;
Within whose circle he might safety seek,
When from the beach the monster of the deep
Might chase him toward the plain ; there Neptune sat, 170
And with him, the other Gods, a veil of cloud
Impenetrable around their shoulders spread.
On the other side, upon the fair hill's brow,
Phœbus with Mars the fort-destroyer sat.
On either side they sat, each facing each   175
With hostile counsels ; yet reluctant both
To take the initiative of ruthless war ;
Till Jove, enthroned on high, the signal gave.
Then all the plain, with men and horses thronged,
The brazen gleam illumined ; rang the earth   180

Beneath their feet, as to the battle-shock
They rushed; but in the midst, both hosts between,
Eager for fight, stood forth two warriors bold,
Proudly pre-eminent; Anchises' son
Æneas, and Achilles' godlike might.   185
    Æneas first with threatening mien advanced,
Nodding his ponderous helm; before his breast
His shield he bore, and poised his brazen spear.
Him met Achilles from the opposing ranks;
Fierce as a ravening lion, whom to slay   190
Pour forth the stalwart youths, the united strength
Of the roused village; he unheeding moves
At first; but wounded by a javelin thrown
By some bold youth, he turns, with gaping jaws,
And frothing fangs, collecting for the spring,   195
His breast too narrow for his mighty heart;
And with his tail he lashes both his flanks
And sides, as though to rouse his utmost rage;
Then on, in pride of strength, with glaring eyes
He dashes, if some hunter he may slay,   200
Or in the foremost rank himself be slain.
So moved his dauntless spirit Peleus' son
Æneas to confront; when near they came,
Thus first Achilles, swift of foot, began:
    "Æneas, why so far before the ranks   205
Advanced? dost thou presume with me to fight?
Perchance expecting that the throne of Troy
And Priam's royal honours may be thine.
E'en if thou slay me, deem not to obtain
Such boon from Priam; valiant sons are his,   210
And he not weak, but bears a constant mind.

Or have the Trojans set apart for thee
Some favoured spot, the fairest of the land,
Orchard or corn-field, shouldst thou work my death;
Which thou shalt find, I trust, too hard a task?   215
Already hast thou fled before my spear;
Hast thou forgotten how amid thy herds
Alone I found thee, and with flying foot
Pursued thee down the steep of Ida's hill?
Nor didst thou dare to turn, or pause in flight.   220
Thou to Lyrnessus fledd'st; Lyrnessus I,
With Pallas' aid and Jove's, assailed and took:
Their women thence, their days of freedom lost,
I bore away, my captives; thee from death
Jove and the other Gods defended then;   225
But will not now bestow, though such thy hope,
Their succour; then I warn thee, while 'tis time,
Ere ill betide thee, to the general throng
That thou withdraw, nor stand to me opposed:
After the event may e'en a fool be wise."   230
    To whom in answer thus Æneas spoke:
"Achilles, think not me, as though a fool,
To daunt with lofty speech; I too could well
With cutting words, and insult, answer thee.
Each other's race and parents well we know   235
From tales of ancient days; although by sight
Nor mine to thee, nor thine to me are known.
To noble Peleus thou, 'tis said, wast born
Of Thetis, fair-haired daughter of the sea;
Of great Anchises, Heaven-descended chief,   240
I boast me sprung, to him by Venus borne.
Of these shall one or other have this day

To mourn their son; since not with empty words
Shall thou and I from mortal combat part.
But if thou farther wouldst enquire, and learn   245
The race I spring from, not unknown to men,
By Dardanus, of cloud-compelling Jove
Begotten, was Dardania peopled first,
Ere sacred Ilion, populous city of men,
Was founded on the plain; as yet they dwelt   250
On spring-abounding Ida's lowest spurs.
To Dardanus was Erichthonius born,
Great King, the wealthiest of the sons of men;
For him were pastured in the marshy mead,
Rejoicing with their foals, three thousand mares;   255
Them Boreas, in the pasture where they fed,
Beheld, enamoured; and amid the herd
In likeness of a coal-black steed appeared;
Twelve foals, by him conceiving, they produced.
These, o'er the teeming corn-fields as they flew,   260
Skimmed o'er the standing ears, nor broke the haulm:
And, o'er wide Ocean's bosom as they flew,
Skimmed o'er the topmost spray of the hoary sea.
Again, to Erichthonius Tros was born,
The King of Troy; three noble sons were his,   265
Ilus, Assaracus, and Ganymede;
The fairest he of all the sons of men;
Him, for his beauty, bore the Gods away,
To minister, as cup-bearer to Jove,
And dwell amid the Immortals: Ilus next   270
Begot a noble son, Laomedon;
Tithonus he, and Priam, Clytius,
Lampus and Icetäon, plant of Mars;

Capys, begotten of Assaracus,
Begot Anchises, and Anchises me:　　　　275
To Priam godlike Hector owes his birth.
Such is my race, and such the blood I boast;
But Jove, at will, to mortals valour gives
Or minishes; for he is Lord of all.
Then cease we now, like babbling fools, to prate　280
Here in the centre of the coming fight.
Terms of reproach we both might find, whose weight
Would sink a galley of a hundred oars;
For glibly runs the tongue, and can at will
Give utterance to discourse in every vein;　　　285
Wide is the range of language; and such words
As one may speak, another may return.
What need that we should insults interchange?
Like women, who some paltry quarrel wage,
Scolding and brawling in the public street,　　　290
And in opprobrious terms their anger vent,
Some true, some false; for so their rage suggests.
With words thou shalt not turn me from the field,
Till we have met in arms; then try we now
Each other's prowess with our brazen spears."　　295
　　He said, and hurled against the mighty shield
His brazen spear; loud rang the weapon's point:
And at arm's length Achilles held the shield
With his broad hand, in fear that through its folds
Æneas' spear would easy passage find;　　　　300
Blind fool! forgetful that the glorious gifts
Bestowed by Gods, are not with ease o'ercome,
Nor yield before the assaults of mortal men.
So broke not through Æneas' sturdy spear,

Stayed by the golden plate, the gift of Heaven;   305
Yet through two plates it passed, but three remained,
For five were in the shield by Vulcan wrought;
Two were of brass, the inner two of tin,
And one of gold, which stayed the brazen spear.
  Achilles threw in turn his ponderous spear,   310
And struck the circle of Æneas' shield
Near the first rim, where thinnest lay the brass,
And thinnest too the o'erlying hide; right through
The Pelian shaft was driven; wide gaped the shield.
Æneas crouched, in fear, as o'er his head   315
He held his shield; the eager weapon passed
Through both the circles of his ample shield,
And in the ground, behind him, quivering, stood.
Escaped the ponderous weapon, sharpest pain
Flashing across his eyes, in fear he stood,   320
So close the spear had passed him; onward then,
Drawing his trenchant blade, Achilles rushed,
With fearful shout; a rocky fragment then
Æneas lifted up, a mighty mass,
Which scarce two men, as men are now, could bear,   325
But he, unaided, lifted it with ease.
Then had Æneas, with the massive stone,
Or on the helmet, or the shield, his death
Averting, struck Achilles; and himself
Had by the sword of Peleus' son been slain,   330
Had not the Earth-shaking God his peril seen,
And to the Immortals thus addressed his speech:
"Oh, woe is me for great Æneas' sake,
Who, by Achilles slain, must visit soon
The viewless shades; insensate, who relied   335

On Phœbus' words; yet nought shall he avail
From death to save him. Yet oh why should he,
Blameless himself, the guilt of others rue?
Who still his grateful sacrifice hath paid
To all the Gods in wide-spread Heaven who dwell. 340
Let us then interpose to guard his life;
Lest, if Achilles slay him, Saturn's son
Be moved to anger; for his destiny
Would have him live; lest, heirless, from the earth
Should perish quite the race of Dardanus;   345
By Saturn's son the best-beloved of all
His sons, to him of mortal women born.
For Jove the race of Priam hath abhorred;
But o'er the Trojans shall Æneas reign,
And his sons' sons, through ages yet unborn."   350
    Whom answered thus the stag-eyed Queen of Heaven:
"Neptune, do thou determine for thyself
Æneas to withdraw, or leave to fall,
Good as he is, beneath Achilles' sword;
But we before the immortal Gods are bound,   355
Both I and Pallas, by repeated oaths,
Ne'er from his doom one Trojan life to save,
Though to devouring flames a prey, all Troy
Were blazing, kindled by the valiant Greeks."
    The Earth-shaker heard; and through the fight he passed,
And through the throng of spears, until he came [360
Where great Achilles and Æneas stood.
Around the eyes of Peleus' son he spread
A veil of mist; then from Æneas' shield
The brass-tipped spear withdrawing, laid it down 365
Before Achilles' feet; and lifting up

Æneas, bore him high above the ground.
O'er many a rank of warriors and of cars
Æneas flew, supported by the God;
Till to the field's extremest verge he came,   370
Where stood the Caucons, arming for the war.
There to Æneas, standing by his side,
The Earth-shaker thus his wingèd words addressed:
" Æneas, say what God has moved thee thus
Against Achilles, reckless, to contend,   375
Thy stronger far, and dearer to the Gods?
If e'er he cross thy path, do thou retire,
Lest, e'en despite of fate, thou find thy death.
But when Achilles hath to fate succumbed,
Then, fearless, with the foremost join the fray: 380
No other Greek shall bear away thy spoils."
    Thus plainly warned, Æneas there he left.
Then from Achilles' eyes he purged the film:
Astonished, he with eyes wide open gazed,
As thus he communed with his mighty heart: 385
    " O Heaven, what marvel do mine eyes behold?
My spear before me laid, and vanished he
At whom I hurled it with intent to slay!
Then is Æneas of the immortal Gods
In truth beloved, though vain I deemed his boast. 390
A curse go with him! yet methinks not soon
Will he again presume to prove my might,
Who gladly now in flight escapes from death.
Then, to the valiant Greeks my orders given,
Let me some other Trojan's mettle prove."   395
    Then toward the ranks he sprang, each several man
Exhorting: " From the Trojans, valiant Greeks,

No longer stand aloof; but man to man
Confront the foe, and nobly dare the fight.
'Twere hard for me, brave warrior though I be,   400
To face such numbers, and to fight with all:
Not Mars, nor Pallas, though immortal Gods,
Could face, and vanquish, such a mighty mass.
But what my single arm, and feet, and strength
May profit, not a jot will I relax;   405
Right through the ranks I mean to force my way;
And small shall be that Trojan's cause for joy,
Who comes within the compass of my spear."
    Thus he, exhorting; Hector cheering on
Meanwhile the Trojans, with assurance given   410
That he himself Achilles would confront.
    "Ye valiant Trojans, fear not Peleus' son;
I too in words could with the Gods contend,
Though not in arms; so much the stronger they.
Not all his words Achilles shall make good;   415
Fulfilling some, in others he shall fail,
His course midway arrested. Him will I
Encounter, though his hands were hands of fire,
Of fire his hands, his strength as burnished steel."
    Thus he, exhorting: with uplifted spears   420
Advanced the Trojans; from the mingling hosts
Loud rose the clamour; then at Hector's side
Apollo stood, and thus addressed the chief:
" Hector, forbear Achilles to defy;
And 'mid the crowd withdraw thee from the fray;   425
Lest with the spear he slay thee, thrown from far,
Or with the sword in combat hand to hand."
    He said; and troubled by the heavenly voice,

Hector amid the throng of men withdrew.

  Then, girt with might, amid the Trojans sprang, 430
With fearful shouts, Achilles; first he slew
Otryntes' son, Iphition, valiant chief
Of numerous warriors; him a Naiad nymph,
In Hyde's fertile vale, beneath the feet
Of snow-clad Tmolus, to Otryntes bore;   435
At him, as on he rushed, Achilles hurled,
And through his forehead drove his glittering spear;
The head was cleft in twain; thundering he fell,
And o'er him thus Achilles made his boast:

  "Son of Otryntes, lie thou there, of men   440
The most vain-glorious; here thou find'st thy death,
Far from thy place of birth, beside the lake
Gygæan; there hadst thou thine heritage
Of old, beside the fish-abounding stream
Of Hyllus, and by Hermus' eddying flood."   445

  Thus he, exulting: o'er Iphition's eyes
Were spread the shades of death; his mangled corpse
Was crushed beneath the Grecian chariot wheels,
In the first shock. Demoleon next he smote,
A helpful aid in war, Antenor's son,   450
Pierced through the temples, through the brass-bound
    helm;
Nor checked the brazen helm the spear, whose point
Went crashing through the bone, that all the brain
Was shattered; onward as he rushed, he fell.
Then through the neck Hippodamas he smote,   455
Flying before him, mounted on his car.
Deep groaned he, breathing out his soul, as groans
A bull, by sturdy youths to the altar dragged

Of Neptune, King divine of Helice;
The Earth-shaking God, well-pleased, the gift receives; 460
E'en with such groans his noble spirit fled.
The godlike Polydore he next assailed,
The son of Priam; him his aged sire
Would fain have kept at home, of all his sons
At once the youngest and the best-beloved;   465
Among them all for speed of foot unmatched;
Whose youthful folly, in the foremost ranks
His speed displaying, cost him now his life.
Him, as he darted by, Achilles' spear
Struck through the centre of the back, where met 470
The golden clasps that held the glittering belt,
And where the breastplate formed a double guard:
Right through his body passed the weapon's point;
Groaning, he fell upon his knees; dark clouds
O'erspread his eyes; supporting with his hand   475
His wounded bowels, on the ground he writhed.
When Hector saw his brother Polydore
Writhing in death, a mist o'erspread his eyes;
Nor longer could he bear to stand aloof,
But sprang to meet Achilles, flashing fire,   480
His keen spear brandishing; at sight of him
Up leaped Achilles, and exulting cried:

"Lo, here the man who most hath wrung my soul,
Who slew my loved companion; now, methinks,
Upon the pass of war not long shall we   485
Stand separate, nor each the other shun."

Then, with stern glance, to godlike Hector thus:
"Draw near, and quickly meet thy doom of death."

To whom thus Hector of the glancing helm,

Unterrified: "Achilles, think not me,　　490
As though a fool and ignorant of war,
To daunt with lofty speech; I too could well
With cutting words and insult answer thee.
I know thee strong and valiant; and I know
Myself to thee inferior; but the event　　495
Is with the Gods; and I, if such their will,
The weaker, with my spear may reach thy life:
My point too hath, ere now, its sharpness proved."

　He said, and, poising, hurled his ponderous spear,
Which from Achilles Pallas turned aside　　500
With lightest breath; and back to Hector sent,
And laid before his feet; intent to slay,
Onward Achilles rushed, with fearful shout;
But Phœbus Hector from the field conveyed,
(As Gods can only,) veiled in thickest cloud.　　505
Thrice Peleus' godlike son, with brazen spear,
His onset made; thrice struck the misty cloud;
But when, with power as of a God, he made
His fourth essay, in fury thus he cried:

　"Yet once again, vile hound, hast thou escaped; 510
Thy doom was nigh, but thee thy God hath saved,
Phœbus, to whom, amid the clash of spears,
Well mayst thou pray! We yet shall meet again;
When I shall end thee, if I too may claim
A guardian God; meanwhile, from thee I turn,　　515
And others seek on whom my hap may light."

　He said, and drove through Dryops' neck his spear,
And stretched him at his feet, and pass'd him by.
Next with his spear he struck below the knee
Philetor's son, Demuchus, stout and tall,　　520

L 2

And checked his forward course; then rushing on
Dealt with his mighty sword the mortal blow.
The sons of Bias next, Laögonus
And Dardanus, he hurled from off their car,
One with the spear, and one by sword-stroke slain. 525
Tros too he slew, Alastor's son, who came
To meet him, and embrace his knees, and pray
To spare his life, in pity of his youth:
Little he knew how vain would be his prayer;
For not of temper soft, nor mild of mood   53ɔ
Was he, but sternly fierce; and as he knelt
And clasped his knees, and would his prayer prefer.
Achilles clove him with his mighty sword,
Gashed through the liver; as from out the wound
His liver dropped, the dark blood gushing forth   535
His bosom filled, and darkness closed his eyes,
As ebbed his life away. Then through the ear
Mulius he thrust; at the other ear came forth
The brazen point. Echeclus next he met,
Son of Agenor, and his hilted sword   540
Full on the centre of his head let fall.
The hot blood dyed the blade; the darkling shades
Of death, and rigorous fate, his eyes o'erspread.
Next, where the tendons bind the elbow-joint,
The brazen spear transfixed Deucalion's arm;   545
With death in prospect, and disabled arm
He stood, till on his neck Achilles' sword
Descending, shared, and flung afar, both head
And helmet; from the spine's dissevered joints
The marrow flowed, as stretched in dust he lay.   550
The noble son of Peireus next he slew,

Rigmus, who came from Thracia's fertile plains;
Him through the waist he struck, the brazen spear
Plunged in his bowels; from the car he fell;
And as Arcithöus, his charioteer,   555
His horses turned, Achilles through the neck
His sharp spear thrusting, hurled him to the ground,
The startled steeds in wild confusion thrown.
   As rage the fires amid the wooded glen
Of some parched mountain's side, and fiercely burns 560
The copse-wood dry, while eddying here and there
The flames are whirled before the gusty wind;
So fierce Achilles raged, on every side
Pursuing, slaughtering; reeked the earth with blood.
As when upon a well-rolled threshing floor,   565
Two sturdy-fronted steers, together yoked,
Tread the white barley out; beneath their feet
Fast flies the grain out-trodden from the husk;
So by Achilles driven, his flying steeds
His chariot bore, o'er bodies of the slain   570
And broken bucklers trampling; all beneath
Was plashed with blood the axle, and the rails
Around the car, as from the horses' feet
And from the felloes of the wheels were thrown
The bloody gouts; and onward still he pressed,   575
Panting for added triumphs, deeply dyed
With gore and carnage his unconquered hands.   577

BOOK XXI.

BUT when they came to eddying Xanthus' ford,
  Fair-flowing stream, born of immortal Jove,
  chilles cut in twain the flying host;
Part driving toward the city, o'er the plain,
Where on the former day the routed Greeks,   5
When Hector raged victorious, fled amain.
On, terror-struck, they rushed; but Juno spread,
To baffle their retreat, before their path,
Clouds and thick darkness; half the fugitives
In the deep river's silvery eddies plunged: 10
With clamour loud they fell; the torrent roared;
The banks around re-echoed; here and there,
They, with the eddies wildly struggling, swam.
As when, pursued by fire, a hovering swarm
Of locusts riverward direct their flight,   15
And, as the insatiate flames advance, they cower
Amid the waters; so a mingled mass
Of men and horses, by Achilles driven,
The deeply-whirling stream of Xanthus choked.
His spear amid the tamarisks on the bank   20
The hero left; on savage deeds intent,
Armed with his sword alone, a God in power,
He sprang amid the torrent; right and left
He smote; then fearful rose the groans of men
Slain with the sword; the stream ran red with blood. 25

As fishes, flying from a dolphin, crowd
The shoal recesses of some open bay,
In fear, for whom he catches he devours;
So crouched the Trojans in the mighty stream
Beneath the banks; and when at length his hand 30
Wearied of slaughter, from the stream, alive,
He dragged twelve youths, whose forfeit lives should be
The bloody fine for slain Patroclus paid.
Helpless from fear, as fawns, he brought them forth;
Their hands secured behind them with the belts 35
Which o'er their shirts of twisted mail they wore,
And bade his comrades lead them to the ships.
Then on again he dashed, athirst for blood;
And first encountered, flying from the stream,
Lycaon, Priam's son; him once before 40
He by a nightly onslaught had surprised,
And from his father's vineyard captive borne:
Where, as he cut, to form his chariot rail,
A fig-tree's tender shoots, unlooked-for ill
O'ertook him in the form of Peleus' son. 45
Thence in his ship to Lemnos' thriving isle
He bore him, ransomed there by Jason's son.
His Imbrian host, Eëtion, set him free
With liberal gifts, and to Arisba sent:
Escaping thence, he reached his native home. 50
Twelve days save one, rejoicing, with his friends
He spent, returned from Lemnos: fate, the twelfth,
Again consigned him to Achilles' hands,
From him, reluctant, to receive his death.
Him when Achilles, swift of foot, beheld, 55
Of helm and shield bereft, no spear in hand,

All flung in haste away, as from the stream,
Reeking with sweat, and faint with toil, he fled,
He communed, wrathful, with his mighty heart:
  "Ye Gods, what marvel do mine eyes behold!   60
Methinks the valiant Trojans slain by me
Ere long will from the realms of darkness rise;
Since, death escaping, but to slavery sold
In Lemnos' isle, this fellow hath returned,
Despite the hoary sea's impediment,   65
Which many a man against his will hath stayed:
Now shall he taste my spear, that I may see
If thence too he return, or if the earth
May keep him safe, which e'en the strongest holds."
  Thus, as he stood, he mused; but all aghast   70
Approached Lycaon; and would fain have clasped
The Hero's knees; for longingly he sought
Escape from bitter death and evil fate.
Achilles raised his spear, in act to strike;
He, stooping, ran beneath, and clasped his knees;   75
Above his back the murderous weapon passed,
And in the earth was fixed: one suppliant hand
Achilles' knees embraced; the other held,
With unrelaxing grasp, the pointed spear;
As he with wingèd words, imploring spoke: 80
  "I clasp thy knees, Achilles! look then down
With pity on my woes; and recognize,
Illustrious chief, a suppliant's sacred claim:
For in thy tent I first broke bread, that day,
When, in my father's fruitful vineyard seized,   85
Thy captive I became, to slavery sold,
Far from my sire and friends, in Lemnos' isle.

A hundred oxen were my ransom then;
At thrice so much I now would buy my life.
This day is but the twelfth, since, sorely tried   90
By lengthened suffering, back to Troy I came.
Now to thy hands once more my cruel fate
Consigns me; surely by the wrath of Jove
Pursued, who gives me to thy power again.
Me, doomed to early death, my mother bore,   95
Old Altes' daughter, fair Läothöe;
Altes, who ruled the warlike Leleges,
In lofty Pedasus, by Satnöis' stream.
His child of Priam's many wives was one;
Two sons she bore, and both by thee must die.   100
Already one, the godlike Polydore,
Amid the foremost ranks thy spear hath slain;
And now my doom hath found me; for from thee,
Since evil fate hath placed me in thy hands,
I may not hope to fly; yet hear but this,   105
And weigh it in thy mind, to spare my life:
I come not of that womb which Hector bore,
Who slew thy comrade, gentle, kind, and brave."
    Thus Priam's noble son, imploring, spoke;
But stern the answer fell upon his ear: 110
    "Thou fool! no more to me of ransom prate!
Before Patroclus met the doom of death,
To spare the Trojans still my soul inclined;
And many captives, ta'en alive, I sold;
But from henceforth, before the walls of Troy,   115
Not one of all the Trojans, whom the Gods
May to my hands deliver, least of all
A son of Priam, shall escape the death.

Thou too, my friend, must die: why vainly wail?
Dead is Patroclus too, thy better far.   120
Me too thou see'st, how stalwart, tall, and fair,
Of noble sire, and Goddess-mother born:
Yet must I yield to death and stubborn fate,
Whene'er, at morn, or noon, or eve, the spear
Or arrow from the bow may reach my life."   125
  He said; and sank Lycaon's limbs and heart;
He loosed the spear, and sat, with both his hands
Upraised, imploring; but Achilles drew,
And on his neck beside the collar-bone
Let fall his trenchant sword; the two-edged blade 130
Was buried deep; prone on the earth he lay;
Forth gushed the crimson blood, and dyed the ground.
Him, dragging by the feet, Achilles threw
In the mid stream, and thus with vaunting speech:
  "Lie there amid the fishes, who shall cleanse,   135
But not with kindly thought, thy gory wounds:
O'er thee, extended on thy bier, shall rise
No mother's wail; Scamander's eddying stream
Shall to the sea's broad bosom roll thee down;
And, springing through the darkly rippling wave,   140
Fishes shall rise, and banquet on thy flesh.
On now the work of death! till, flying ye,
And slaughtering I, we reach the city wall.
Nor this fair-flowing, silver-eddying stream,
Shall aught avail ye, though to him ye pay   145
In sacrifice the blood of countless bulls,
And living horses in his waters sink.
Ye all shall perish, till Patroclus' death
Be fully avenged, and slaughter of the Greeks,

Whom, in my absence, by the ships ye slew."   150
He said: the mighty River at his words
Indignant chafed, and pondered in his mind
How best to check Achilles' warlike toil,
And from destruction guard the Trojan host.
    Meantime Achilles with his ponderous spear   155
Asteropæus, son of Pelegon,
Assailed with deadly purpose; Pelegon
To broadly-flowing Axius owed his birth,
The River-God commingling with the blood
Of Peribœa, daughter eldest born   160
Of Acessamenus: on him he sprang;
He, from the river rising, stood opposed,
Two lances in his hand; his courage roused
By Xanthus, who, indignant, saw his stream
Polluted by the blood of slaughtered youths,   165
By fierce Achilles' hand, unpitying, slain.
When near the warriors, each to other, came,
Achilles, swift of foot, took up the word:
" What man, and whence art thou, who dar'st to stand
Opposed to me? of most unhappy sires   170
The children they, who my encounter meet!"
    To whom the illustrious son of Pelegon:
" Great son of Peleus, why enquire my race?
From far Pæonia's fertile fields I come,
The leader of the long-speared Pæon host.   175
Ten days have passed since I to Ilion came.
From widely-flowing Axius my descent,
Axius, the purest stream on earth that flows.
He Pelegon begot, the spear-renowned;
Of Pelegon I boast me sprung; and now   180

Address thee, brave Achilles, to the fight."
    Threatening he spoke: Achilles raised on high
The Pelian spear; but, ambidexter, he
From either hand at once a javelin launched.
One struck, but pierced not through, the mighty shield, 185
Stayed by the golden plate, the gift of Heaven:
Achilles' right fore-arm the other grazed:
Forth gushed the crimson blood; but, glancing by,
And vainly longing for the taste of flesh,
The point behind him in the earth was fixed.   190
Then at Asteropæus in his turn
With deadly intent the son of Peleus threw
His straight-directed spear; his mark he missed,
But struck the lofty bank, where, deep infixed
To half its length, the Pelian ash remained.   195
Then from beside his thigh Achilles drew
His trenchant blade, and, furious, onward rushed;
While from the cliff Asteropæus strove
In vain, with stalwart hand, to wrench the spear.
Three times he shook it with impetuous force,   200
Three times relaxed his grasp; a fourth attempt
He made to bend and break the sturdy shaft;
But him, preventing, Peleus' godlike son
With deadly stroke across the belly smote,
And gushed his bowels forth; upon the ground   205
Gasping he lay, and darkness sealed his eyes.
Then on his breast Achilles sprang, and stripped
His armour off, and thus with vaunting speech:
"So lie thou there! 'tis hard for thee to fight,
Though river-born, against the progeny   210
Of mighty Jove; a widely-flowing stream

Thou claim'st as author of thy parentage;
My high descent from Jove himself I boast.
My father Peleus, son of Æacus,
Reigns o'er the numerous race of Myrmidons;   215
The son of Jove himself was Æacus.
High o'er all rivers, that to the ocean flow,
Is Jove exalted; and in like degree
Superior is his race in power to theirs.
A mighty River hast thou here at hand,   220
If that might aught avail thee; but his power
Is impotent to strive with Saturn's son.
With him, not Achelöus, King of streams,
Presumes to vie; nor e'en the mighty strength
Of deeply-flowing, wide Oceanus;   225
From whom all rivers, all the boundless sea,
All fountains, all deep wells derive their source;
Yet him appals the lightning bolt of Jove,
And thunder, pealing from the vault of Heaven."
He said, and from the cliff withdrew his spear.   230
Him left he lifeless there upon the sand
Extended; o'er him the dark waters washed,
And eels and fishes, thronging, gnawed his flesh.
Then 'mid the Pæons' plumèd host he rushed,
Who fled along the eddying stream, when him,   235
Their bravest in the stubborn fight, they saw
Slain by the sword and arm of Peleus' son.
Thersilochus and Mydon then he slew,
Mnesus and Thrasius and Astypylus,
Ænius and Ophelestes; and yet more   240
Had been the slaughter by Achilles wrought,
But from his eddying depths, in human form,

With wrathful tone the mighty River spoke:
"In strength, Achilles, and in deeds of arms,
All mortals thou surpassest; for the Gods   245
Themselves attend thee, and protect from harm;
If Saturn's son have given thee utterly
The Trojans to destroy, yet, ere thou slay,
Far from my waters drive them o'er the plain;
For now my lovely stream is filled with dead;   250
Nor can I pour my current to the sea,
With floating corpses choked, whilst thou pursuest
The work of death, insatiate: stay thy hand!
With horror I behold thee, mighty chief!"
Whom answered thus Achilles, swift of foot: 255
"Be it as thou wilt, Scamander, Heaven-born stream;
Yet cease I not to slay until I drive
These vaunting Trojans to their walls, and prove
The force of Hector, if, in single fight,
I be by him, or he by me, subdued."   260
He said, and fiercely on the Trojans rushed,
A God in might! to Phœbus then his speech
The deeply-eddying River thus addressed:
"God of the silver bow, great son of Jove,
Obey'st thou thus the will of Saturn's son,   265
Who charged thee by the Trojans still to stand,
And aid their cause, till evening's late approach
Should cast its shadows o'er the fertile earth?"
Thus as he spoke, from off the lofty bank
Achilles springing in mid current plunged;   270
Then high the swelling stream, tumultuous, rose
In all its angry flood; and with a roar
As of a bellowing bull, cast forth to land

The numerous corpses by Achilles slain;
And many living, in his caverned bed   275
Concealed, behind the whirling waters saved.
Fierce, round Achilles, rose the boiling wave,
And on his shield descending, drove him down;
Nor might he keep his foothold; but he grasped
A lofty elm, well-grown, which from the cliff   280
Uprooted, all the bank had torn away,
And with its tangled branches checked the flow
Of the fair river, which with all its length
It bridged across; then, springing from the deep,
Swiftly he fled in terror o'er the plain.   285
Nor ceased the mighty River, but pursued,
With darkly-ruffling crest, intent to stay
Achilles' course, and save the Trojan host.
Far as a javelin's flight he rushed, in speed
Like the dark hunter eagle, strongest deemed,   290
And swiftest winged of all the feathered race.
So on he sped; loud rattled on his breast
His brazen armour, as before the God,
Cowering, he fled; the God behind him still
With thundering sound pursued. As when a man 295
From some dark-watered spring through trenches leads,
'Mid plants and gardens, the irrigating stream,
And, spade in hand, the appointed channel clears:
Down flows the stream anon, its pebbly bed
Disturbing; fast it flows with bubbling sound,   300
Down the steep slope, o'ertaking him who leads.
Achilles so the advancing wave o'ertook,
Though great his speed; but man must yield to Gods.
Oft as Achilles, swift of foot, essayed

To turn and stand, and know if all the Gods,   305
Who dwell in Heaven, were leagued to daunt his soul;
So oft the Heaven-born River's mighty wave
Above his shoulders dashed; in deep distress
He sprang on high; then rushed the flood below,
And bore him off his legs, and wore away   310
The soil beneath his feet; then, groaning, thus,
As up to Heaven he looked, Achilles cried:
"O Father Jove, will none of all the Gods
In pity save me from this angry flood?
Content, thereafter, would I meet my fate.   315
Of all the powers of Heaven, my mother most
Hath wronged me, who hath buoyed me up with hope
Delusive, that, before the walls of Troy,
I should by Phœbus' swift-winged arrows fall.
Would that by Hector's hand 'twere mine to die,   320
The bravest of their brave! a warrior so
Were by a warrior slain! now am I doomed
Ignobly here to sink, the mighty flood
O'erwhelming me, like some poor shepherd lad,
Borne down in crossing by a wintry brook."   325
     He said; and quickly, clothed in mortal form,
Neptune and Pallas at his side appeared;
With cheering words they took him by the hand,
And thus the Earth-shaking God his speech began:
     "Achilles, fear not thou, nor be dismayed;   330
Such powerful aid, by Jove's consent, we bring,
Pallas and I, from Heaven; 'tis not decreed
That thou shouldst by the River be o'erwhelmed;
He shall retire ere long, and thou shalt see;
And more, if thou wilt hear, we undertake   335

That from the war thine arm shall not be stayed,
Till thou shalt drive beneath the walls of Troy
The crowd of flying Trojans; thou thyself
Shalt Hector slay, and safe regain the ships:
Such high renown we give thee to achieve."   340
    They to the other Gods, this said, returned;
He, greatly strengthened by the voice divine,
Pressed onwards to the plain; the plain he found
All flooded o'er; and, floating, armour fair,
And many a corpse of men in battle slain;   345
Yet onward, lifting high his feet, he pressed
Right toward the stream; nor could the mighty stream
Check his advance, such vigour Pallas gave;
Nor did Scamander yet his fury stay,
But fiercer rose his rage; and rearing high   350
His crested wave, to Simöis thus he cried:
    "Dear brother, aid me with united force
This mortal's course to check; he, unrestrained,
Will royal Priam's city soon destroy,
Nor will the Trojans his assault endure.   355
Haste to the rescue then, and from their source
Fill all thy stream, and all thy channels swell;
Rouse thy big waves, and roll a torrent down
Of logs and stones, to whelm this man of might,
Who triumphs now, and bears him as a God.   360
Nought shall his strength or beauty then avail,
Or gallant arms, beneath the waters sunk,
Deep buried in the mud: himself will I
In sand imbed, and o'er his corpse a pile
Of shingly gravel heap; nor shall the Greeks   365
Be able to collect his bones, encased

By me so deep in slime. His monument
They here may raise; but when they celebrate
His funeral rites, no mound will he require."
　　He said; and on Achilles, from on high   370
Came boiling, rushing down, with thundering roar,
With foam and blood and corpses intermixed.
High rose the Heaven-born River's darkling wave,
And bore Achilles downward; then in fear
Lest the broad waters of the eddying stream   375
Should quite o'erwhelm him, Juno cried aloud,
And Vulcan thus, her son, in haste addressed:
　　"Up, Vulcan; up, my son; for we had deemed
That eddying Xanthus stood to thee opposed:
Haste thee to aid; thy fiery strength display;   380
While from the sea I call the stormy blast
Of Zephyr and brisk Notus, who shall drive
The raging flames ahead, and burn alike
The Trojans and their arms: do thou the while
Burn down the trees on Xanthus' banks; himself   385
Assail with fire, nor by his honeyed words
Nor by his menaces be turned aside;
Nor, till thou hear my voice, restrain thy power;
Then stay the raging flames' unwearied course."
　　Thus Juno spoke; and Vulcan straight prepared 390
The heavenly fire; and first upon the plain
The flames he kindled, and the dead consumed,
Who lay, promiscuous, by Achilles slain:
The plain was dried, and stayed the watery flood.
As when the breath of Boreas quickly dries   395
In Autumn-time a newly-watered field,
The tiller's heart rejoicing: so was dried

The spacious plain; then he, the dead consumed,
Against the river turned the fiery glare:
Burnt were the willows, elms, and tamarisk shrubs.   400
The lotus, and the reeds, and galingal,
Which by the lovely river grew profuse.
The eels and fishes, 'mid the eddying whirl,
'Mid the clear wave were hurrying here and there,
In dire distress from Vulcan's fiery breath: 405
Scorched by the flames, the mighty River spoke:
  " Vulcan, no God against thy power can stand,
Nor with thy fiery flames will I contend;
Restrain thy wrath; though Peleus' godlike son
Should from their city drive the Trojans straight,   410
With rival parties what concern have I?"
  All scorched he spoke; his fair stream bubbling up,
As when a caldron, on a blazing fire,
Filled with the melting fat of well-fed swine,
Boils up within, and bubbles all around,   415
With well-dried wood beneath, so bubbling up
The waters of the lovely River boiled:
Nor onward would he flow, but checked his course,
By the hot blast o'er-borne, and fiery strength
Of skilful Vulcan; and to Juno thus,   420
Imploring, he his wingèd words addressed:
  " Juno, what cause impels thy son, my stream,
O'er all the rest, to visit with his wrath?
E'en less than others who the Trojans aid,
Have I offended; yet at thy command   425
Will I withdraw; but bid that he too cease;
And this I swear, no Trojan more to save,
Though to devouring flames a prey, all Troy

Were blazing, kindled by the valiant Greeks."
This when the white-armed Goddess Juno heard, 430
To Vulcan straight she thus addressed her speech :
"Vulcan, my glorious son, restrain thy hand :
In mortal men's behalf, it is not meet
To press thus hardly an Immortal God."
She said, and Vulcan stayed his fiery strength,　435
And, back returning, in his wonted bed
Flowed the fair River. Xanthus thus subdued,
These two their warfare ceased, by Juno checked,
Despite her wrath ; but 'mid the other Gods
Arose contention fierce, and discord dire,　　　440
Their warring passions roused on either side.
With fearful crash they met: the broad Earth groaned ;
Loud rang the Heaven as with a trumpet's sound :
Jove, on Olympus' height, the tumult heard,
And in his heart he laughed a joyous laugh,　　445
To see the Gods in angry battle met.
Not long they stood aloof, led on by Mars
The buckler-breaker, who to Pallas first,
Poising his spear, his bitter speech addressed :
"What dost thou here, thou saucy jade, to war　450
The Gods exciting, over-bold of mood,
Led by thy haughty spirit ? dost thou forget
How thou the son of Tydeus, Diomed,
Didst urge against me, and with visible spear
Direct his aim, and aid to wound my flesh ?　　455
For all I suffered then, thou now shalt pay."
Thus as he spoke, he struck the tasselled shield,
Awful to view, which not the lightning bolt
Of Jove himself could pierce : the blood-stained Mars

Against it thrust in vain his ponderous spear.   460
The Goddess stooped, and in her ample hand
Took up a stone that lay upon the plain,
Dark, rugged, vast, which men of elder days
Had set to mark the limits of their land.
Full on the neck of Mars she hurled the mass,   465
His limbs relaxing: o'er seven hundred feet
Prostrate he lay, his hair defiled with dust:
Loud rang his armour; and with scornful smile
Pallas addressed him thus with vaunting speech:
     "Fool, hast thou yet to learn how mightier far   470
My strength than thine, that me thou dar'st to meet?
Bear thus the burthen of thy mother's curse,
Who works thee harm, in wrath that thou the Greeks
Deserting, aid'st the haughty Trojans' cause."
     She said, and turned away her piercing glance: 475
Him, deeply groaning, scarce to life restored,
Jove's daughter Venus taking by the hand,
Led from the field; which when the white-armed Queen
Beheld, in haste to Pallas thus she cried:
"O Heaven, brave child of ægis-bearing Jove,   480
Undaunted! lo again this saucy jade
Amid the press, the bane of mortals, Mars
Leads from the field; but haste thee in pursuit."
     Thus Juno: Pallas hastened in pursuit
Well pleased; and Venus with her powerful hand   485
Assailing, struck upon the breast; at once
The Goddess' courage and her limbs gave way.
There on the ground the two together lay,
While Pallas o'er them thus with vaunting speech:
     "Would all were such, who aid the Trojan cause,   490

Whene'er they meet in fight the warlike Greeks,
As valiant and as stout as Venus proves,
Who brings her aid to Mars, confronting me;
Then had our warlike labours long been o'er,
And Ilion's strong-built citadel o'erthrown."   495
      Thus Pallas spoke: the white-armed Goddess smiled,
And to Apollo thus the Earth-shaker spoke:
"Phœbus, why stand we idly thus aloof?
The war begun by others, 'tis not meet;
And shame it were that to Olympus' height   500
And to the brazen-floored abode of Jove
We two without a contest should return.
Thou then begin, as younger: 'twere not well
For me, in age and practice more advanced.
Feeble of soul, how senseless is thy heart!   505
Hast thou forgotten all the cruel wrongs
We two, alone of all the Immortals, bore,
When here, in Ilion, for a year, we served,
By Jove's command, the proud Laomedon,
For promised hire; and he our tasks assigned?   510
His fortress, and a wall both broad and fair
I built, the town's impregnable defence;
While thou didst on his plodding herds attend,
In many-crested Ida's woody glens.
But when the joyous seasons in their course,   515
Had brought our labour's term, the haughty King
Denied our guerdon, and with threats dismissed.
Bound hand and foot he threatened thee to send
And sell to slavery in the distant isles,
And with the sword cut off the ears of both.   520
So in indignant sorrow we returned,

Robbed of the hire he promised, but denied.
For this thy favour dost thou show to Troy;
And dost not rather join thy force to ours,
That down upon their knees the Trojans all   525
Should perish, with their babes and matrons chaste."

Whom answered thus the far-destroying King:
"Earth-shaking God, I should not gain with thee
The esteem of wise, if I with thee should fight
For mortal men; poor wretches, who like leaves   530
Flourish awhile, and eat the fruits of earth,
But, sapless, soon decay: from combat then
Refrain we, and to others leave the strife."

He turned, thus saying: for he deemed it shame
His father's brother to assail in arms;   535
But him his sister, Goddess of the chase,
Rebuked, and thus with scornful speech addressed:

"Fliest thou, Apollo? and to Neptune leav'st
The easy victory and baseless fame?
Why o'er thy shoulder hangs thine idle bow?   540
Ne'er in our father's halls again, as erst
Among the Immortals, let me hear thee boast
How thou with Neptune wouldst in arms contend."

Thus she; Apollo answered not a word;
But Jove's imperial consort, filled with wrath,   545
Assailed with bitter words the Archer-Queen.

"How canst thou dare, thou saucy minx,* to stand

---

* L. 547. The terms made use of in this line, and in 481, may appear somewhat coarse, as addressed by one Goddess to another: but I assure the English
reader that in this passage especially I have greatly softened down the expression
of the original; a literal translation of which, however forcible, would shock
even the least fastidious critic. It must, indeed, be admitted that the mode in

Opposed to me, too great for thine assault,
Despite thy bow? though Jove hath given thee power
O'er feeble women, whom thou wilt, to slay,   550
E'en as a lion; better were't for thee
To chase the mountain beasts and flying hinds,
Than thy superiors thus to meet in arms.
But since thou dar'st confront me, thou shalt know
And feel how far my might surpasses thine."   555
　　She said; and with the left hand both the wrists
Of Dian grasping, with her ample right
The bow and quiver from her shoulders tore;
And with them, as she turned away her head,
With scornful laughter buffeted her ears: 560
The arrows keen were scattered on the ground:
Weeping, the Goddess fled; as flies a dove
The hawk's pursuit, and in a hollow rock
Finds refuge, doomed not yet to fall a prey;
So, weeping, Dian fled, and left her bow.   565
　　Then Hermes to Latona thus: "With thee
I strive not; shame it were to meet in fight
A consort of the cloud-compelling Jove.
Freely amid the Immortals make thy boast,
That by thy prowess thou hast vanquished me."   570
　　Thus he: Latona gathered up the bow,
And fallen arrows, scattered here and there
Amid the whirling dust; then, these regained,
Following her daughter, from the field withdrew.
Meanwhile to high Olympus fled the Maid,   575

And to the brazen-floored abode of Jove.
There, weeping, on her father's knees she sat,
While quivered round her form the ambrosial robe.
The son of Saturn towards him drew his child,
And thus, with gracious smile, enquiry made: 580
" Which of the heavenly powers hath wronged thee thus,
My child, as guilty of some open shame?"
  To whom the bright-crowned Goddess of the chase:
"Thy wife, my father, white-armed Juno; she
Hath dealt thus rudely with me; she, from whom 585
All jars and strife among the Gods proceed."
  Such converse while they held, the gates of Troy
Apollo entered, for the well-built wall
Alarmed, lest e'en against the will of fate
The Greeks that day should raze it to the ground. 590
The other Gods were to Olympus gone,
Triumphant these, and those in angry mood,
And took their seats before the cloud-girt Sire.
But on the Trojans pressing, Peleus' son
Horses and men alike, promiscuous, slew.   595
As in a city, which the Gods in wrath
Have fired, whose volleying smoke ascends to Heaven,
On all her people grievous toil is cast,
On many, harm and loss; such toil, such loss
Achilles wrought amid the Trojan host.   600
  Upon a lofty tower, the work of Gods,
The aged Priam stood, and looking down,
He marked Achilles' giant might, and saw
Before him driven in panic flight confused,
Their courage quite subdued, the Trojan host: 605
Then, groaning, from the tower he hastened down,

And to the warders cried along the wall:
"Stand to the gates, and hold them opened wide,
That in the crowd of fugitives may pour,
And refuge find: for close upon their flight   610
Achilles hangs; disaster now is near.
But while our friends, received within the walls,
Find time to breathe again, replace in haste
The closely-fitting portals, for I fear
That man of blood may e'en the city storm."   615
    He said; the gates they opened, and drew back
The solid bars; the portals, opening wide,
Let in the light; but in the vacant space
Apollo stood, the Trojan host to save.
The flyers, parched with thirst and dust-begrimed,   620
Straight for the city and the lofty wall
Made from the plain; Achilles, spear in hand,
Pressed hotly on the rearmost; for his soul
Was filled with rage, and maddening lust of fame.
And now the lofty-gated city of Troy   625
The sons of Greece had won; but Phœbus roused
Agenor's spirit, a valiant youth and strong,
Son of Antenor; he his bosom filled
With dauntless courage, and beside him stood
To turn aside the heavy hand of death,   630
As, veiled in cloud, against the oak he leaned.
He, when Achilles' awful form he knew,
Yet firmly stood, though much perplexed in mind
As thus he communed with his mighty heart:
    "Oh woe is me! should I attempt to fly   635
Before Achilles' might, where fly the rest
Across the plain, disordered, he would soon

O'ertake me, and in flight ignoble slay.
Or should I leave the others to their fate,
Scattered by Peleus' son, and from the wall   640
And o'er the plain of Troy direct my flight,
Far as the foot of Ida's hill, and there
Lie hid in thickest covert; and at eve,
Refreshed by bathing in the cooling stream,
And purged the sweat, retrace my steps to Troy? 645
Yet why, my soul, admit such thoughts as these?
For should he mark me flying from the town,
And overtake me by his speed of foot,
No hope were left me of escape from death,
So far his strength exceeds the strength of man.   650
But how if boldly I await him here
Before the wall? his flesh is not to wounds
Impervious: but a single life is his,
Nor is he more, they say, than mortal man,
Though Jove assists him, and his triumph wills."   655
   He said, and stood collected, to await
Achilles' onset; and his manly heart,
With courage filled, was eager for the fray.
As when a panther from the thicket's depth
Comes forth to meet the hunter, undismayed,   660
Nor turned to flight by baying of the hounds;
Nor, wounded or by javelin or by sword,
Or by the spear transfixed, remits her rage,
But fights, until she reach her foe, or die;
Agenor so, Antenor's godlike son,   665
Disdained to fly, ere proved Achilles' might.
Before his breast his shield's broad orb he bore,
And poised his spear, as thus he called aloud:

"Thy hope, renowned Achilles, was this day
The valiant Trojans' city to destroy;　　　670
Unconscious of the toils, the woes, that yet
Around her walls await ye! for within
Are warriors brave and numerous, who will fight
In her defence, for parents, children, wives.
Thou too, Achilles, here shalt meet thy doom,　　675
All-powerful as thou art, and warrior bold."
He said, and threw with stalwart hand the spear;
Achilles' leg he struck, below the knee,
Nor missed his aim, and loudly rang the greaves
Of new-wrought tin; but back the brazen point　　680
Rebounded, nor the heavenly armour pierced.
In turn Achilles on Agenor sprang:
But Phœbus robbed him of his hoped-for prize,
Who, veiled in thickest cloud, conveyed away
Antenor's son, and from the battle bore　　685
To rest in peace, while he by guile withdrew
The son of Peleus from the flying crowd:
For in Agenor's very likeness clad,
Before him stood the far-destroying King:
Then fled, Achilles hastening in pursuit.　　690
He o'er the fertile plain with flying foot
Pursued; beside Scamander's eddying stream
Apollo turned, and still but little space
Before him flying, subtly lured him on,
Each moment hoping to attain his prize.　　695
Meantime the general crowd, in panic flight,
With eager haste the city's refuge sought,
And all the town with fugitives was filled.

Nor did they dare without the walls to stand
For mutual aid; nor halt to know what friends 700
Were safe, who left upon the battle-field;
But through the gates poured in the hurrying mass
Who to their active limbs their safety owed. 703

BOOK XXII.

THUS they from panic flight, like timorous fawns,
   Within the walls escaping, dried their sweat,
And drank, and quenched their thirst, reclining safe
On the fair battlements; but nearer drew,
With slanted shields, the Greeks; yet Hector still   5
In front of Ilion and the Scæan gate,
Stayed by his evil doom, remained without.
Then Phœbus thus to Peleus' godlike son:
" Achilles, why with active feet pursue,
Thou mortal, me Immortal? know'st thou not   10
My Godhead, that so hot thy fury burns?
Or heed'st thou not that all the Trojan host
Whom thou hast scared, while thou art here withdrawn,
Within the walls a refuge safe have found?
On me thy sword is vain! I know not death!"   15
   Enraged, Achilles, swift of foot, replied:
"Deep is the injury, far-darting King,
Most hostile of the Gods, that at thy hand
I bear, who here hast lured me from the walls,
Which many a Trojan else had failed to reach,   20
Ere by my hand they bit the bloody dust.
Me of immortal honour thou hast robbed,
And them, thyself from vengeance safe, hast saved:
Had I the power, that vengeance thou shouldst feel."
   Thus saying, and on mightiest deeds intent,   25

He turned him city-ward, with fiery speed;
As when a horse contending for the prize,
Whirls the swift car, and stretches o'er the plain,
E'en so, with active limbs, Achilles raced.

Him first the aged Priam's eyes discerned,   30
Scouring the plain, in arms all dazzling bright,
Like to the autumnal star, whose brilliant ray
Shines eminent amid the depth of night,
Whom men the dog-star of Orion call;
The brightest he, but sign to mortal man   35
Of evil augury, and fiery heat:
So shone the brass upon the warrior's breast.

The old man groaned aloud, and lifting high
His hands, he beat his head, and with loud voice
Called on his son, imploring; he, unmoved,   40
Held post before the gates, awaiting there
Achilles' fierce encounter; him his sire,
With hands outstretched and piteous tone addressed:

"Hector, my son, await not here alone
That warrior's charge, lest thou to fate succumb,   45
Beneath Pelides' arm, thy better far!
Accursed be he! would that the immortal Gods
So favoured him as I! then should his corpse
Soon to the vultures and the dogs be given!
(So should my heart a load of anguish lose)   50
By whom I am of many sons bereaved,
Many and brave, whom he has slain, or sold
To distant isles in slavery; and e'en now,
Within the city walls I look in vain
For two, Lycaon brave, and Polydore,   55
My gallant sons, by fair Laothöe;

If haply yet they live, with brass and gold
Their ransom shall be paid; good store of these
We can command; for with his daughter fair
A wealthy dowry aged Altes gave.   60
But to the viewless shades should they have gone,
Deep were their mother's sorrow and my own;
But of the general public, well I know
Far lighter were the grief, than if they heard
That thou hadst fallen beneath Achilles' hand.   65
Then enter now, my son, the city gates,
And of the women and the men of Troy
Be still the guardian; nor to Peleus' son,
With thine own life, immortal glory give.
Look too on me with pity; me, on whom,   70
E'en on the threshold of mine age, hath Jove
A bitter burthen cast, condemned to see
My sons struck down, my daughters dragged away
In servile bonds; our chambers' sanctity
Invaded; and our babes by hostile hands   75
Dashed to the ground, and by ferocious Greeks
Enslaved the widows of my slaughtered sons.
On me at last the ravening dogs shall feed,
When by some foeman's hand, by sword or lance,
My soul shall from my body be divorced;   80
Those very dogs which I myself have bred,
Fed at my table, guardians of my gate,
Shall lap my blood, and over-gorged shall lie
E'en on my threshold. That a youth should fall
Victim to Mars, beneath a foeman's spear,   85
May well beseem his years, and if he fall
With honour, though he die, yet glorious he!

But when the hoary head and hoary beard,
And naked corpse to ravening dogs are given,
No sadder sight can wretched mortals see." 90
  The old man spoke, and from his head he tore
The hoary hair; yet Hector firm remained.
Then to the front his mother rushed, in tears,
Her bosom bare, with either hand her breast
Sustaining, and with tears addressed him thus: 95
"Hector, my child, thy mother's breast revere;
And on this bosom if thine infant woes
Have e'er been hushed, bear now in mind, dear child,
The debt thou ow'st; and from within the walls
Ward off this fearful man, nor in the field 100
Encounter; cursed be he! should he prevail,
And slay thee, not upon the funeral bed,
My child, my own, the offspring of my womb,
Shall I deplore thee, nor thy widowed wife,
But far away, beside the Grecian ships, 105
Thy corpse shall to the ravening dogs be given."
  Thus they, with tears and earnest prayers imploring,
Addressed their son; yet Hector firm remained,
Waiting the approach of Peleus' godlike son.
As when a snake upon the mountain side, 110
With deadly venom charged, beside his hole
Awaits the traveller, and filled with rage,
Coiled round his hole, his baleful glances darts;
So filled with dauntless courage Hector stood,
Scorning retreat, his gleaming buckler propped 115
Against the jutting tower; then, deeply moved,
Thus with his warlike soul communion held:
  "Oh woe is me! if I should enter now

The city gates, I should the just reproach
Encounter of Polydamas, who first   120
His counsel gave within the walls to lead
The Trojan forces, on that fatal night
When great Achilles in the field appeared.
I heeded not his counsel; would I had!
Now, since my folly hath the people slain,   125
I well might blush to meet the Trojan men,
And long-robed dames of Troy, lest some might say,
To me inferior far, 'This woful loss
To Hector's blind self-confidence we owe.'
Thus shall they say; for me, 'twere better far,   130
Or from Achilles, slain in open fight,
Back to return in triumph, or myself
To perish nobly in my country's cause.
What if my bossy shield I lay aside,
And stubborn helmet, and my ponderous spear   135
Propping against the wall, go forth to meet
The unmatched Achilles? What if I engage
That Helen's self, and with her all the spoil,
And all that Paris in his hollow ships
Brought here to Troy, whence first this war arose, 140
Should be restored, and to the Greeks be paid
An ample tribute from the city's stores,
Her secret treasures; and hereafter bind
The Trojans by their Elders' solemn oaths
Nought to withhold, but fairly to divide   145
Whate'er of wealth our much-loved city holds?
But wherefore entertain such thoughts, my soul?
Should I so meet him, what if he should show
Nor pity nor remorse, but slay me there,

Defenceless as a woman, and unarmed?   150
Not this the time, nor he the man, with whom
By forest oak or rock, like youth and maid,
To hold light talk, as youth and maid might hold.
Better to dare the fight, and know at once
To whom Olympian Jove the triumph wills."   155
    Thus, as he stood, he mused; but near approached
Achilles, terrible as plumèd Mars;
From his right shoulder brandishing aloft
The ashen spear of Peleus, while around
Flashed his bright armour, dazzling as the glare   160
Of burning fire, or of the rising sun.
Hector beheld, and trembled at the sight;
Nor dared he there await the attack, but left
The gates behind, and, terror-stricken, fled.
Forward, with flying foot, Pelides rushed.   165
As when a falcon, bird of swiftest flight,   •
From some high mountain-top, on timorous dove
Swoops fiercely down; she, from beneath, in fear,
Evades the stroke; he, dashing through the brake,
Shrill-shrieking, pounces on his destined prey;   170
So, winged with desperate hate, Achilles flew,
So Hector, flying from his keen pursuit,
Beneath the walls his active sinews plied.
They by the watch-tower, and beneath the wall
Where stood the wind-beat fig-tree, raced amain   175
Along the public road, until they reached
The fairly-flowing fount whence issued forth,
From double source, Scamander's eddying streams.
One with hot current flows, and from beneath,
As from a furnace, clouds of steam arise;   180

N 2

'Mid summer's heat the other rises cold
As hail, or snow, or water crystallized;
Beside the fountains stood the washing-troughs
Of well-wrought stone, where erst the wives of Troy
And daughters fair their choicest garments washed, 185
In peaceful times, ere came the sons of Greece.
There raced they, one in flight, and one pursuing;
Good he who fled, but better who pursued,
With fiery speed; for on that race was staked
No common victim, no ignoble ox :   190
The prize at stake was mighty Hector's life.
As when the solid-footed horses fly
Around the course, contending for the prize,
Tripod, or woman of her lord bereft;
So raced they thrice around the walls of Troy   195
With active feet; and all the Gods beheld.
Then thus began the Sire of Gods and men :
" A woful sight mine eyes behold; a man
I love in flight around the walls! my heart
For Hector grieves, who, now upon the crown   200
Of deeply-furrowed Ida, now again
On Ilion's heights, with fat of choicest bulls
Hath piled mine altar; whom around the walls,
With flying speed, Achilles now pursues.
Give me your counsel, Gods, and say, from death   205
If we shall rescue him, or must he die,
Brave as he is, beneath Pelides' hand ? "
   To whom the blue-eyed Goddess, Pallas, thus :
" O Father, lightning-flashing, cloud-girt King,
What words are these ? wouldst thou a mortal man, 210
Long doomed by fate, again from death preserve ?

Do as thou wilt, but not with our consent."
  To whom the Cloud-compeller thus replied:
"Be of good cheer, my child! unwillingly
I speak, yet loth thy wishes to oppose: 215
Have then thy will, and draw not back thy hand."
  His words fresh impulse gave to Pallas' zeal,
And from Olympus' heights in haste she sped.
  Meanwhile on Hector, with untiring hate,
The swift Achilles pressed: as when a hound,   220
Through glen and tangled brake, pursues a fawn,
Roused from its lair upon the mountain side;
And if awhile it should evade pursuit,
Low crouching in the copse, yet quests he back,
Searching unwearied, till he find the trace;   225
So Hector sought to baffle, but in vain,
The keen pursuit of Peleus' active son.
Oft as he sought the shelter of the gates
Beneath the well-built towers, if haply thence
His comrades' weapons might some aid afford;   230
So oft his foeman, with superior speed,
Would cut him off, and turn him to the plain.
He toward the city still essayed his flight;
And as in dreams, when one pursues in vain,
One seeks in vain to fly, the other seeks   235
As vainly to pursue; so could not now
Achilles reach, nor Hector quit, his foe.
Yet how should Hector now the doom of death
Have 'scaped, had not Apollo once again,
And for the last time, to his rescue come,   240
And given him strength and suppleness of limb?
  Then to the crowd Achilles with his head

Made sign that none at Hector should presume
To cast a spear, lest one might wound, and so
The greater glory obtain, while he himself   245
Must be contented with the second place.
But when the fourth time in their rapid course
The founts were reached, the Eternal father hung
His golden scales aloft, and placed in each
The lots of doom, for great Achilles one,   250
For Hector one, and held them by the midst:
Down sank the scale, weighted with Hector's death,
Down to the shades, and Phœbus left his side.
      Then to Pelides came the blue-eyed Maid,
And stood beside him, and bespoke him thus: 255
"Achilles, loved of Heaven, I trust that now
To thee and me great glory shall accrue
In Hector's fall, insatiate of the fight.
Escape he cannot now, though at the feet
Of ægis-bearing Jove, on his behalf,   260
With earnest prayer Apollo prostrate fall.
But stay thou here and take thy breath, while I
Persuade him to return and dare the fight."
      So Pallas spoke; and he with joy obeying,
Stood leaning on his brass-barbed ashen spear.   265
The Goddess left him there, and went (the form
And voice assuming of Deiphobus)
In search of godlike Hector; him she found,
And standing near, with wingèd words addressed:
"Sorely, good brother, hast thou been bested   270
By fierce Achilles, who around the walls
Hath chased thee with swift foot; now stand we both
For mutual succour and his onset wait."

To whom great Hector of the glancing helm:
" Deiphobus, of all my brothers, sons   275
Of Hecuba and Priam, thou hast been
Still dearest to my heart; and now the more
I honour thee who dar'st on my behalf,
Seeing my peril, from within the walls
To sally forth, while others skulk behind."   280
To whom the blue-eyed Goddess thus replied:
" With many prayers, good brother, both our sire
And honoured mother, and our comrades all
Successively implored me to remain;
Such fear is fallen on all; but in my soul   285
On thine account too deep a grief I felt.
Now, forward boldly! spare we not our spears;
Make trial if Achilles to the ships
From both of us our bloody spoils can bear,
Or by thine arm himself may be subdued."   290
    Thus Pallas lured him on with treacherous wile;
But when the two were met, and close at hand,
First spoke great Hector of the glancing helm:
" No more before thee, Peleus' son, I fly:
Thrice have I fled around the walls, nor dared   295
Await thine onset; now my spirit is roused
To stand before thee, to be slain, or slay.
But let us first the immortal Gods invoke;
The surest witnesses and guardians they
Of compacts: at my hand no foul disgrace   300
Shalt thou sustain, if Jove with victory
Shall crown my firm endurance, and thy life
To me be forfeit; of thine armour stripped
I promise thee, Achilles, to the Greeks

Thy body to restore; do thou the like."   305
  With fierce regard Achilles answered thus:
" Hector, thou object of my deadly hate,
Talk not to me of compacts; as 'tween men
And lions no firm concord can exist,
Nor wolves and lambs in harmony unite,   310
But ceaseless enmity between them dwells:
So not in friendly terms, nor compact firm,
Can thou and I unite, till one of us
Glut with his blood the mail-clad warrior Mars.
Mind thee of all thy fence; behoves thee now   315
To prove a spearman skilled, and warrior brave.
For thee escape is none; now, by my spear,
Hath Pallas doomed thy death; my comrades' blood,
Which thou hast shed, shall all be now avenged."
  He said, and poising, hurled his weighty spear;   320
But Hector saw, and shunned the blow; he stooped,
And o'er his shoulder flew the brass-tipped spear,
And in the ground was fixed; but Pallas drew
The weapon forth, and to Achilles' hand,
All unobserved of Hector, gave it back.   325
Then Hector thus to Peleus' matchless son:
  " Thine aim has failed; nor truly has my fate,
Thou godlike son of Peleus, been to thee
From Heaven revealed; such was indeed thy boast;
But flippant was thy speech, and subtly framed   330
To scare me with big words, and make me prove
False to my wonted prowess and renown.
Not in my back will I receive thy spear,
But through my breast, confronting thee, if Jove
Have to thine arm indeed such triumph given.   335

Now, if thou canst, elude in turn my spear;
May it be deeply buried in thy flesh!
For lighter were to Troy the load of war,
If thou, the greatest of her foes, wert slain."
　　He said, and poising, hurled his ponderous spear; 340
Nor missed his aim; full in the midst he struck
Pelides' shield; but glancing from the shield
The weapon bounded off. Hector was grieved,
That thus his spear had bootless left his hand.
He stood aghast; no second spear was nigh:　　345
And loudly on Deiphobus he called
A spear to bring; but he was far away.
Then Hector knew that he was duped, and cried,
" Oh Heaven! the Gods above have doomed my death!
I deemed indeed that brave Deiphobus　　350
Was near at hand; but he within the walls
Is safe, and I by Pallas am betrayed.
Now is my death at hand, nor far away:
Escape is none; since so hath Jove decreed,
And Jove's far-darting son, who heretofore　　355
Have been my guards; my fate hath found me now.
Yet not without a struggle let me die,
Nor all inglorious; but let some great act,
Which future days may hear of, mark my fall."
Thus as he spoke, his sharp-edged sword he drew, 360
Ponderous and vast, suspended at his side;
Collected for the spring, and forward dashed:
As when an eagle, bird of loftiest flight,
Through the dark clouds swoops downward on the plain,
To seize some tender lamb, or cowering hare;　　365
So Hector rushed, and waved his sharp-edged sword.

Achilles' wrath was roused: with fury wild
His soul was filled: before his breast he bore
His well-wrought shield; and fiercely on his brow
Nodded the four-plumed helm, as on the breeze   370
Floated the golden hairs, with which the crest
By Vulcan's hand was thickly interlaced;
And as amid the stars' unnumbered host,
When twilight yields to night, one star appears,
Hesper, the brightest star that shines in Heaven,   375
Gleamed the sharp-pointed lance, which in his right
Achilles poised, on godlike Hector's doom
Intent, and scanning eagerly to see
Where from attack his body least was fenced.
All else the glittering armour guarded well,   380
Which Hector from Patroclus' corpse had stripped;
One chink appeared, just where the collar-bone
The neck and shoulder parts, beside the throat,
Where lies exposed the swiftest road of death.
There levelled he, as Hector onward rushed;   385
Right through the yielding neck the lance was driven,
But severed not the windpipe, nor destroyed
His power of speech; prone in the dust he fell;
And o'er him, vaunting, thus Achilles spoke:
 "Hector, Patroclus stripping of his arms,   390
Thy hope was that thyself wast safe; and I,
Not present, brought no terror to thy soul:
Fool! in the hollow ships I yet remained,
I, his avenger, mightier far than he;
I, who am now thy conqueror. By the dogs   395
And vultures shall thy corpse be foully torn,
While him the Greeks with funeral rites shall grace."

Whom answered Hector of the glancing helm,
Prostrate and helpless: "By thy soul, thy knees,
Thy parents' heads, Achilles, I beseech,   400
Let not my corpse by Grecian dogs be torn.
Accept the ample stores of brass and gold,
Which as my ransom by my honoured sire
And mother shall be paid thee; but my corpse
Restore, that so the men and wives of Troy   405
May deck with honours due my funeral pyre."
To whom, with fierce aspect, Achilles thus:
"Knee me no knees, vile hound! nor prate to me
Of parents! such my hatred, that almost
I could persuade myself to tear and eat   410
Thy mangled flesh; such wrongs I have to avenge.
He lives not, who can save thee from the dogs;
Not though with ransom ten and twenty fold
He here should stand, and yet should promise more;
No, not though Priam's royal self should sue   415
To be allowed for gold to ransom thee;
No, not e'en so, thy mother shall obtain
To lay thee out upon the couch, and mourn
O'er thee, her offspring; but on all thy limbs
Shall dogs and carrion vultures make their feast."   420
    To whom thus Hector of the glancing helm,
Dying: "I know thee well; nor did I hope
To change thy purpose; iron is thy soul.
But see that on thy head I bring not down
The wrath of Heaven, when by the Scæan gate   425
The hand of Paris, with Apollo's aid,
Brave warrior as thou art, shall strike thee down."
    E'en as he spoke, his eyes were closed in death;

And to the viewless shades his spirit fled,
Mourning his fate, his youth and vigour lost.   430
  To him, though dead, Achilles thus replied:
"Die thou! my fate I then shall meet, whene'er
Jove and the immortal Gods shall so decree."
  He said, and from the corpse his spear withdrew,
And laid aside; then stripped the armour off,   435
With blood besmeared; the Greeks around him thronged,
Gazing on Hector's noble form and face,
And none approached that did not add a wound:
And one to other looked, and said, "Good faith,
Hector is easier far to handle now,   440
Than when erewhile he wrapped our ships in fire."
Thus would they say, then stab the dead anew.
  But when the son of Peleus, swift of foot,
Had stripped the armour from the corpse, he rose,
And, standing, thus the assembled Greeks addressed: 445
"O friends, the chiefs and councillors of Greece,
Since Heaven hath granted us this man to slay,
Whose single arm hath wrought us more of ill
Than all the rest combined, advance we now
Before the city in arms, and trial make   450
What is the mind of Troy; if, Hector slain,
They from the citadel intend retreat,
Or still, despite their loss, their ground maintain.
But wherefore entertain such thoughts, my soul?
Beside the ships, unwept, unburied, lies   455
Patroclus; whom I never can forget,
While numbered with the living, and my limbs
Have power to move; in Hades though the dead
May be forgotten, yet even there will I

The memory of my loved companion keep.　　460
Now to the ships return we, sons of Greece,
Glad pæans singing! with us he shall go;
Great glory is ours, the godlike Hector slain,
The pride of Troy, and as a God revered."
He said, and foully Hector's corpse misused;　　465
Of either foot he pierced the tendon through,
That from the ancle passes to the heel,
And to his chariot bound with leathern thongs,
Leaving the head to trail along the ground;
Then mounted, with the captured arms, his car,　　470
And urged his horses; nothing loth they flew.
A cloud of dust the trailing body raised:
Loose hung his glossy hair; and in the dust
Was laid that noble head, so graceful once;
Now to foul insult doomed by Jove's decree,　　475
In his own country, at a foeman's hand.
So lay the head of Hector; at the sight
His aged mother tore her hair, and far
From off her head the glittering veil she threw,
And with loud cries bewailed her slaughtered son.　　480
Piteous, his father groaned; and all around
Was heard the voice of wailing and of woe.
Such was the cry, as if the beetling height
Of Ilion all were smouldering in the fire.
Scarce in his anguish could the crowd restrain　　485
The old man from issuing through the Dardan gates;
Low in the dust he rolled, imploring all,
Entreating by his name each several man:
" Forbear, my friends; though sorrowing, stay me not;
Leave me to reach alone the Grecian ships,　　490

And there implore this man of violence,
This haughty chief, if haply he my years
May reverence, and have pity on my age.
For he too has a father, like to me;
Peleus, by whom he was begot, and bred,   495
The bane of Troy; and, most of all, to me
The cause of endless grief, who by his hand
Have been of many stalwart sons bereft.
Yet all, though grieved for all, I less lament,
Than one, whose loss will sink me to the grave,   500
Hector! oh would to Heaven that in mine arms
He could have died; with mourning then and tears
We might have satisfied our grief, both she
Who bore him, hapless mother, and myself."
Weeping, he spoke; and with him wept the crowd: 505
Then 'mid the women, Hecuba poured forth
Her vehement grief: "My child, oh whither now,
Heart-stricken, shall I go, of thee bereft,
Of thee, who wast to me by night and day
A glory and a boast; the strength of all   510
The men of Troy, and women? as a God
They worshipped thee: for in thy life thou wast
The glory of all; but fate hath found thee now."
Weeping, she spoke; but nought as yet was known
To Hector's wife; to her no messenger   515
Had brought the tidings, that without the walls
Remained her husband; in her house withdrawn
A web she wove, all purple, double woof,
With varied flowers in rich embroidery,
And to her neat-haired maidens gave command   520
To place the largest caldrons on the fire,

That with warm baths, returning from the fight,
Hector might be refreshed; unconscious she,
That by Achilles' hand, with Pallas' aid,
Far from the bath, was godlike Hector slain.   525
The sounds of wailing reached her from the tower;
Tottered her limbs, the distaff left her hand,
And to her neat-haired maidens thus she spoke:
"Haste, follow me, some two, that I may know
What mean these sounds; my honoured mother's voice 530
I hear; and in my breast my beating heart
Leaps to my mouth; my limbs refuse to move;
Some evil, sure, on Priam's house impends.
Be unfulfilled my words! yet much I fear
Lest my brave Hector be cut off alone,   535
By great Achilles, from the walls of Troy,
Chased to the plain, the desperate courage quenched,
Which ever led him from the general ranks
Far in advance, and bade him yield to none."
Then from the house she rushed, like one distract, 540
With beating heart; and with her went her maids.
But when she reached the tower, where stood the crowd,
And mounted on the wall, she looked around,
And saw the body which with insult foul
The flying steeds were dragging towards the ships; 545
Then sudden darkness overspread her eyes;
Backward she fell, and gasped her spirit away.
Far off were flung the adornments of her head,
The net, the fillet, and the woven bands;
The nuptial veil by golden Venus given,   550
That day when Hector of the glancing helm
Led from Eëtion's house his wealthy bride.

The sisters of her husband round her pressed,
And held, as in the deadly swoon she lay.
But when her breath and spirit returned again,   555
With sudden burst of anguish thus she cried:
"Hector, oh woe is me! to misery
We both were born alike; thou here in Troy
In Priam's royal palace; I in Thebes,
By wooded Placos, in Eëtion's house,   560
Who nursed my infancy; unhappy he,
Unhappier I! would I had ne'er been born!
Now thou beneath the depths of earth art gone,
Gone to the viewless shades; and me hast left
A widow in thy house, in deepest woe;   565
Our child, an infant still, thy child and mine,
Ill-fated parents both! nor thou to him,
Hector, shalt be a guard, nor he to thee:
For though he 'scape this tearful war with Greece,
Yet nought for him remains but ceaseless woe,   570
And strangers on his heritage shall seize.
No young companions own the orphan boy:
With downcast eyes, and cheeks bedewed with tears,
His father's friends approaching, pinched with want,
He hangs upon the skirt of one, of one   575
He plucks the cloak; perchance in pity some
May at their tables let him sip the cup,
Moisten his lips, but scarce his palate touch;
While youths, with both surviving parents blessed,
May drive him from their feast with blows and taunts, 580
'Begone! thy father sits not at our board:'
Then weeping, to his widowed mother's arms
He flies, that orphan boy, Astyanax,

Who on his father's knees erewhile was fed
On choicest marrow, and the fat of lambs;　　585
And, when in sleep his childish play was hushed,
Was lulled to slumber in his nurse's arms
On softest couch, by all delights surrounded.
But grief, his father lost, awaits him now,
Astyanax, of Trojans so surnamed,　　590
Since thou alone wast Troy's defence and guard.
But now on thee, beside the beakèd ships,
Far from thy parents, when the ravening dogs
Have had their fill, the wriggling worms shall feed;
On thee, all naked; while within thy house　　595
Lies store of raiment, rich and rare, the work
Of women's hands; these will I burn with fire;
Not for thy need—thou ne'er shalt wear them more,—
But for thine honour in the sight of Troy."

　　Weeping she spoke; the women joined her wail.　600

BOOK XXIII.

THUS they throughout the city made their moan;
   But when the Greeks had come where lay their ships
By the broad Hellespont, their several ways
They each pursued, dispersing; yet not so
Achilles let his Myrmidons disperse,   5
But thus his warlike comrades he addressed:
  "My faithful comrades, valiant Myrmidons,
Loose we not yet our horses from the cars;
But for Patroclus mourn, approaching near,
With horse and car; such tribute claim the dead; 10
Then, free indulgence to our sorrows given,
Loose we the steeds, and share the evening meal."
  He said; and they with mingled voices raised
The solemn dirge; Achilles led the strain;
Thrice round the dead they drove their sleek-skinned
    steeds,   15
Mourning, with hearts by Thetis grief-inspired;
With tears the sands, with tears the warriors' arms,
Were wet; so mighty was the chief they mourned.
Then on his comrade's breast Achilles laid
His blood-stained hands, and thus began the wail: 20
  "All hail, Patroclus, though in Pluto's realm;
All that I promised, lo! I now perform;
That on the corpse of Hector, hither dragged,
Our dogs should feed; and that twelve noble youths,

The sons of Troy, before thy funeral pyre,   25
My hand, in vengeance for thy death, should slay."
    He said, and foully Hector's corpse misused,
Flung prostrate in the dust, beside the couch
Where lay Menœtius' son. His comrades then
Their glittering armour doffed, of polished brass,   30
And loosed their neighing steeds; then round the ship
Of Peleus' son in countless numbers sat,
While he the abundant funeral feast dispensed.
There many a steer lay stretched beneath the knife,
And many a sheep, and many a bleating goat,   35
And many a white-tusked porker, rich in fat,
There lay extended, singeing o'er the fire;
And blood, in torrents, flowed around the corpse.
To Agamemnon then the Kings of Greece
The royal son of Peleus, swift of foot,   40
Conducted; yet with him they scarce prevailed;
So fierce his anger for his comrade's death.
But when to Agamemnon's tent they came,
He to the clear-voiced heralds gave command
An ample tripod on the fire to place;   45
If haply Peleus' son he might persuade
To wash away the bloody stains of war:
But sternly he, and with an oath refused.
    "No, by great Jove I swear, of all the Gods
Highest and mightiest, water shall not touch   50
This head of mine, till on the funeral pyre
I see the body of Patroclus laid,
And build his tomb, and cut my votive hair;
For while I live and move 'mid mortal men,
No second grief like this can pierce my soul.   55

Observe we now the mournful funeral feast;
But thou, great Agamemnon, King of men,
Send forth at early dawn, and to the camp
Bring store of fuel, and all else prepare,
That with provision meet the dead may pass   60
Down to the realms of night; so shall the fire
From out our sight consume our mighty dead,
And to their wonted tasks the troops return."
    He said; they listened, and his words obeyed;
Then busily the evening meal prepared,   65
And shared the social feast; nor lacked there aught.
But when their thirst and hunger were appeased,
Each to their several tents the rest repaired;
But on the many-dashing ocean's shore
Pelides lay, amid his Myrmidons,   70
With bitter groans; in a clear space he lay,
Where broke the waves, continuous, on the beach.
There, circumfused around him, gentle sleep,
Lulling the sorrows of his heart to rest,
O'ercame his senses; for the hot pursuit   75
Of Hector round the breezy heights of Troy
His active limbs had wearied: as he slept,
Sudden appeared Patroclus' mournful shade,
His very self; his height, and beauteous eyes,
And voice; the very garb he wont to wear: 80
Above his head it stood, and thus it spoke:
    "Sleep'st thou, Achilles, mindless of thy friend,
Neglecting, not the living, but the dead?
Hasten my funeral rites, that I may pass
Through Hades' gloomy gates; ere those be done,   85
The spirits and spectres of departed men

Drive me far from them, nor allow to cross
The abhorrèd river; but forlorn and sad
I wander through the wide-spread realms of night.
And give me now thy hand, whereon to weep;　　90
For never more, when laid upon the pyre,
Shall I return from Hades; never more,
Apart from all our comrades, shall we two,
As friends, sweet counsel take; for me, stern Death,
The common lot of man, has oped his mouth;　　95
Thou too, Achilles, rival of the Gods,
Art destined here beneath the walls of Troy
To meet thy doom; yet one thing must I add,
And make, if thou wilt grant it, one request.
Let not my bones be laid apart from thine,　　100
Achilles, but together, as our youth
Was spent together in thy father's house,
Since first my sire Menœtius me a boy
From Opus brought, a luckless homicide,
Who of Amphidamas, by evil chance,　　105
Had slain the son, disputing o'er the dice:
Me noble Peleus in his house received,
And kindly nursed, and thine attendant named
So in one urn be now our bones enclosed,
The golden vase, thy Goddess-mother's gift."　　110
　　Whom answered thus Achilles, swift of foot:
"Why art thou here, loved being? why on me
These several charges lay? whate'er thou bidd'st
Will I perform, and all thy mind fulfil;
But draw thou near; and in one short embrace,　　115
Let us, while yet we may, our grief indulge."
　　Thus as he spoke, he spread his longing arms,

But nought he clasped; and with a wailing cry,
Vanished, like smoke, the spirit beneath the earth.
Up sprang Achilles, all amazed, and smote　　　　120
His hands together, and lamenting cried:
"Oh Heaven, there are then, in the realms below,
Spirits and spectres, unsubstantial all;
For all night long Patroclus' shade hath stood,
Weeping and wailing, at my side, and told　　　　125
His bidding; the image of himself it seemed."
　He said; his words the general grief aroused:
To them, as round the piteous dead they mourned,
Appeared the rosy-fingered morn; and straight,
From all the camp, by Agamemnon sent,　　　　130
Went forth, in search of fuel, men and mules,
Led by a valiant chief, Meriones,
The follower of renowned Idomeneus.
Their felling axes in their hands they bore,
And twisted ropes; their mules before them driven;　135
Now up, now down, now sideways, now aslope,
They journeyed on; but when they reached the foot
Of spring-abounding Ida, they began
With axes keen to hew the lofty oaks;
They, loudly crashing, fell: the wood they clove,　140
And bound it to the mules; these took their way
Through the thick brushwood, hurrying to the plain.
The axe-men too, so bade Meriones,
The follower of renowned Idomeneus,
Were laden all with logs, which on the beach　　　145
They laid in order, where a lofty mound,
In memory of Patroclus and himself,
Achilles had designed. When all the store

Of wood was duly laid, the rest remained
In masses seated; but Achilles bade   150
The warlike Myrmidons their armour don,
And harness each his horses to his car;
They rose and donned their arms, and on the cars
Warriors and charioteers their places took.
  First came the horse, and then a cloud of foot,   155
Unnumbered; in the midst Patroclus came,
Borne by his comrades; all the corpse with hair
They covered o'er, which from their heads they shore.
Behind, Achilles held his head, and mourned
The noble friend whom to the tomb he bore.   160
Then on the spot by Peleus' son assigned,
They laid him down, and piled the wood on high.
Then a fresh thought Achilles' mind conceived:
Standing apart, the yellow locks he shore,
Which as an offering to Sperchius' stream,   165
He nursed in rich profusion; sorrowing then
Looked o'er the dark-blue sea, as thus he spoke:
  "Sperchius, all in vain to thee his prayer
My father Peleus made, and vowed that I,
Returned in safety to my native land,   170
To thee should dedicate my hair, and pay
A solemn hecatomb, with sacrifice
Of fifty rams, unblemished, to the springs
Where on thy consecrated soil is placed
Thine incense-honoured altar; so he vowed;   175
But thou the boon withhold'st; since I no more
My native land may see, the hair he vowed,
To brave Patroclus thus I dedicate."
  He said, and on his comrade's hand he laid

The locks; his act the general grief aroused;   180
And now the setting sun had found them still
Lamenting o'er the dead; but Peleus' son
Approaching, thus to Agamemnon spoke:
  "Atrides, for to thee the people pay
Readiest obedience, mourning too prolonged   185
May weary; thou then from the pyre the rest
Disperse, and bid prepare the morning meal;
Ours be the farther charge, to whom the dead
Was chiefly dear; yet let the chiefs remain."
The monarch Agamemnon heard, and straight   190
Dispersed the crowd amid their several ships.
The appointed band remained, and piled the wood.
A hundred feet each way they built the pyre,
And on the summit, sorrowing, laid the dead.
Then many a sheep and many a slow-paced ox   195
They flayed and dressed around the funeral pyre;
Of all the beasts Achilles took the fat,
And covered o'er the corpse from head to foot,
And heaped the slaughtered carcases around;
Then jars of honey placed, and fragrant oils,   200
Resting upon the couch; next, groaning loud,
Four powerful horses on the pyre he threw;
Then, of nine dogs that at their master's board
Had fed, he slaughtered two upon his pyre;
Last, with the sword, by evil counsel swayed,   205
Twelve noble youths he slew, the sons of Troy.
The fire's devouring might he then applied,
And, groaning, on his loved companion called:
  "All hail, Patroclus, though in Pluto's realm!
All that I promised, lo! I now perform: 210

On twelve brave sons of Trojan sires, with thee,
The flames shall feed; but Hector, Priam's son,
Not to the fire, but to the dogs I give."
　Such was Achilles' threat, but him the dogs
Molested not; for Venus, night and day,　　　　　215
Daughter of Jove, the ravening dogs restrained;
And all the corpse o'erlaid with roseate oil,
Ambrosial, that though dragged along the earth,
The noble dead might not receive a wound.
Apollo too a cloudy veil from Heaven　　　　　　220
Spread o'er the plain, and covered all the space
Where lay the dead, nor let the blazing sun
The flesh upon his limbs and muscles parch.
Yet burnt not up Patroclus' funeral pyre;
Then a fresh thought Achilles' mind conceived:　225
Standing apart, on both the Winds he called,
Boreas and Zephyrus, and added vows
Of costly sacrifice; and pouring forth
Libations from a golden goblet, prayed
Their presence, that the wood might haste to burn, 230
And with the fire consume the dead; his prayer
Swift Iris heard, and bore it to the Winds.
They in the hall of gusty Zephyrus
Were gathered round the feast; in haste appearing,
Swift Iris on the stony threshold stood.　　　　235
They saw, and rising all, besought her each
To sit beside him; she with their requests
Refused compliance, and addressed them thus:
　"No seat for me; for I o'er the ocean stream
From hence am bound to Æthiopia's shore,　　　240
To share the sacred feast, and hecatombs,

Which there they offer to the immortal Gods;
But, Boreas, thee, and loud-voiced Zephyrus,
With vows of sacrifice, Achilles calls
To fan the funeral pyre, whereon is laid   245
Patroclus, mourned by all the host of Greece."
     She said, and vanished; they, with rushing sound,
Rose, and before them drove the hurrying clouds:
Soon o'er the sea they swept; the stirring breeze
Ruffled the waves; the fertile shores of Troy   250
They reached, and falling on the funeral pyre,
Loud roared the crackling flames; they all night long
With current brisk together fanned the fire.
All night Achilles with a double cup
Drew from a golden bowl the ruddy wine,   255
Wherewith, outpoured, he moistened all the earth,
Still calling on his lost Patroclus' shade.
As mourns a father o'er a youthful son,
Whose early death hath wrung his parents' hearts;
So mourned Achilles o'er his friend's remains,   260
Prostrate beside the pyre, and groaned aloud.
But when the star of Lucifer appeared,
The harbinger of light, whom following close
Spreads o'er the sea the saffron-robèd morn,
Then paled the smouldering fire, and sank the flame; 265
And o'er the Thracian sea, that groaned and heaved
Beneath their passage, home the Winds returned;
And weary, from the pyre a space withdrawn,
Achilles lay, o'ercome by gentle sleep.
     Anon, awakened by the tramp and din   270
Of crowds that followed Atreus' royal son,
He sat upright, and thus addressed his speech:

" Thou son of Atreus, and ye chiefs of Greece,
Far as the flames extended, quench we first
With ruddy wine the embers of the pyre;   275
And of Menœtius' son, Patroclus, next
With care distinguishing, collect the bones;
Nor are they hard to know; for in the midst
He lay, while round the edges of the pyre,
Horses and men commixed, the rest were burnt.   280
Let these, between a double layer of fat
Enclosed, and in a golden urn remain,
Till I myself shall in the tomb be laid;
And o'er them build a mound, not over-large,
But of proportions meet; in days to come,   285
Ye Greeks, who after me shall here remain,
Complete the work, and build it broad and high."
Thus spoke Achilles; they his words obeyed:
Far as the flames had reached, and thickly strown
The embers lay, they quenched with ruddy wine; 290
Then tearfully their gentle comrade's bones
Collected, and with double layers of fat
Enclosed, and in a golden urn encased;
Then in the tent they laid them, overspread
With veil of linen fair; then meting out   295
The allotted space, the deep foundations laid
Around the pyre, and o'er them heaped the earth.
Their task accomplished, all had now withdrawn;
But Peleus' son the vast assembly stayed,
And bade them sit; then, prizes of the games,   300
Tripods and caldrons from the tents he brought,
And noble steeds, and mules, and sturdy steers,
And women fair of form, and iron hoar.

First, for the contest of the flying cars
The prizes he displayed: a woman fair,   305
Well skilled in household cares; a tripod vast,
Two-handled, two and twenty measures round;
These both were for the victor: for the next,
A mare, unbroken, six years old, in foal
Of a mule colt; the third, a cauldron bright,   310
Capacious of four measures, white and pure,
By fire as yet untarnished; for the fourth,
Of gold two talents; for the fifth, a vase
With double cup, untouched by fire, he gave.
Then, standing up, he thus addressed the Greeks: 315
"Thou son of Atreus, and ye well-greaved Greeks,
Before ye are the prizes, which await
The contest of the cars; but if, ye Greeks,
For any other cause these games were held,
I to my tent should bear the foremost prize;   320
For well ye know how far my steeds excel,
Steeds of immortal race, which Neptune gave
To Peleus, he to me, his son, transferred.
But from the present strife we stand aloof,
My horses and myself; they now have lost   325
The daring courage and the gentle hand
Of him who drove them, and with water pure
Washed oft their manes, and bathed with fragrant oil.
For him they stand and mourn, with drooping heads
Down to the ground, their hearts with sorrow filled; 330
But ye in order range yourselves, who boast
Your well-built chariots and your horses' speed."
He said: up sprang the eager charioteers;
The first of all, Eumelus, King of men,

Son of Admetus, matchless charioteer;   335
Next, Tydeus' son, the valiant Diomed,
Beneath whose car were yoked the steeds of Tros,
His prize, when Phœbus saved Æneas' life;
Then Heaven-born Meneläus, Atreus' son,
Two flying coursers harnessed to his car;   340
His own, Podargus, had for yokefellow
Æthe, a mare by Agamemnon lent:
Her to Atrides Echepolus gave,
Anchises' son, that to the wars of Troy
He might not be compelled, but safe at home   345
Enjoy his ease; for Jove had blessed his store
With ample wealth, in Sicyon's wide domain.
Her now he yoked, impatient for the course.
The fourth, Antilochus, the gallant son
Of Nestor, son of Neleus, mighty chief,   350
Harnessed his sleek-skinned steeds; of Pylian race
Were they who bore his car; to him, his sire
Sage counsel poured in understanding ears:
  "Antilochus, though young in years thou art,
Yet Jove and Neptune love thee, and have well   355
Instructed thee in horsemanship; of me
Thou need'st no counsel; skilled around the goal
To whirl the chariot; but thou hast, of all,
The slowest horses: whence I augur ill.
But though their horses have the speed of thine,   360
In skill not one of them surpasses thee.
Then thou, dear boy, exert thine every art,
That so thou mayst not fail to gain a prize.
By skill, far more than strength, the woodman fells
The sturdy oak; by skill the steersman guides   365

His flying ship across the dark-blue sea,
Though shattered by the blast; 'twixt charioteer
And charioteer 'tis skill that draws the line.
One, vainly trusting to his coursers' speed,
Drives reckless here and there; o'er all the course,   370
His horses, unrestrained, at random run.
Another, with inferior horses far,
But better skilled, still fixing on the goal
His eye, turns closely round, nor overlooks
The moment when to draw the rein; but holds   375
His steady course, and on the leader waits.
A mark I give thee now, thou canst not miss:
There stands a withered trunk, some six feet high,
Of oak, or pine, unrotted by the rain;
On either side have two white stones been placed,   380
Where meet two roads; and all around there lies
A smooth and level course; here stood perchance
The tomb of one who died long years ago;
Or former generations here have placed,
As now Achilles hath decreed, a goal.   385
There drive, as only not to graze the post;
And leaning o'er the wicker body, leave
Close on the left the stones; thine offside hors ·
Then urge with voice and whip, and slack his rein,
And let the nearside horse so closely graze,   390
As that thy nave may seem to touch, the goal:
But yet beware, lest, striking on the stone,
Thy steeds thou injure, and thy chariot break,
A source of triumph to thy rivals all,
Of shame to thee; but thou sage caution use;   395
For, following, if thou make the turn the first,

Not one of all shall pass thee, or o'ertake;
Not though Arion's self were in the car,
Adrastus' flying steed, of heavenly race,
Nor those which here Laomedon possessed."   400
    This said, and to his son his counsels given,
The aged Nestor to his seat withdrew.
Fifth in the lists Meriones appeared.
They mounted on their cars, and cast their lots:
Achilles shook the helmet; first leaped forth   405
The lot of Nestor's son, Antilochus;
Next came the King Eumelus; after whom
The valiant Mencläus, Atreus' son;
The fourth, Meriones; and last of all,
But ablest far, Tydides drew his place.   410
They stood in line; Achilles pointed out,
Far on the level plain, the distant goal;
And there in charge the godlike Phœnix placed,
His father's ancient follower, to observe
The course assigned, and true report to make.   415
Then all at once their whips they raised, and urged
By rein, and hand, and voice, their eager steeds.
They from the ships pursued their rapid course
Athwart the distant plain; beneath their chests
Rose like a cloud, or hurricane, the dust;   420
Loose floated on the breeze their ample manes;
The cars now skimmed along the fertile ground,
Now bounded high in air; the charioteers
Stood up aloft, and every bosom beat
With hope of victory; each with eager shout   425
Cheering his steeds, that scoured the dusty plain.
But when, the farthest limits of the course

Attained, they turned beside the hoary sea,
Strained to their utmost speed, were plainly seen
The qualities of each; then in the front   430
Appeared Eumelus' flying mares, and next
The Trojan horses of Tydides came:
Nor these were far behind, but following close
They seemed in act to leap upon the car.
Eumelus, on his neck and shoulders broad,   435
Felt their warm breath; for o'er him, as they flew,
Their heads were downward bent; and now, perchance,
Had he or passed, or made an even race,
But that, incensed with valiant Diomed,
Apollo wrested from his hands the whip.   440
Then tears of anger from his eyelids fell,
As gaining more and more the mares he saw,
While, urged no more, his horses slacked their speed.
But Pallas marked Apollo's treacherous wile;
And hasting to the chief, restored his whip,   445
And to his horses strength and courage gave.
The Goddess then Admetus' son pursued,
And snapped his chariot yoke; the mares, released,
Swerved from the track; the pole upon the ground
Lay loosened from the car; and he himself   450
Beside the wheel was from the chariot hurled.
From elbows, mouth, and nose, the skin was torn;
His forehead crushed and battered in; his eyes
Were filled with tears, and mute his cheerful voice.
Tydides turned aside, and far ahead   455
Of all the rest, passed on; for Pallas gave
His horses courage, and his triumph willed.
Next him, the fair-haired Meneläus came,

The son of Atreus; but Antilochus
Thus to his father's horses called aloud: 460
   "Forward, and stretch ye to your utmost speed;
I ask you not with those of Diomed
In vain to strive, whom Pallas hath endued
With added swiftness, and his triumph willed;
But haste ye, and o'ertake Atrides' car,   465
Nor be by Æthe, by a mare, disgraced.
Why, my brave horses, why be left behind?
This too I warn ye, and will make it good:
No more at Nestor's hand shall ye receive
Your provender, but with the sword be slain,   470
If by your faults a lower prize be ours;
Then rouse ye now, and put forth all your speed,
And I will so contrive, as not to fail
Of slipping past them in the narrow way."
   He said; the horses, of his voice in awe,   475
Put forth their powers awhile; before them soon
Antilochus the narrow pass espied.
It was a gully, where the winter's rain
Had lain collected, and had broken through
A length of road, and hollowed out the ground: 480
There Mencläus held his cautious course,
Fearing collision; but Antilochus,
Drawing his steeds a little from the track,
Bore down upon him sideways: then in fear
The son of Atreus to Antilochus   485
Shouted aloud, "Antilochus, thou driv'st
Like one insane; hold in awhile thy steeds;
Here is no space; where wider grows the road,
There thou mayst pass; but here, thou wilt but cause

Our cars to clash, and bring us both to harm."   490
   He said; but madlier drove Antilochus,
Plying the goad, as though he heard him not.
   Far as a discus' flight, by some stout youth,
That tests his vigour, from the shoulder hurled,
So far they ran together, side by side: 495
Then dropped Atrides' horses to the rear,
For he himself forbore to urge their speed,
Lest, meeting in the narrow pass, the cars
Should be o'erthrown, and they themselves, in haste
To gain the victory, in the dust be rolled.   500
Then thus, reproachful, to Antilochus:
   "Antilochus, thou most perverse of men!
Beshrew thy heart! we Greeks are much deceived
Who gave thee fame for wisdom! yet e'en now
Thou shalt not gain, but on thine oath, the prize."   505
   He said, and to his horses called aloud:
"Slack not your speed, nor, as defeated, mourn;
Their legs and feet will sooner tire than yours,
For both are past the vigour of their youth."
Thus he; the horses, of his voice in awe,   510
Put forth their powers, and soon the leaders neared.
   Meanwhile the chieftains, seated in the ring,
Looked for the cars, that scoured the dusty plain.
The first to see them was Idomeneus,
The Cretan King; for he, without the ring,   515
Was posted high aloft; and from afar
He heard and knew the foremost horseman's voice;
Well too he knew the gallant horse that led,
All bay the rest, but on his front alone
A star of white, full-orbèd as the moon: 520

Then up he rose, and thus the Greeks addressed :
" O friends, the chiefs and councillors of Greece
Can ye too see, or I alone, the cars?
A different chariot seems to me in front,
A different charioteer; and they who first   525
Were leading, must have met with some mischance.
I saw them late, ere round the goal they turned,
But see them now no more; though all around
My eyes explore the wide-spread plain of Troy.
Perchance the charioteer has dropped the reins,   530
Or round the goal he could not hold the mares:
Perchance has missed the turn, and on the plain
Is lying now beside his broken car,
While from the course his mettled steeds have flown.
Stand up, and look yourselves; I cannot well   535
Distinguish; but to me it seems a chief,
Who reigns o'er Greeks, though of Ætolian race,
The son of Tydeus, valiant Diomed."
    Sharply Oïleus' active son replied :
" Idomeneus, why thus, before the time,   540
So rashly speak? while the high-stepping steeds
Are speeding yet across the distant plain.
Thine eyes are not the youngest in the camp,
Nor look they out the sharpest from thy head;
But thou art ever hasty in thy speech,   545
And ill becomes thee this precipitance,
Since others are there here, thy betters far.
The same are leading now, that led at first,
Eumelus' mares; 'tis he that holds the reins."
    To whom in anger thus the Cretan chief: 550
" Ajax, at wrangling good, in judgment naught,

And for aught else, among the chiefs of Greece
Of small account—so stubborn is thy soul;
Wilt thou a tripod or a caldron stake,
And Agamemnon, Atreus' son, appoint   555
The umpire to decide whose steeds are first?
So shalt thou gain thy knowledge at thy cost."
    He said: up sprang Oïleus' active son,
In anger to reply; and farther yet
Had gone the quarrel, but Achilles' self   560
Stood up, and thus the rival chiefs addressed:
    "Forbear, both Ajax and Idomeneus,
This bitter interchange of wordy war;
It is not seemly; and yourselves, I know,
Another would condemn, who so should speak.   565
But stay ye here, and seated in the ring,
Their coming wait; they, hurrying to the goal,
Will soon be here; and then shall each man know
Whose horses are the second, whose the first."
    Thus he; but Tydeus' son drew near, his lash   570
Still laid upon his horses' shoulder-points;
As lightly they, high-stepping, scoured the plain.
Still on the charioteer the dust was flung;
As close upon the flying-footed steeds
Followed the car with gold and tin inlaid;   575
And lightly, as they flew along, were left
Impressed the wheel-tracks on the sandy plain.
There in the midst he stood, the sweat profuse
Down-pouring from his horses' heads and chests;
Down from the glittering car he leaped to earth,   580
And leaned his whip against the chariot yoke;
Nor long delayed the valiant Sthenelus,

But eagerly sprang forth to claim the prize;
Then to his brave companions gave in charge
To lead away the woman, and to bear   585
The tripod, while himself unyoked the steeds.
    Next came the horses of Antilochus,
Who had by stratagem, and not by speed,
O'er Meneläus triumphed; yet e'en so
Atrides' flying coursers pressed him hard;   590
For but so far as from the chariot-wheel
A horse, when harnessed to a royal car;
Whose tail, back-streaming, with the utmost hairs
Brushes the felloes; close before the wheel,
Small space between, he scours the wide-spread plain: 595
So far was Meneläus in the rear
Of Nestor's son; at first, a discus' cast
Between them lay; but rapidly his ground
He gained—so well the speed and courage served
Of Æthe, Agamemnon's beauteous mare;   600
And, but a little farther were the course,
Had passed him by, nor left the race in doubt.
Behind the noble son of Atreus came,
A javelin's flight apart, Meriones,
The faithful follower of Idomeneus: 605
His were the slowest horses, and himself
The least experienced in the rapid race.
Dragging his broken car, came last of all,
His horses driven in front, Admetus' son;
Achilles swift of foot with pity saw,   610
And to the Greeks his wingèd words addressed:
    " See where the best of all the last appears;
But let him take, as meet, the second prize:

The first belongs of right to Tydeus' son."
    Thus he; they all assented to his words;   615
And, by the general voice of Greece, the mare
Had now been his; but noble Nestor's son,
Antilochus, stood up, his right to claim,
And to Achilles, Peleus' son, replied:
"Achilles, thou wilt do me grievous wrong,   620
If thou thy words accomplish; for my prize
Thou tak'st away, because mishap befell
His car and horses, by no fault of his;
Yet had he to the Immortals made his prayer,
He surely had not thus been last of all.   625
But, pitying him, if so thy mind incline,
Thy tents contain good store of gold, and brass,
And sheep, and female slaves, and noble steeds;
For him, of these, hereafter mayst thou take
A prize of higher value; or e'en now,   630
And with the applause of all; but for the mare,
I will not give her up; and let who will
Stand forth, my own right hand shall guard my prize."
    He said; and smiled Achilles swift of foot,
Delighted: for he loved the noble youth,   635
To whom his wingèd words he thus addressed:
    "Antilochus, if such be thy request,
That for Eumelus I should add a prize,
This too I grant thee; and to him I give
My breastplate, from Asteropæus won,   640
Of brass, around whose edge is rolled a stream
Of shining tin; a gift of goodly price."
    He said, and bade Automedon, his friend
And comrade, bring the breastplate from his tent;

He went, and brought it; in Eumelus' hand   645
He placed it; he with joy the gift received.
Then Meneläus, sad at heart, arose,
Burning with wrath against Antilochus;
And while the herald in the monarch's hand
His royal sceptre placed, and bade the Greeks   650
Keep silence, thus the godlike hero spoke:
  "Antilochus, till now reputed wise,
What hast thou done? thou hast disgraced my skill,
And shamed my horses, who hast brought thine own,
Inferior far, before them to the goal.   655
But come, ye chiefs and councillors of Greece,
Judge ye between us, favouring neither side:
That none of all the brass-clad Greeks may say
That Meneläus hath by false reports
O'erborne Antilochus, and holds his prize: 660
His horses fairly worsted, and himself
Triumphant only by superior power.
Or come now, I myself will judgment give;
Nor deem I any Greek will find to blame
In my decision, for 'tis fair and just.   665
Antilochus, come forward, noble chief;
And standing, as 'tis meet, before the car
And horses, in thy hand the slender whip
Wherewith thou drov'st, upon the horses lay
Thy hand, and by Earth-shaking Neptune swear   670
That not of malice, and by set design,
Thou didst by fraud impede my chariot's course."
  To whom Antilochus with prudent speech:
"Have patience with me yet; for I, O King,
O Meneläus, am thy junior far;   675

My elder and superior thee I own.
Thou know'st the o'er-eager vehemence of youth,
How quick in temper, and in judgment weak.
Set then thy heart at ease; the mare I won
I freely give; and if aught else of mine   680
Thou shouldst desire, would sooner give it all,
Than all my life be lowered, illustrious King,
In thine esteem, and sin against the Gods."
    Thus saying, noble Nestor's son led forth,
And placed in Meneläus' hands the mare: 685
The monarch's soul was melted, like the dew
Which glitters on the ears of growing corn,
That bristle o'er the plain; e'en so thy soul,
O Meneläus, melted at his speech;
To whom were thus addressed thy wingèd words: 690
    "Antilochus, at once I lay aside
My anger; thou art prudent, and not apt
To be thus led astray; but now thy youth
Thy judgment hath o'erpowered; seek not henceforth
By trickery o'er thine elders to prevail.   695
To any other man of all the Greeks
I scarce so much had yielded; but for that
Thyself hast laboured much, and much endured,
Thou, thy good sire, and brother, in my cause;
I yield me to thy prayers; and give, to boot,   700
The mare, though mine of right; that these may know
I am not of a harsh, unyielding mood."
    He said, and to Noëmon gave in charge,
The faithful comrade of Antilochus,
The mare; himself the glittering caldron took.   705

Of gold two talents, to the fourth assigned,
Fourth in the race, Meriones received;
Still the fifth prize, a vase with double cup,
Remained; Achilles this to Nestor gave,
Before the assembled Greeks, as thus he spoke: 710
" Take this, old man, and for an heir-loom keep,
In memory of Patroclus' funeral games,
Whom thou no more amid the Greeks shalt see.
Freely I give it thee; for thou no more
Canst box, or wrestle, or in sportive strife 715
The javelin throw, or race with flying feet;
For age with heavy hand hath bowed thee down."
He said, and placed it in his hand; the old man
Received with joy the gift, and thus replied:
" All thou hast said, my son, is simple truth: 720
No firmness now my limbs and feet retain,
Nor can my arms with freedom, as of old,
Straight from the shoulder, right and left, strike out.
Oh that such youth and vigour yet were mine,
As when the Epeians in Buprasium held 725
The royal Amaryuceus' funeral games,
And when the monarch's sons his prizes gave!
Then could not one of all the Epeian race,
Or Pylians, or Ætolians vie with me.
In boxing, Clytomedes, Œnops' son, 730
I vanquished; then Anchæus, who stood up
To wrestle with me, I with ease o'erthrew;
Iphiclus I outran, though fleet of foot;
In hurling with the spear, with Phyleus strove,
And Polydorus, and surpassed them both. 735

The sons of Actor in the chariot-race
Alone o'ercame me; as in number more,*
And grudging more my triumph, since remained,
This contest to reward, the richest prize.
They were twin brothers; one who held the reins, 740
Still drove, and drove; the other plied the whip.
Such was I once; but now must younger men
Engage in deeds like these; and I, the chief
Of heroes once, must bow to weary age.
But honour thou with fitting funeral games   745
Thy comrade; I accept, well-pleased, thy gift,
My heart rejoicing that thou still retain'st
Of me a kindly memory, nor o'erlook'st
The place of honour, which among the Greeks
Belongs to me of right; for this, the Gods   750
Reward thee with a worthy recompense!"
    He said; Achilles listened to the praise
Of Neleus' son; then joined the general throng.
Next, he set forth the prizes, to reward
The labours of the sturdy pugilists;   755
A hardy mule he tethered in the ring,
Unbroken, six years old, most hard to tame;
And for the vanquished man, a double cup;
Then rose, and to the Greeks proclaimed aloud:
    "Thou son of Atreus, and ye well-greaved Greeks, 760

---

* They being two, while I was only one. Such I believe to be the true
interpretation of this passage, which, however, is one of admitted difficulty.
According to our modern notions, it is not very evident what advantage two
men in a car would have over one in another; nor what would be gained by
the division of labour which assigned the reins to one and the whip to the
other; but such, from l. 740-741, appears to have been the view taken by
Homer.

For these we bid two champions brave stand forth,
And in the boxer's manly toil contend;
And he, whose stern endurance Phœbus crowns
With victory, recognized by all the Greeks,
He to his tent shall lead the hardy mule; 765
The loser shall the double cup receive."
  He said; up sprang Epeius, tall and stout,
A boxer skilled, the son of Panopeus,
Who laid his hand upon the mule, and said:
  "Stand forth, if any care the cup to win; 770
The mule, methinks, no Greek can bear away
From me, who glory in the champion's name.
Is't not enough, that in the battle-field
I claim no special praise? 'tis not for man
In all things to excel; but this I say, 775
And will make good my words, who meets me here,
I mean to pound his flesh, and smash his bones.
See that his seconds be at hand, and prompt
To bear him from the ring, by me subdued."
  He said; they all in silence heard his speech: 780
Only Euryalus, a godlike chief,
Son of Mecistheus, Talaïon's son,
Stood forth opposing; he had once in Thebes
Joined in the funeral games of Œdipus,
And there had vanquished all of Cadmian race. 785
On him attended valiant Diomed,
With cheering words, and wishes of success.
Around his waist he fastened first the belt,
Then gave the well-cut gauntlets for his hands,
Of wild bull's hide. When both were thus equipped, 790
Into the centre of the ring they stepped:

There, face to face, with sinewy arms upraised,
They stood awhile, then closed; strong hand with hand
Mingling, in rapid interchange of blows.
Dire was the clatter of their jaws; the sweat   795
Poured forth, profuse, from every limb; then rushed
Epeius on, and full upon the cheek,
Half turned aside, let fall a staggering blow;
Nor stood Euryalus; but, legs and feet
Knocked from beneath him, prone to earth he fell; 800
And as a fish, that flounders on the sand,
Thrown by rude Boreas on the weedy beach,
Till covered o'er by the returning wave;
So floundered he beneath that stunning blow.
But brave Epeius took him by the hand,   805
And raised him up; his comrades crowded round
And bore him from the field, with dragging steps,
Spitting forth clotted gore, his heavy head
Rolling from side to side; within his tent
They laid him down, unconscious; to the ring   810
Then back returning, bore away the cup.

Achilles next before the Greeks displayed
The prizes of the hardy wrestler's skill:
The victor's prize, a tripod vast, fire-proof,
And at twelve oxen by the Greeks appraised;   815
And for the vanquished man, a female slave
Priced at four oxen, skilled in household work.
Then rose, and loudly to the Greeks proclaimed,
"Stand forth, whoe'er this contest will essay."

He said; and straight uprose the giant form   820
Of Ajax Telamon: with him uprose
Ulysses, skilled in every crafty wile.

Girt with the belt, within the ring they stood,
And each, with stalwart grasp, laid hold on each;
As stand two rafters of a lofty house,   825
Each propping each, by skilful architect
Designed the tempest's fury to withstand.
Creaked their backbones beneath the tug and strain
Of those strong arms; their sweat poured down like rain;
And bloody weals of livid purple hue   830
Their sides and shoulders streaked, as sternly they
For victory and the well-wrought tripod strove.
Nor could Ulysses Ajax overthrow,
Nor Ajax bring Ulysses to the ground,
So stubbornly he stood; but when the Greeks   835
Were weary of the long-protracted strife,
Thus to Ulysses mighty Ajax spoke:
"Ulysses sage, Laertes' godlike son,
Or lift thou me, or I will thee uplift:
The issue of our struggle rests with Jove."   840
     He said, and raised Ulysses from the ground;
Nor he his ancient craft remembered not,
But locked his leg around, and striking sharp
Upon the hollow of the knee, the joint
Gave way; the giant Ajax backwards fell,   845
Ulysses on his breast; the people saw,
And marvelled. Then in turn Ulysses strove
Ajax to lift; a little way he moved,
But failed to lift him fairly from the ground;
Yet crooked his knee, that both together fell,   850
And side by side, defiled with dust, they lay.
     And now a third encounter had they tried
But rose Achilles, and the combat stayed:

"Forbear, nor waste your strength in farther strife;
Ye both are victors; both then bear away　　　　　855
An equal meed of honour; and withdraw,
That other Greeks may other contests wage."
Thus spoke Achilles; they his words obeyed,
And brushing off the dust, their garments donned.
The prizes of the runners, swift of foot,　　　　860
Achilles next set forth; a silver bowl,
Six measures its content, for workmanship
Unmatched on earth, of Sidon's costliest art
The product rare; thence o'er the misty sea
Brought by Phœnicians, who, in port arrived,　　　865
Gave it to Thoas: by Eunëus last,
The son of Jason, to Patroclus paid,
In ransom of Lycaon, Priam's son;
Which now Achilles, on his friend's behalf,
Assigned as his reward, whoe'er should prove　　　870
The lightest foot, and speediest in the race.
A steer, well fattened, was the second prize,
And half a talent, for the third, of gold.
He rose, and to the Greeks proclaimed aloud,
"Stand forth, whoe'er this contest will essay."　　875
He said: uprose Oïleus' active son;
Uprose Ulysses, skilled in every wile,
And noble Nestor's son, Antilochus,
Who all the youth in speed of foot surpassed.
They stood in line: Achilles pointed out　　　　880
The limits of the course; as from the goal
They stretched them to the race, Oïleus' son
First shot ahead; Ulysses following close;
Nor farther than the shuttle from the breast

Of some fair woman, when her outstretched arm　885
Has thrown the woof athwart the warp, and back
Withdraws it toward her breast; so close behind
Ulysses pressed on Ajax, and his feet
Trod in his steps, ere settled yet the dust.
His breath was on his shoulders, as the plain　890
He lightly skimmed; the Greeks with eager shouts
Still cheering, as he strained to win the prize.
But as they neared the goal, Ulysses thus
To blue-eyed Pallas made his mental prayer:
"Now hear me, Goddess, and my feet befriend."　895
　Thus as he prayed, his prayer the Goddess heard,
And all his limbs with active vigour filled;
And, as they stretched their hands to seize the prize,
Tripped up by Pallas, Ajax slipped and fell,
Amid the offal of the lowing kine　900
Which o'er Patroclus Peleus' son had slain.
His mouth and nostrils were with offal filled.
First in the race Ulysses bore away
The silver bowl; the steer to Ajax fell;
And as upon the horn he laid his hand,　905
Sputtering the offal out, he called aloud:
"Lo, how the Goddess has my steps bewrayed,
Who guards Ulysses with a mother's care."
Thus as he spoke, loud laughed the merry Greeks.
Antilochus the sole remaining prize　910
Received, and, laughing, thus the Greeks addressed:
　"I tell you, friends, but what yourselves do know,
How of the elder men the immortal Gods
Take special care; for Ajax' years not much
Exceed mine own; but here we see a man,　915

One of a former age, and race of men;
A hale old man we call him; but for speed
Not one can match him, save Achilles' self."
    Thus he, with praise implied of Peleus' son;
To whom in answer thus Achilles spoke :   920
"Antilochus, not unobserved of me,
Nor unrewarded shall thy praise remain :
To thy half talent add this second half."
    Thus saying, in his hand he placed the gold;
Antilochus with joy the gift received.   925
    Next, in the ring the son of Peleus' laid
A ponderous spear, a helmet, and a shield,
The spoil Patroclus from Sarpedon won;
Then rose, and loudly to the Greeks proclaimed :
"For these we call upon two champions brave   930
To don their arms, their sharp-edged weapons grasp,
And public trial of their prowess make;
And he who first his rival's flesh shall reach,
And, through his armour piercing, first draw blood,
He shall this silver-studded sword receive,   935
My trophy from Asteropæus won,
Well-wrought, of Thracian metal; but the arms
In common property they both shall hold,
And in my tent a noble banquet share."
    He said; uprose great Ajax Telamon,   940
And Tydeus' son, the valiant Diomed.
First, from the crowd apart they donned their arms;
Then, eager for the fight, with haughty stare
Stood in the midst; the Greeks admiring gazed.
When, each approaching other, near they came,   945
Thrice rushed they on, and thrice in combat closed.

Then through the buckler round of Diomed
Great Ajax drove his spear, nor reached the point
Tydides' body, by the breastplate stayed:
While, aimed above the mighty shield's defence,   950
His glittering weapon flashed at Ajax' throat.
For Ajax fearing, shouted then the Greeks
To cease the fight, and share alike the prize;
But from Achilles' hand the mighty sword,
With belt and scabbard, Diomed received.   955
    Next in the ring the son of Peleus placed
A mass of solid iron, as a quoit
Once wielded by Eëtion's giant strength,
But to the ships with other trophies borne,
When by Achilles' hand Eëtion fell.   960
Then rose, and loudly to the Greeks proclaimed:
" Stand forth, whoe'er this contest will essay.
This prize who wins, though widely may extend
His fertile fields, for five revolving years
It will his wants supply, nor to the town   965
For lack of iron, with this mass in store,
Need he his shepherd or his ploughman send."
    He said; and valiant Polypœtes rose,
Epeius, and Leonteus' godlike strength,
And mighty Ajax, son of Telamon.   970
In turns they took their stand; Epeius first
Upraised the ponderous mass, and through the air
Hurled it, amid the laughter of the Greeks.
Next came Leonteus, scion true of Mars;
The third was Ajax; from whose stalwart hand,   975
Beyond the farthest mark the missile flew.
But when the valiant Polypœtes took

The quoit in hand, far as a herdsman throws
His staff, that, whirling, flies among the herd;
So far beyond the ring's extremest bound   980
He threw the ponderous mass; loud were the shouts;
And noble Polypœtes' comrades rose,
And to the ships the monarch's gift conveyed.
    The archer's prizes next, of iron hoar,
Ten sturdy axes, doubly-edged, he placed,   985
And single hatchets ten; then far away
Reared on the sand a dark-prowed vessel's mast,
On which, with slender string, a timorous dove
Was fastened by the foot, the archers' mark;
That who should strike the dove, should to his tent   990
The axes bear away; but who the string
Should sever, but should fail to strike the bird,
As less in skill, the hatchets should receive.
    Thus spoke Achilles; straight uprose the might
Of royal Teucer, and Meriones,   995
The faithful follower of Idomeneus.
They in a brass-bound helmet shook the lots.
The first was Teuecr's; with impetuous force
He shot; but vowed not to the Archer-King
Of firstling lambs a solemn hecatomb,   1000
The dove he struck not, for the Archer-God
Withheld his aid; but close beside her foot
The arrow severed the retaining string.
The bird released, soared heavenward; while the string
Dropped, from the mast suspended, towards the earth, 1005
And loudly shouted their applause the Greeks.
Then snatched Meriones in haste the bow
From Teucer's hand; his own already held

His arrow, pointed straight; he drew the string,
And to the far-destroying King he vowed   1010
Of firstling lambs a solemn hecatomb.
Aloft amid the clouds he marked the dove,
And struck her, as she soared, beneath the wing:
Right through the arrow passed; and to the earth
Returning, fell beside Meriones.   1015
The bird upon the dark-prowed vessel's mast
Lighted awhile; anon, with drooping head,
And pinions fluttering vain, afar she fell,
Lifeless; the admiring crowd with wonder gazed.
Meriones the axes bore away,   1020
While Teucer to the ships the hatchets bore.
    Last, in the ring the son of Peleus laid
A ponderous spear, and caldron, burnished bright,
Priced at an ox's worth, untouched by fire,
For those who with the javelin would contend.   1025
Uprose then Agamemnon, King of men,
The son of Atreus, and Meriones,
The faithful follower of Idomeneus;
But Peleus' godlike son addressed them thus:
  "How far, Atrides, thou excell'st us all,   1030
And with the javelin what thy power and skill
Pre-eminent, we know; take thou this prize
And bear it to thy ships, and let us give
To brave Meriones the brazen spear;
If so it please thee, such were my advice."   1035
    He said; and Agamemnon, King of men,
Assenting, gave to brave Meriones
The brazen spear; while in Talthybius' care,
His herald, placed the King his noble prize.   1039

BOOK XXIV.

THE games were ended, and the multitude
   Amid the ships their several ways dispersed
Some to their supper, some to gentle sleep
Yielding, delighted; but Achilles still
Mourned o'er his loved companion; not on him   5
Lighted all-conquering sleep, but to and fro
Restless he tossed, and on Patroclus thought,
His vigour and his courage; all the deeds
They two together had achieved; the toils,
The perils they had undergone, amid   10
The strife of warriors, and the angry waves,
Stirred by such memories, bitter tears he shed;
Now turning on his side, and now again
Upon his back; then prone upon his face;
Then starting to his feet, along the shore   15
All objectless, despairing, would he roam;
Nor did the morn, o'er sea and shore appearing,
Unmarked of him arise; his flying steeds
He then would harness, and, behind the car
The corpse of Hector trailing in the dust,   20
Thrice make the circuit of Patroclus' tomb;
Then would he turn within his tent to rest,
Leaving the prostrate corpse with dust defiled;
But from unseemly marks the valiant dead
Apollo guarded, who with pity viewed   25

The hero, though in death; and round him threw
His golden ægis; nor, though dragged along,
Allowed his body to receive a wound.
   Thus foully did Achilles in his rage
Misuse the mighty dead; the blessed Gods   30
With pitying grief beheld the sight, and urged
That Hermes should by stealth the corpse remove.
The counsel pleased the rest; but Juno still,
And Neptune, and the blue-eyed Maid, retained
The hatred, unappeased, with which of old   35
Troy and her King and people they pursued;
Since Paris to the rival Goddesses,
Who to his sheepfold came, gave deep offence,
Preferring her who brought him in return
The fatal boon of too successful love.   40
But when the twelfth revolving day was come,
Apollo thus the assembled Gods addressed:
" Shame on ye, Gods, ungrateful! have ye not,
At Hector's hand, of bulls and choicest goats
Received your offerings meet? and fear ye now   45
E'en his dead corpse to save, and grant his wife,
His mother, and his child, his aged sire
And people, to behold him, and to raise
His funeral pile, and with due rites entomb?
But fell Achilles all your aid commands;   50
Of mind unrighteous, and inflexible
His stubborn heart; his thoughts are all of blood;
E'en as a lion, whom his mighty strength
And dauntless courage lead to leap the fold,
And 'mid the trembling flocks to seize his prey;   55
E'en so Achilles hath discarded ruth,

And conscience, arbiter of good and ill.
A man may lose his best-loved friend, a son,
Or his own mother's son, a brother dear:
He mourns and weeps, but time his grief allays,   60
For fate to man a patient mind hath given:
But godlike Hector's body, after death,
Achilles, unrelenting, foully drags,
Lashed to his car, around his comrade's tomb.
This is not to his praise; though brave he be,   65
Yet thus our anger he may justly rouse,
Who in his rage insults the senseless clay."
    To whom, indignant, white-armed Juno thus:
"Some show of reason were there in thy speech,
God of the silver-bow, could Hector boast   70
Of equal dignity with Peleus' son.
A mortal one, and nursed at woman's breast;
The other, of a Goddess born, whom I
Nurtured and reared, and to a mortal gave,
In marriage; gave to Peleus, best beloved   75
By all the Immortals, of the race of man.
Ye, Gods, attended all the marriage rites;
Thou too, companion base, false friend, wast there,
And, playing on thy lyre, didst share the feast."
    To whom the Cloud-compeller answered thus: 80
"Juno, restrain thy wrath; they shall not both
Attain like honour; yet was Hector once,
Of all the mortals that in Ilion dwell,
Dearest to all the Gods, and chief to me;
For never did he fail his gifts to bring,   85
And with burnt-offerings and libations due
My altars crown; such worship I received.

Yet shall bold Hector's body, not without
The knowledge of Achilles, be removed;
For day and night his Goddess-mother keeps   90
Her constant watch beside him. Then, some God
Bid Thetis hither to my presence haste;
And I with prudent words will counsel her,
That so Achilles may at Priam's hand
Large ransom take, and set brave Hector free."   95
    He said; and promptly on his errand sprang
The storm-swift Iris; in the dark-blue sea
She plunged, midway 'twixt Imbros' rugged shore
And Samos' isle; the parting waters plashed,
As down to ocean's lowest depths she dropped,   100
Like to a plummet, which the fisherman
Lets fall, encased in wild bull's horn, to bear
Destruction to the sea's voracious tribes.
There found she Thetis in a hollow cave,
Around her ranged the Ocean Goddesses: 105
She, in the midst, was weeping o'er the fate
Her matchless son awaiting, doomed to die
Far from his home, on fertile plains of Troy.
Swift-footed Iris at her side appeared,
And thus addressed her: "Hasten, Thetis; Jove,   110
Lord of immortal counsel, summons thee."
To whom the silver-footed Goddess thus:
"What would with me the mighty King of Heaven?
Pressed as I am with grief, I am ashamed
To mingle with the Gods; yet will I go: 115
Nor shall he speak in vain, whate'er his words."
    Thus as she spoke, her veil the Goddess took,
All black, than which none deeper could be found;

She rose to go; the storm-swift Iris led
The way before her; ocean's parted waves   120
Around their path receded; to the beach
Ascending, upwards straight to Heaven they sprang.
The all-seeing son of Saturn there they found,
And ranged around him all the immortal Gods.
Pallas made way; and by the throne of Jove   125
Sat Thetis, Juno proffering to her hand
A goblet fair of gold, and adding words
Of welcome; she the cup received, and drank.
Then thus began the sire of Gods and men:
"Thou, Thetis, sorrowing to Olympus com'st,   130
Borne down by ceaseless grief; I know it well;
Yet hear the cause for which I summoned thee.
About Achilles, thy victorious son,
And valiant Hector's body, for nine days
Hath contest been in heaven; and some have urged   135
That Hermes should by stealth the corpse remove.
This to Achilles' praise I mean to turn,
And thus thy reverence and thy love retain.
Then haste thee to the camp, and to thy son
My message bear; tell him that all the Gods   140
Are filled with wrath; and I above the rest
Am angry, that beside the beakèd ships,
He, mad with rage, the corpse of Hector keeps:
So may he fear me, and restore the dead.
Iris meantime to Priam I will send,   145
And bid him seek the Grecian ships, and there
Obtain his son's release; and with him bring
Such presents as may melt Achilles' heart."
    He said; the silver-footed Queen obeyed;

Down from Olympus' heights in haste she sped,   150
And sought her son; him found she in his tent,
Groaning with anguish, while his comrades round
Plying their tasks, prepared the morning meal.
For them a goodly sheep, full-fleeced, was slain.
Close by his side his Goddess-mother stood,   155
And gently touched him with her hand, and said,
"How long, my son, wilt thou thy soul consume
With grief and mourning, mindful nor of food
Nor sleep? nor dost thou wisely to abstain
From woman's love; for short thy time on earth: 160
Death and imperious fate are close at hand.
Hear then my words; a messenger from Jove
To thee I come, to tell thee that the Gods
Are filled with wrath, and he above the rest
Is angry, that beside the beakèd ships   165
Thou, mad with rage, the corpse of Hector keep'st.
Then ransom take, and liberate the dead."
     To whom Achilles, swift of foot, replied:
"So be it; ransom let him bring, and bear
His dead away, if such the will of Jove."   170
     Thus, in the concourse of the ships, they two,
Mother and son, their lengthened converse held.
     Then Saturn's son to Iris gave command:
"Haste thee, swift Iris, from Olympus' height,
To Troy, to royal Priam bear my words;   175
And bid him seek the Grecian ships, and there
Obtain his son's release; and with him take
Such presents as may melt Achilles' heart.
Alone, no Trojan with him, must he go;
Yet may a herald on his steps attend,   180

Some aged man, his smoothly-rolling car
And mules to drive; and to the city back
To bring his dead, whom great Achilles slew.
Nor let the fear of death disturb his mind:
Hermes shall with him, as his escort, go,   185
And to Achilles' presence safely bring.
Arrived within the tent, nor he himself
Will slay him, but from others will protect.
Not ignorant is he, nor void of sense,
Nor disobedient to the Gods' behest;   190
But will with pitying eyes his suppliant view."
    He said; and on his errand sped in haste
The storm-swift Iris; when to Priam's house
She came, the sounds of wailing met her ear.
Within the court, around their father, sat   195
His sons, their raiment all bedewed with tears;
And in the midst, close covered with his robe,
Their sire, his head and neck with dirt defiled,
Which, wallowing on the earth, himself had heaped,
With his own hands, upon his hoary head.   200
Throughout the house his daughters loudly wailed
In memory of the many and the brave
Who lay in death, by Grecian warriors slain.
Beside him stood the messenger of Jove,
And whispered, while his limbs with terror shook: 205
"Fear nothing, Priam, son of Dardanus,
Nor let thy mind be troubled; not for ill,
But here on kindly errand am I sent:
To thee I come, a messenger from Jove,
Who from on high looks down on thee with eyes 210
Of pitying love; he bids thee ransom home

The godlike Hector's corpse; and with thee take
Such presents as may melt Achilles' heart.
Alone, no Trojan with thee, must thou go;
Yet may a herald on thy steps attend,   215
Some aged man, thy smoothly-rolling car
And mules to drive, and to the city back
To bring thy dead, whom great Achilles slew.
Nor let the fear of death disturb thy mind:
Hermes shall with thee, as thine escort, go,   220
And to Achilles' presence safely bring.
Arrived within the tent, nor he himself
Will slay thee, but from others will protect;
Not ignorant is he, nor void of sense,
Nor disobedient to the Gods' behest,   225
But will with pitying eyes his suppliant view."
     Swift-footed Iris said, and vanished straight:
He to his sons commandment gave, the mules
To yoke beneath the smoothly-rolling car,
And on the axle fix the wicker seat.   230
Himself the lofty cedar-chamber sought,
Fragrant, high-roofed, with countless treasures stored;
And called to Hecuba his wife, and said,
"Good wife, a messenger from Jove hath come,
Who bids me seek the Grecian ships, and there   235
Obtain my son's release; and with me take
Such presents as may melt Achilles' heart.
Say then, what think'st thou? for my mind inclines
To seek the ships within the Grecian camp."
     So he; but Hecuba lamenting cried,   240
"Alas, alas! where are thy senses gone?
And where the wisdom, once of high repute

'Mid strangers, and 'mid those o'er whom thou reign'st ?
How canst thou think alone to seek the ships,
Entering his presence, who thy sons hath slain,   245
Many and brave ? an iron heart is thine !
Of that bloodthirsty and perfidious man,
If thou within the sight and reach shalt come,
No pity will he feel, no reverence show :
Rather remain we here apart and mourn;   250
For him, when at his birth his thread of life
Was spun by fate, 'twas destined that afar
From home and parents he should glut the maw
Of ravening dogs, by that stern warrior's tent,
Whose inmost heart I would I could devour :   255
Such for my son were adequate revenge,
Whom not in ignominious flight he slew;
But standing, thoughtless of escape or flight,
For Trojan men and Troy's deep-bosomed dames."
    To whom in answer Priam, godlike sire :   260
" Seek not to hinder me; nor be thyself
A bird of evil omen in my house;
For thou shalt not persuade me. If indeed
This message had been brought by mortal man,
Prophet, or seer, or sacrificing priest,   265
I should have deemed it false, and laughed to scorn
The idle tale; but now (for I myself
Both saw and heard the Goddess) I must go;
Nor unfulfilled shall be the words I speak :
And if indeed it be my fate to die   270
Beside the vessels of the brass-clad Greeks,
I am content! by fierce Achilles' hand
Let me be slain, so once more in my arms

I hold my boy, and give my sorrow vent."
Then raising up the coffer's polished lid,   275
He chose twelve gorgeous shawls, twelve single cloaks,
As many rugs, as many splendid robes,
As many tunics; then of gold he took
Ten talents full; two tripods, burnished bright,
Four caldrons; then a cup of beauty rare,   280
A rich possession, which the men of Thrace
Had given, when there he went ambassador;
E'en this he spared not, such his keen desire
His son to ransom. From the corridor
With angry words he drove the Trojans all: 285
    "Out with ye, worthless rascals, vagabonds!
Have ye no griefs at home, that here ye come
To pester me? or is it not enough
That Jove with deep affliction visits me,
Slaying my bravest son? ye to your cost   290
Shall know his loss: since now that he is gone,
The Greeks shall find you easier far to slay.
But may my eyes be clothed in death, ere see
The city sacked, and utterly destroyed."
    He said, and with his staff drove out the crowd; 295
Before the old man's anger fled they all;
Then to his sons in threatening tone he cried;
To Paris, Helenus, and Agathon,
Pammon, Antiphonus, Polites brave,
Deiphobus, and bold Hippothöus,   300
And godlike Dius; all these nine with threats
And angry taunts the aged sire assailed:
"Haste, worthless sons, my scandal and my shame!
Would that ye all beside the Grecian ships

In Hector's stead had died! Oh woe is me,   305
Who have begotten sons, in all the land
The best and bravest; now remains not one;
Mestor, and Troïlus, dauntless charioteer,
And Hector, who a God 'mid men appeared,
Nor like a mortal's offspring, but a God's: 310
All these hath Mars cut off; and left me none,
None but the vile and refuse; liars all,
Vain skipping coxcombs, in the dance alone,
And in nought else renowned; base plunderers,
From their own countrymen, of lambs and kids.   315
When, laggards, will ye harness me the car
Equipped with all things needed for the way?"
    He said; they quailed beneath their father's wrath,
And brought the smoothly-running mule-wain out,
Well-framed, new-built; and fixed the wicker-seat; 320
Then from the peg the mule-yoke down they took,
Of boxwood wrought, with boss and rings complete;
And with the yoke, the yoke-band brought they forth,
Nine cubits long; and to the polished pole
At the far end attached; the breast-rings then   325
Fixed to the pole-piece; and on either side
Thrice round the knob the leathern thong they wound,
And bound it fast, and inward turned the tongue.
Then the rich ransom, from the chambers brought,
Of Hector's head, upon the wain they piled;   330
And yoked the strong-hoofed mules, to harness trained,
The Mysians' splendid present to the King:
To Priam's car they harnessed then the steeds,
Which he himself at polished manger fed.
    Deep thoughts revolving, in the lofty halls   335

Were met the herald and the aged King,
When Hecuba with troubled mind drew near;
In her right hand a golden cup she bore
Of luscious wine, that ere they took their way
They to the Gods might due libations pour;   340
Before the car she stood, and thus she spoke:
"Take, and to father Jove thine offering pour,
And pray that he may bring thee safely home
From all thy foes; since sore against my will
Thou needs wilt venture to the ships of Greece.   345
Then to Idæan Jove, the cloud-girt son
Of Saturn, who the expanse of Troy surveys,
Prefer thy prayer, beseeching him to send,
On thy right hand, a wingèd messenger,
The bird he loves the best, of strongest flight;   350
That thou thyself mayst see and know the sign,
And, firm in faith, approach the ships of Greece.
But should all-seeing Jove the sign withhold,
Then not with my consent shouldst thou attempt,
Whate'er thy wish, to reach the Grecian ships."   355
    To whom, in answer, godlike Priam thus:
"O woman, I refuse not to obey
Thy counsel; good it is to raise the hands
In prayer to Heaven, and Jove's protection seek."
The old man said; and bade the attendant pour   360
Pure water on his hands; with ewer she,
And basin, stood beside him: from his wife,
The due ablutions made, he took the cup;
Then in the centre of the court he stood,
And as he poured the wine, looked up to Heaven, 365
And thus with voice uplifted prayed aloud:

"O father Jove, who rul'st on Ida's height,
Most great, most glorious! grant that I may find
Some pity in Achilles' heart; and send,
On my right hand, a wingèd messenger,   370
The bird thou lov'st the best, of strongest flight,
That I myself may see and know the sign,
And, firm in faith, approach the ships of Greece."
     Thus as he prayed, the Lord of counsel heard;
And sent forthwith an eagle, feathered king,   375
Dark bird of chase, and Dusky thence surnamed:
Wide as the portals, well secured with bolts,
That guard some wealthy monarch's lofty hall,
On either side his ample pinions spread.
On the right hand appeared he, far above   380
The city soaring; they the favouring sign
With joy beheld, and every heart was cheered.
Mounting his car in haste, the aged King
Drove through the court, and through the echoing porch,
The mules in front, by sage Idæus driven,   385
That drew the four-wheeled wain; behind them came
The horses, down the city's steep descent
Urged by the old man to speed; the crowd of friends
That followed mourned for him, as doomed to death.
Descended from the city to the plain,   390
His sons and sons-in-law to Ilion took
Their homeward way; advancing o'er the plain
They two escaped not Jove's all-seeing eye;
Pitying he saw the aged sire; and thus
At once to Hermes spoke, his much-loved son: 395
"Hermes, for thou in social converse lov'st
To mix with men, and hear'st whome'er thou wilt;

Haste thee, and Priam to the Grecian ships
So lead, that none of all the Greeks may see
Ere to Achilles' presence he attain."　　400
　　He said; nor disobeyed the heavenly Guide;
His golden sandals on his feet he bound,
Ambrosial work; which bore him o'er the waves,
Swift as the wind, and o'er the wide-spread earth;
Then took his rod, wherewith he seals at will　　405
The eyes of men, and wakes again from sleep.
This in his hand he bore, and sprang for flight.
Soon the wide Hellespont he reached, and Troy,
And passed in likeness of a princely youth,
In opening manhood, fairest term of life.　　410
　　The twain had passed by Ilus' lofty tomb,
And halted there the horses and the mules
Beside the margin of the stream to drink;
For darkness now was creeping o'er the earth.
When through the gloom the herald Hermes saw　　415
Approaching near, to Priam thus he cried:
"O son of Dardanus, bethink thee well;
Of prudent counsel great is now our need.
A man I see, and fear he means us ill.
Say, with the horses shall we fly at once,　　420
Or clasp his knees, and for his mercy sue?"
The old man heard, his mind confused with dread;
So grievously he feared, that every hair
Upon his bended limbs did stand on end;
He stood astounded; but the Guardian-God　　425
Approached, and took him by the hand, and said:
"Where, father, goest thou thus with horse and mule
In the still night, when men are sunk in sleep?

And fear'st thou not the slaughter-breathing Greeks,
Thine unrelenting foes, and they so near?   430
If any one of them should see thee now,
So richly laden in the gloom of night,
How wouldst thou feel? thou art not young thyself,
And this old man, thy comrade, would avail
But little to protect thee from assault.   435
I will not harm thee, nay will shield from harm,
For like my father's is, methinks, thy face."
    To whom in answer Priam, godlike sire:
" 'Tis as thou say'st, fair son; yet hath some God
Extended o'er me his protecting hand,   440
Who sends me such a guide, so opportune.
Blessed are thy parents in a son so graced
In face and presence, and of mind so wise."
    To whom in answer thus the Guardian-God:
"O father, well and wisely dost thou speak;   445
But tell me this, and truly: dost thou bear
These wealthy treasures to some foreign land,
That they for thee in safety may be stored?
Or have ye all resolved to fly from Troy
In fear, your bravest slain, thy gallant son,   450
Who never from the Greeks' encounter flinched?"
    To whom in answer Priam, godlike sire:
"Who art thou, noble Sir, and what thy race,
That speak'st thus fairly of my hapless son?"
    To whom in answer thus the Guardian-God: 455
"Try me, old man; of godlike Hector ask;
For often in the glory-giving fight
These eyes have seen him; chief, when to the ships
The Greeks he drove, and with the sword destroyed.

We gazed in wonder; from the fight restrained　　460
By Peleus' son, with Agamemnon wroth.
His follower I; one ship conveyed us both;
One of the Myrmidons I am; my sire
Polyctor, rich, but aged, e'en as thou.
Six sons he hath, besides myself, the seventh;　　465
And I by lot was drafted for the war.
I from the ships am to the plain come forth;
For with the dawn of day the keen-eyed Greeks
Will round the city marshal their array.
They chafe in idleness; the chiefs in vain　　470
Strive to restrain their ardour for the fight."
　To whom in answer Priam, godlike sire:
"If of Achilles, Peleus' son, thou art
Indeed a follower, tell me all the truth;
Lies yet my son beside the Grecian ships,　　475
Or hath Achilles torn him limb from limb,
And to his dogs the mangled carcase given?"
　To whom in answer thus the Guardian-God:
"On him, old man, nor dogs nor birds have fed,
But by the ship of Peleus' son he lies　　480
Within the tent; twelve days he there hath lain,
Nor hath corruption touched his flesh, nor worms,
That wont to prey on men in battle slain.
The corpse, indeed, with each returning morn,
Around his comrade's tomb Achilles drags,　　485
Yet leaves it still uninjured; thou thyself
Mightst see how fresh, as dew-besprent, he lies,
From blood-stains cleansed, and closed his many wounds,
For many a lance was buried in his corpse.
So, e'en in death, the blessed Gods above,　　490

Who loved him well, protect thy noble son."

He said; the old man rejoicing heard his words,
And answered, "See, my son, how good it is
To give the immortal Gods their tribute due;
For never did my son, while yet he lived,   495
Neglect the Gods who on Olympus dwell;
And thence have they remembered him in death.
Accept, I pray, this goblet rich-embossed;
Be thou my guard, and, under Heaven, my guide,
Until I reach the tent of Peleus' son."   500
To whom in answer thus the Guardian-God:
"Old father, me thy younger wouldst thou tempt,
In vain; who bidd'st me at thy hands accept
Thy proffered presents, to Achilles' wrong.
I dread his anger; and should hold it shame   505
To plunder him, through fear of future ill.
But, as thy guide, I could conduct thee safe,
As far as Argos, journeying by thy side,
On ship-board or on foot; nor by the fault
Of thy conductor shouldst thou meet with harm."   510
Thus spoke the Guardian-God, and on the car
Mounting in haste, he took the whip and reins,
And with fresh vigour mules and horses filled.
When to the ship-towers and the trench they came,
The guard had late been busied with their meal;   515
And with deep sleep the heavenly Guide o'erspread
The eyes of all; then opened wide the gates,
And pushed aside the bolts, and led within
Both Priam and the treasure-laden wain.
But when they reached Achilles' lofty tent,   520
(Which for their King the Myrmidons had built

Of fir-trees felled, and overlaid the roof
With rushes mown from off the neighbouring mead;
And all around a spacious court enclosed
With cross-set palisades; a single bar   525
Of fir the gateway guarded, which to shut
Three men, of all the others, scarce sufficed,
And three to open; but Achilles' hand
Unaided shut with ease the massive bar)
Then for the old man Hermes oped the gate,   530
And brought within the court the gifts designed
For Peleus' godlike son; then from the car
Sprang to the ground, and thus to Priam spoke:
"Old man, a God hath hither been thy guide;
Hermes I am, and sent to thee from Jove,   535
Father of all, to bring thee safely here.
I now return, nor to Achilles' eyes
Will I appear; beseems it not a God
To greet a mortal in the sight of all.
But go thou in, and clasp Achilles' knees,   540
And supplicate him for his father's sake,
His fair-haired mother's, and his child's, that so
Thy words may stir an answer in his heart."
    Thus saying, Hermes to Olympus' heights
Returned; and Priam from his chariot sprang,   545
And left Idæus there, in charge to keep
The horses and the mules, while he himself
Entered the dwelling straight, where wont to sit
Achilles, loved of Heaven. The chief he found
Within, his followers seated all apart;   550
Two only in his presence ministered,
The brave Automedon, and Alcimus,

A warrior bold; scarce ended the repast
Of food and wine; the table still was set.
Great Priam entered, unperceived of all;   555
And standing by Achilles, with his arms
Embraced his knees, and kissed those fearful hands,
Blood-stained, which many of his sons had slain.
As when a man, by cruel fate pursued,
In his own land hath shed another's blood,   560
And flying, seeks beneath some wealthy house
A foreign refuge; wondering, all behold:
On godlike Priam so with wonder gazed
Achilles; wonder seized the attendants all,
And one to other looked; then Priam thus   565
To Peleus' son his suppliant speech addressed:
"Think, great Achilles, rival of the Gods,
Upon thy father, e'en as I myself
Upon the threshold of unjoyous age:
And haply he, from them that dwell around   570
May suffer wrong, with no protector near
To give him aid; yet he, rejoicing, knows
That thou still liv'st; and day by day may hope
To see his son returning safe from Troy;
While I, all hapless, that have many sons,   575
The best and bravest through the breadth of Troy,
Begotten, deem that none are left me now.
Fifty there were, when came the sons of Greece;
Nineteen the offspring of a single womb;
The rest, the women of my household bore.   580
Of these have many by relentless Mars
Been laid in dust; but he, my only one,
The city's and his brethren's sole defence,

He, bravely fighting in his country's cause,
Hector, but lately by thy hand hath fallen : 585
On his behalf I venture to approach
The Grecian ships ; for his release to thee
To make my prayer, and priceless ransom pay.
Then thou, Achilles, reverence the Gods ;
And, for thy father's sake, look pitying down 590
On me, more needing pity ; since I bear
Such grief as never man on earth hath borne,
Who stoop to kiss the hand that slew my son."
  Thus as he spoke, within Achilles' breast
Fond memory of his father rose ; he touched 595
The old man's hand, and gently put him by ;
Then wept they both, by various memories stirred :
One, prostrate at Achilles' feet, bewailed
His warrior son ; Achilles for his sire,
And for Patroclus wept, his comrade dear ; 600
And through the house their weeping loud was heard.
But when Achilles had indulged his grief,
And eased the yearning of his heart and limbs,
Uprising, with his hand the aged sire,
Pitying his hoary head and hoary beard, 605
He raised, and thus with gentle words addressed :
  " Alas, what sorrows, poor old man, are thine !
How couldst thou venture to the Grecian ships
Alone, and to the presence of the man
Whose hand hath slain so many of thy sons, 610
Many and brave ? an iron heart is thine !
But sit thou on this seat ; and in our hearts,
Though filled with grief, let us that grief suppress ;
For woful lamentation nought avails.

Such is the thread the Gods for mortals spin,   615
To live in woe, while they from cares are free.
Two coffers lie beside the door of Jove,
With gifts for man : one good, the other ill ;
To whom from each the Lord of lightning gives,
Him sometimes evil, sometimes good befalls ;   620
To whom the ill alone, him foul disgrace
And grinding misery o'er the earth pursue :
By God and man alike despised he roams.
Thus from his birth the Gods to Peleus gave
Excellent gifts ; with wealth and substance blessed 625
Above his fellows ; o'er the Myrmidons
He ruled with sovereign sway ; and Heaven bestowed
On him, a mortal, an immortal bride.
Yet this of ill was mingled in his lot,
That in his house no rising race he saw   630
Of future Kings ; one only son he had,
One doomed to early death ; nor is it mine
To tend my father's age ; but far from home
Thee and thy sons in Troy I vex with war.
Much have we heard too of thy former wealth ;   635
Above what Lesbos northward, Macar's seat,
Contains, and Upper Phrygia, and the shores
Of boundless Hellespont, 'tis said that thou
In wealth and number of thy sons wast blessed.
But since on thee this curse the Gods have brought,   640
Still round thy city war and slaughter rage.
Bear up, nor thus with grief incessant mourn ;
Vain is thy sorrow for thy gallant son ;
Thou canst not raise him, and mayst suffer more."
     To whom in answer Priam, godlike sire :   645

" Tell me not yet, illustrious chief, to sit,
While Hector lies, uncared for, in the tent;
But let me quickly go, that with mine eyes
I may behold my son; and thou accept
The ample treasures which we tender thee :   650
Mayst thou enjoy them, and in safety reach
Thy native land, since thou hast spared my life,
And bidd'st me still behold the light of Heaven."
    To whom Achilles thus with stern regard :
" Old man, incense me not; I mean myself   655
To give thee back thy son; for here of late
Despatched by Jove, my Goddess-mother came,
The daughter of the aged Ocean-God :
And thee too, Priam, well I know, some God
(I cannot err) hath guided to our ships.   660
No mortal, though in venturous youth, would dare
Our camp to enter; nor could hope to pass
Unnoticed by the watch, nor easily
Remove the ponderous bar that guards our doors.
But stir not up my anger in my grief;   665
Lest, suppliant though thou be, within my tent
I brook thee not, and Jove's command transgress."
    He said; the old man trembled, and obeyed;
Then to the door-way, with a lion's spring,
Achilles rushed; not unaccompanied;   670
With him Automedon and Alcimus,
His two attendants, of his followers all,
Next to the lost Patroclus, best-esteemed;
They from the yoke the mules and horses loosed;
Then led the herald of the old man in,   675
And bade him sit; and from the polished wain

The costly ransom took of Hector's head.
Two robes they left, and one well-woven vest,
To clothe the corpse, and send with honour home.
Then to the female slaves he gave command　　680
To wash the body, and anoint with oil,
Apart, that Priam might not see his son;
Lest his grieved heart its passion unrestrained
Should utter, and Achilles, roused to wrath,
His suppliant slay, and Jove's command transgress.　685
When they had washed the body, and with oil
Anointed, and around it wrapped the robe
And vest, Achilles lifted up the dead
With his own hands, and laid him on the couch;
Which to the polished wain his followers raised.　　690
Then groaning, on his friend by name he called:
"Forgive, Patroclus! be not wroth with me,
If in the realm of darkness thou shouldst hear
That godlike Hector to his father's arms,
For no mean ransom, I restore; whereof　　695
A fitting share for thee I set aside."
　This said, Achilles to the tent returned;
On the carved couch, from whence he rose, he sat
Beside the wall; and thus to Priam spoke:
　"Old man, thy son, according to thy prayer,　　700
Is given thee back; upon the couch he lies;
Thyself shalt see him at the dawn of day.
Meanwhile the evening meal demands our care.
Not fair-haired Niobe abstained from food,
When in the house her children lay in death,　　705
Six beauteous daughters and six stalwart sons.
The youths, Apollo with his silver bow,

The maids, the Archer-Queen, Diana, slew,
With anger filled that Niobe presumed
Herself with fair Latona to compare,   710
Her many children with her rival's two;
So by the two were all the many slain.
Nine days in death they lay; and none was there
To pay their funeral rites; for Saturn's son
Had given to all the people hearts of stone.   715
The tenth, the immortal Gods entombed the dead.
Nor yet did Niobe, when now her grief
Had worn itself in tears, from food refrain.
And now in Sipylus, amid the rocks,
And lonely mountains, where the Goddess nymphs 720
That love to dance by Achelöus' stream,
'Tis said, were cradled, she, though turned to stone,
Broods o'er the wrongs inflicted by the Gods.
So we too, godlike sire, the meal may share;
And later, thou thy noble son mayst mourn,   725
To Troy restored—well worthy he thy tears."
    This said, he slaughtered straight a white-fleeced sheep;
His comrades then the carcase flayed and dressed:
The meat prepared, and fastened to the spits;
Roasted with care, and from the fire withdrew.   730
The bread Automedon from baskets fair
Apportioned out; the meat Achilles shared.
They to the food prepared their hands addressed.
But when their thirst and hunger were appeased,
In wonder Priam on Achilles gazed,   735
His form and stature; as a God he seemed;
And he too looked on Priam, and admired
His venerable face, and gracious speech.

With mutual pleasure each on other gazed,
Till godlike Priam first addressed his host :   740
  "Dismiss me now, illustrious chief, to rest;
And lie we down, in gentle slumbers wrapped ;
For never have mine eyes been closed in sleep,
Since by thy hand my gallant son was slain :
But groaning still, I brood upon my woes,   745
And in my court with dust my head defile.
Now have I tasted bread, now ruddy wine
Hath o'er my palate passed ; but not till now."
  Thus he ; his comrades and the attendant maids
Achilles ordered in the corridor   750
Two mattresses to place, with blankets fair
Of purple wool o'erlaid ; and on the top
Rugs and soft sheets for upper covering spread.
They from the chamber, torch in hand, withdrew,
And with obedient haste two beds prepared.   755
Then thus Achilles spoke in jesting tone :
  "Thou needs must sleep without, my good old friend;
Lest any leader of the Greeks should come,
As is their custom, to confer with me ;
Of them whoe'er should find thee here by night   760
Forthwith to Agamemnon would report,
And Hector might not be so soon restored.
But tell me truly this ; how many days
For godlike Hector's funeral rites ye need;
That for so long a time I may myself   765
Refrain from combat, and the people stay."
  To whom in answer Priam, godlike sire ·
  "If by thy leave we may indeed perform
His funeral rites, to thee, Achilles, great

Will be our gratitude, if this thou grant.   770
Thou know'st how close the town is hemmed around;
And from the mountain, distant as it is,
The Trojans well may fear to draw the wood.
Nine days to public mourning would we give;
The tenth, to funeral rites and funeral feast;   775
Then on the eleventh would we raise his mound;
The twelfth, renew the war, if needs we must."
    To whom Achilles swift of foot replied:
"So shall it be, old Priam; I engage
To stay the battle for the time required."   780
    Thus speaking, with his hand the old man's wrist
He grasped, in token that he need not fear.
Then in the corridor lay down to rest
Old Priam and the herald, Elders sage;
While in his tent's recess Achilles slept,   785
The fair Briseïs resting by his side.
    In night-long slumbers lay the other Gods,
And helmèd chiefs, by gentle sleep subdued;
But on the eyes of Hermes, Guardian-God,
No slumber fell, deep pondering in his mind   790
How from the ships in safety to conduct
The royal Priam, and the guard elude.
Above the sleeper's head he stood, and cried:
"Old man, small heed thou tak'st of coming ill,
Who, when Achilles gives thee leave to go,   795
Sleep'st undisturbed, surrounded by thy foes.
Thy son hath been restored, and thou hast paid
A generous price; but to redeem thy life,
If Agamemnon and the other Greeks
Should know that thou art here, full thrice so much   800

Thy sons, who yet are left, would have to pay."
  He said; the old man trembled, and aroused
The herald; while the horses and the mules
Were yoked by Hermes, who with silent speed
Drove through the encampment, unobserved of all. 805
But when they came to eddying Xanthus' ford,
Fair-flowing stream, born of immortal Jove,
To high Olympus Hermes took his flight,
As morn, in saffron robe, o'er all the earth
Was light diffusing; they with funeral wail   810
Drove cityward the horses; following came
The mules that drew the litter of the dead.
The plain they traversed o'er, observed of none,
Or man or woman, till Cassandra, fair
As golden Venus, from the topmost height   815
Of Pergamus, her father in his car
Upstanding saw, the herald at his side.
Him too she saw, who on the litter lay;
Then lifted up her voice, and cried aloud
To all the city, "Hither, Trojans, come,   820
Both men and women, Hector see restored;
If, while he lived, returning from the fight,
Ye met him e'er rejoicing, who indeed
Was all the city's chiefest joy and pride."
  She said: nor man nor woman then was left   825
Within the city; o'er the minds of all
Grief passed, resistless; to the gates in throngs
They pressed, to crowd round him who brought the dead.
The first to clasp the body were his wife
And honoured mother; eagerly they sprang   830
On the smooth-rolling wain, to touch the head

Of Hector; round them, weeping, stood the crowd.
Weeping, till sunset, all the live-long day
Had they before the gates for Hector mourned;
Had not old Priam from the car addressed   835
The crowd: "Make way, that so the mules may pass;
When to my house I shall have brought my dead,
Ye there may vent your sorrow as ye will."
    Thus as he spoke, obedient to his word
They stood aside, and for the car made way: 840
But when to Priam's lordly house they came,
They laid him on a rich-wrought couch, and called
The minstrels in, who by the hero's bed
Should lead the melancholy chorus; they
Poured forth the music of the mournful dirge,   845
While women's voices joined in loud lament.
White-armed Andromache the wail began,
The head of Hector clasping in her hands:
"My husband, thou art gone in pride of youth,
And in thine house hast left me desolate;   850
Thy child an infant still, thy child and mine,
Unhappy parents both! nor dare I hope
That he may reach the ripeness of his youth;
For ere that day shall Troy in ruin fall,
Since thou art gone, her guardian! thou whose arm 855
Defended her, her wives, and helpless babes!
They now shall shortly o'er the sea be borne,
And with them I shall go; thou too, my child,
Must follow me, to servile labour doomed,
The suffering victim of a tyrant Lord;   860
Unless perchance some angry Greek may seize
And dash thee from the tower—a woful death!

Whose brother, or whose father, or whose son
By Hector hath been slain; for many a Greek
By Hector's hand hath bit the bloody dust;   865
Not light in battle was thy father's arm;
Therefore for him the general city mourns;
Thou to thy parents bitter grief hast caused,
Hector! but bitterest grief of all hast left
To me! for not to me was given to clasp   870
The hand extended from thy dying bed,
Nor words of wisdom catch, which night and day,
With tears, I might have treasured in my heart."
  Weeping she spoke—the women joined the wail.
Then Hecuba took up the loud lament: 875
"Hector, of all my children dearest thou!
Dear to the Immortals too in life wast thou,
And they in death have borne thee still in mind;
For other of my sons, his captives made,
Across the watery waste, to Samos' isle   880
Or Imbros, or the inhospitable shore
Of Lemnos, hath Achilles, swift of foot,
To slavery sold; thee, when his sharp-edged spear
Had robbed thee of thy life, he dragged indeed
Around Patroclus' tomb, his comrade dear,   885
Whom thou hadst slain; yet so he raised not up
His dead to life again; now liest thou here,
All fresh and fair, as dew-besprent; like one
Whom bright Apollo, with his arrows keen,
God of the silver bow, hath newly slain."   890
  Weeping, she spoke; and roused the general grief.
Then Helen, third, the mournful strain renewed:
"Hector, of all my brethren dearest thou;

True, godlike Paris claims me as his wife,
Who bore me hither—would I then had died!   895
But twenty years have passed since here I came,
And left my native land; yet ne'er from thee
I heard one scornful, one degrading word;
And when from others I have borne reproach,
Thy brothers, sisters, or thy brothers' wives,   900
Or mother (for thy sire was ever kind
E'en as a father), thou hast checked them still
With tender feeling, and with gentle words.
For thee I weep, and for myself no less;
For, through the breadth of Troy, none love me now, 905
None kindly look on me, but all abhor."

Weeping she spoke, and with her wept the crowd.
At length the aged Priam gave command:
" Haste now, ye Trojans, to the city bring
Good store of fuel; fear no treacherous wile;   910
For when he sent me from the dark-ribbed ships,
Achilles promised that from hostile arms
Till the twelfth morn we should no harm sustain."

He said; and they the oxen and the mules
Yoked to the wains, and from the city thronged: 915
Nine days they laboured, and brought back to Troy
Good store of wood; but when the tenth day's light
Upon the earth appeared, weeping, they bore
Brave Hector out; and on the funeral pile
Laying the glorious dead, applied the torch.   920

While yet the rosy-fingered morn was young
Round noble Hector's pyre the people pressed:
When all were gathered round, and closely thronged,
First on the burning mass, as far as spread

The range of fire, they poured the ruddy wine,   925
And quenched the flames: his brethren then and friends
Weeping, the hot tears flowing down their cheeks,
Collected from the pile the whitened bones;
These in a golden casket they enclosed,
And o'er it spread soft shawls of purple dye;   930
Then in a grave they laid it, and in haste
With stone in ponderous masses covered o'er;
And raised a mound, and watched on every side,
From sudden inroad of the Greeks to guard.
The mound erected, back they turned; and all   935
Assembled duly, shared the solemn feast
In Priam's palace, Heaven-descended King.
      Such were the rites to glorious Hector paid.   938

END OF THE ILIAD.

TRANSLATIONS.

FROM THE GREEK.

ANACREON.

Od. 1.

ATREUS' Sons I fain would sing .
Fain to Cadmus touch the string;
But my lyre no theme will own,
Save the theme of Love alone.
All the chords I late withdrew,   5
And my lyre I strung anew;
Then essayed, in lofty strain,
Great Alcides' praise—in vain!
For my lyre's responsive tone
Gave back notes of Love alone.   10
Heroes all, farewell! with you,
Henceforth, I have nought to do;
For my lyre no theme will own,
Save the theme of Love alone.

Od. 3.

AT the hour of deep midnight,
When the star of Arctos bright
Wheels beneath Boötes' hand;
And, throughout the drowsy land,
Sleep its gentle influence sheds   5
On o'erwearied mortals' heads;
Cupid stood my gate before,
Knocking at the bolted door.

"Who," I cried, "is he who shakes
Thus my door—my slumber breaks?"   10
"Open quick, be not afraid,
'Tis a Child that knocks," he said:
"In the moonless night astray,
Wet and cold, I've lost my way."
I with pity heard, and straight   15
Lit my lamp, unbarred my gate;
And a Child indeed was there,
Who a bow and quiver bare.
By my hearth I made him stand;
Chafed with mine each icy hand,   20
Wringing from his hair the rain.
Soon restored to warmth again,
"Come," he said, "I fain would know
If the wet have marred my bow."
Straight he aimed, and through my heart   25
Shot, as 'twere a gadfly's smart.
Up then leaped the laughing Boy;
"Host," he chuckled, "share my joy;
All uninjured is my bow,
As by proof thy heart shall know."   30

Qd. 11.

"Thou'rt old, Anacreon," say the girls;
"Take thy mirror, and look for thy curls,
And see thy forehead all bald and bare."
Whether or no the curls be there,
I know not, and care not; this I know,   5
That year by year, as older we grow,
'Tis reason the more to be joyous and gay,
As nearer we draw to our closing day.

FROM THE LATIN.

HORACE.

Od. i. 4.

STERN Winter melts as genial airs the balmy Spring
    restore,
    And keels, long dry, are carried to the shore;
The ploughman now the fireside leaves, nor herds in stalls
    remain,
    Nor hoar-frost glitters o'er the whitened plain;
And Venus now by moonlight leads her revelry and mirth,   5
    And Nymphs, with Graces mingling, make the earth
Ring with the music of their feet; while with his Cyclops
    train,
    At sweltering forge, stout Vulcan toils amain.
Our glossy hair should now with wreaths of myrtle green
    be bound,
    Or flowers new-burst from out the loosened ground.   10
And now the wonted sacrifice, beneath the forest's shade,
    Of lamb or kid, to Faunus should be paid.
Pale Death upon the peasant's door and prince's lordly gate
    Impartial knocks.   O Sextius, rich and great!

SOLVITUR acris hiems grata vice veris et Favoni,
    Trahuntque siccas machinæ carinas;
Ac neque jam stabulis gaudet pecus, aut arator igni;
    Nec prata canis albicant pruinis.
Jam Cytherea choros ducit Venus imminente Luna;   5
    Junctæque Nymphis Gratiæ decentes
Alterno terram quatiunt pede; dum graves Cyclopum
    Vulcanus ardens urit officinas.
Nunc decet aut viridi nitidum caput impedire myrto,
    Aut flore, terræ quem ferunt solutæ.   10
Nunc et in umbrosis Fauno decet immolare lucis,
    Seu poscat agna, sive mallt hædo.
Pallida mors æquo pulsat pede pauperum tabernas,
    Regumque turres. O beate Sexti,

Our life's short span should moderate our lengthened hope's
　　excess;
　　Round thee shall Night and bodiless Phantoms press　16
Ere long in Pluto's meagre halls, where ne'er at festive board
Shalt thou by lot be crowned the banquet's Lord.

Vitæ summa brevis spem nos vetat inchoare longam.　　　15
　　Jam te premet nox, fabulæque manes,
Et domus exilis Plutonia; quo simul meâris,
　　Nec regna vini sortiere talis;
Nec tenerum Lycidam mirabere, quo calet juventus
　　Nunc omnis, et mox virgines tepebunt.　　　20

Od. i. 5.

What slender youth, on rosy couch reclining,
Breathing sweet odours, courts thee, Pyrrha, now
Beneath some pleasant grot?　For whom dost thou,
With simple grace thy golden tresses twining,

Put forth thy beauty?　Ah, how oft shall he　　　5
Thy broken faith, and Gods estranged, bewail;
And see, aghast, beneath the darkling gale,
The unwonted ruffle of the angry sea,

Quis multa gracilis te puer in rosa
Perfusus liquidis urget odoribus
Grato, Pyrrha, sub antro?
Cui flavam religas comam,

　　Simplex munditiis?　Heu, quoties fidem,　　　5
Mutatosque Deos flebit, et aspera
Nigris æquora ventis
Emirabitur insolens,

Who now, confiding, revels in thy charms,
Deeming thee purest gold! and hopes that thou   10
Shalt still remain as he beholds thee now,
As kind, as open to his longing arms,

Nor knows the breeze how fickle! Hapless those
On whom thou shin'st untried! To Ocean's King
How I, escaped, my dripping garments bring,   15
On Neptune's wall my votive tablet shows.

Qui nunc te fruitur credulus aurea,
Qui semper vacuam, semper amabilem   10
Sperat, nescius aurae
Fallacis! Miseri quibus

Intentata nites. Me tabula sacer
Votiva paries indicat uvida
Suspendisse potenti   15
Vestimenta maris Deo.

Od. i. 8.

Lydia, by all the Gods above,
Why Sybaris destroy with fatal love?
    Why now the Campus does he shun,
Unshrinking once from dust and scorching sun?
    Why now no more, in martial pride,   5
Among his youthful comrades does he ride,
    Curbing his fiery Gallic horse?
Why fear with active limb to stem the force
    Of yellow Tiber's swollen flood?
Why, with abhorrence as of viper's blood,   10

Lydia dic, per omnes
Te deos oro, Sybarin cur properes amando
    Perdere? cur apricum
Oderit campum, patiens pulveris atque solis?
    Cur neque militaris   5
Inter æquales equitat, Gallica nec lupatis
    Temperat ora frænis?
Cur timet flavum Tiberim tangere? cur olivum
    Sanguine viperino
Cautius vitat? neque jam livida gestat armis   10

The lubricating oil refuse?
Why leave no weapons now their livid bruise
  On arms, which oft the discus round
Or javelin hurled beyond the extremest bound?
  Why lurks he now, as erst, they say,   15
When near approached proud Ilion's fatal day,
  The son of Thetis lurked, amid
The train of virgins, ignominious, hid,
  Lest, by his manly garb betrayed,
The toils of war should claim the seeming maid?   20

    Brachia, sæpe disco,
Sæpe trans finem jaculo nobilis expedito?
    Quid latet, ut marinæ
Filium dicunt Thetidis sub lacrimosa Trojæ
    Funera, ne virilis   15
Cultus in cædem et Lycias proriperet catervas?

Od. i. 9.

SEE where Soracte stands, his brow
White with deep snow; the labouring woods
Beneath the unwonted burthen bow;
And stay their course the ice-bound floods.

Pile, Thaliarchus, pile on high   5
The blazing logs, and mock at cold:
This generous flagon freely ply
Of Sabine vintage four years old.

VIDES, ut alta stet nive candidum
Soracte, nec jam sustineant onus
  Silvæ laborantes, geluque
    Flumina constiterint acuto.

Dissolve frigus, ligna super foco   5
Large reponens: atque benignius
  Deprome quadrimum Sabina,
    O Thaliarche, merum diota.

Leave to the Gods all else: when they
Compose the warring winds and seas, 10
The cypress bough, the ashen spray,
No longer quiver in the breeze.

Think for the morrow nought; enjoy
Each day the boons bestowed by chance;
Nor rudely spurn, too happy boy, 15
Or love's delights, or joyous dance,

Ere crabbed age have bleached thy brow.
The Campus now may claim thy care,
The gay promenade, the whispered vow,
At twilight breathed to willing fair; 20

And tell-tale laugh of merry maid
In corner hid; and slender wrist
Of bracelet spoiled, or ring conveyed
From fingers that but half resist.

Permitte divis cætera; qui simul
Stravere ventos æquore fervido 10
 Deprœliantes; nec cupressi,
  Nec veteres agitantur orni.

Quid sit futurum cras, fuge quærere; et
Quem sors dierum cunque dabit, lucro
 Appone; nec dulces amores 15
  Sperne puer, neque tu choreas,

Donec virenti canities abest
Morosa. Nunc et campus, et arcæ,
 Lenesque sub noctem susurri
  Composita repetantur hora: 20

Nunc et latentis proditor intimo
Gratus puellæ risus ab angulo,
 Pignusque dereptum lacertis
  Aut digito male pertinaci.

Od. i. 11.

SEEK not, Leuconoë, ('tis sinful) to explore
What term of life for thee or me may be in store,
Nor tempt Chaldean mysteries! wiser far, whate'er
Our future fate may send, with cheerful mind to bear.
Whether long years be ours, or this may be the last,　5
Which hears the Tuscan waves, driven by the wintry
　　blast
Break on the opposing rocks.　Be wise; pour forth the
　　wine;
Within our narrow span thy wandering hopes confine:
Ev'n while we speak, cur years are slipping fast away;
Trust not the uncertain future, grasp the fleeting day.　10

Tu ne quæsieris, scire nefas, quem mihi, quem tibi
Finem Di dederint, Leuconoë; nec Babylonios
Tentaris numeros.　Ut melius, quicquid erit, pati !
Seu plures hiemes, seu tribuit Jupiter ultimam,
Quæ nunc oppositis debilitat pumicibus mare　　　　　　5
Tyrrhenum.　Sapias, vina liques, et spatio brevi
Spem longam reseces.　Dum loquimur, fugerit invida
Ætas; carpe diem, quam minimum credula postero.

Od. i. 24.

WHAT bounds to grief for loss of one so dear
Shall reason fix? the mournful verse inspire,
Melpomene, whose accents, soft and clear,
　　Suit well the tuneful lyre.

Quis desiderio sit pudor aut modus
Tam cari capitis?　Præcipe lugubres
Cantus, Melpomene, cui liquidam pater
　　Vocem cum cithara dedit.

And does Quinctilius sleep in endless death?   5
Oh, where, for modest worth and truthful mind,
And, twin with Justice, uncorrupted Faith,
    Shall we his equal find?

For him shall many a good man's tears be given:
And none shall bitterer weep, than, Virgil, thou;   10
Who for thy loved Quinctilius weariest Heaven
    With unavailing vow.

No, not thy strains, though sweet as those of yore
With which the listening forests Orpheus led,
To that cold corpse the life-blood can restore,   15
    Which, with his wand of dread,

Mercurius, deaf to sounds of human grief,
Hath summoned to the grisly band below:
'Tis hard; yet Patience may afford relief
    Where none can ward the blow!   20

Ergo Quinctilium perpetuus sopor   5
Urguet! cui Pudor, et Justitiæ soror
Incorrupta Fides, nudaque Veritas
    Quando ullum invenient parem?

Multis ille bonis flebilis occidit;
Nulli flebilior quam tibi, Virgili.   10
Tu frustra pius, heu! non ita creditum
    Poscis Quinctilium deos.

Quod si Thrëicio blandius Orpheo
Auditam moderere arboribus fidem;
Non vanæ redeat sanguis imagini,   15
    Quam virga semel horrida,

Non lenis precibus fata recludere,
Nigro compulerit Mercurius gregi.
Durum! sed levius fit patientia,
    Quicquid corrigere est nefas.   20

Od. i. 31.

With what petition at the shrine
Of Phœbus shall the Bard appear?
And, as he pours the sacred wine,
What prayer shall reach his Patron's ear?
He asks not, he, the golden grain   5
That waves o'er rich Sardinia's plain,

Nor flocks, nor herds, that wander o'er
Calabria's sultry mountains steep:
Nor gold, nor wealthy India's store
Of ivory, nor pastures deep,   10
Through whose rich soil of mouldering clay
Smooth Liris eats his silent way.

Let those who Fortune's favours gain,
Prune the rank growth of Cales' vines;
Let the rich merchant freely drain   15
From golden goblets costly wines,
The prizes of his prosperous trade,
By Syrian merchandize repaid.

Quid dedicatum poscit Apollinem
Vates? quid orat, de patera novum
  Fundens liquorem?   Non opimas
    Sardiniæ segetes feracis;

Non æstuosæ grata Calabriæ   5
Armenta; non aurum, aut ebur Indicum;
  Non rura, quæ Liris quieta
    Mordet aqua, taciturnus amnis.

Premant Calena falce, quibus dedit
Fortuna, vitem; dives et aureis   10
  Mercator exsiccet culullis
    Vina Syra reparata merce,

He to the Gods must sure be dear,
Whose daring vessels scatheless brave,   20
Or thrice or more within the year,
The perils of the Atlantic wave.
For me be still with olives stored,
And cooling herbs, my frugal board.

Though small it be, my share of wealth   25
Grant me to enjoy; and, that I may,
O Phœbus, add the boon of health;
A mind uninjured by decay,
A green old age, with honour blessed,
And of my lyre not dispossessed.   30

Dis carus ipsis; quippe ter et quater
Anno revisens æquor Atlanticum
   Impune. Me pascant olivæ,   15
    Me cichorea levesque malvæ.

Frui paratis et valido mihi,
Latoë, dones, et, precor, integra
   Cum mente; nec turpem senectam
    Degere, nec cithara carentem.   20

Od. ii. 8.

Barine, did not perjuries fail
To leave on thee one angry trace;
If one discoloured tooth, one nail
Less perfect, marred thy wondrous grace,

Ulla si juris tibi pejerati
Pœna, Barine, nocuisset unquam;
Dente si nigro fieres, vel uno
    Turpior ungui,

I might believe; but with each vow   5
Thou heap'st on thy perfidious head,
More radiant beams thy glorious brow,
And wider still thy conquests spread.

'Tis gainful, o'er a mother's urn
To invoke, with false and perjured breath,   10
The silent stars that nightly burn,
The Gods above who know not death.

Laughs at such fraud the Cyprian Queen:
Laugh the kind Nymphs in gamesome mood;
And Cupid, who his arrows keen   15
Sharpens on whetstone stained with blood.

The rising race thy fetters wear;
Fresh bands of slaves embrace their chain;
And, though their bonds they oft forswear,
Thy former lovers still remain.   20

Thee for their sons grave matrons shun,
And cautious sires; and brides, new-made,
Fear, lest by thine enchantments won,
Their husbands' homeward steps be stayed.

Crederem: sed tu, simul obligasti   5
Perfidum votis caput, enitescis
Pulchrior multo, juvenumque prodis
    Publica cura.

Expedit matris cineres opertos
Fallere, et toto taciturna noctis   10
Signa cum cœlo, gelidaque divos
    Morte carentes.

Ridet hoc, inquam, Venus ipsa, rident
Simplices Nymphæ, ferus et Cupido
Semper ardentes acuens sagittas   15
    Cote cruenta.

Adde quod pubes tibi crescit omnis;
Servitus crescit nova; nec priores
Impiæ tectum dominæ relinquunt,
    Sæpe minati.   20

Te suis matres metuunt juvencis,
Te senes parci, miseræque nuper
Virgines nuptæ, tua ne retardet
    Aura maritos.

Od. ii. 10.

WOULDST thou, Licinius, safely steer,
Tempt not too far the uncertain deep:
Nor, while the storm you wisely fear,
The treacherous shore too closely keep.

Who loves of life the golden mean,   5
Escapes alike the squalid cell,
And turmoils, that too oft are seen
In grandeur's envied halls to dwell.

The giant pine-trees most invite
The stormy winds; with heaviest crash   10
Fall proudest towers; the mountain height
The first attracts the lightning's flash.

The balanced mind, in weal or woe
Alike for fortune's change prepares;
Since he, who sends the winter's snow,   15
Himself that winter's loss repairs.

RECTIUS vives, Licini, neque altum
Semper urguendo; neque, dum procellas
Cautus horrescis, nimium premendo
  Littus iniquum.

Auream quisquis mediocritatem   5
Diligit, tutus caret obsoleti
Sordibus tecti, caret invidenda
  Sobrius aula.

Sæpius ventis agitatur ingens
Pinus; et celsæ graviore casu   10
Decidunt turres; feriuntque summos
  Fulgura montes.

Sperat infestis, metuit secundis
Alteram sortem bene præparatum
Pectus.   Informes hiemes reducit   15
  Jupiter, idem

If hard be now thy lot, ere long
A change will come: so Phœbus wakes
At times the slumbering Muses' song,
And for the lyre his bow forsakes.   20

In narrow straits firm courage show:
But, prudent, when propitious gales
On broader seas too favouring blow,
Contract betimes thy swelling sails.

Summovet. Non, si male nunc, et olim
Sic erit. Quondam cithara tacentem
Suscitat Musam, neque semper arcum
     Tendit Apollo.   20

Rebus angustis animosus atque
Fortis appare; sapienter idem
Contrahes vento nimium secundo
     Turgida vela.

Od. ii. 14.

ALAS, my Posthumus, alas!
The fleeting years too quickly pass,
     And none may stay their course;
Nor purest life delay bespeak
Of wrinkled age, and furrowed cheek,   5
     And death's resistless force.

EHEU! fugaces, Postume, Postume,
Labuntur anni; nec pietas moram
Rugis et instanti senectæ
     Afferet, indomitæque morti.

Three hundred bullocks, daily slain,
Would seek to mitigate in vain
  The inexorable King;
Whose drear dominion Tityus holds,   10
And Geryon's giant bulk enfolds
  Within the watery ring

Of that sad flood, which all, whoe'er
Draw here the breath of vital air,
  Must cross, whate'er their lot,   15
Whether be theirs on earth to shine
In kingly palaces, or pine
  In peasant's lowly cot.

In vain from war's alarms we run;
In vain of Adria's billows shun   20
  The hoarse and broken flood;
In vain we dread the subtle death
Wherewith the south wind's poisonous breath
  In Autumn taints the blood.

Non, si trecenis, quotquot eunt dies,   5
Amice, places illacrimabilem
  Plutona tauris; qui ter amplum
    Geryonen Tityonque tristi

Compescit unda, scilicet omnibus,
Quicunque terræ munere vescimur,   10
  Enaviganda, sive reges
    Sive inopes erimus coloni.

Frustra cruento Marte carebimus,
Fractisque rauci fluctibus Adriæ;
  Frustra per auctumnos nocentem   15
    Corporibus metuemus Austrum:

We all must see Cocytus flow   25
With sullen current, black and slow;
    And Danäus' hateful brood;
And Sisyphus, condemned by fate
His mortal crimes to expiate
    By labours still renewed.   30

Thy land, thy house, thy pleasing wife,
Must all be left with parting life:
    The cypress, tree of gloom,
Alone, of all thou lov'st to tend,
Shall on its short-lived lord attend,   35
    And wave above thy tomb.

Thy cellars, guarded with such care
By hundred locks, thy worthier heir
    Shall ransack of their hoard;
And wine thy marble floors shall drown   40
More rich than e'er was seen to crown
    A pontiff's splendid board.

Visendus ater flumine languido
Cocytos errans, et Danai genus
    Infame, damnatusque longi
        Sisyphus Æolides laboris.   20

Linquenda tellus, et domus, et placens
Uxor; neque harum, quas colis, arborum
    Te, præter invisas cupressos,
        Ulla brevem dominum sequetur.

Absumet hæres Cæcuba dignior   25
Servata centum clavibus; et mero
    Tinguet pavimentum superbo
        Pontificum potiore cœnis.

Od. iii. 9.

Hor. While I was dear to thee,
   While with encircling arms
   No youth, preferred to me,
Dared to profane thy bosom's snowy charms;
   I envied not, by thee adored,   5
   The wealth, the bliss of Persia's lord.

Lyd. While all thy bosom glowed
   With love for me alone;
   While Lydia there abode,
Where Chloe now has fixed her hateful throne; 10
   Well pleased, our Roman Ilia's fame
   I deemed eclipsed by Lydia's name.

Hor. 'Tis true, my captive heart
   The fair-haired Chloe sways,
   Skilled with transcendent art   15
To touch the lyre, and breathe harmonious lays;
   For her my life were gladly paid,
   So Heaven would spare my Thracian maid.

Hor. Donec gratus eram tibi,
   Nec quisquam potior brachia candidæ
Cervici juvenis dabat;
   Persarum vigui rege beatior.

Lyd. Donec non alia magis   5
   Arsisti, neque erat Lydia post Chloën;
Multi Lydia nominis
   Romana vigui clarior Ilia.

Hor. Me nunc Thressa Chloë regit,
   Dulces docta modos, et citharæ sciens; 10
Pro qua non metuam mori,
   Si parcent animæ fata superstiti.

LYD.   My breast with fond desire
       For youthful Calaïs burns;   20
       Touched with a mutual fire
The son of Ornithus my love returns;
       For him I'd doubly die with joy,
       So Heaven would spare my Thurian boy.

HOR.   What if the former chain,   25
       That we too rashly broke,
       We yet should weave again,
And bow once more beneath the accustomed yoke?
       If Chloe's sway no more I own,
       And Lydia fill the vacant throne?   30

LYD.   Though bright as Morning Star
       My Calaïs' beaming brow;
       Though more inconstant far,
And easier chafed than Adria's billows thou,
       With thee my life I'd gladly spend,   35
       Content with thee that life to end.

LYD.   Me torret face mutua
       Thurini Calais filius Ornyti;
       Pro quo bis patiar mori,   15
       Si parcent puero fata superstiti.

HOR.   Quid si prisca redit Venus,
       Diductosque jugo cogit aheneo?
       Si flava excutitur Chloë,
       Rejectæque patet janua Lydiæ?   20

LYD.   Quamquam sidere pulchrior
       Ille est, tu levior cortice, et improbo
       Iracundior Adria;
       Tecum vivere amem, tecum obeam libens.

Od. iii. 13.

Bandusia, purest fount, as crystal bright,
Well worthy floral wreaths and festal rite,
    To thee shall bleed, to-morrow morn,
    A kid, whose newly budding horn

Gives hopes of future loves, and battle's shock: 5
Vain hopes! the scion of the wanton flock
    With the red tribute of his blood
    Must stain thy cold and silvery flood.

Thou by the fiery Dog-Star's fiercest heat
Remain'st untouched; thy sheltering cool retreat   10
    Is welcome to the o'er-laboured ox,
    Loosed from the plough, and wandering flocks.

Nor shalt thou want, 'mid founts, an honoured name;
While I, thy bard, consign to future fame
    The caverned rocks, with ilex crowned,   15
    Down which thy babbling waters bound.

O fons Bandusiæ, splendidior vitro,
Dulci digne mero, non sine floribus,
    Cras donaberis hædo,
    Cui frons turgida cornibus

Primis et Venerem et prœlia destinat,   5
Frustra; nam gelidos inficiet tibi
    Rubro sanguine rivos
    Lascivi soboles gregis.

Te flagrantis atrox hora Caniculæ
Nescit tangere: tu frigus amabile   10
    Fessis vomere tauris
    Præbes, et pecori vago.

Fies nobilium tu quoque fontium,
Me dicente cavis impositam ilicem
    Saxis, unde loquaces   15
    Lymphæ desiliunt tuæ.

Od. iv. 2.

Who seeks to rival Pindar's fame
With waxen wings, Iulus, flies;
To give, like Icarus, a name
To seas, where quenched his folly lies.

As mountain torrents, swoll'n by rain,　　　　5
O'erpass their banks, and boil along,
So Pindar, boundless, rolls amain
The deep-mouthed volume of his song:

With Phœbus' laurel justly crowned,
Whether in Dithyrambics free,　　　　10
From trammels loosed, with words new-found,
He pour his lawless harmony:

Whether of Gods, or kings, the seed
Of Gods, he sing, who gave to death,
Well-merited, the Centaur breed,　　　　15
And quenched Chimæra's fiery breath;

Pindarum quisquis studet æmulari, I-
ule, ceratis ope Dædalea
Nititur pennis, vitreo daturus
　　　Nomina ponto.

Monte decurrens velut amnis, imbres　　　　5
Quem super notas aluere ripas,
Fervet immensusque ruit profundo
　　　Pindarus ore,

Laurea donandus Apollinari,
Seu per audaces nova Dithyrambos　　　　10
Verba devolvit, numerisque fertur
　　　Lege solutis;

Seu deos, regesve canit, deorum
Sanguinem, per quos cecidere justa
Morte Centauri, cecidit tremendæ　　　　15
　　　Flamma Chimæræ;

Or honour with a richer meed
Than all the sculptor's art could trace,
The pugilist, or victor steed,
Triumphant in the Elean race; 20

Or with the widowed bride condole,
Reft of her lord in manhood's bloom,
Extol his grace, his heart, his soul,
And rescue from the oblivious tomb.

Riding the gale on pinions proud, 25
The Swan of Dirce soars sublime
Amid the expanse of storm and cloud;
While, as the bee from fragrant thyme,

Laborious, draws her honied spoil;
Moist Tibur's groves and banks along 30
Musing I rove, and ceaseless toil
To weave my unaspiring song.

Sive, quos Elea domum reducit
Palma coelestes, pugilemve equumve
Dicit, et centum potiore signis
    Munere donat; 20

Flebili sponsæ juvenemve raptum
Plorat; et vires animumque mores-
que aureos educit in astra, nigro-
    que invidet Orco.

Multa Dircæum levat aura cycnum, 25
Tendit, Antoni, quoties in altos
Nubium tractus: ego, apis Matinæ
    More modoque

Grata carpentis thyma per laborem
Plurimum, circa nemus uvidique 30
Tiburis ripas operosa parvus
    Carmina fingo.

But thou shalt strike a loftier strain,
When Cæsar, on some glorious day,
Shall lead the fierce Sicambrian train　　　35
Of captives, up the sacred way:

Cæsar, than whom, in mercy given,
No greater, better boon we hold;
Nor should do, though indulgent Heave
Restored the fabled age of gold.　　　　40

Thou shalt the joyful days record,
The city's public games, decreed
For Cæsar to our prayers restored,
The courts from anxious suitors freed.

Then shall be heard my joyous lay　　　45
(Should aught of mine such honour earn),
Oh, glorious sun! oh, happy day!
That sees Augustus' safe return!

Concines majore Poëta plectro
Cæsarem, quandoque trahet feroces
Per Sacrum clivum, merita decorus　　　35
　　　Fronde, Sicambros;

Quo nihil majus meliusve terris
Fata donavere bonique divi,
Nec dabunt, quamvis redeant in aurum
　　　Tempora priscum.　　　40

Concines lætosque dies, et urbis
Publicum ludum, super impetrato
Fortis Augusti reditu, forumque
　　　Litibus orbum.

Tum meæ (si quid loquar audiendum)　　　45
Vocis accedet bona pars; et, o Sol
Pulcher, o laudande, canam recepto
　　　Cæsare felix.

And, as you **pass**, from every tongue
Triumphant shouts renewed shall rise;
And thousands to the temples throng,
To pay their grateful sacrifice.

For thee ten bulls, as many cows;
For me a weanling calf shall bleed
In satisfaction of my vows,
Who revels now in grassy mead:

Dun-coloured, save of snowy white,
Upon his front a crescent blaze;
Shaped like the horns of silvery light
The moon, at three days old, displays.

Tuque dum procedis, Io Triumphe !
Non semel dicemus, Io Triumphe !
Civitas omnis; dabimusque divis
    Tura benignis.

Te decem tauri totidemque vaccæ,
Me tener solvet vitulus, relicta
Matre, qui largis juvenescit herbis
    In mea vota,

Fronte curvatos imitatus ignes
Tertium Lunæ referentis ortun:,
Qua notam duxit, niveus videri,
    Cætera fulvus.

Od. iv. 7.

THE snows are gone, the fields resume their grassy hue;
    The trees their leaves renew:
The earth is freshly clad; the late swoll'n streams, now low,
    Within their limits flow:
The sister Graces three, and Nymphs unzoned advance,   5
    And lead the festive dance.
The seasons' change, the hours that steal our days, explain
    Immortal hopes how vain!
Springs banish Winter's frosts—Summers succeed to Springs,
    Then fruitful Autumn brings   10
Her ripened treasures forth; and soon the earth again
    Is bound in wintry chain.
But Nature's losses soon the circling months repair;
    We, when we journey, where
Æneas, Tullus, Ancus, all have gone before,   15
    Are shades and dust—no more!
That Heaven to this day's sum will add another day,
    Who shall presume to say?

DIFFUGERE nives; redeunt jam gramina campis,
    Arboribusque comæ:
Mutat terra vices, et decrescentia ripas
    Flumina prætereunt:
Gratia cum Nymphis geminisque sororibus audet   5
    Ducere nuda choros.
Immortalia ne speres monet annus, et almum
    Quæ rapit hora diem.
Frigora mitescunt Zephyris: ver proterit æstas
    Interitura, simul   10
Pomifer auctumnus fruges effuderit; et mox
    Bruma recurrit iners.
Damna tamen celeres reparant cœlestia lunæ:
    Nos, ubi decidimus
Quo pius Æneas, quo dives Tullus et Ancus,   15
    Pulvis et umbra sumus.
Quis scit, an adjiciant hodiernæ crastina summæ
    Tempora Di superi?

Whate'er with liberal hand thy generous bounty shares,
    Shall 'scape thy greedy heirs;   20
When thou shalt once have died, and Minos hath on thee
    Passed his august decree,
Torquatus, not thy blood, thine eloquence, thy worth,
    Can bring thee back to earth.
Not pure Hippolytus could 'scape, with Dian's aid,   25
    From that Tartarean shade;
Nor Theseus break the slumbrous chains of Lethe, round
    His loved Pirithöus bound.

Cuncta manus avidas fugient hæredis, amico
    Quæ dederis animo.   20
Cum semel occideris, et de te splendida Minos
    Fecerit arbitria;
Non, Torquate, genus, non te facundia, non te
    Restituet pietas.
Infernis neque enim tenebris Diana pudicum   25
    Liberat Hippolytum;
Nec Lethæa valet Theseus abrumpere caro
    Vincula Pirithoo.

CATULLUS.

Car. xxxi.

SIRMIO.

Sirmio, fair eye of all the laughing isles
And jutting capes that rise from either main,
Or crown our inland waters, with glad smiles
Of heartfelt joy I greet thee once again,
Scarce daring to believe mine eyes, that see   5
No more Bithynia's plains, but fondly rest on thee,

My own, my chosen Home! Oh, what more blest
Than that sweet pause of troubles, when the mind
Flings off its burthen, and when, long oppressed
By cares abroad and foreign toil, we find   10
Our native home again, and rest our head
Once more upon our own, long-lost, long-wished-for bed!

This, this alone, o'erpays my every pain!
Hail! loveliest Sirmio, hail! with joy like mine
Receive thy happy lord! Thou liquid plain   15
Of Laria's lake, in sparkling welcome shine!
Put all your beauties forth! laugh out! be glad!
In universal smiles this day must all be clad!

Peninsularum, Sirmio, insularumque
Ocelle, quascunque in liquentibus stagnis,
Marique vasto fert uterque Neptunus:
Quam te libenter, quamque lætus inviso!
Vix mî ipse credens Thyniam, atque Bithynos   5
Liquisse campos, et videre te in tuto.
O quid solutis est beatius curis?
Cum mens onus reponit, ac peregrino
Labore fessi venimus larem ad nostrum,
Desideratoque acquiescimus lecto.   10
Hoc est, quod unum est pro laboribus tantis;
Salve, o venusta Sirmio, atque hero gaude:
Gaudete vosque, Lariæ lacus undæ:
Ridete quidquid est domi cachinnorum.

Epitaph

ON

HIS DAUGHTER.

BY BISHOP LOWTH.

———◦◦———

Dear Child, farewell! that didst in worth,
   Wit, piety, so far excel!
By closer ties than those of birth
   Knit to my heart, dear Child, farewell!

Dear Child, farewell! till Time bring round   5
   Those blessed ages, yet in store,
When I, if haply worthy found,
   Shall meet thee face to face once more!

Dear Child, oh come, no more to part,
   Shall I exclaim in rapture then;   10
To bless a Father's arms and heart,
   My Child, my Mary, come again!

———————————

Cara, vale! ingenio præstans, pietate, pudore,
   Et plusquam natæ nomine cara, vale!

Cara, vale! donec veniat felicius ævum,
   Quando iterum tecum, sim modo dignus, ero.

Cara, redi, lætâ tum dicam voce, paternos   5
   Eia age in amplexus, cara Maria, redi!

𝔈𝔭𝔦𝔱𝔞𝔭𝔥

ON THE

MARQUIS OF WELLESLEY,

BY HIMSELF

Long tost on Fortune's waves, I come to rest,
Eton, once more on thy maternal breast.
On loftiest deeds to fix the aspiring gaze,
To seek the purer lights of ancient days,
To love the simple paths of manly truth,—   5
These were thy lessons to my opening youth.
If on my later life some glory shine,
Some honours grace my name, the meed is thine!
My Boyhood's nurse, my aged dust receive,
And one last tear of kind remembrance give!   10

Fortunæ rerumque vagis exercitus undis,
   In gremium redeo serus, Etona, tuum.
Magna sequi, et summæ mirari culmina famæ,
   Et purum antiquæ lucis adire jubar,
Auspice te didici puer ; atque in limine vitæ   5
   Ingenuas veræ laudis amare vias.
Siqua meum vitæ decursæ gloria nomen
   Auxerit, aut aliquis nobilitârit honor,
Muneris, alma, tui est. Altrix da terra sepulcrum,
   Supremam lacrymam da, memoremque mei.   10

FROM THE FRENCH.

MILLEVOYE.

THICKLY amid the groves were laid
　　The leafy spoils of Autumn's gale;
Each woody nook to light displayed,
And hushed the voiceless nightingale.

Ev'n in his dawn of life decaying,　　　　5
A youthful poet sadly roved;
Yet once again with faint steps straying
Amid the scenes his childhood loved.

Dear woods, farewell! your mournful hue
Foretells the doom that waits on me;　　　10
And in each blighted leaf, anew
I learn to read my death's decree.

DE la dépouille de nos bois
　　L'Automne avait jonché la terre ;
Le bocage était sans mystère,
Le rossignol était sans voix.

Triste, et mourant dans son aurore,　　　5
Un jeune malade, à pas lents,
Parcourait une fois encore
Les bois chers à ses premiers ans.

Bois chéris, adieu ! je succombe ;
Votre deuil prédit mon sort ;　　　　10
Et dans chaque feuille qui tombe
Je vois l'arrêt de ma mort.

Yes he, the boding sage, has said,
Perchance thine eye may see once more
The Autumnal forest's mellowing red,   15
Yet once again, and then 'tis o'er.

Round thy young front, all dark and sere,
Is twined e'en now the cypress wreath;
And paler than the paling year
Thou bendest toward the bed of death.   20

Ere yonder russet grass shall fade,
Ere droop upon yon vine-clad height
The last remains of lingering shade,
Thy youth shall feel the nipping blight.

And I must die! the chilling blast   25
Congeals me with its icy touch,
And ere my spring of life is past,
I feel my winter's near approach.

Fatal oracle d'Epidaure,
Tu l'as dit, les feuilles du bois
A tes yeux jauniront encore,   15
Mais c'est pour la dernière fois.

Le sombre cyprès t'environne;
Plus pâle que le pâle Automne,
Tu t'inclines vers le tombeau;
Et ta jeunesse sera flétrie   20
Avant l'herbe de la prairie,
Avant le pampre du côteau.

Et je meurs! de leur froide haleine
Les vents funestes m'ont touché;
Et mon printemps s'achève à peine,   25
Que mon hiver s'est approché.

Fall, blighted foliage, chill and pale;
Hide from the sight this road of sorrow, 30
And from a mother's anguish veil
The spot where I must lie to-morrow!

But if to this sequestered brake
Kind pity lead one much-loved Maid;
Sweetly her fairy step shall wake, 35
And soothe awhile my troubled shade!

He past—and never to return!—
The last leaf quivering in the glade
Fell on the youthful Poet's urn.
Beneath the oak his tomb was made. 40

But never to that lowly stone
The Maiden came, by pity led;
The passing Shepherd's step alone
Disturbed that still sepulchral bed.

Tombe, tombe, feuille éphémère !
Voile aux yeux ce triste chemin !
Cache au désespoir de ma mère
La place où je serai demain ! 30

Mais vers la solitaire allée
Si mon amante désolée
Venait pleurer quand le jour fuit.
Eveillée par son léger bruit
Mon ombre un instant consolée . . . 35

Il dit—s'éloigne, et sans retour !
La dernière feuille qui tombe
A signalé son dernier jour.
Sous le chêne on creusa sa tombe.

Mais son amante ne vint pas 40
Visiter la pierre isolée ;
Et le pâtre de la vallée
Troubla seul, du bruit de ses pas,
Le silence du mausolée.

FROM THE ITALIAN

METASTASIO.

THE PARTING.

THE hour is come! Love, fare thee well!
  Farewell, my Love, my first, my last!
For me the charms of life are past
  When far away from thee, Love!
For me nor joys nor peace remain,   5
But wakeful thoughts and ceaseless pain;
While thou, perchance, wilt never more—
  Oh, never, think on me, Love!

Yet canst thou not forbid my thoughts
Lingering around those charms to stay,   10
Which sweetly stole my peace away,
  And hover still round thee, Love!

ECCO quel fiero istante;
  Nice, mia Nice, addio.
Come vivrò, ben mio,
Così lontan da te?
  Io vivrò sempre in pene,   5
Io non avrò più bene;
E tu, chi sa se mai
Ti sovverrai di me!

Soffri che in traccia almeno
  Di mia perduta pace   10
  Venga il pensier seguace
  Sull' orme del tuo piè.

Still, still about thy path, where'er
Thy steps are turned, my heart is there;
While thou, perchance, wilt never more—   15
   Oh, never, think on me, Love!

While I through distant climes shall roam,
And sadly to the desert shore
My constant strain of sorrow pour,
   And vainly call on thee, Love!   20
From morn to morn one theme of woe,
One only theme, my heart can know;
While thou, perchance, wilt never more—
   Ah, never, think on me, Love!

And on those scenes of vanished joys,   25
Those pleasant scenes, I oft shall gaze,
Where swiftly passed the blissful days,
   The days I passed with thee, Love!
For me shall every spot I view
My bleeding memory's wounds renew;   30

   Sempre nel tuo cammino
   Sempre m' avrai vicino;
   E tu, chi sa se mai   15
   Ti sovverrai di me!

Io fra remote sponde
   Mesto volgendo i passi
   Andrò chiedendo ai sassi,
   La ninfa mia dov' è?   20
   Dall' una all' altra aurora
   Te andrò chiamando ognora.
   E tu, chi sa se mai
   Ti sovverrai di me!

Io rivedrò sovente   25
   Le amene piagge, o Nice,
   Dove vivea felice,
   Quando vivea con te.
   A me saran tormento
   Cento memorie e cento;   30

While thou, perchance, wilt never more—
    Ah, never, think on me, Love!

Beside this fount I saw thy brow
A moment cloud, but soon appeased
That beauteous hand with rapture seized,   35
    The pledge of peace with thee, Love!
Here first I heard Hope's flattering tone;
There fondly sighed, but not alone;
Yet thou, perchance, wilt never more—
    Ah, never, think on me, Love!   40

And now around thy new abode,
Full many a heart like mine shall swell,
And many a tale of passion tell,
    With vows of truth to thee, Love!
And thou, while all their homage pay,   45
And fondly weep, or softly pray,
Wilt thou, perchance, one moment ever,—
    Oh, wilt thou think on me, Love?

E tu, chi sa se mai
    Ti sovverrai di me!

Ecco, dirò, quel fonte,
    Dove avvampò di sdegno,
    Ma poi di pace in pegno   35
    La bella man mi diè.
      Qui si vivea di spene,
Là si languiva insieme;
    E tu, chi sa se mai
    Ti sovverrai di me!   40

Quanti vedrai giungendo
    Al nuovo tuo soggiorno,
    Quanti venirti intorno
    A offrirti amore, e fe!
      O Dio! chi sa fra tanti   45
    Teneri omaggi, e pianti,
    O Dio! chi sa se mai
    Ti sovverrai di me!

Oh, think on all the pangs I feel,
The wound that rankles in my breast: 50
I dared not hope—but, hope suppressed,
   Still fondly worshipped thee, Love!
Oh, think what anguished feelings swell
In this last, bitterest fare-thee-well!
Oh, think—but thou wilt never more—   55
   No, never, think on me, Love!

Pensa qual dolce strale,
   Cara, mi lasci in seno :   50
Pensa che amò Fileno
Senza sperar mercè !
   Pensa, mia vita, a questo
Barbaro addio funesto ;
Pensa . . . Ah chi sa se mai   55
Ti sovverrai di me !

FILICAIA.

SONNETS TO ITALY.

Son. i.

Italia! oh, Italia! thou on whom
The fatal gift of beauty brings e'en now
The dower of anguish, which thy constant doom
Hath graven for ages on thy furrowed brow!
Wert thou less fair, or more renowned in arms!   5
That they might love thee less, or fear thee more,
Who, basking in the sunshine of thy charms,
Yet on thy beauties war and rapine pour.
Then should not I behold the war-cloud burst
Down from the Alps; nor France's legions bending 10
In the Po's bloodstained waves to quench their thirst;
Nor thee, on valour not thine own depending,
With foreign friends from foreign foes to save,
Conquering or conquered, still alike a hopeless slave! 14

Italia, Italia, o tu cui feo la sorte
   Dono infelice di bellezza, ond' hai
   Funesta dote d' infiniti guai
   Che in fronte scritti per gran doglia porte ;
Deh fossi tu men bella, o almen più forte,   5
   Onde assai più ti paventasse, o assai
   T' amasse men chi del tuo bello ai rai
   Par che si strugga, e pur ti sfida a morte !
Che or giù dall' Alpi non vedrei torrenti
   Scender d' armati, nè di sangue tinta   10
   Bever l' onda del l'o gallici armenti ;
Nè te vedrei, del non tuo ferro cinta,
   Pugnar col braccio di stranigere enti,
   Per servir sempre o vincitrice o vinta.   14

Son. ii.

WHERE is thine arm, Italia? why employ
A stranger's hand to guard thee? he who saves
Is not less fierce than they who now destroy:
Both are thy foes, and both were once thy slaves.
Preserv'st thou thus thine honour? dar'st thou show 5
Such memory of thy once all-glorious reign?
To Valour, ancient Valour, keep'st thou so
The plighted faith he swore to thee again?
Go, then! divorce thy wedded lord! espouse
Foul, helpless Sloth! sleep on, 'mid cries abhorred, 10
And groans, and murder, mindless of thy vows!
Sleep, vile adulteress, till the avenging sword
Find thee a naked, slumbering, guilty prey,
Ev'n in thy leman's arms, and wake thee but to slay! 14

Dov' è, Italia, il tuo braccio? e a che ti servi
   Tu dell' altrui? non è, s' io scorgo il vero,
   Di chi t' offende il difensor men fero:
   Ambo nemici sono, ambo fur servi.
Così dunque l' onor, così conservi   5
   Gli avanzi tu del glorioso impero?
   Così al valor, così al valor primiero
   Che a te fede giurò, la fede osservi?
Or va'; repudia il valor prisco, e sposa
   L' ozio; e fra il sangue, i gemiti e le strida,   10
   Nel periglio maggior dormi e riposa:
Dormi, adultera vil, fin che omicida
   Spada ultrice ti svegli, e sonnacchiosa
   E nuda in braccio al tuo fedel t' uccida.   14

Son. iii.

WITH equal steps, Italia, toward their close
Approach the winter, and thine hours of life;
Nor know'st thou yet with what a storm of woes
For thee the clouds of destiny are rife.
But as the Nile pursues his hidden course,　　　　5
Till all at once his mighty waters rise;
Ev'n so on thee in fury from their source
Shall burst the torrent of thy miseries.
Then shalt thou see, beneath that whelming tide
Shipwrecked and sunk, thine over-jealous fears,　　10
Thy helpless prudence and vainglorious pride!
Then see how weak disjointed power appears!
Then learn how vain the coward statesman's art,
Who fears to guard the whole, yet hopes to save a
　　part.　　　　　　　　　　　　　　　　14

VANNO a un termine sol con passi eguali
　　Del verno, Italia, e di tua vita l' ore;
　　Nè ancor sai quante di sua man lavore
　　A tuo danno il destin saette e strali.
Ma qual per sotterranei canali　　　　5
　　Scorre 'l Nilo, e improvviso esce poi fuore;
　　Tai, schiuso il fonte del natio furore,
　　Tutte in te sboccheran l' acque dei mali:
E vedrai tosto in sì turbata e fiera
　　Onda naufraghe andar tema gelosa,　　10
　　Prudenza inerme, e vanitate altera:
Vedrai che imperio disunito posa
　　Sempre in falso; e che parte indarno spera
　　Salvar, chi tutto di salvar non osa.　　　　14

Son. iv.

For thee, Italia, Death and Discord are
Two names, one thing; and with this ill thou hast
Another greater; that too weak for war,
Thou art too strong to be in silence past.
In such perplexing state of doubt and care,   5
To yield is bitter, hopeless to contend:
Whence, as conflicting winds in middle air,
Now here, now there, their balanced pinions bend;
So mingled Jealousy, and Fear, and Rage,
Self-poised between thy weakness and thy power, 10
Within thy breast their whirlwind battle wage;
And down on thee such storms of misery shower,
That, hope—despair—or crouch, or nobly strike,
Though varying still the risk, thy doom is scaled alike! 14

Sono, Italia, per te discordia e morte
    In due nomi una cosa; e a sì gran male
    Un mal s' aggiugne non minor, che frale
    Non se' abbastanza nè abbastanza forte.
In tale stato, in così dubbia sorte   5
    Ceder non piace, e contrastar non vale:
    Onde come a mezz' aria impennan l' ale,
    E a fiera pugna i venti apron le porte;
Tra 'l frale e 'l forte tuo non altrimenti
    Nascon quasi a mezz' aria, e guerra fanno 10
    D' ira, invidia e timor turbini e venti;
E tai piovono in te nembi d' affanno,
    Che se speri o disperi, osi o paventi,
    Diverso è 'l rischio, e sempre ugual fia 'l danno. 14

Son. v.

WHEN darker still the embrowning shade declines
From the huge mountain-top, "our dying light,"
Musing I cry, "on other nations shines,
Nor reigns o'er all one universal night."
But thou, Italia! in what gloom departs   5
The vanished glory of thy mid-day sun!
Glories of wit and valour, arms and arts,
All once were thine, and now remains not one!
Amid such gloomy darkness, seest thou not
The flame of war that kindles all around?   10
Or dost thou see, nor yet believe thy lot?
But if by suffering still delay be found,
Yes, suffer still! yet shalt thou sometime see
That death deferred awhile, is far from victory! 14

QUANDO giù dai gran monti bruna bruna
  Cade l' ombra, un pensiero a dir mi sforza:
  S' accende altrove il dì, se quù si smorza;
  Nè tutto a un tempo l' universo imbruna.
Indi esclamo: Qual notte atra importuna   5
  Tutte l' ampie tue glorie a un tratto ammorza?
  Glorie di senno, di valor, di forza
  Già mille avesti; or non hai tu pur una.
E in così buie tenebre non vedi
  L' alto incendio di guerra, onde tutt' ardi?   10
  E non credi al tuo mal, se agli occhi credi?
Ma se tue stragi col soffrir ritardi,
  Soffri, misera, soffri; indi a te chiedi
  Se sia forse vittoria il perder tardi.   14

Son. vi.

Yes, hapless, suffer still! victorious France
Cheers in thy milder clime the wintry gloom;
And toward their close the rigorous months advance,
That interpose between thee and thy doom.
But ere the murderous trump of war have given   5
Its fearful prelude to the battle shock,
Hear how thy destiny is sealed in Heaven;
And wilt thou still the awful warning mock?
Thy fate draws near—thine hour is come—thy foes
Have sworn, ere earth be clad in verdure yet,   10
To reap the harvest of thy ripened woes;
No dubious language, no ambiguous threat:
Read then thy sentence in their warning voice—
To die, or live a slave! Reflect, and take thy choice!   14

Soffri, misera, soffri. Ecco al tuo foco
  Tempran l' inverno i Franchi; e s' interpone
  Sol fra' tuoi scempi e te la rea stagione
  Che omai s' avanza, e al nuovo april dà loco.
Ma pria che tromba micidial col fioco   5
  Suo canto accenda la fatal tenzone,
  Odi ciò che in tuo danno il ciel dispone.
  Estremo è il danno; e 'l prenderai tu a gioco?
Freme il nemico, e ti vuol morta; e giura,
  Giura di far, pria che 'l terren verdeggi,   10
  L' infausta messe de' tuo' guai matura.
Non oscuro è il linguaggio: ancor non leggi
  Nelle minacce sue la tua sciagura?
  O servire, o morir. Pensa, ed eleggi.   14

LOST FREEDOM.

Oh, break my golden fetters, and restore
The happy hours when I with thee was blessed;
Or, if I lose thee, let me keep no more
The memory of the bliss I once possessed.
That I love thee, O Freedom, Heaven can tell,   5
The mountain echoes, and the lonely vale;
The ocean flood that with my tears I swell;
The desert air that hears my constant wail.
But if indeed thy wrath I justly feel,
Become the slave of slavish dignity,   10
Increase thine anger, but thy charms conceal.
When Heaven is wroth, nor sun nor stars we see,
Nor sign of beauty cheers the darkened air;
But thou art still more wroth, and still art doubly fair!

O 'l dolce tempo ch' io di te godei,
  Rendi, e 'l forte mio laccio aureo recidi :
  O fa' ch' io perda, poichè te perdei,
  L' alta imago del bel che in te già vidi.
S' io t' amo, o bella Libertà, gl' Iddei   5
  Il sanno, e 'l san le valli e i monti e i lidi,
  E 'l mar che cresce de' gran pianti miei.
  E l' aere ch' empio de' miei alti stridi.
Ma se degli odi tuoi son io ben degno
  Dal dì ch' io servo a dignitate ancella,   10
  Purchè scemi 'l tuo bel, cresca 'l tuo sdegno.
Quando s' adira il ciel, nè sol nè stella,
  Nè in lui pur veggio di bellezza un segno :
  Tu più sempre t' adiri, e più sei bella.   15

DISPARAGEMENT OF EARTHLY GLORY.

Oꜰ, vanquished oft, but never quite subdued,
Desire of Glory, child of mortal birth,
That art all earth thyself, and earth thy food,
And mak'st thy subjects, like thyself, all earth!
Oh, what avails it, that with constant toil   5
I strive, and stifle thee within my heart;
If still thy contact with thy native soil
Fresh strength and life, Antæus-like, impart?
That soil accurst, my own too fond conceit;
Whence could I tear thee once, and so destroy,   10
Then would I celebrate that glorious feat
With far more triumph, more exulting joy,
Than Hercules on Libya's plains could know,
When he Antæus slew, a far less dangerous foe.   14

O ᴠɪɴᴛᴏ sì, ma non mai vinto appieno,
  Desío di gloria, che di terra nasci,
  E sei terra, e di terra anco ti pasci,
  E fai l' uom, come te, tutto terreno;
Qual pro che ad or ad or dentro al mio seno   5
  Te quasi estinto e tramortito io lasci,
  Se ognor più forte, qual Anteo, rinasci
  Tocco appena al materno empio terreno?
Empio terren della mia propria stima,
  Dal cui contatto sì malvagio e reo,   10
  S' unqua fia ch' io ti stacchi e poi t' opprima
Del grande scempio d'un più forte Anteo
  Andrò superbo, e n' avrò spoglia opima,
  E farò più che in Libia Ercol non feo.   14

COUNTRY IN SPRING.

THESE lonely hills possess such charms for me,
These glades in all their native wildness dressed,
That day by day unwearied still I see,
And plant their image in my thoughtful breast.
Pleased, I behold the new-born verdure grow,   5
The tender shoots put forth their leafy green;
Or sit beside the stream, whose limpid flow
Bathes, and reflects at once, the forest scene.
Here all unseen, long tranquil days I lead;
Here from my heart's pernicious soil I cast   10
Each evil thought, each noxious mental weed:
Here muse in silence o'er my errors past;
And on some tree my self-inflicted woes
Record, and bathe with tears; and there repentance grows!

Io son sì vago dell' orror natío
   Di questi alpestri e solitari colli,
   Che non fian gli occhi mai stanchi o satolli
   Di mandarne l' imago al pensier mio.
Crescer qui l' erbe nuove, e qui vegg' io   5
   Spuntar sul tronco i giovani rampolli;
   E alle verd' ombre di rugiada molli
   Spegner la sete, e farsi specchio il rio.
Qui le reliquie de' miei giorni al lido
   Traggo; e quei germi che 'l maligno suolo   10
   Di mia mente nodrì, svello e recido:
E dei passati error, pensoso e solo,
   Mentre l' istoria in ogni tronco incido,
   Di pianto il bagno; e vi germoglia il duolo.   14

MANZONI.

THE FIFTH OF MAY.

'TIS past; as, motionless and pale,
The mortal struggle o'er, but late
With that proud spirit animate,
   Now lies the senseless clay:
   So, awe-struck, in dismay,   5
Earth stands in breathless trance, and listens to the tale.
That fated Mortal's dying hour
She muses o'er, and ponders when
With iron heel such earthly power
Shall tread her bloodstained fields again.   10

Ei fù !—siccome immobile
Dato il mortal sospiro
Stette la spoglia immemore
Orba di tanto spiro ;
Così percossa, attonita,   5
   La terra al nunzio sta ;
Muta pensando all' ultima
Ora dell' uom fatale,
Nè sa quando una simile
Orma di piè mortale   10
La sua cruenta polvere
   A calpestar verrà.

Him, uninspired, my soul beheld,
Enthroned in glory's glittering hall;
I marked him from his splendour flung,
Again to rise, again to fall;
And when a thousand harps were strung,   15
My voice the chorus never swelled;
By servile flattery ne'er disgraced,
By coward insult undebased.
But now, o'er such a planet's last eclipse,
She wakes, and haply not in vain,   20
    From unpolluted lips,
Pours o'er the funeral urn a long-surviving strain.

From Alpine heights to Egypt's shore,
From Rhine to Tagus, far around
Was heard his thunder's vengeful roar;   25
    And Death was in the sound!
His red-winged lightning flashed from Scylla's rock:
The frozen North re-echoed to the shock.
Was this true glory? let succeeding Time
    That arduous question ask;   30

Lui, folgorante in soglio,
Vide il mio genio, e tacque;
Quando con vice assidua   15
Cadde, risorse, e giacque,
Di mille voci al sonito
    Mista la sua non ha;
Vergin di servo encomio,
E di codardo oltraggio,   20
Sorge or commosso al subito
Sparir di tanto raggio,
E scioglie all' urna un cantico,
    Che forse non morrà.

Dall' Alpi alle Piramidi,   25
Dal Manzanarre al Rheno,
Di quel securo il fulmine
Scorrea dietro al baleno:
Scoppiò da Scilla a Tanai,
    Dall' uno all' altro mar.   30
Fu vera gloria? ai Posteri
L' ardua sentenza! Nui

Ours be the simpler task
Before the mighty Maker's throne to bow,
Who in that towering genius deigned to show
Of His Creator Spirit an image, how sublime!

The stormy, tremulous delight   35
   Of some exalted plan;
The fever of the haughty soul
   Of more than mortal scope:
Scarce curbed to serve, with eager scan
Still fixed on Empire as its goal;   40
And reaching such a dizzy height
'Twere madness to have dared to hope—
All this he knew; he too had known
The blaze of glory, brighter from defeat;
   The flight—the victory—the throne—   45
   The Exile's lone retreat;
Twice in the dust; and twice, in sterner pride,
A god, by countless myriads deified.

He comes: two centuries are seen
Arrayed in hostile arms to stand; ·   50

Chiniam la fronte al massimo
Fattor, che volle in lui
Del Creator suo Spirito   35
   Più vasta orma stampar.

La procellosa e trepida
Gioja d' un gran disegno;
L' ansia d' un cor che indocile
Serve, pensando al regno;   40
E'l giugne, e ottiene un premio
   Ch' era follìà sperar;

Tutto ei provò! la gloria
Maggior dopo il periglio,
La fuga e la vittoria,   45
Il regno, e il tristo esilio;
Due volte nella polvere,
   Due volte in sull' altar.

Ei si nomò; due secoli
L' un contro l' altro armato,   50

To him they turn, from his command,
Submiss, their destiny await:
He bids be still; and, high between,
He sits, the arbiter of fate!
He vanished—and in dull repose,   55
In narrow bounds his life must close;
By turns, in every changing state,
Object of envy, love, and fear;
Pursued by unextinguished hate,
And wept by Pity's tenderest tear.   60
        As o'er the drowning wretch
The incumbent wave rolls its o'erwhelming weight;
That very wave, on which of late
Upborne, his anxious gaze would stretch,
And, o'er the billows' summit strain,   65
To reach the distant shore—in vain!
        So o'er that haughty soul
Must the dark tide of recollection roll!
How oft, to each succeeding age
To paint himself he vainly planned!   70

Sommessi a lui si volsero,
Come aspettando il fato
Ei fè silenzio, ed arbitro
    S' assise in mezzo a lor.
E sparve; e i dì nell' ozio   55
Chiuse in sì breve sponda,
Segno d' immensa invidia,
E di pietà profonda;
D' inestinguibil odio,
    E d' indomato amor.   60

Come, sul capo al naufrago,
L' onda s' avvolve, e pesa;
L' onda, su cui del misero
Alta pur dianzi e tesa
Scorrea la vista a scernere   65
    Prode remote invan;
Tal su quell' alma il cumulo
Delle memorie scese.

Ahi, quante volte ai posteri
Narrar se stesso imprese!   70

As oft, upon the eternal page
  Sank overpowered his weary hand.
Oft, as in silence died some listless day,
  His eyeball's lightning ray
Bent idly on the tumbling flood,   75
  With folded arms he stood;
And bitterly he numbered o'er
The days that had been, and that were no more!

He saw the quick-struck tents again,
The hot assault, the battle-plain,   80
The troops in martial pomp arrayed,
The pealing of the artillery,
The torrent charge of cavalry;
  The hasty word
  In thunder heard—   85
Heard, and at once obeyed!

Beneath such suffocating thought
Perchance the panting soul at times
  Would sink in chill despair;

Ma sull' eterna pagina
  Cadde la stanca man!
Ahi, quante volte al tacito
Morir d' un giorno inerte,
Chinati i rai fulminei,   75
Le braccia al sen conserte,
Stette, e dei dì che furono
  L' assalse il sovvenir!

E ripensò le mobili
Tende, e i percossi valli,   80
E 'l campo dei manipoli,
E l 'onda dei cavalli;
E 'l concitato imperio,
  E 'l celere ubbedir!

Ahi, forse a tanto strazio   85
Cadde lo spirito anelo,
E disperò; ma valida

But Heaven in mercy consolation brought,   90
And bore his weary spirit to purer climes
Of holier light, and more refreshing air!
  By viewless hands his steps were led,
  The flowery paths of Hope to tread,
  Toward those enchanting fields of rest,   95
  By unimagined joys possess'd;
  Where mortal glory's feeble ray
  Is quenched in one unclouded day.
O Thou, whose triumphs who can tell?
Pure, heavenly Faith! amid the rest   100
Let this the glorious number swell!
Rejoice! for never haughtier crest,
To Him, on Golgotha who died,
  Hath vailed his stubborn pride.
From foul reproach, angelic Friend,   105
Do thou his weary dust defend!
Since on that lonely couch, and suffering breast,
  He, who alone hath power the soul
  To raise, depress, afflict, console,
  The Mighty God hath deigned to rest!   110

  Venne una man dal cielo,
  E in più spirabil aere
    Pietosa il trasportò.   90
  E l' avviò sui floridi
  Sentier della speranza
  Ai campi eterni, al premio
  Che 'l desiderio avanza;
  Ov' è silenzio e tenebre   95
    La gloria che passò.
  Bella, Immortal, benefica
  Fede, ai trionfi avvezza,
  Scrivi ancor questo; allegrati,
  Che più superba altezza   100
  Al disonor del Golgota
    Giammai non si chinò.
  Tu dalle stanche ceneri
  Sperdi ogni ria parola;
  Il Dio, che atterra e suscita,   105
  Che affanna e che consola,
  Sulla deserta coltrice
    Accanto a lui posò!

FROM THE GERMAN.

SCHILLER.

THE IDEAL.

AND wilt thou then desert me quite
　　With all thy glowing phantasy?
With all thy pangs, thy keen delight,
Oh wilt thou thus, relentless, fly?

Can nought persuade thee? nought delay,　　　5
Oh golden time of youthful bliss?
'Tis vain! thy waves have forced their way
To join the eternal Past's abyss.

Quenched are the suns, whose cloudless rays
My path of youth and fancy blest;　　　10
Sunk the high thoughts, whose generous blaze
With joyous frenzy fired my breast.

SO willst du treulos von mir scheiden
　　Mit deinen holden Phantasien,
Mit deinen Schmerzen, deinen Freuden,
Mit allen unerbittlich fliehn?

Kann nichts dich, Fliehende, verweilen,
O meines Lebens goldne Zeit?
Vergebens, deine Wellen eilen
Hinab ins Meer der Ewigkeit.

Erloschen sind die heitern Sonnen,
Die meiner Jugend Pfad erhellt;　　　10
Die Ideale sind zerronnen,
Die einst das trunkne Herz geschwellt;

'Tis gone, the hope to find indeed
The world my youthful fancy dreamed;
And stern realities succeed 15
What once so bright, so Godlike seemed.

As round the stone with fond desire
Pygmalion threw his eager arms,
Till the cold marble's answering fire
Glowed in her cheek with tenfold charms; 20

To Nature thus, with arms of love,
Entranced I clung, till, fondly pressed,
The Goddess seemed to breathe, to move,
To warm beneath my poet-breast.

With kindling fire she seemed to burn, 25
To speak in accents soft and sweet;
My glowing kisses to return,
Throb heart to heart, and beat for beat.

Er ist dahin, der süsse Glaube
An Wesen, die mein Traum gebar,
Der rauhen Wirklichkeit zum Raube, 15
Was einst so schön, so göttlich war.

Wie einst mit flehendem Verlangen
Pygmalion den Stein umschloss,
Bis in des Marmors kalte Wangen
Empfindung glühend sich ergoss, 20

So schlang ich mich mit Liebesarmen
Um die Natur, mit Jugendlust,
Bis sie zu athmen, zu erwarmen
Begann an meiner Dichterbrust,

Und, theilend meine Flammentriebe, 25
Die Stumme eine Sprache fand,
Mir wiedergab den Kuss der Liebe
Und meines Herzens Klang verstand;

Then grove and field with life were fraught;
With life the flashing waters sang;   30
Ev'n soulless things my feeling caught,
And forth a new creation sprang.

How swelled my bosom's narrow space!
A boundless world of thought was there!
I panted to begin my race,   35
To see, to feel, to do, to dare!

How glorious seemed this world of ours,
While but the opening buds were seen!
How few are now the expanded flowers,
And ev'n those few, how poor and mean!   40

How, winged with hope, with ardour blessed,
Unchilled by doubt, unchecked by dread,
The young enthusiast onward pressed,
His fiery path of life to tread!

Da lebte mir der Baum, die Rose,
Mir sang der Quellen Silberfall,   30
Es fühlte selbst das Seelenlose
Von meines Lebens Wiederhall.

Es dehnte mit allmächt'gem Streben
Die enge Brust ein kreissend All,
Herauszutreten in das Leben,   35
In That und Wort, in Bild und Schall.

Wie gross war diese Welt gestaltet,
So lang die Knospe sie noch barg;
Wie wenig, ach! hat sich entfaltet,
Dies Wenige, wie klein und karg!   40

Wie sprang, von kühnem Muth beflügelt,
Beglückt in seines Traumes Wahn,
Von keiner Sorge noch gezügelt,
Der Jüngling in des Lebens Bahn.

Above the farthest, palest star, 45
On Fancy's soaring wings he flew;
Was nought so high, was nought so far,
To check his flight, to bound his view!

How easy seemed each toilsome strife!
What might he hope, and hope in vain? 50
Around his chariot-wheels of life
How cheerly danced the joyous train!

Fortune, with golden chaplets dressed;
Young Love, with all his visions bright;
And star-crowned Glory's haughty crest; 55
And Truth, that loves the clear sunlight.

But long ere half the way was done,
My gay companions all were flown;
They turned aside, and, one by one,
Forsook me, cheerless and alone. 60

Bis an des Aethers bleichste Sterne 45
Erhob ihn der Entwürfe Flug;
Nichts war so hoch und nichts so ferne,
Wohin ihr Flügel ihn nicht trug.

Wie leicht ward er dahin getragen,
Was war dem Glücklichen zu schwer! 50
Wie tanzte vor des Lebens Wagen,
Die luftige Begleitung her!

Die Liebe mit dem süssen Lohne,
Das Glück mit seinem goldnen Kranz,
Der Ruhm mit seiner Sternenkröne, 55
Die Wahrheit in der Sonne Glanz!

Doch, ach! schon auf des Weges Mitte
Verloren die Begleiter sich,
Sie wandten treulos ihre Schritte,
Und einer nach dem andern wich. 60

Soon, light of foot, was Fortune fled :
Unquenched the thirst of knowledge staid;
And clouds of doubt began to spread
Round Truth's fair front their envious shade.

I saw on vulgar brows profaned 65
The laurel wreath that Glory wore;
Love's visions bright awhile remained,
Then faded, to return no more.

And darker still and drearier grew
Around my steps the lonely way: 70
Ev'n Hope, the lingerer, scarcely threw,
To cheer my path, a glimmering ray.

Of all that swelled my youthful pride,
Who now remained to light the gloom?
Who still adhered my faithful guide, 75
My trust, my comfort, to the tomb?

Leichtfüssig war das Glück entflogen,
Des Wissens Durst blieb ungestillt,
Des Zweifels finstre Wetter zogen
Sich um der Wahrheit Sonnenbild.

Ich sah des Ruhmes heil'ge Kränze 65
Auf der gemeinen Stirn' entweiht.
Ach, allzuschnell, nach kurzem Lenze
Entfloh die schöne Liebeszeit!

Und immer stiller ward's und immer
Verlassner auf dem rauhen Steg; 70
Kaum warf noch einen bleichen Schimmer
Die Hoffnung auf den finstern Weg.

Von all dem rauschenden Geleite
Wer harrte liebend bei mir aus?
Wer steht mir tröstend noch zur Seite 75
Und folgt mir bis finstern Haus?

Thou, whose soft hand and tender care
Can lull to rest each fevered wound;
Thou, Friendship, sent our woes to share!
Thou, fondly sought, and early found!   80

And thou, with Friendship well combined,
Like her, the passions' storm to lay;
Employment, formed the tortured mind
With sober, gradual force to sway,

And though the Eternal Future's pile   85
But grain by grain its fabric rears:
From off the account of Time the while
Thus strik'st thou minutes, days, and years.

Du, die du alle Wunden heilest,
Der Freundschaft leise, zarte Hand,
Des Lebens Bürden liebend theilest,
Du, die ich frühe sucht' und fand.   80

Und du, die gern sich mit ihr gattet,
Wie sie, der Seele Sturm beschwört,
Beschäftigung, die nie ermattet,
Die langsam schafft, doch nie zerstört,

Die zu dem Bau der Ewigkeiten   85
Zwar Sandkorn nur für Sandkorn reicht,
Doch von der grossen Schuld der Zeiten
Minuten, Tage, Jahre streicht.

HONOUR TO WOMAN.

ALL honour to Woman! to her it is given
To entwine with Earth's garlands the roses of Heaven,
To weave all the bliss-giving chains of the heart;
And in Modesty's veil while she chastely retires,
To kindle the brightest, the holiest fires, 5
The pure beam of feeling that ne'er can depart.

  Man's wild soul, in fierce commotion,
  Still beyond the bounds of reason,
  Varies like the varying season,
  Tost on Passion's stormy ocean. 10
  On the future still he gazes,
  Ne'er contented, still aspiring,
  Still some phantom good desiring,
  Which his dreaming fancy raises.

EHRET die Frauen! sie flechten und weben
Himmlische Rosen ins irdische Leben,
Flechten der Liebe beglückendes Band,
Und in der Grazie züchtigem Schleier
Nähren sie wachsam das ewige Feuer 5
Schöner Gefühle mit heiliger Hand.

  Ewig aus der Wahrheit Schranken
  Schweift des Mannes wilde Kraft;
  Unstät treiben die Gedanken
  Auf dem Meer der Leidenschaft; 10
  Gierig greift er in die Ferne,
  Nimmer wird sein Herz gestillt;
  Rastlos durch entlegne Sterne
  Jagt er seines Traumes Bild.

But the soft voice of woman's all-eloquent glance   15
Calls the wanderer home from his wearisome trance;
To the present recalls him, no longer to roam,
To the path, to the cot, where, contented to rest,
Her thoughts, like herself, have been tranquilly blest,
True daughter of Nature, the sweet'ner of Home!   20

> Man, 'mid storms, and wrath, and strife,
> Breaking with resistless force
> All that bars his headlong course,
> Hurries down his path of life;
> Slaves to each capricious mood,   25
> Still his feverish wishes flow;
> Still like Hydra's heads they grow,
> Still destroyed, and still renew'd.

But Woman, with milder enjoyment contented,
Plucks the bloom of each hour in succession presented;
'Mid cares that distract not, but sweetly employ,   31

Aber mit zauberisch fesselndem Blicke   15
Winken die Frauen dem Flüchtling zurücke,
Warnend zurück in der Gegenwart Spur.
In der Mutter bescheidener Hütte
Sind sie geblieben mit schamhafter Sitte,
Treue Töchter der frommen Natur.   20

> Feindlich ist des Mannes Streben,
> Mit zermalmender Gewalt
> Geht der wilde durch das Leben,
> Ohne Rast und Aufenthalt.
> Was er schuf, zerstört er wieder,   25
> Nimmer ruht der Wünsche Streit,
> Nimmer, wie das Haupt der Hyder
> Ewig fällt und sich erneut.

Aber, zufrieden mit stillerem Ruhme,
Brechen die Frauen des Augenblicks Blume,
Nähren sie sorgsam mit liebendem Fleiss,   31

More rich and more free in her limited sphere,
Than he in his wisdom's, his glory's career,
And all the wide circle of fanciful joy.

    Self-reliant, proud and high,   35
    Haughty man can never know
    All the mutual charms that flow
    From the heart's mysterious tie,
    From the soul's unfettered union
    He who melts not, weeps not, steeled   40
    By the storms, the strife revealed
    In the world's unblest communion.

But ev'n as the harp, when the zephyr's light wings
Play with flutt'ring delight o'er its tremulous strings,
So the warm heart of Woman to feeling replies;   45
Her smile casts a gleam upon Misery's hues,
Her breast heaves with sorrow, and Heaven's own dews
Are the tear-drops of pity, that steal from her eyes.

Freier in ihrem gebundenen Wirken,
Reicher, als er, in des Wissens Bezirken
Und in der Dichtung unendlichem Kreis.

    Streng und stolz, sich selbst genügend,   35
    Kennt des Mannes kalte Brust,
    Herzlich an ein Herz sich schmiegend,
    Nicht der Liebe Götterlust,
    Kennet nicht den Tausch der Seelen,
    Nicht in Thränen schmilzt er hin;   40
    Selbst des Lebens Kämpfe stählen
    Härter seinen harten Sinn.

Aber, wie leise vom Zephyr erschüttert,
Schnell die äolische Harfe erzittert,
Also die fühlende Seele der Frau.   45
Zärtlich geängstigt vom Bilde der Quälen,
Wallet der liebende Busen, es strahlen
Perlend die Augen von himmlischem Thau.

Man, tyrannically brave,
Tyrant force alone obeys;   50
By the sword the Scythian sways,
And the Persian lives a slave.
Still within his troubled breast
Passions wild and fierce are raging;
And their angry battle waging,   55
Banish peace, and love, and rest.

'Tis for Woman's dear pleading to soften the soul,
To wield the mild sceptre of moral control;
To quench the fierce embers of passion; to call
On the strong arm of power its dissensions to end; 60
Each jarring material in unison blend,
Compose the wild discord, and harmonise all!

In der Männer Herrschgebiete
Gilt der Stärke trotzig Recht;   50
Mit dem Schwert beweist der Scythe,
Und der Perser wird zum Knecht.
Es befehden sich im Grimme
Die Begierden wild und roh,
Und der Eris rauhe Stimme   55
Waltet, wo die Charis floh.

Aber mit sanft überredender Bitte
Führen die Frauen den Scepter der Sitte,
Löschen die Zwietracht, die tobend entglüht,
Lehren die Kräfte, die feindlich sich hassen,   60
Sich in der lieblichen Form zu umfassen,
Und vereinen, was ewig sich flicht.

THE KNIGHT OF TOGGENBURG.

A Ballad.

"Sir Knight, a sister's love for thee
This breast shall still retain;
But ask none other love of me;
Thou wouldst not give me pain?

"I feel no throb when thy form appears,   5
Unmoved, I see thee go;
And the pang that fills thine eyes with tears,
I do not, cannot know."

Speechless he heard with grief suppressed;
Then with bitter feeling stung,   10
He clasped her once to his throbbing breast,
And then on his steed he sprung.

"Ritter, treue Schwesterliebe
"Widmet euch dies Herz;
"Fordert keine andre Liebe,
"Denn es macht mir Schmerz.

"Ruhig mag ich euch erscheinen,   5
"Ruhig gehen sehn.
"Eurer Augen stilles Weinen
"Kann ich nicht verstehn."

Und er hört's mit stummem Harme,
Reisst sich blutend los,   10
Presst sie heftig in die Arme,
Schwingt sich auf sein Ross,

He hath summoned his vassals, one and all,
  Through the whole of Switzerland;
With the Cross on their breast, they are gone at his call
  To fight in the Holy Land.   16

And the might of that Warrior's arm was shown
  By his deeds on that blood-stained coast,
And well that Warrior's plume was known
  In the ranks of the Paynim host.   20

And Toggenburg was a name of dread
  That made the Moslem quail,
But inly that Warrior's bosom bled
  With a wound that nought could heal.

A long, long year he hath borne his pain,   25
  He can bear it now no more;
He finds no rest on the battle-plain,
  And he quits the holy shore.

Schickt zu seinen Mannen allen
  In dem Lande Schweiz;
Nach dem heil'gen Grab sie wallen,   15
  Auf der Brust das Kreuz.

Grosse Thaten dort geschehen
  Durch der Helden Arm;
Ihres Helmes Büsche wehen
  In der Feinde Schwarm;   20

Und des Toggenburgers Name
  Schreckt den Muselmann;
Doch das Herz von seinem Grame
  Nicht genesen kann.

Und ein Jahr hat er's getragen,   25
  Trägt's nicht länger mehr;
Ruhe kann er nicht erjagen
  Und verlässt das Heer;

He hath found a ship on Joppa's strand,
  He hath spread the willing sail;   30
And home he is gone to his own dear land,
  Where blew the favouring gale.

The Pilgrim came to the Lady's hall;
  He knocks at the Castle gate;
And the words on his ear like thunder fall,   35
  That tell him he comes too late:

"The maid you seek the veil has ta'en,
  She is now the Bride of Heaven;
And yestermorn at the holy fane
  Her plight to God was given."   40

He has left for ever the fortress-height,
  Where his fathers dwelt of yore;
He looks no more on his armour bright,
  On his trusty steed no more.

Sieht ein Schiff an Joppes Strande,
  Das die Segel bläht,   30
Schiffet heim zum theuren Lande,
  Wo ihr Athem weht.

Und an ihres Schlosses Pforte
  Klopft der Pilger an;
Ach, und mit dem Donnerworte   35
  Wird sie aufgethan:

" Die ihr suchet, trägt den Schleier,
  " Ist des Himmels Braut,
"Gestern war des Tages Feier,
  " Der sie Gott getraut."   40

Da verlässet er auf immer
  Seiner Väter Schloss,
Seine Waffen sieht er nimmer,
  Noch sein treues Ross.

And down he passed, unmarked and unknown, 45
  From Toggenburg's lofty mound;
For a humble vest of hair was thrown
  His manly limbs around.

And there he hath built him a lowly hut
  Beneath the sacred chimes; 50
Where the walls of the bosomed convent jut
  From a grove of shady limes.

And there from the early dawn of day
  Till the star of evening shone,
Hope tinging his cheek with a sickly ray, 55
  The Warrior sat alone.

His eye was fixed on the Convent above,
  And the live-long day did he wait,
And gaze on the window that held his Love,
  Till he heard the window grate: 60

Von der Toggenburg hernieder 45
  Steigt er unbekannt,
Denn es deckt die edeln Glieder
  Härenes Gewand.

Und erbaut sich eine Hütte
  Jener Gegend nah, 50
Wo das Kloster aus der Mitte
  Düstrer Linden sah;

Harrend von des Morgens Lichte
  Bis zu Abends Schein,
Stille Hoffnung im Gesichte, 55
  Sass er da allein.

Blickte nach dem Kloster drüben,
  Blickte stundenläng
Nach dem Fenster seiner Lieben,
  Bis das Fenster klang, 60

Till that loved one's form from the window leant,
  Till he saw her placid brow,
And her angel-smile of meek content,
  As she looked on the vale below.

And then would he turn to his lowly bed,   65
  And peacefully sleep the night,
Rejoicing still when the morning shed
  Its beams of returning light.

And many a day, and many a year,
  The Warrior there did wait,   70
Without a murmur, without a tear,
  Till he heard the window grate:

Till that loved one's form from the window leant,
  Till he saw her placid brow,
And her angel-smile of meek content,   75
  As she looked on the vale below.

Bis die Liebliche sich zeigte,
  Bis das theure Bild
Sich ins Thal herunter neigte,
  Ruhig, engelmild.

Und dann legt' er froh sich nieder,   65
  Schlief getröstet ein,
Still sich freuend, wenn es wieder
  Morgen würde sein.

Und so sass er viele Tage,
  Sass viel Jahre lang,   70
Harrend ohne Schmerz und Klage,
  Bis das Fenster klang,

Bis die Liebliche sich zeigte,
  Bis das theure Bild
Sich ins Thal herunter neigte,   75
  Ruhig, engelmild.

And there one morning, stiff and chill,
  He was found a corpse at last;
And the gaze of his cold, fixed eye was still
  On that Convent window cast.   80

Und so sass er, eine Leiche,
  Eines Morgens da;
Nach dem Fenster noch das bleiche
  Stille Antlitz sah.   80

HERO AND LEANDER.

SEE how each on other gaze
Yon grey towers of elder days,
In the golden sunshine glowing,
Where the Hellespontine waves
Brawling through the rock-girt caves   5
Of the Dardanelles are flowing.
Hear'st thou how the breakers thunder?
How the storm-rent cliffs are shivering?
Europe here from Asia severing,
Love they could not tear asunder.   10

SEHT ihr dort die altergrauen
Schlösser sich entgegenschauen,
Leuchtend in der Sonne Gold,
Wo der Hellespont die Wellen
Brausend durch der Dardanellen   5
Hohe Felsenpforte rollt?
Hört ihr jene Brandung stürmen,
Die sich an den Felsen bricht?
Asien riss sie von Europen;
Doch die Liebe schreckt sie nicht.   10

Hero's and Leander's hearts,
With his sweetly-painful darts,
Love, the mighty god, had fired;
She, as Hebe, fair and young;
He, in health and vigour strong,　　　　15
In the mountain-chase acquired.
But their fathers' feuds had blighted
All their hopes, of wedded bliss;
And o'er danger's dark abyss
Hung the fruit that Love had plighted.　　　20

There, on Sestos' fortress-rock,
Where with ceaseless tempest-shock
Hellespont in fury swells;
Sat the maid, alone and sighing,
Far Abydos vainly eyeing,　　　　25
Where the fondly-worshipped dwells.
Ah! that stormy sea above
Rose no bridge from shore to shore;
Path was none the dark waves o'er;
But the way was found by Love.　　　30

Heros und Leanders Herzen
Rührte mit dem Pfeil der Schmerzen
Amors heil'ge Göttermacht.
Hero, schön wie Hebe blühend,
Er durch die Gebirge ziehend　　　　15
Rüstig im Geräusch der Jagd.
Doch der Väter feindlich Zürnen
Trennte das verbundne Paar,
Und die süsse Frucht der Liebe
Hing am Abgrund der Gefahr.　　　　20

Dort auf Sestos' Felsenthurme,
Den mit ew'gem Wogensturme
Schäumend schlägt der Hellespont,
Sass die Jungfrau, einsam grauend,
Nach Abydos' Küste schauend,　　　　25
Wo der Heissgeliebte wohnt.
Ach, zu dem entfernten Strande
Baut sich keiner Brücke Steg,
Und kein Fahrzeug stösst vom Ufer;
Doch die Liebe fand den Weg.　　　　30

Love, who taught by faithful thread
Creta's labyrinth to tread:
Love, who warms the dullest souls:
He the brute creation rules;
And the fiery-breathing bulls   35
With his iron yoke controls.
Not the Styx, that nine-fold flowed,
Could his dauntless might restrain:
Nor the loved one could detain,
Ev'n in Pluto's dark abode.   40

Love, and youth's impetuous blood,
Through the Hellespontine flood
Led Leander to his bride.
When morn pale began to glimmer
Fading day, the hardy swimmer   45
Plunged amid the foaming tide:
Stoutly stemmed the dark waves' might,
Straining to the friendly shore,
Where, to guide the wanderer o'er,
Flashed the wakeful beacon light.   50

Aus des Labyrinthes Pfaden
Leitet sie mit sicherm Faden,
Auch den Blöden macht sie klug,
Beugt ins Joch die wilden Thiere,
Spannt die feuersprühnden Stiere   **35**
An den diamantnen Pflug.
Selbst der Styx, der neunfach fliesset,
Schliesst die Wagende nicht aus;
Mächtig raubt sie das Geliebte
Aus des Pluto finstern Haus.   40

Auch durch des Gewässers Fluthen
Mit der Sehnsucht feur'gen Gluthen
Stachelt sie Leanders Muth.
Wenn des Tages heller Schimmer
Bleichet, stürzt der kühne Schwimmer   45
In des Pontus finstre Fluth,
Theilt mit starkem Arm die Woge,
Strebend nach dem theuren Strand,
Wo, auf hohem Söller leuchtend,
Winkt der Fackel heller Brand.   50

There, by glowing Love carest,
Sweetly, fondly shall he rest,
From his journey hard and long;
There in mutual bliss embraced,
He the heavenly joys shall taste,   55
Which to Love alone belong:
Till the morn the lingerers wake,
And their dreams of transport chase;
And for Ocean's cold embrace
Bid him those soft arms forsake.   60

Thus, amid their stolen delight,
Thirty times the orb of light
O'er his course too swiftly flew;
Rapturous as the bridal hours,
Envied by the immortal powers,   65
Ever young, and ever new.
Happiness has ne'er been his,
Who has never, where it stood
On the verge of Hell's black flood,
Plucked the heavenly fruit of bliss.   70

Und in weichen Liebesarmen
Darf der Glückliche erwarmen
Von der schwer bestandnen Fahrt,
Und den Götterlohn empfangen,
Den in seligem Umfangen   55
Ihm die Liebe aufgespart,
Bis den Säumenden Aurora
Aus der Wonne Träumen weckt,
Und ins kalte Bett des Meeres
Aus dem Schooss der Liebe schreckt.   60

Und so flohen dreissig Sonnen
Schnell, im Raub verstohlner Wonnen
Dem beglückten Paar dahin,
Wie der Brautnacht süsse Freuden,
Die die Götter selbst beneiden,   65
Ewig jung und ewig grün.
Der hat nie das Glück gekostet,
Der die Frucht des Himmels nicht
Raubend an des Höllenflusses
Schauervollem Rande bricht.   70

On the Earth by turns arose
Morn, and dewy evening's close:
They, in heedless transports lost,
Marked not how the leaves were falling,
Marked not how stern Boreas, brawling,   75
Ushered in the Winter's frost:
Gladly saw the hours of light
Shorter yet, and shorter grow,
Blessing Heaven with many a vow,
For the lengthened joys of night.   80

Soon the balance equal lay
In the sky 'twixt night and day;
And the Maiden still at even
Watched upon the fortress' height,
When the fiery steeds of light   85
Sank beneath the verge of Heaven.
And the sea lay still and sleeping
As a polished mirror sheen;
O'er the expanse of crystal green,
Not a breath of Zephyr sweeping.   90

Hesper und Aurora zogen
Wechselnd auf am Himmelsbogen;
Doch die Glücklichen, sie sahn
Nicht den Schmuck der Blätter fallen,
Nicht aus Nords beeisten Hallen   75
Den ergrimmten Winter nahn.
Freudig sahen sie des Tages
Immer kürzern, kürzern Kreis;
Für das längere Glück der Nächte
Dankten sie bethört dem Zeus.   80

Und es gleichte schon die Wage
An dem Himmel Nächt' und Tage,
Und die holde Jungfrau stand
Harrend auf dem Felsenschlosse,
Sah hinab die Sonnenrosse   85
Fliehen an des Himmels Rand.
Und das Meer lag still und eben,
Einem reinen Spiegel gleich,
Keines Windes leises Weben
Regte dasstall kryne Reich.   90

Frolic shoals of dolphins here
Up and down amid the clear
Silver-flashing waters played:
There amid the sea-shore rocks,
Thetis' darkly-shining flocks   95
On the oozy sand were laid.
And to these alone revealed
Were the secret vows of Love:
These, whose lips the Powers above
Had in endless silence sealed.   100

And with joy her bosom swelled,
As in flattering tone she held
Converse with the laughing Sea:
"Glorious God, canst thou deceive?
No, I ne'er will him believe,   105
Who with falsehood taxes thee.
Harsh is oft a father's care,
False and treacherous mankind;
Thou alone art ever kind;
Thou canst feel for Love's despair.   110

Lustige Delphinenschaaren
Scherzten in dem silbeklaren,
Reinen Element umher,
Und in schwärzlich grauen Zügen,
Aus dem Meergrund aufgestiegen,   95
Kam der Tethys buntes Heer.
Sie, die Einzigen, bezeugten
Den verstohlnen Liebesbund;
Aber ihnen schloss auf ewig
Hekate den stummen Mund.   100

Und sie freute sich des schönen
Meeres, und mit Schmeicheltönen
Sprach sie zu dem Element:
"Schöner Gott, du solltest trügen?
Nein, den Frevler straf' ich Lügen,   105
Der dich falsch und treulos nennt.
Falsch ist das Geschlecht der Menschen,
Grausam ist des Vaters Herz;
Aber du bist mild und gütig,
Und dich rührt der Liebe Schmerz."   110

" 'Mid these dreary walls alone,
Hopeless, joyless must I moan,
And my youth in sorrow spend:
Didst not thou in mercy bear,
Trusted blindly to thy care,   115
To my arms my only friend.
Dread is thine unfathomed flood,
O'er the rocks in fury beating:
But thou bend'st to Love's entreating,
And to valour's hardihood!   120

" Thou, too, Monarch of the ocean,
Thou wast touched with soft emotion,
When across thy watery way
Helle, in her homeward flight,
In resplendent beauty bright,   125
Bore the golden fleece away.
Vanquished by the Maiden's charms,
Soon thou bad'st thy floods arise,
To convey the beauteous prize
Gently to thy longing arms.   130

" In den öden Felsenmauern
Müsst' ich freudlos einsam trauern
Und verblühn in ew'gem Harm;
Doch du trägst auf deinem Rücken,
Ohne Nachen, ohne Brücken,   115
Mir den Freund in meinen Arm.
Grauenvoll ist deine Tiefe,
Furchtbar deiner Wogen Fluth,
Aber dich erflcht die Liebe,
Dich bezwingt der Heldenmuth."   120

" Denn auch dich, den Gott der Wogen,
Rührte Eros mächt'ger Bogen,
Als des goldnen Widders Flug
Helle, mit dem Bruder fliehend,
Schön in Jugendfülle blühend,   125
Ueber deine Tiefe trug.
Schnell, von ihrem Reiz besiegt,
Griffst du aus dem finstern Schlund,
Zogst sie von des Widders Rücken
Nieder in den Meeresgrund."   130

"There, a goddess of the waves,
In the deepest ocean's caves,
Lives she, ne'er again to die;
Persecuted Love befriending,
Oft thy stubborn fury bending,　　　　135
At the affrighted sailor's cry.
Fairest Helle!　Goddess bright!
I thy friendly aid implore;
Bid my lover hasten o'er
To my arms again to-night!"　　　　140

Darkness mounted up the sky;
And upon the platform high
Beamed the wonted beacon-light,
Faithful pledge of love and bliss,
Which across the dark abyss　　　　145
Should the wanderer guide aright.
Hark! from far a thundering sound!
Curls the sea in darker ire,
And the stars have hid their fire,
And the storm is blackening round.　　　　150

"Eine Göttin mit dem Gotte,
In der tiefen Wassergrotte,
Lebt sie jetzt unsterblich fort;
Hilfreich der verfolgten Liebe,
Zähmt sie deine wilden Triebe,　　　　135
Führt den Schiffer in den Port.
Schöne Helle, holde Göttin,
Selige, dich fleh' ich an:
Bring' auch heute den Geliebten
Mir auf der gewohnten Bahn!"　　　　140

Und schon dunkelten die Fluthen,
Und sie liess der Fackel Gluthen
Von dem hohen Söller wehn.
Leitend in den öden Reichen
Sollte das vertraute Zeichen　　　　145
Der geliebte Wandrer sehn.
Und es saust und dröhnt von ferne,
Finster kräuselt sich das Meer,
Und es löscht das Licht der Sterne,
Und es naht gewitterschwer.　　　　150

Night upon the waters lay;
Gleamed the forky lightning's ray;
From the bosom of the cloud
Heavily the torrents fell;
Each from forth his rocky cell 155
Raved the loosened winds aloud:
And in awful whirlpools driven
Raged the restless flashing tide,
As a hell-gulf yawning wide,
To its deep foundations riven. 160

"Ah!" exclaimed the weeping fair,
"What was late my idle prayer?
Jove, be that rash prayer forgiven.
Should the Gods have heard that vow!
Should his life a prey e'en now 165
To yon angry sea be given!
Home the wave-borne sea-mew hies
To his shelter in the rock;
Trembling at the tempest's shock
Close in port the sailor lies. 170

Auf des Pontus weite Fläche
Legt sich Nacht, und Wetterbäche
Stürzen aus der Wolken Schooss;
Blitze zucken in den Lüften,
Und aus ihren Felsengrüften 155
Werden alle Stürme los,
Wühlen ungeheure Schlünde
In den weiten Wasserschlund;
Gähnend, wie ein Höllenrachen
Oeffnet sich des Meeres Grund. 160

"Wehe, weh mir!" ruft die Arme
Jammernd. "Grosser Zeus, erbarme!
Ach, was wagt' ich zu erflehn!
Wenn die Götter mich erhören,
Wenn er sich den falschen Meeren 165
Preis gab in des Sturmes Wehn!
Alle meergewohnten Vögel
Ziehen heim, in eil'ger Flucht;
Alle sturmerprobten Schiffe
Bergen sich in sichrer Bucht." 170

"Ah! too sure that dauntless breast,
By imperious Love possessed,
Will the dangerous journey take:
For by all Love's oaths he swore
Yet again to venture o'er;   175
Death alone that vow can break.
Ah! perchance with efforts vain,
Wrestling with the tempest's power,
Sinks he in this very hour,
Whelmed beneath that angry main.   180

"Oh, thy calm, perfidious sea
Was the hell of treachery!
Smooth as glass thou lay'st erewhile
Slumbering in thy crystal bed,
Till thou hadst thy victim led   185
To believe thy lying smile;
Till upon thy dupe, seduced
Far from the protecting shore,
Now amid thy torrent's roar,
All thy wrath at once is loosed."   190

"Ach, gewiss, der Unverzagte
Unternahm das oft Gewagte,
Denn ihn trieb ein mächt'ger Gott.
Er gelobte mir's beim Scheiden
Mit der Liebe heil'gen Eiden,   175
Ihn entbindet nur der Tod.
Ach, in diesem Augenblicke
Ringt er mit des Sturmes Wuth,
Und hinab in ihre Schlünde
Reisst ihn die empörte Fluth!"   180

"Falscher Pontus, deine Stille
War nur des Verrathes Hülle,
Einem Spiegel warst du gleich;
Tückisch ruhten deine Wogen,
Bis du ihn heraus betrogen   185
In dein falsches Lügenreich.
Jetzt, in deines Stromes Mitte,
Da die Rückkehr sich verschloss,
Lässest du auf den Verrathnen
Alle deine Schrecken los!"   190

Fiercer yet the tempest raves;
Swell on high the mountain waves;
And the angry billows roar
'Gainst the rocks in thunder broke.
Ev'n the ship with ribs of oak   195
Dares not near that sea-beat shore.
And the beacon light was drowned,
Which should lend its cheering ray;
Terror on the waters lay;
Terror on the landing frowned.   200

And to Venus for her aid,
'Gainst the hurricane she prayed,
'Gainst the flashing thunder-cloud:
And a steer with horns of gold
(Would they so their wrath withhold)   205
To the stubborn winds she vowed.
Every Goddess of the deep,
All the Gods in Heaven who dwell
She besought, the restless swell
Of the waves to lull to sleep.   210

Und es wächst des Sturmes Toben.
Hoch, zu Bergen aufgehoben,
Schwillt das Meer, die Brandung bricht
Schäumend sich am Fuss der Klippen;
Selbst das Schiff mit Eichenrippen   195
Nahte unzerschmettert nicht.
Und im Wind erlischt die Fackel,
Die des Pfades Leuchte war;
Schrecken bietet das Gewässer,
Schrecken auch die Landung dar.   200

Und sie fleht zur Aphrodite,
Dass sie dem Orkan gebiete,
Sänftige der Wellen Zorn,
Und gelobt, den strengen Winden
Reiche Opfer anzuzünden,   205
Einen Stier mit goldnem Horn.
Alle Göttinnen der Tiefe,
Alle Götter in der Höh'
Fleht sie, lindernd Oel zu giessen
In die sturmbewegte See.   210

Hear thy suppliant when she calls!
Hear me in thy coral halls,
Ever-blest Leucothoe!
Whom, their utmost need befriending,
Thy protecting hand extending,　　　　　215
Oft the shipwrecked sailors see.
Lend thy veil, which from the grave
(Woven in mysterious woof,
From profaner eyes aloof)
Boasts a magic power to save.　　　　　220

Hushed and still the wild winds lay;
Brightly rose the new-born day
In serenest lustre mild;
To its ancient bed again,
Glassy smooth, returned the main;　　　　225
Sea and sky in union smiled.
Light the puny billows played,
Rippling on the unbroken sand;
Gently wafted to the land,
On the shore a corpse was laid.　　　　　230

" Höre meinen Ruf erschallen,
Steig' aus deinen grünen Hallen,
Selige Leukothea!
Die der Schiffer in dem öden
Wellenreich, in Sturmesnöthen　　　　　215
Rettend oft erscheinen sah.
Reich' ihm deinen heil'gen Schleier,
Der, geheimnissvoll gewebt,
Die ihn tragen, unverletzlich
Aus dem Grab der Fluthen hebt!"　　　　220
Und die wilden Winde schweigen,
Hell an Himmels Rande steigen
Eos Pferde in die Höh'.
Friedlich in dem alten Bette
Fliesst das Meer in Spiegelglätte,　　　　225
Heiter lächeln Luft und See.
Sanfter brechen sich die Wellen
An des Ufers Felsenwand,
Und sie schwemmen, ruhig spielend,
Einem Leichnam an den Strand.　　　　　230

Yes! 'tis he, who e'en in death
Scorned to break his plighted faith:
One quick glance was darted there—
Not a tear was seen to flow—
Not a word of anguished woe;   235
Fixed she gazed in chill despair.
Yet a glance upon the sky,
On the deep a glance she turned;
And the while a bright flame burned
In that pale and haggard eye.   240

"Yes, I hear, relentless Fate!
Whom no prayer can mitigate:
Yes, thou claim'st thy right divine!
Though, alas! too quickly flown,
Happiness I yet have known,   245
And the fairest lot was mine.
Venus, in thy temple I
Have a faithful Priestess been;
Now to thee, immortal Queen,
I a willing victim die!"   250

Ja, er ist's, der auch entseelet
Seinem heil'gen Schwur nicht fehlet!
Schnellen Blicks erkennt sie ihn.
Keine Klage läs-t sie schallen,
Keine Thräne sieht man fallen,   235
Kalt, verzweifelnd starrt sie hin.
Trostlos in die öde Tiefe
Blickt sie, in des Aethers Licht,
Und ein edles Feuer röthet
Das erbleichte Angesicht.   240

"Ich erkenn' euch, ernste Mächte!
Strenge treibt ihr eure Rechte,
Furchtbar, unerbittlich ein.
Früh schon ist mein Lauf beschlossen,
Doch das Glück hab' ich genossen,   245
Und das schönste Loos war mein.
Lebend hab' ich deinem Tempel
Mich geweiht als Priesterin;
Dir ein freudig Opfer sterb' ich,
Venus, grosse Königin!"   250

Light in air her garments hung,
As from off the rock she sprung
Downward to the expecting wave.
High from out his watery reign
Rose the Monarch of the main, 255
And his arms became her grave.
Then, contented with his prize,
Sank he back, and, peaceful, pours
From his unexhausted stores
The ocean stream, that never dies. 260

Und mit fliegendem Gewande
Schwingt sie von des Thurmes Rande
In die Meerfluth sich hinab.
Hoch in seinen Fluthenreichen
Wälzt der Gott die heil'gen Leichen 255
Und er selber ist ihr Grab.
Und mit seinem Raub zufrieden,
Zieht er freudig fort und giesst
Aus der unerschöpften Urne
Seinen Strom, der ewig fliesst. 260

HOPE.

We talk and we dream of the future years,
And hope for better and brighter days;
And ever some distant bliss appears,
The golden scope of our eager gaze.
The world grows old, and grows young again,   5
But "The Better" is ever the dream of men!

Hope smiles on the infant's dawn of day;
To boyhood she opens her liveliest page;
Gilds the visions of youth with her magic ray,
Nor is buried at length in the grave of age;   10
For there when our weary career we close,
Still Hope is the plant from the tomb that grows.

Es reden und träumen die Menschen viel
  Von besseren künftigen Tagen;
Nach einem glücklichen, goldenen Ziel
  Sieht man sie rennen und jagen.
Die Welt wird alt und wird wieder jung,   5
Doch der Mensch hofft immer Verbesserung.

Die Hoffnung führt ihn ins Leben ein,
  Sie umflattert den fröhlichen Knaben,
Den Jüngling locket ihr Zauberschein,
  Sie wird mit dem Greis nicht begraben;   10
Denn beschliesst er im Grabe den müden Lauf,
Noch am Grabe pflanzt er—die Hoffnung auf.

'Tis no brain-kindled phantom, whose meteor flames
Gleam but to mislead with their wandering fire;
From the depth of the heart a voice proclaims,   15
The end of our being is something higher;
Nor e'er from the trustful soul shall fade
The hope by that inward voice conveyed.

Es ist kein leerer, schmeichelnder Wahn,
  Erzeugt im Gehirne des Thoren.
Im Herzen kündet es laut sich an:
  Zu was Besserm sind wir geboren;
Und was die innere Stimme spricht,
Das täuscht die hoffende Seele nicht.   15

THE END.

LONDON: PRINTED BY WILLIAM CLOWES AND SONS, STAMFORD STREET,
AND CHARING CROSS.

The Shield of Achilles.
    XVIII : 530

Helen's Farewell to Hector
    XXIV : 891.
to[illegible] — p. 192 p. 255